"Towsley keeps you on the edge of your s̶e̶a̶t̶ ̶a̶n̶d̶ ̶b̶e̶g̶g̶i̶n̶g̶ ̶f̶o̶r̶ ̶t̶h̶e̶ ̶n̶e̶x̶t̶ turn of the page!"

NINO BOSAZ — TACTICAL WEAPONS MAGAZINE EDITOR

"How many times have you picked up a thriller, only to have the author make some egregious gaffe concerning guns and blow all credibility? Towsley's in-depth firearm knowledge shines through and carries the reader through a roll-ercoaster narrative of post-apocalyptic times."

IAIN HARRISON — "TOP SHOT" SEASON ONE WINNER

"Towsley's novel brings **drama***, action, and suspense, as current as tomorrow's headlines. You won't want to put this one down!"*

JIM WILSON — RETIRED SHERIFF OF CROCKETT COUNTY, TEXAS,
TACTICAL FIREARMS INSTRUCTOR.
SENIOR FIELD EDITOR FOR NRA
PUBLICATIONS AND TELEVISION PERSONALITY

This book captures the future we are headed for if we as a people don't alter our course. Captivating, non-stop action packed and backed with the very substanti-ated facts on the course of what could become of us.

RANDALL CURTIS — US ARMY SPECIAL FORCES MSG (RET)

"While most post-apocalyptic fiction depends on the writer's vivid imagination, Bryce Towsley's vision of the future in "The 14th Reinstated" may be all too real. The book's detailed passages on firearms and survival are top-notch, just what I would expect from one of America's most knowledgeable and entertaining out-door writers."

JOHN ZENT — EDITORIAL DIRECTOR, NRA MEDIA

"A fantastic ride through a post-apocalyptic world of chaos and man's visceral drive to survive. Towsley's knowledge and experience with hunting and firearms makes for an authentic and sometimes terrifying adventure."

SCOTT BALLARD —WEAPONS AND TACTICS INSTRUCTOR, SIG SAUER ACADEMY

"This book hooks the reader immediately, the up to date story and concept applies to a scenario that engages the reader into a whole different concept of what could happen during our life cycle. Towsley's knowledge and description of the hardware and scenarios is not only written with excitement and intrigue but also described in detail by experience from his firearms background and training."

RANDY E. LUTH — FOUNDER OF THE DPMS FIREARMS COMPANY
MANAGING DIRECTOR DEL-TONE / LUTH GUN RANGE
USA OLYMPIC SHOOTING TEAM FOUNDATION DIRECTOR

"Is this a novel or a future history book? Thought provoking and exciting, you might actually learn from this quick moving, post-apocalyptic scenario."

KYLE LAMB — SGM RETIRED, US ARMY SPECIAL OPERATIONS

"One of the key ingredients of any robust, rollicking adventure story is the ring of authenticity. Bryce Towsley, who has long been recognized as one of America's leading sporting scribes when it comes to guns and hunting, brings his expertise in those areas to bear in fine fashion. This is a delightful inaugural foray into fiction. There's an underlying message which any patriotic American would be well advised not only to read but to heed, but that message is a mere subtext. In the bargain we get a heady mix of first-rate craftsmanship and titillating mystery; precisely the stuff it takes to make a real page turner. Sit back, perhaps with a comforting libation at hand or a warming fire toasting your toes, and settle in for a splendid session of armchair adventure."

JIM CASADA, PHD —WORLD RENOWNED EXPERT ON SPORTING LITERATURE

"A fast-moving read that not only serves as a grisly warning against thinly-veiled socialist policies but also provides an action-packed solution. Towsley is a guy who knows his guns and is not afraid to let his characters use them."

ADAM HEGGENSTALLER — EXECUTIVE EDITOR, NRA'S SHOOTING ILLUSTRATED MAGAZINE

"Finally! A book with a great story line, incredible suspense, and firearms and tactics information that is spot on. Something this masterful could only be written by both a great writer and incredibly knowledgeable shooter. It's extremely rare to find both in one package. Read this book, you will NOT be able to put it down!"

MIKE SEEKLANDER —WORLD CHAMPION COMPETITIVE PISTOL SHOOTER
TACTICAL FIREARMS AND PERSONAL DEFENSE INSTRUCTOR
CO-HOST OF "THE BEST DEFENSE" TELEVISION SHOW

"Bryce Towsley is the most knowledgeable mind I've ever met in the world of guns and shooting, as well as a world class critic of liberal politics. Bottom line, he's just a damned good writer. It's no wonder his first novel figures to be a classic adventure."

DAVE HENDERSON — OUTDOOR AND FIREARMS WRITER

"In a post-collapse America, Towsley's 'man with no name' is the kind of protagonist who forever has been part of our lore. He's part everyman, part hero, part statesman, a hundred percent human. Read Towsley's tale, then load and lock.

J. SCOTT OLMSTED — EDITOR IN CHIEF OF NRA'S AMERICAN HUNTER MAGAZINE

Unlike other similar novels available today, this work is penned by a true firearms expert with real-world knowledge of the ins and outs of not only how these weapons work, but also their capabilities. The fact that he is an entertaining and clever writer just makes the work even more notable. Pick up a copy. You won't regret it.

MICHAEL O. HUMPHRIES — EDITOR-AT-LARGE, SPECIAL WEAPONS FOR MILITARY & POLICE

For John
It was your road they traveled.

"It carries me back to the times when, beset with difficulties and dangers, we were fellow laborers in the same cause, struggling for what is most valuable to man, his right to self-government. Laboring always at the same oar, with some wave ever ahead threatening to overwhelm us, and yet passing harmless ... we rode through the storm with heart and hand."

THOMAS JEFFERSON IN A LETTER TO JOHN ADAMS

"If not us — who? If not now — when?

RONALD REAGAN

The 14th

Reinstated

Bryce M. Towsley

TABLE OF CONTENTS

CHAPTER 1

The guy was dead.

I knew that when I pulled the trigger, but I checked anyway.

It's like we used to say back when we hunted Cape buffalo, "It's the dead ones that get back up and kill you."

Then I picked up his pistol and made sure it was still loaded.

I already knew it worked.

The currencies today are bullets, guns, antibiotics and food, in that order. Most people used their dollar bills years ago to start a fire or to wipe their asses. Both, if they were smart. Those who hoarded gold now have some shiny metal to look at while they starve to death. It's a barter system and guns fetch a premium. This handgun can feed my family for a month and stockpile some medicine for future problems.

What bothered me was I had no idea he was waiting for me until the first bullet flew past my head. I should have been dead, but he started too soon. Rather than let me get close, he shot from sixty yards away. Only the best can make that shot under stress and he clearly was not the best.

After he missed, he really panicked and started spraying bullets. I took cover behind a trashed car and waited. He finally stepped out to see where I had gone; assuming, I suppose, that he had somehow hit me. I used my M-4 carbine to double tap his chest, and then I put another shot in his head after he fell, just in case he wore body armor. Few do, but like I said, it's the dead ones that get you. Another cartridge is cheap insurance. I make them by the thousands.

I had just put his pistol in my backpack when my breakfast, little that there was, spewed onto the cracked pavement. Then I started shaking like a dog shitting peach pits as I sat down to wait it out.

I knew it would pass, because I had been there before. It was, of course, a reaction to killing the guy. But not like in the old movies where the hero is so upset about taking a human life that he gets sick. That's fiction — Hollywood's idea of how we should act. They used to think that killing somebody should leave us conflicted and ruined.

I never felt that way; not even the first time, because I never killed anybody who didn't need killing. Sure I had a reaction, any human would, but it was because I lived; not because they died. Killing an asshole who is trying to kill me or my family doesn't cause any more moral conflict than shooting a coyote trying to eat my chickens. It is simply solving a problem that I didn't create.

The movies "back before" were mostly made by people leaning to the left with their political and social beliefs. Socialists, communists, liberals: No matter what you called them, it was a class of people who are all but extinct today because they were hit hard by the social wars. Too bad, because I would like to find a few so I could kick them in the nuts for doing this to us. America used to be a great place to live until they decided to "improve" it.

It turned out they were wrong on so many counts; not just how we would react after killing somebody in self-defense. Those of us left were never much conflicted about killing. At least not killing a guy like this. It was him or me and he started it. My moral obligation was to stay alive and make it back home because my family needs me. My violent reaction was from the adrenaline dump after the action was over.

Well, that and the understanding that I had survived another one and that sooner or later the odds were going to catch up with me.

No matter how good you are, it's a guy like this, a worthless little piece of shit, who will finally get you. He will do it by shooting from ambush without you having a clue he was anywhere around. It doesn't take skill to do that and skill won't save you. Only luck can do that. If this guy had been a better shot or more disciplined, it would be me lying on the road instead of him. I just hoped that when it happened it would be quick, like it was for him. I think what I fear most is rotting away with infection after a gut shot.

I went over and over it in my mind, trying to see where I had gone wrong, what mistakes I had made, but there was nothing. It is just like deer hunting. The whitetail deer has more acute senses than any human and it is extremely wary. It should be impossible to ever shoot one, especially a big, old well-educated buck. But, hunters do it all the time. Or at least they used to.

The secret is to hide and wait for the deer. If you make sure the wind is in your face so he can't smell you and if you don't make any noise so he can't hear you and you hide so he can't see you, it doesn't matter how sharp his senses are. Still, a lot of those crafty old bucks managed to escape. They did it because of other mistakes the hunter made. Mistakes like a footprint in the wrong place that the deer could smell, or passing upwind of where he was sleeping so he could smell you on your way to your blind, or spooking a bird that made noise as it flew off so the deer knew you were coming. A smart buck notices those things. That's how they stay alive for years. I tried to learn from that and always be watching for clues. But even with all that, if you did it right, you still shot the deer, and it was the same thing here. A guy waiting in hiding, who doesn't make any mistakes, should be able to kill you every time. This morning I was lucky, but luck can't hold forever.

The bigger lesson is you make the most mistakes when you are moving. Moving puts you at a disadvantage. The smartest bucks only move at night when hunters are not out and about, because they know that moving in day-light will result in getting shot.

I was moving, but I had no choice. I had something I had to do and where I had to do it was miles down the road.

CHAPTER 2

This guy should not have been there. At first I thought it was just random; that he saw me coming and decided to kill me on the spur of the moment and take what I had. But, nobody still alive would have risked that today. If they were still around and not dead, after everything that had happened, they should have learned from the fools who tried stupid things and got themselves killed.

I guess this guy didn't learn much. First of all, he never should have shot at me. At least not once he saw the rifle. Those odds are just not good, and knowing the odds is what is keeping all of us alive these days. Defying them, like I am now, is what is likely to kill you. Sometimes, though, you just don't have a choice.

One man traveling all alone is so unusual now that it should have raised a red flag for this guy. People rarely travel at all these days, but when they do it's almost always in large, well-armed groups. Somebody with a rifle and traveling alone is either crazy or a badass. Either way, he is probably not the guy to mess with. There are easier targets. Lone bandits are smarter than that, or they are dead and rotting. It's a tough world out there and only the sharp and smart survive.

So what's the story with this guy?

Was this random, just a chance meeting with a guy dumb enough to try to kill me? I didn't think anybody in the outside world knew what I was doing, but it sure looks like he was waiting for me. Could this somehow be related to why I am making this trip?

If it was, how did he know I was coming? How could anybody possibly know that I would be passing by here today? For that matter, why here? Even if they were somehow expecting me, this was not the place that a smart bandit would pick for a robbery. It was too remote and it was a poor location, tactically.

I was after some bad people and the more I thought about it, the more I believed that somebody must have known I was coming. It looks like they were planning to stop me. It's the only thing that made sense. I started to think that maybe the location was exactly why they left this guy here, because nobody would expect it. When you are deer hunting you don't put your blind where the buck will be looking for it, but in the place he least expects it. That's what they did. It should have worked, it would have worked; they just left the wrong guy.

On the other hand, as far as I know, it was the only mistake they made, which made me realize who I was dealing with and it scared me. Scared is good, scared keeps you sharp, scared keeps you alive. Just as long as you don't get too scared.

CHAPTER 3

What led to this? Well, it's very complicated and really simple. The simple version is that it was the softness, the weakness that had pervaded our society. I suppose it was fine in theory. The concept of being a better people and a better country is admirable. But, we let it get out of control and allowed it to be hijacked and to blind a nation to reality. The idea that America could be better, more generous, was the right one. Until it mutated into something different. We were trying to be a "kinder, gentler" nation, but we turned weak, divided and so self-absorbed that we forgot that the world can be an evil place. We let our own society falter to the brink of disaster. Then disaster came knocking on the door.

What many in America thought was being a better society was perceived as weakness by the rest of the world and, looking back, it's clear that their perception was right. We were weak, we were pathetic. When we grew soft and vulnerable enough, the predators came hunting.

Nobody can say exactly when it started because it crept in so slowly, so silently and just grew almost unnoticed in the background. Some say it started with F.D.R. and the "New Deal." Others say it was the sixties. Me? Well, I think it was always there, but we needed to mature as a nation to let it loose. Once the Great Depression and World War II were over, after the United States of America became the most prosperous nation in the history of the world and life turned easy, the infection had an entry point.

America was a good place with good people, but that goodness led to weak leaders with hidden agendas. Leaders we elected for the wrong reasons. Not because they could bring good things to America, but out of guilt for perceived sins of our past. It also led to weak and lazy citizens. As entitlements grew, our country declined. Too many voted for a handout and we ended up with corrupt leadership. Once those living off the government outnumbered those working to pay the taxes to fund them, it was over.

We got so caught up in the shame of living well that we forgot that it could all be taken away. Those of us who warned it could happen were dismissed as the lunatic fringe. We were laughed at, scorned and ridiculed. Still, I take little solace today in knowing we were right.

Those who didn't believe it could happen, who thought the government would take care of them, who didn't think violence was ever the answer, those unwilling to protect themselves, who denied it all, died quickly. Some of them were people I loved.

A few years before the collapse I was with my family in Florida for my father's 80th birthday. A group of the extended family wound up together one afternoon in a beach house, discussing how our experimental president and our foolish Congress were selling out America. We were talking about how it was going to end up and we put together a tentative plan for the family to meet at a central location and try to survive. How I wish now that we had followed through.

Mine was a large extended family and there were probably just as many gathered there for the birthday who disagreed with our point of view. Most of them had voted for the very politicians who were trashing the country and they continued to blindly support them. They called us names, laughed at our theories and dismissed us as fools, so we had not invited them to the meeting that day because we knew what their reactions would be. But, we decided we would help them anyway if things got bad, because after all they were family. One guy, David, I think, (whom I have not seen again) joked, "Sure, we will take them in, feed them and protect them, but the deal is we get to make them our bitches!"

If only that had happened.

My brother Bradley is a good example. He fancied himself an intellectual and he lived in the world of theory, not reality. He attended college until he was in his late thirties. Then he got a job sucking on a government tit as a "grant writer," meaning he spent his days begging Washington for money. He rarely left the big city and he spent his time with academics and government employees. With so small a focus he lost his perspective on reality. He voted for every left-wing, liberal candidate who ran for office and promised a hand out. He was immune to the corruption that our "leaders" had come to epitomize and as long as the checks kept coming he could turn a blind eye to almost anything.

One boozy evening years back, after a vacation day of water skiing at our family's lakeside camp, the fireside talk turned to self-defense. He argued that he could never take a human life.

"Not even if the guy was about to kill your kids and rape your wife?" somebody asked.

"No, violence against him would just bring me down to his level. I would reason with him instead."

Well, he died with his morals intact. But he died too young and he died horribly. I hope it was worth it. From what we know, his son and his wife died with him. His daughter was in her mid-twenties, rebellious and beautiful. That saved her. They took her away and (I hoped) kept her alive. Maybe she doesn't think "alive" is such a good thing after what they probably have done to her over the past months, but that's not for me to say. She is family and she is the reason I was walking down this particular road. I thought I knew where she was and I was going to bring her home. The problem was, now that they knew I was coming, things just got a lot more complicated.

But at least I figured that this guy shooting at me the way he did might be a good sign that I was moving in the right direction. Until now, I wasn't one hundred percent sure I was even on the right track.

It took me three months just to find out who "they" were. Once again, it wasn't like the movies. There was no central "kingpin" who controlled all the gangs, holding the beautiful girl locked away for his own pleasure. The reality was chaos.

After the collapse, two things quickly happened on the same timeline. The government checks stopped coming and the police disappeared. Those who lived in the city and had existed on handouts for years either joined a gang, or they perished. Nobody ever "controlled" the gangs, they just did their thing — some lived and some died. It was bad for a long time while they fought for "turf," but the upside is that they pretty much stayed in the urban areas as they killed each other off, which was a good way of taking out the trash.

In the end, there were a lot fewer of those parasites running around. But, those who were left were a bad lot and they epitomized evil. The selection process meant that the worst of the worst survived. The law of the jungle, "only the strong survive," was a romantic notion that missed one important point. It's not just the strong; it's the strong and the mean that survive. A strong, moral man might hesitate, but the man with no morals will not, and he will kill the hesitant moral man.

The selection process favors those without a conscience. The gangs that are running things now are the meanest, the nastiest and the quickest to kill. They are perhaps the worst people to ever populate the earth.

That's who I was looking for.

The gang I was hunting were mostly guys who should have died in prison years ago. But, our soft society kept them on the streets. The left-wing, activist judges who kept turning them back into society to commit more crimes are probably all dead, but these guys are just getting stronger.

At first, that didn't matter too much to me. I live in Vermont, or at least what used to be Vermont. It's funny how we all still identify our homes by what (or where) they used to be. Anyway, I live away from the cities and all that mess. I have always been self-sufficient and while life has changed and gotten much harder, it's still good. For a while, the bad guys battled it out in the cities and didn't bother us, so we didn't bother them.

With every city a battleground, we begged them to join us, but my brother and his family were convinced that Philadelphia still held their best hope. He thought that having a lot of people around would keep them safe. I argued that a remote area with fewer people was safer because there were fewer people to attack you or to take what is yours. I explained that we could protect ourselves better because of our remote location. But then, he never listened to me.

They survived for a few years by moving to a gated community with like-minded people. Of course the residents sold out their "principles" and hired armed guards to keep the community safe. Somehow, paying somebody else to do the killing, even in self-defense, was more morally acceptable.

Then somebody got careless and made a mistake. They let their guard down, trusted in the goodness of human nature and there were predators waiting to pounce. One of the paid guards got a better offer, let the bad guys into the compound and what followed was a bloodbath. As far as I know, the only resident of that walled community to leave alive was Sarah, my niece.

I wanted to just stay in my home for the rest of my life with my wife and family, to mind my own business and live my own life. I expected to, actually; then word got to me that they had moved her to Vermont and well, here I am, far outside my comfort zone, heading for who knows what.

But she is family, and you don't mess with family.

CHAPTER 4

While I really couldn't spare the time, I stayed hidden and waited. Like I said, you make mistakes when you move. So, I waited to see if anybody else would show up. I had no idea if it was just this one guy, or if there was an army waiting around the corner.

We were at a junction of several roads where a little village had been. The main two-lane highway ran up the valley, following the small river and passing, on the other side of the river, to the north of the empty village. It was connected to this junction by a short street with a bridge. Normally I would try to stay off the main roads, but an old friend, Jack Kelly, offered me a ride.

Jack lived in Moultrie, which is about twenty miles to the east of where I live. He has a shipping company that hires on to bring supplies to the various small communities. There is enough emerging commerce that a train comes into Ridgeland, a few miles north of me, about once a month with whatever supplies are available at the time – food, medicine, clothing, soap, cooking utensils, toilet paper and sometimes books. I might get by without toilet paper, but life wouldn't be worth living if I didn't have something to read at night.

Sometimes there isn't much, but on this trip the railroad cars were full of cargo. They dropped whatever was needed in Ridgeland before continuing north to Middlebury and Burlington. From there, they pass through the old border for Canada and continue to the recently repopulated city of Montreal. There, with luck, they could refill the cars for another trip back. Montreal has become a destination for a few sporadic shipments from what remained of the rest of the world, as it is accessible by ship through the St. Lawrence Seaway and for now is stable and calm.

The train runs up and down the East Coast, from Jacksonville, Florida to Montreal, picking up whatever people have to trade and leaving what they need. It all runs on barter, and the Farnsworth brothers who had taken the initiative to restart the railroad lived well, someplace in Georgia.

They found an old steam locomotive in a museum and converted it to run on wood. They began locally, just running to a few towns. But they kept working on the tracks to repair them and steadily expanded in both directions. It only took a couple of years before they were running up and down the entire East Coast, providing jobs for quite a few people.

It was the beginning of a new economy, a revival of capitalism, which was the only economic model that ever truly worked. They issued company scrip as payment to their employees, redeemable for any goods they carried on the train. For now it was working, but if this trend continued, sooner or later we would need a new form of currency. Barter was getting difficult to manage and even the Farnsworth brothers recognized that some kind of money was going to be needed. Some of the places they traded with had their own local scrip, but it was worthless anyplace else. The people needed a common currency, but one they could trust.

The brothers had been talking to a few of us along the route about creating a national currency. They are among the contingent, as am I, that is hopeful we can move even further beyond that and reestablish a working national government. Several of us have created local governments, but it was becoming clear that we needed to unite in a larger, central government for what was left of America.

The truth is we were planning a meeting in a few weeks in Virginia where the Farnsworths had a warehouse, so the train stopping for a while would not attract attention. We had invited a small number of men, all the leaders of the local governments as well as some other important community leaders, to discuss forming a new national government. Word was that most would agree to simply follow the lead of our founding fathers and revive the original republic that was the United States of America. The same constitution, the same structure, the same hopes and dreams, only this time we would try to keep it on track.

Of course, there are multiple opinions on how we need to accomplish that, but the one thing we all agree on is that we will return to the gold bullion standard for our money. We will not make the mistake that the United States had made in the seventies when the government removed the gold standard and decided that the dollar needed nothing of value backing it. The resulting "fiat currency" had nothing more than the "full faith and credit of the United States" insuring its value. But, our country become a cesspool of corruption and it turned out that the faith was betrayed and the credit was destroyed.

Many of us believe that leaving the gold standard was the catalyst for the events that created the huge inflation and the severe devaluation of the U.S. dollar in the last years of the Republic.

"Republic."

Every time I hear that word I am reminded of what Ben Franklin said when exiting the Constitutional Convention of 1787. A lady shouted out, "Well Doctor, what have we got, a Republic or a Monarchy?" To which Franklin replied, "A Republic, if you can keep it."

Sadly, we could not. It just took a few hundred years longer than the good Dr. Franklin had feared.

Too many people were burned by the lies and betrayals of the American politicians. If we are to expect any of the citizens of our new country, and the rebuilding world, to trust the currency it must have tangible backing.

For all of mankind's history gold has been the accepted standard and we intend to return to that with the new currency. A big side effect will be making all those who hoarded gold happy. Their shiny metal will again have value, although that value will likely be a fraction of the highly inflated price they paid for it. At least in actual paper dollars, the buying power will be about the same.

Jack was hired to meet the train and to haul all the supplies they could fit in their trucks back to the towns that hired them. This time it was his hometown of Moultrie. He and his small crew sometimes stopped at my place on the way back to trade for some fresh meat. They had to overnight while we butchered and packaged it for them. Without reliable refrigeration, the best way to keep meat fresh is to keep it alive until it's needed.

I always remind him that he can send word ahead and we will have everything ready. But, to tell you the truth, I think he enjoys the down time. Our place is safe, so he and the crew can let down their guard for a little while. Most of his guys are younger, about the same age as my daughter, her husband and my son, who are all in their twenties. When word leaks out that Jack's crew is here, it's never long before other young people from miles around drop by. Somebody always has a guitar or two and pretty soon they are dancing and having a good time.

The guys fire up my big grill with maple and cherry cordwood. Then they usually tap a bottle or two of hard cider to sip while they wait for the wood to burn down and for the coals to get just right for grilling meat. Times might be hard, but life can still be fun.

We always have meat available because my wife and I run a small, custom processing butcher shop. It started back when I was hunting and we would process all our own big game. I had all the tools to do the work and after everything crashed people started bringing their game and livestock for me to process. It just kind of morphed into a small business for us. Our fee is twenty percent of the meat; we eat some and barter with the rest. As a result we always have meat on hand, but you never know what it might be, moose, venison, pork or even "beefalo" which is half cow and half bison. A farm down in Pawlet run by the Mason brothers raises them and we butcher a few every year.

Today it was beef. Jack had picked up fresh vegetables, some potatoes and several loaves of bread from the train. He even had a couple of watermelons, something I had not tasted in years.

The youngsters worked while they partied and they prepared everything, getting it ready for the grill once we had finished our work and could join them in relaxing with a little cider.

Jack sipped from his cup and we talked about the old days as he watched my wife and I work. He had offered to help, but we had learned from hard experience that's a bad idea. We have a routine that works and we move fast. From all the years of working together, we always know what the other person is going to do next. Butchering involves using large, very sharp knives. When a "helper" joins in, sooner or later somebody zigs when they should zag and human blood starts flowing. It's much easier to just let us do our jobs until the meat is cut up. Then everybody can help with packaging and the cleanup.

"What's with the rifle and the backpack?" Jack asked, pointing to my gear stacked up in the corner.

"I have a little family problem to deal with over in Indian Country," I said, not wanting to give too much away. "I am going to head over there in a couple of days."

"I can give you a ride tomorrow if you like. We will be happy to have another gun along."

It's still a dangerous place out on the roads and this was a much bigger expedition than normal, so he had a lot of goods. That made his crew a target. They hate to waste valuable fuel by running so many trucks, as gasoline is extremely hard to find. Nobody has made fresh gasoline for years and gas has a shelf life. The supplies left are starting to go bad very quickly, even the stuff we had the foresight to treat with stabilizer.

Jack had brought all three of his trucks and filled them to the top with supplies. Some of the goods would have to go into storage until they were needed. But he figured stockpiling was a good idea, because soon enough the trucks would be worthless. Without gas, they couldn't move and it was just a matter of months before the little gas he had would be worthless. It made more sense to use the fuel while the engines could still digest it and to move as much freight as possible in the time left.

I was just glad they had room for me as it would save me miles of walking. They never traveled in the dark because it's too dangerous. So, just as the sun was hinting at a new day, I gathered my gear and jumped into the back of the lead truck.

"Glad to have you aboard," the young driver growled as he stuck his hand though the port from the cab for me to shake. "I heard you are pretty good with that rifle. They say you used to be the New England champ back when they had shooting competitions. We can always use an old guy like you along for the ride, as long as you have that rifle, of course. "

He laughed as his hand retracted back into the cab and I looked away. A grunt brought my attention back to the port and this time the hand was holding a fresh peach.

"Try this," he said before starting the engine. "My mom grows them in a greenhouse out in back of the barn."

Like the watermelon, I had not had a fresh peach in years and that first bite was like tasting all the good memories of the world we left behind. The succulent texture was perfect and the wonderful taste exploded in my mouth. You don't realize how important the little things like this can be, the things that we took for granted, until you rediscover them. For some reason the peach brought on a bout of depression.

I sat down on a bag of grain and lost myself in regret.

CHAPTER 5

Each truck had a driver and an armed gunner in the front. The old term "shotgun" used to describe the passenger seat might have come from the Old West and the stagecoach days, but the guy in my truck believed it. He had a Benelli 12-gauge semi-auto stuck out of a slot in the side door, ready for action. I noticed he shot left handed, which is probably why he was sitting on the right side of the truck. A right-handed shooter is at a disadvantage trying to shoot out of the right side of a vehicle, because he has to twist in the seat to get the stock on his right shoulder.

The shotgun was mounted to the door with a swivel, so that he could let go of it and not risk losing the gun. I assumed that was so he could take over after the driver was hurt or killed.

"These supply runs are big targets for the bad guys," the guy sitting next to me said, as if he was reading my thoughts. "But they don't like to disable the vehicles because any running truck with gas in its tank is a valuable piece of plunder. So the bastards will lie in ambush on the left side, usually near a bad piece of road or at an intersection where the truck is going slow. A sniper with a rifle shoots the driver in the head. Usually the truck rolls to a stop and the bad guys swarm over it, killing everybody else. I lost a couple of good friends to those assholes, and I ain't got that many friends to spare. That's why I volunteer for every one of these trips."

He paused for a moment, then continued, his voice a little softer. "Sure he pays me, but I like the payback when those son of a bitches try to rob us now. I can't get my friends back, but I figure with every one of those assholes I kill I might help keep somebody else's friends alive."

He was a little older than most of the rest of the crew, probably early to mid-thirties. He wasn't small, but he also was not a big man. He was one of those guys whose looks are deceptive. If you were young and stupid and looking for trouble you might think he was an easy mark, but I suspect you would be making a big mistake. He was almost thin, but it was all muscle and sinew. His face was scarred and his nose had been broken. Most wouldn't even notice, they would just think he had some character. But, I know a little about fighting and I recognized the scars on his eyebrows and on his bottom lip and figured he was a brawler. He had a thatch of black hair, a dark three day beard and deep, piercing blue eyes. I had seen him on some other runs, but he kind of kept to himself. He would sit back and watch the others drinking and dancing, but I never saw him join in. At least not the dancing. He always had a cup of something he was sipping slowly as he sat by himself, just watching.

I knew his name was David Keenan and that everybody just called him Davy. Jack had once mentioned that he was the best man he ever hired for these runs. He said the guy was fearless and had an intuitive knack in any kind of a fight for predicting what the other guy was going to do next.

My mother used to say it was the Irish in me that made me so moody and that people didn't like it when I brooded. I didn't want to seem ungrateful for the ride and figured some conversation would help bring me out of my funk.

"You a fighter?" I asked. "A pro?"

"I was, back before," he answered as his face lit up. I could tell instantly that he was one of those guys who loved to fight and that I had picked a good topic.

"I was fighting in mixed martial arts the last few years it was around. I was a lot more pumped up then and I fought as a light heavyweight. Actually I was about one-ninety, so I was one of the smaller guys in the class. I guess I could have dropped five pounds and fought in middleweight, but I liked fighting the bigger guys. I was undefeated in twenty-three pro fights. I even had a title shot all lined up when everything fell apart.

"How about you, did you ever get in the cage?"

"A little bit, but we didn't call it that," I replied. "It was before MMA came along. I did Golden Gloves boxing for a while then I got into Taekwondo for a few years. I even did some full contact fighting, the predecessor for MMA. But, it wasn't for me. I didn't like hurting people and that always meant I got hurt. You need to be ruthless and relentless and I just wasn't."

"Yeah," he said. "I know exactly what you mean. A lot of guys had the skills and were tough enough to go all the way, but just like you said, they weren't mean enough. Well, maybe mean isn't exactly the right word. You gotta love fighting, all of it, even the pain, to go all the way. It's not really about being mean, a lot of fighters are really good guys. We all know the deal when we step in the ring and nobody expects mercy. It's just that most guys don't have that fire in their belly. I always did, still do. In fact, I pick up some smoker fights now and then. The trouble is, word got around and nobody wants to fight me anymore.

"Billy Farnsworth says there is a guy down in South Carolina who is pretty good. I think he is going to try to set up a match and I might ride on down there with him on the next run south. Might be fun. Hell, he is even going to pay us.

"But, on the other hand, I probably ought to retire. I am getting a bit too old for this. These kids who fight today might not have all the formal training that I got, but that "young" shit counts for a lot, especially stamina. You gotta take them young guys out fast or else they tire your ass out."

I asked him about the plate steel where the doors and windshields used to be, leaving small slits to look and shoot through. This was new and different from the last time they had stopped by several months ago.

"After losing a couple of shipments we got smarter," my new friend continued. "We are not just a bunch of guys with a couple of trucks; everybody Jack uses is well trained. A lot of the guys who started with Jack were military or law enforcement, back before. We use what we know to help train the younger guys. When we are not on a run, we train daily in shooting, hand-to-hand fighting and in tactics. Jack hired me as an instructor for my fighting skills. I had to talk him into letting me come on the runs. When I started with him I had never fired a gun, but with cross training I found out I am pretty good. I wish I knew about shooting years ago, I love it and I would really like to have tried some of those shooting competitions that you used to do back before. Heck, if they were still around now I probably would retire from fighting and start shooting. Anything to keep up some kind of competition, I love kicking the other guy's ass.

"I guess for now I'll just have to settle for whacking the assholes who try to steal from Jack. In a lot of ways that's the ultimate competition."

I laughed. "I suppose it is, but losing must suck a lot more than when I was competing. I just had to deal with my shattered ego then. With this, you wind up in the ground."

"Well, then, the best plan is don't lose!

"Anyway, we drill for the kind of attack I told you about over and over. Particularly the driver and the front seat gunner. They practice until the gunner can pull a dead or unconscious driver out of his seat, climb over him and take control of the truck in just a couple of seconds. We keep the truck moving no matter what.

"These were dump trucks back before, so they already had thick metal dump bodies. We doubled the weak areas with AR 550 armor plating steel. We also used that for the cab to make it bulletproof. We got that steel from a guy in Massachusetts who made targets for you guys to shoot in competition back before. They say that the 3/8 plate we used will stop, or at least slow down, just about any rifle those bastards have. Most of those assholes don't know anything about guns anyway. They think a 9mm is a giant killer and if they have an AK they think they are the baddest motherfucker that ever walked. I love to watch their faces when they find out they ain't."

"Doesn't that add a lot of weight to the trucks?" I asked.

"Yup, it's one reason we go so slow. You probably noticed from the rough ride, the springs are doubled up to handle the extra weight and we have solid tires so they can't shoot them out. We plated the engine compartment so they can't shoot out the power plant. We use a double baffle system to get air to the radiator but block any bullets.

"We scrounged the parts wherever we could find them to make these modifications. That windshield used to be a snow plow on a state road crew's truck. They are hardened steel so they wouldn't wear out so fast while plowing the roads. We reverse them so the curve is facing frontwards, and the bullets usually roll off when they hit. We cut a few slits so we can see to drive, just like a tank.

It took us a couple of months and quite a bit of gas for the welding rig's engine to build these trucks, but it paid off. A couple of well-trained guys in the back of the truck with AR-15 rifles can hide behind the plating, shoot though the ports and hold off any attackers. The trucks are not very fast with all this extra weight, but with the poor condition of the roads that doesn't matter much anyway. Hell, a Corvette couldn't go any faster on most of this shit.

"Once we plated up the trucks and implemented these strategies the attacks all but stopped.

"Pissed me off," he said with a chuckle. "It's all kinda boring now."

He went silent for a while and I thought he was done. Then he said quietly, "I got quite a few of those bastards before they figured it out.

"It don't matter now," he continued. "With the little bit of gas we have left going bad with old age, we only got a few more runs with these trucks. After that, I don't know what we will do. If nobody starts making gasoline again, I guess we will go back to horses and wagons. The problem is, I don't know how the hell we will armor plate a horse."

I noticed that the truck I was in had an armor plated box with a chair mounted on a pedestal, high above the truck bed. There was a guy sitting up there, listening to us but watching, never taking his eyes off the road and always scanning. He could swivel the chair 360 degrees and cover any approach with his rifle. I noticed that on the inside of the box the walls were covered with welded on magazine holders, every one of them stuffed with a full rifle magazine. When he shot his gun dry, he could drop the empty magazine into the bed of the truck and a reload was just inches away. Clearly these guys knew their jobs.

"I used to ride up there," Davy said with a smirk. "But, they said I used too much ammo, so they made me trade places with Bobby up there. He don't use nearly as much ammo, but then again, after I got done, he don't have nearly as many targets."

CHAPTER

Several miles out I would turn south while they continued to the east on the two lane highway. They dropped me off at the end of the connecting street and I stood in the early-morning light until the trucks were gone.

I didn't like the wide-open expanse I had to cross, but the bridge was the only way across the river. Normally in the late spring I could wade the river, but this year had been very rainy and all our brooks and rivers were running at near flood stage.

The road ran a straight two hundred yards before it connected to another two lane road, which again crossed the river before it hooked south and then followed the course of that river. South was where I was headed and I wondered what waited for me there.

The two-lane blacktop I planned to follow would run through some remote, empty country, rising two thousand feet over the mountain pass before topping out and leading me down through the gulf and into the small town on the other side where I was pretty sure they were holding my niece. I didn't like sticking to the roads, but it was the only way as the brush was much too thick on the sides to walk through.

I planned on getting to the town about dark and that's where I figured I would find trouble. I had not really counted on hitting it here.

In retrospect, I should have used the abandoned cars lining the road for cover, stopping every now and then to look with my binoculars. But, I made the mistake of thinking nobody was around. I hadn't expected any problems, so instead of being cautious I walked right along, trying to make some time.

That nearly got me killed.

I dragged the dead guy through the side door, into the closest building and out the back door to the loading dock, locking the door behind me. It was an old hardware store and this concrete dock was high enough so that trucks could back up to it and unload the heavy merchandise. I was up about five feet above the road and hidden behind some old shipping crates. This gave me a pretty good view of the approach from the north and west sides, while the building covered me on the other two.

I reloaded the magazine in my rifle from the spare ammo in my pack. Then I checked his pistol to see how many rounds were left. There was one in the chamber and two more left in the magazine. That meant if the gun was full when he started, he had shot eleven times at me. It's odd that I don't remember that much shooting, but I know from experience that your mind shuts down into sort of a tunnel vision mode when you are in a firefight. My only focus was on shooting him, not counting his rounds.

His pistol was chambered in .40 S&W while mine is a .45 APC. The two are much different. I didn't have any spare ammo to reload his gun, so I put it back in my pack.

My habit is to check all my guns after a fight. Sometimes you get so lost in the moment you don't remember a lot of what happened. The gun might be empty and you don't have any recollection of shooting; it's that "tunnel vision" thing again.

I already had taken care of my rifle, so I did a press check on my pistol to make sure the chamber was loaded. I popped out the eight round magazine and did a double check that it was full. After I re-seated the magazine I smacked it hard with the heel of my hand to make one hundred percent sure it was fully seated.

Given what I was likely heading into, I thought I could probably use another loaded pistol, so I started to search the body for spare magazines and ammo.

It occurred to me that while the Glock is a great pistol, it is part of what got him killed. With a different handgun, say a custom 1911 like the one I carry, he might have pulled off that shot. But he had a Glock 23, their compact model. It's designed for close quarters fighting. The shorter barrel means a shorter sight radius, which makes it a bit more difficult to aim. The Glock has what is called a "striker-fired" trigger system which has a much harder trigger pull than my 1911. I built the gun myself in my shop and tuned it for a light three-pound trigger pull. A Glock trigger will usually be about double that weight. Out of curiosity I unloaded his gun and checked the trigger. I was surprised to find it was fitted with a "New York Trigger" which had a twelve-pound pull. My guess is that it was taken off a dead cop sometime in the past as few civilians installed that abomination on their guns. The harder pulling trigger was favored by some police departments back before, because it was believed it made the gun safer. Under the circumstances, my guess is that you would have a hard time convincing this guy right now. He didn't exactly have a "safe" day.

That hard trigger pull and short barrel make it more difficult to keep the sights aligned for a long-range, precision shot. My gun has a longer sight radius and a much lighter trigger pull, which makes shooting it accurately at longer ranges easier, while it is still deadly at close quarters. It's a small thing, but those small things sometimes keep you alive, or get you killed.

Just ask this guy.

As my head cleared from the after-action brain muddle that always seems to follow a fight, I thought about things and it started to make sense that they had somebody waiting here. But how had they known I was coming? I didn't even know myself. I hadn't planned to leave for at least another day, probably two, but when the offer for a ride came along I knew it would cut miles off my walk so I changed my plans. Had my friends with the trucks betrayed me? I really didn't think so, they just were not the type.

I found three loaded pistol magazines on his belt and two more in his pockets. I also found three loaded AR-15 rifle magazines. I had not seen a rifle, which was curious. I walked back outside to where he was shooting from and for the first time noticed a puddle on the pavement. I bent down and smelled it. The guy had stepped out to take a leak. I guess he had just finished up and when he turned around to go back into the building, he spotted me.

I went back into the building and out to the front where the old showroom had been. There, on a dusty desk, was a Bushmaster carbine. Apparently he had been guarding the south side, watching out the windows. Inside the building he probably didn't hear the trucks drop me off.

I understood now that the location made sense, because no matter which road I came in on I would have to walk past the front of the building. If he played it smart I would pass and he could shoot me in the back. I guess he got bored and wandered out for a piss, leaving his rifle behind. He had seen me coming from the north, panicked and started shooting. It was a foolish mistake that ultimately cost him his life.

The rifle was fitted with an ACOG sight, which was unusual to see these days. They were very expensive and even back before you mostly saw them on military rifles. A few civilians used them but the price was so high that they were not hugely popular. This one looked pretty new, as did the rifle. I carried the gun back to the loading dock where I had hidden the body and propped it against one of the old packing crates.

There was something bothering me about the guy (other than the obvious fact that he had tried to kill me). It finally dawned on me. While he did have some tattoos, so did most everybody these days. But his were professionally done by somebody with some talent. His hair was cut short; he was clean shaven with no facial hair other than a day's stubble. His clothes were dirty from where he fell after I shot him, but not worn or frayed. The dirt was not the ground-in filth from weeks without washing as you would expect after months on the road. In fact, they had a para-military, uniform look to them, but carried no identifying patches, insignias or badges. Most of the tattoos were standard issue with the generation born around the turn of the century, a tribal band on his left bicep and a total "sleeve" of scrolls and art on his right arm. The only writing I could see was buried inside that right arm's elaborate and very well done art. It read, *"Treue zur Welt für ein größeres gut"* I wasn't sure, but I thought it might be German.

Other than the well-armed trade ships, there had been very little international travel in recent times. Most airlines went bankrupt years ago and few passenger ships roamed the pirate infested seas.

After Congress passed the "America First" trade bill, foreign trade ground to a halt. In fact, that one act alone had a lot to do with what China did to our country. We owed them trillions of dollars and the congressional bill was a slimy attempt to default on our debt. There was no way we could have paid everything we owed, the debt was simply too high. We knew it and China knew it. Congress thought they could bully them, but they were wrong. China was not awed by the U.S. or the big stick we thought we carried. They knew that stick might have been powerful once upon a time, but by then it was cracked and splintered. China shut off all trade with the U.S. in retaliation. After a hasty vote to repeal the act failed, China nationalized all the U.S. owned factories in their country and forced the other Pacific-rim countries to do the same. Then they shut off all shipments to America.

Because most of our products were being made overseas by then, store shelves were soon empty. The U.S. companies that were nationalized sued Congress and Congress started impeachment proceedings against the president. While that was being battled out in the courts and on television every night, China called their loans due.

The U.S. government didn't have any money to pay them. They tried to print more dollars, but China refused to accept them. The global currency standard had switched from the United States Dollar to the new world currency called "One Earth" a year earlier. But the U. S. was holding out from joining, insisting that we wanted to phase it in for a "seamless" transition.

The truth was our dollar had become so weak and the exchange rate so low that switching to the new world currency would have wiped out ninety percent of the remaining wealth in America. So Congress claimed it was working out the details for the transition while actually doing nothing. The stalling tactic, along with the continued printing of more and more money by the Fed, had driven the U.S. dollar to a record low. Mexico was another hold-out. Their peso was one thousand to one value against the One Earth currency and it was said that a peso was worth three U. S. dollars.

China wanted payment in One Earth currency and the United States simply didn't have the funds. So China demanded that we turn over the Western public lands and mineral rights that had been put up as collateral for the loans. That deal had been made in secret by the U. S. government and the first time the people heard about it was when the ranchers were kicked off their leased BLM land in Wyoming and Montana by armed Chinese troops.

The Chinese army came in and took over all the mining and oil production in the West as well as the cattle lands. They took all the BLM land as well as the national forests and park lands.

The people revolted and started shooting up the buildings and vehicles as well as sabotaging the oil rigs and mining equipment. A bunch of the more level headed formed up the poorly named "Citizen's Militia" to begin a legal fight against Chinese intrusion. Despite its name, it was more of a lobbying and lawyers' group and had nothing to do with the violence and attacks. Still, they were the only visible target.

China demanded the United States stop the revolt, so the president ordered the Army to attack the Citizen's Militia. Ignoring the Posse Comitatus Act, he ordered soldiers to fire on their own people. Many in the military had friends and family in the Citizen's Militia, and, as the armed forces hadn't been paid in months, figured they no longer owed the military a damn thing. Thousands decided to ignore the orders and deserted to join the militia. The Army was already depleted due to budget cuts and soon it was decimated to the point where those remaining soldiers surrendered to China. The Navy and Air Force simply quit after that. I guess they just didn't want to serve the corruption that had invaded our government. The Marines held on a little longer, saying it was a matter of honor, until the president, fearing China, issued an executive order to disband them.

A lot of airplanes, trucks and tanks disappeared during that time. Thousands of guns and a lot of ammo also went missing. Most just figured that the soldiers who were left high and dry wanted a ride home and a way to protect that home when they got there. With nobody left around to say no, they simply "borrowed" some equipment from Uncle Sam. I suppose most of them were owed back wages anyway, although it would have taken a lot of missed paychecks to pay for a tank.

Once that happened China realized our government had lost control, so they seized all the land they claimed they were owed. Our government protested that the deal was only for the land belonging to the U. S. government, but China claimed that the deal was for the entire western United States, including all the private property. Who knows which side was telling the truth? Both failed to produce any sort of legal document or even proof of any deal.

It didn't matter, because when more and more of the Chinese army showed up, they met little resistance. Those who did fight were killed fast and effectively. To make an example, they wiped out the entire city of Denver, Colorado. They bombed it flat, saying the headquarters for the resistance was located there. Then they said they would do the same to any other city or town that wanted to fight.

The Citizen's Militia took the leadership role and convinced most people it was a lost cause. They knew if they fought back it would be a long and bloody battle that they could not win. The American fighting spirit was willing, but there was no supply chain, no way to feed the people and no way to resupply arms and ammo.

The CM rallied the people to understand that and to peaceably accept China's offer for transportation to the East or West coasts, along with enough food for the first month. Most took the offer. Those who chose to fight died quickly.

Now China had everything west of the Mississippi under their control, except for a narrow strip along the Pacific coastline. That was full of people and had few natural resources, so China in a gesture of "good faith" gave back everything from the coast to two hundred miles inland, except the sea ports. They kept the major ports and a twenty-mile-wide corridor along the east/west major highways to the ports. They allow passage across the corridors at specific points so that people can move up and down the land mass, but movement is strictly controlled. At least that was the last thing we heard. There has been no communication from the west for a few years now. We can only assume they suffered the same melt down as we did here in the east.

China's intent in giving back the West Coast was to create a place to live for those they displaced. They never counted on the social collapse that followed.

As the displaced citizens of the Rocky Mountain and Plains states moved, either to this West Coast strip, or to the Eastern cities, they overburdened the already wobbly infrastructure. These refugees had no food or shelter so they turned to the government, expecting help. Our government didn't have the resources or the answers and panicked. They simply refused to help and tried to control the mobs with the ineffective and bankrupt Federal Police Force. Riots broke out and when the few police left tried to stop them and started shooting, they were ripped apart in the streets.

The angry hordes descended on Washington and occupied the Capital and the White House. They hung the president and first lady from a tree on the Mall. They beat several members of Congress to death and the remaining members scattered and hid. Oddly enough, the Secret Service and other federal agencies that should have prevented this from happening sustained very few casualties. Of course, by then budget cuts had them down below a skeleton crew level and I suppose they were owed back pay as well. Or more likely, they figured if they could turn a blind eye to the corruption for all those years, they could also turn another blind eye while justice played out.

After that, China fortified their clearly defined boundaries with their military and forbade any non-Chinese persons from entering or traveling through the territories. They cut all communication lines and destroyed all our communications satellites. They also banned air traffic overhead, so they effectively cut off the East and West Coast survivors from each other.

I have family in California, but I have no idea if they are dead or alive. We have no way to communicate. Travel has been nonexistent with airlines and shipping shut down, except for the few boats we are now seeing from Europe. There isn't a ground route through the former heartland of America where you can pass without being shot by the Chinese. Mexico is controlled by China and trying to travel through Canada is impossible. That vast land is empty; almost everybody is gone, killed in their own social wars and by a plague that ravaged the entire border area after the wars.

I used to spend a lot of time in Canada. I knew a lot of the tough people who lived in the North Country and I have no doubt some of them are still alive. But most of the population was in the south, close to the U. S. border. They were urban dwellers, dependent on the system and didn't do well without the support of government. Most of those people didn't understand the implications of being unarmed. When Canada banned guns they complied fully, as was expected of any good Canadian. When the riots started, it was bloody.

They say the plague that pretty well finished off the few survivors came from the millions of rotting bodies, but who knows? The timing was right and it seemed to die off once there were no more living people to act as carriers. I am sure that in better times the government and medical people would have gotten it under control quickly. But then again, in better times, there would not have been millions of rotting bodies to set it off.

No matter, what's done is done and the result is that if you plan to travel through Canada, there is no way to refuel or find food. The rumor is that China planned to take over Canada as well, but was scared off by the plague. Now their troops refuse to cross the border. Who knows what's true or just a myth. Without communications or media, nothing can be verified. But, the one thing I do know is that attempting to transverse North America would be certain death no matter where you plotted your route. Take your choice; starve in the North or catch a Chinese bullet anyplace else.

But, this guy was not part of that. He was white, looked to be European, and the tattoo would seem to confirm that. As far as I knew, we were not at war with Germany. In fact, Germany and most of old Europe was going through the same economic and social problems as us and they too were struggling for their continued existence.

CHAPTER 7

We were back in the shadows, where it was a bit dark, and I noticed a slight red glow in his shirt. The shirt had double pockets, which I had not noticed when I searched him the first time. I dug into the rear pocket and pulled out a small black box with a glowing red LED. I vaguely remembered seeing a similar box sometime in the past, but what the thing was remained just outside my memory.

A flock of crows had been eating something dead on the road across the river and they suddenly all flew off at once. I picked up my rifle and started watching the river. I knew the first thing I would see was movement, so I was careful to keep my eyes scanning, as humans see movement better out of the sides of their eyes. The sun was bright and low from the east, on my right, and I caught a flash. Actually, it wasn't a flash, but something had momentarily blocked a small section of glare on the river. The top of one riffle was shining like a mirror and then, just for a moment, it wasn't. Somebody was coming up the river, trying to stay out of sight and he had momentarily blocked the ray of sun reflecting off the top of the riffle. Then the glare winked again, and again and again.

This was not good.

I remembered what that box was I found in the dead guy's shirt. Old people living alone used them and cops carried them into dangerous situations. When the person went down and remained motionless for more than a few minutes it transmitted a signal indicating they were in trouble. That must be how these guys knew to show up at the river, their dead buddy told them.

I thought about that old Ron White joke, "I don't know how many guys it would take to kick my ass, but I knew how many they were sending." I had this bunch at four, but I figured they were not alone.

There was a loud crash behind me and when I turned, the door to the loading dock suddenly had a huge crack in it. That probably saved my life, at least for the moment. If it had opened with the first hit I would have been a goner. I never heard them sneaking though the old store, which meant either I was getting old and losing my hearing or they were very, very good.

I didn't wasting any time debating that question, or mourning my lost youth. I pulled my pistol from my belt holster and started shooting at the door. The guy came at it to kick again and I could see him through the crack just as I fired three fast shots. One bullet splintered the edge of the crack, but the other two went through. I heard a thud as the guy fell back.

I did a tactical reload, dumping the still half full magazine into my pocket and recharging the pistol with a new magazine. It was a calculated risk, as I figured I had the two seconds I needed to do that while somebody else stepped up to hit the door.

Instead of a guy with a gun, a big, cast iron wood burning stove came crashing through the door, followed by three very big guys. I dodged left to avoid the stove and fired three shots as fast as I could get the front sight on their centers of mass, all the while moving and ducking for cover. One guy went down and another staggered and grabbed his shoulder. I rolled under the piled up shipping crates as bullets pounded where I had just been. Knocking the crates out of my way, I kept rolling until I fell off the loading dock, landing on my backpack, which cushioned the blow. Luckily my rifle was on a sling and hanging in front of me, but I had lost the Bushmaster, which was still on the loading dock.

The guy I had missed was at the edge of the loading dock and tracking me with his pistol, so I dumped a double tap at his center of mass. I used point shooting techniques as he was so close and I needed to be faster than him. The first shot caught him in the pelvis, breaking it and toppling him over. The second shot rode the recoil and went high, and as he fell it hit him in the mouth, exiting the back of his neck and shutting off the switch. He landed on top of me, knocking the wind out of me. But, the second guy was right there, bleeding from his right shoulder and holding his pistol in his left hand. I pointed and emptied the rest of the magazine into him, then I moved out of the way as he fell on his buddy.

I scrambled to my feet just as bullets started hitting the cement loading dock behind me, which mean they were coming from the bunch I had spotted sneaking up the river.

I ran forward towards the shooters as I holstered the empty pistol. There was an abandoned car ten feet ahead and to the right of me and I dove toward it face first, sliding up against the front tire. More rifle fire hit the car, shattering the windshield. I could hear bullets hitting the motor and some metal fragments sprayed from the car and hit my leg. It hurt like hell, but it also gave me an idea.

I rolled under the car, holding my rifle sideways so it would fit in the narrow space, and picked up a set of legs in my scope. I fired three quick shots and one leg bent at an abnormal angle. As the guy fell through my line of vision I dumped two more shots into his body.

I rolled out from under the car and back behind the wheel just as a burst of bullets skidded along the pavement where I had been. I huddled behind the front tire, trying to make myself small and hoping it and the motor would give me a little shelter. People think a car will stop bullets. The engine will, but there are several inches of open air underneath the engine on most cars. A tire will not stop a rifle bullet, but your best hope is to hide behind the front tire. At least there you have the suspension, the steering, the frame, some brake parts and maybe the tire and wheel on the other side blocking for you. It's the place that puts the most car parts between you and the gun, but don't kid yourself, there are holes where an industrious bullet can get through.

I put the rifle over the hood, keeping my head down, and fired a few shots. I wasn't aiming, but then my plan was not to hit anybody, just to get them used to me shooting from there. I did it again. When bullets skidded across the hood I figured I was both pushing my luck and had accomplished my goal. So, I put the gun to my left shoulder and quickly moved out around the front of the car. I picked up a guy in the scope, aiming at the hood assuming I would pop up to shoot again, and I shot him in the chest. I pulled back behind the car while they opened up again. I did a tactical reload with the rifle so I would have a fully charged magazine, smacking it hard to be sure it was seated. Then I put the partially emptied magazine in my pocket.

The car was backed about halfway into a wooden garage that was missing its doors. Staying low, I ran around the back of the car. Inside the garage, sitting with its feet sunk into the dirt floor, was an old fashioned cast iron bathtub. I peeked around the side of the garage door and saw one of the first guys who had come out of the river duck behind a car about twenty feet away. Behind him, close to the river, were about twenty more men, coming in from the west. They were across the bridge, still a hundred yards away, but they were working their way along the buildings and abandoned cars that lined the side of the road and closing the distance fast.

I waited for the closest guy to poke his head over the car and I shot him in the forehead. Actually, I aimed at his forehead, but I forgot about the scope off-set that makes you shoot low on close targets and I hit the roof of the car just in front of him. The bullet fragmented and slammed into his face. Same result, just more dramatic.

Then I ran like hell, dove into the bathtub and started screaming bad words.

CHAPTER 8

As I expected, the bunch coming down the road opened up. Bullets slammed through the board siding of the garage and filled the air. Several hit the bathtub. Most just pinged off, but a couple punched through. Both the through shots were above my body, so I wasn't hurt, but it told me that at least one guy had a much more powerful rifle.

I was used to dealing with gangs and bad guys with civilian style guns. These guys clearly had some military training and were using full-auto carbines. I think the big gun was some sort of sniper rifle in a bigger cartridge, like the very powerful .338 Lapua that was so popular with military and wanna-be snipers, back before.

That changed the rules, the tub might have been protective cover when I was dealing with carbine fire, but now they could shoot though the wall, the tub and me without slowing the damn bullet down much at all.

After what seemed like days, but was probably less than a minute, they stopped firing. I dared to peek over the tub and look at the wall. These guys were pros. They had systematically covered every square inch of the wall and then stopped firing. They knew that anything on the other side had to have been hit.

I scrambled back behind the car and looked underneath. I could see a lot of feet heading my way, so I slid my rifle underneath and started shooting at legs. Then, when there were no more legs, I swung back and shot at every body lying on the ground I could find. Then I scrambled back behind the front wheel.

As my back hit the wheel I realized my mistake. I had not looked back at the store even once after taking out that first team.

It's a wonder I didn't get shot in the back. But luck was again in sync with me, because I looked through the splintered back door and glimpsed a guy weaving through the debris in the store's old showroom. I didn't think he had seen me yet, because there was no shooting. I duck-walked back to the garage, well aware of all the bullets hitting the car and how little protection it was giving me. They clearly didn't see me move, because they continued to pour fire into the car.

When I went past the cast iron tub I noticed the bottom was smeared with blood. I was aware that my right leg hurt like hell and when I looked my pants were bloody below the knee. But everything still worked okay and I didn't have time to worry about it now.

Once inside the garage I made my way to the south end. There was a small woodshed off the garage with an open door between them. I ran into the shed and peeked out the window, just as the guy cautiously exited the store He was only about ten feet from me, but I wasn't sure what the window glass would do to the bullet. So, I held on the center of mass in order to have the biggest target in case the glass deflected the bullet and pulled the trigger three times, as fast as I could get the sights back on the guy's belly. He fell and rolled onto the two other dead guys. I shot him twice more in the head. He was going to be behind me and I didn't need him rising from the dead to shoot me in the back.

The shooting had stopped, so I got back behind the front wheel of the car and risked a peek around the bumper. There were three more bodies in the road from my burst, but that still left something like seventeen more. I was never good at math and who the hell wastes time counting when they can be shooting, anyway? Whatever the number, it was too damn many.

Somebody must have seen me take that quick look and they lit up the car one more time. Now they knew exactly where I was, so they were focusing on the front tires. There is no way those tires would stop the big gun, so I dove for the garage, landing about halfway there. Luckily, they were still shooting back where they thought I was, so no bullets were there to greet me as I belly crawled into the garage.

My eyes adjusted to the light and I saw a dusty, cobweb covered ladder nailed to the back wall. I scrambled up and through the opening at the top into an attic over the garage. It was filled with piles of debris, the collection of a couple of lifetimes' worth of stuff. On the northwest side I could see a filthy window. I made my way to it, standing back so nobody would see me as I looked out at the street.

What I saw was not good. I guess they figured I was dead, but they were still being careful. They advanced in pairs, running a jagged course to make a tougher target. As the first two advanced, the rest remained behind the cars with their rifles, ready to cover them. Once the pair was behind cover, two more started forward. They had closed up so that the nearest were only about thirty yards from the car I had been hiding behind.

It was just a matter of time before they found me here and there were way too many of them to fight. I might get a few, but the old wooden walls of this building wouldn't stop enough bullets to keep me from ending up with a lot more holes in my body than I started the day with.

Ten feet to the right of the window was another ladder with a small wooden door at the top, about thirty inches square. I climbed up the ladder and balanced on it as I reached up and opened the sliding latch. The door opened on old creaky hinges to reveal a short passageway, just big enough to crawl through with my pack. I moved to another door at the far end. That opened to the main attic on the third floor of the house. The roof was pitched so that it was about nine feet off the floor in the center, but the walls were only three feet high on the sides.

There was junk piled everywhere, with trails and paths running through it at odd angles. It looked like a giant maze, so I stuck to the main path. The light was filtered through a couple of dirty windows and as soon as I entered my movement filled the air with dust. About halfway to the other end I spotted a trap door and when I opened it there was a narrow set of enclosed stairs with a door at the bottom. I hoped the door would lead to something.

I moved back to the last window and waited for the next two guys to make their run. When they started I smashed out the window with the AR-15's flash hider and shot the closest head I could see peeking over a car. Then I transitioned to the next guy hiding behind a car and shot him. The rest caught on and every head disappeared. That left the two guys running across the thirty yards of open space. They knew they were in trouble and were running as hard as they could. I held just in front of the rear guy, swinging the gun with him, and shot. I didn't even look for a result, but sped up the movement of the gun and as the crosshair passed through the second runner, I pulled the trigger. They both went down. I brought the gun back and double tapped both in the head, then ran like hell for the stairs. I dumped the magazine on the way, pulled a fresh one out of my vest pocket and smacked it into the carbine. I hated to lose a valuable magazine, but I didn't have time to pick it up and put it in a pocket. Bullets were shattering the walls of the attic as I ran down the stairs as quietly as possible. The door was locked, or stuck. It didn't matter which, it wouldn't open. I had hoped to be quiet, but it wasn't to be. I backed up and slammed my shoulder into the old wooden door with all I had. It crashed open and I fell into a tiny room filled with old clothes piled in heaps and a table with an antique sewing machine. Just as I looked at the sewing machine the thread bobbin on top exploded. Bullets started ripping though the wall, so I guess there was no doubt they heard the door open.

Falling to the floor had saved me, as the bullets were all going over my head. I belly crawled to the next room, a tiny bedroom, and then worked to the center hall off that. From there I kept moving east, trying to put as many walls between me and the shooters as possible.

This old house had walls that were made of wooden laths covered with plaster that was mixed with horsehair. They were much thicker and denser than a modern house's interior walls and a couple of them would stop most of the bullets.

When I got to the east bedroom I risked a look out the window. There were a bunch of guys coming around the house and diving for cover behind the big maple trees that were scattered around the back lawn. Before they could start shooting I ran for the center hall and down the stairs to the ground floor.

There was a guy coming through the front door at the end of the stairs and I shot him as I ran past. When he fell I could see more behind him, but they got the message and ducked for cover.

I ran into the kitchen and spotted an old wooden door off the back wall. I headed for that while bullets filled the space I had just vacated. The door was not latched, so I flung it open and ran into the dark. I tripped over a box and fell face first down a flight of steep wooden stairs, landing on the dirt floor of the cellar.

The fall knocked the wind out of me, but I didn't have time to lie there and breathe, I had to keep moving and hope it would work out. I looked around and spotted a deep root cellar off the backside of the main basement that was dug into the earth under the lawn. I hid in there, safe for now and looked back to the main cellar for a way out while I tried to get some air back in my lungs.

There was a bulkhead door and a couple of ground level windows. I picked up a piece of lumber off a wall rack, ran out and waved it past the first window. A three shot burst splintered the board in my hand. So now they knew where I was, and at least one of them could really shoot. But there were no walls to shoot though like upstairs, so I just needed to stay away from the windows.

I heard a board creak above my head, so I shot five times at the sound, stringing out the shots to cover more area. I was rewarded with a thump and the sound of more running feet. I emptied the magazine at the sounds and after another thump, everything went deathly quiet.

Blood started running through the cracks in two different locations. I backed into the root cellar, just as bullets started pouring down from above. I guess they figured if I could shoot up through it, they could shoot down through it. Judging from the number of bullets, there had to be ten guys shooting, but I couldn't tell where they were. If they were smart, they were behind cover. I only had a couple of loaded magazines left, so I held my fire and waited.

It was deathly quiet for several minutes. The blood kept dripping down through the ceiling, but with all the new bullet holes there seemed to be a lot of it. Then I noticed the smell of kerosene and knew it wasn't just blood. They must have found the fuel tank for the old space heater I had spotted in the living room. That only meant one thing and I knew I had to get the hell out of there fast.

I could hear a truck's horn blasting and a motor racing off to the north, followed by a lot more rifle fire. I ran to the window and waved the board again. Again, they shot at it. I repeated, but this time they must have figured out it was a decoy. I did it twice more then I jumped up on an old apple crate under the window and stuck my carbine out the window. I saw two guys looking at me with that "aw shit" look in their eyes and I shot them both.

Luckily, kerosene is not as volatile as gasoline. If they had used gas the air would have filled with fumes, then there would have been an explosion and my lungs would be burned to a crisp by now. But kerosene is harder to ignite and the flames spread much slower when lit. I could smell the fire and hear the flames above me, but so far they had not followed me down to the cellar. The sound of the truck horn was louder and mixed with a lot of shouting. I hoped the two guys I just shot were all that had been left guarding the back side of the house. I didn't dare open the bulkhead, as they would expect that.

It occurred to me that when I was a kid, everybody called them "hatchways." It's odd what pops into your head when you are stressed.

To the left of the hatchway was a half-height wooden wall. I looked over the top to see coal heaped up in the corner. Coal was a popular fuel used to heat houses in this part of the country back in the early years of the 20th century. No doubt the old boiler had been replaced with one that burned fuel oil, but the coal bin remained. At the top of the foundation wall was a chute that had been used to run the coal from the delivery trucks into this storage bin.

I climbed up the pile of coal and into the opening. There was a wooden trap door at the top. I was afraid it would be nailed shut, but it pushed open easily enough, a testament to how crime free Vermont was back before.

I peeked through and a guy was off to my right, standing with his rifle at the ready, covering the window. I fired three fast shots, trying to make them sound like their full-auto, three-shot burst rifles, so the guys in front would think it was them shooting at me. Then I jumped out of the coal chute and started running like hell.

When I rounded the corner of the house I could see two of the three trucks from Jack's convoy. They had turned the trucks around so they were ready to head back across the bridge. Everybody inside was in a hot gun battle with the rest of the bad guys, who were all looking at the trucks and had their backs to me. I started picking them off as fast as I could, while running like hell for the trucks. I shot three or four more before they all started ducking for cover. That let me get around the back of the first truck, so it shielded me from them. I jumped onto the step on the driver's side, grabbed the cargo rack on the roof and screamed "Go! Go! Go!" As loud as I could. Bullets smacked the armor plating on the truck as the driver floored the big engine. We drove across the bridge and turned right on the main road. The truck stopped, a cargo door opened from the bed and Davy's face peered through with a huge grin.

"It looks like you have been busy and probably have worked up an appetite, so I figured you needed another one of Clay's mom's peaches."

Bullets were still pounding the other side of the truck, so I didn't bother to answer. I just dove headfirst through the door and then pulled it shut behind me.

CHAPTER

"A few miles down the road from where we let you out we noticed some fresh tire tracks going up one of those old logging roads," Jack told me after I had transferred to the cab of his truck a few miles down the road. "So we decided to check it out. There was a big truck parked just out of sight of the main road, and nobody around to guard it. We found a bunch of guns and ammo and several fifty-five gallon drums. We opened one of them and it was filled with gasoline. Not that yellow, cruddy, odd-smelling old gas we are burning, but fresh, clear gasoline. I haven't seen any of that in so long I forgot what it looked like. Somebody is refining petroleum again and making new gasoline. But, who?

"We heard your first shots" he continued, "but figured that it was finished one way or the other. I could tell from the sound that the first shots were a pistol, and then I heard your rifle, so I thought you came out okay. Then, while we were looking through the truck, the shit hit the fan and we heard all that shooting.

"It had to be the guys from this truck and, judging from all the footprints, we knew you were a goner. But there seemed be no end to it all. I figured a few shots and done, yet this thing just kept going and going. I guess all that stuff we heard about you is true, huh?"

"What stuff?" I asked.

"How you fought off the hordes by yourself during the social wars and then taught the rest of the valley how to protect their homes."

"I didn't do anything alone; my family was there too, it was a joint effort. We got lucky a few times, that's all," I replied.

"Not how I heard it," he said with a grin.

"Anyway, after awhile somebody pointed out that maybe you needed some help and Davy here wanted to shoot some more bad guys. Those arrogant bastards were so sure they were the only people coming back they left the keys in the truck. I sent one of my trucks with another driver and a shooter along to guard it and the rest of us took the other two trucks back for you."

"I guess I owe you all another steak dinner for that."

"Hell, you owe us the whole damned cow!"

"Not me, I had fun," Davy shouted through the port. "Hell, I would much rather shoot assholes than eat."

CHAPTER 10

We live okay now, growing most of our own food. In addition to a big garden, we have chickens, pigs and a few cows. So there is a supply of milk, butter, meat and eggs. But, the first years were pretty rough.

Like a lot of macho guys, I used to brag that as long as I had a gun and some bullets we would have food on the table, even if it meant turning a blind eye to the game laws. It turns out the game wardens were never an issue. They were gone long before the collapse. Vermont had created so many entitlement programs that needed to be funded that by the time Washington's policies had trashed the economy, the state had started to feed on itself like a starving man cutting off and cooking his own leg so he could have some protein.

When the decline started, one of the first cuts they made eliminated the Fish & Wildlife Department and with it the game wardens. Caving in to pressure from PETA and the animal-rights whackos, they banned hunting and fishing. After that, they reasoned that we didn't need Fish & Wildlife any longer.

The State Police soon followed into oblivion and then the road maintenance crews. By then, our inept and corrupt governor didn't even bother trying to rationalize why.

It was obvious to all of us that it was to keep the welfare flowing, because through it all the entitlement programs remained fully funded. By that time there were more people feeding at the government trough than working, and they all voted.

The "leaders" we kept electing, against any form of logic, neglected the fact that the taxpayers, those who funded the state, needed roads and police to function, so of course it didn't last long.

Vermont was one of the very first states to declare bankruptcy. We struggled along on federal money for a while, but that dried up too. Vermonters, like the citizens of most of the "blue" states, have been on our own since well before the collapse.

Trying to use my guns to feed my family only worked for a very short time. The trouble was the state only had about eighty-thousand whitetail deer and nearly seven hundred-thousand people. It didn't take long for the woods to empty and protein to run to short supply.

I knew that would happen because I had seen it before. In 2009 I made my third hunting safari to Zimbabwe. For years, the country had been under the control of a horrible dictator named Robert Mugabe. A decade earlier, he had panicked when his support began to slip and turned to extremely racist policies to curry favor with the blacks who made up eighty percent of the country's population. He forced all the white landowners and farmers off their land, grabbing their property and killing them if they resisted, and gave the farms to his black supporters.

Within just a few years the country went from a thriving economy with a currency on par with the then-strong U. S. dollar, a country that was called the "bread-basket of sub-Sahara Africa" because of all the food it produced, to total desolation. The economy collapsed to the point where they no longer had a currency. Commerce stopped and people began to starve.

On that trip we drove from Harare to the southeast corner of Zimbabwe, a trip of several hundred miles that took most of the day. I was shocked by the miles and miles of total desolation we traveled through. Every animal had been killed, every tree cut down, every blade of grass torn up. There was nothing but raw dirt for mile after mile. This was done by starving people trying to survive. People without a plan. People who were no doubt now dead.

I understood that it was about to happen in the United States as well, so I took action. Sure, I shot deer and other game when I could find it. I also shot a cow I found wandering on the road near my house. I suppose I could have tried to find the owner, but my family was hungry. I am not proud, but we are alive. We even ate a feral dog or two when things got really bad.

My guns fed us for those first awful months, but I knew that couldn't last. I had to come up with a way to survive long-term.

I still had my truck then and I borrowed a horse trailer. I traded a few guns and a bunch of ammo for some livestock and seeds from a guy in New York, about thirty miles away. He needed protection, as he had obeyed the tough gun laws of his state and was caught in the collapse with nothing more than a shotgun. I spent a day teaching him about his new guns, but he couldn't tell me a damn thing about the cows or the seeds. He was a school teacher, had picked them up in another trade and knew less than I did about farming — which wasn't much.

All I knew about farming was from shoveling manure and bailing hay during a summer job on a farm when I was thirteen. There had not been a working dairy farm in my part of Vermont in years, so I didn't even know who to ask about livestock.

It took a while to figure out how it all worked and we nearly lost everything to sickness a couple of times. I found some people who had run a farm years ago who were willing to help for a cut of the milk and meat. I also traded some of the milk for some books on planting, so I learned enough to grow a garden.

Now we know what to look for and who to call for help when the livestock gets sick. More importantly, we know how to keep them from getting sick.

We are careful about only killing the surplus, like the old investors used to say about their money, "Never touch the principal." If we keep enough critters around to breed, we always have meat to eat and to trade. By rotating our stock we keep them young and healthy.

We are also careful about making sure the livestock we keep are well fed and well-tended, so for now things are fine. In fact, we usually have a surplus each year and have a pretty good business trading the fresh meat. Like I mentioned earlier, we also do custom butchering for our neighbor's livestock and game.

We also sell a lot of the ammo I handload during the winter and I barter a few guns, but just like the investors, I never touch the principal. One thing I make sure of is that we have a lot of guns and ammo for ourselves and our family. With guns we can always survive.

There is no money, but we trade our goods and services for things we need, like clothing, building supplies or toilet paper. I might have said I would rather have books than toilet paper, but the best approach is to have both. I dread the day when we run out of the stuff.

Several years ago I made a trip to Russia to tour a gun factory and hunt brown bears. We had a day's layover in Moscow, where we went for lunch at a restaurant in a nearly vacant mall just off Red Square. I needed to use the men's room after lunch and was surprised to find a lady with a table set up outside the door, selling toilet paper. I had my interpreter tell her I needed some and she handed me about eighteen inches off the roll.

"Take a good look at me," I told the interpreter. "I am a big guy and for the past two days I have been eating food I can't identify that was prepared by people with questionable hygiene. Things are happening that are not going to be pretty. That little scrap wouldn't serve to wipe my runny nose. Tell her I want the entire roll."

"Five dollars American," he said, without bothering to check with the lady selling the toilet paper.

I handed the crook a five, took the roll and saw with clarity what I would fear most if our society ever went to hell.

Of course, back then I never believed it would.

So today, I have a standing order for toilet paper or baby wipes from any-body selling it. While I pride myself on my book collection, I also take pride in the cases of ass wipes I have hoarded in my garage. Both, I think, are the mark of a civilized man.

Without a freezer, it's tough to keep meat but sometimes it makes more sense to butcher rather than feed. So we had to re-learn some of the old ways and we can a lot of meat. We also can the vegetables we grow. The berries and apples we pick are turned into preserves. There is still enough commerce to barter for sugar, salt and other things we need.

We dry some of everything; meat, berries and fruit, by the wood stove in the winter. Our summers are much too humid for making jerky or dried fruit, but in the winter our house is filled with the wonderful smell of food being preserved.

We heat with wood, which is a lot tougher to cut now that gas is so hard to find. Perhaps the best invention of our time was the chain saw. I used to curse them as I have always hated to cut firewood, but now I long to hear that annoy-ing buzz again. The upside is that running a hand powered buck saw, along with all the other work we have to do, has gotten me into pretty good shape. It has put some muscles on my aging arms and shoulders and has really built up my endurance. That's all come in pretty handy a few times over the past years.

I dropped a lot of weight and found out that I can live without a bunch of the drugs that the doctors were shoving down my throat for decades.

That's a good thing, because most of them are not available anymore. I am one of the lucky ones. I had a few rough months while I dumped the weight and my body adjusted to not having the drugs, but those who were totally dependent on insulin or other medicines didn't live long.

The shortages started well before the collapse. The implementation of government run health care, coupled with a huge increase in regulation, had resulted in widespread shortages of medical supplies. The system struggled on for years while the government tried to regulate the industry out of the mess it had become, which of course just made things worse.

Once the concept of a capitalist, free-market based economy was abandoned by the United States, and ultimately the world, most of the drug manufacturers got fed up and just closed their doors.

The government tried to force them to continue operations, but how are you going to force somebody to stay in business when that business is failing? It was just more of the muddled "we are the world" thinking that pervaded our government in the last years. You might force them to stay open, but if they can't pay their suppliers or their employees, they are not going to produce much of anything.

Congress tried to force the suppliers to send product anyway, but it was more of the same story. When they didn't get paid, they couldn't pay their suppliers and it didn't take long for it all to collapse.

The government tried to nationalize the drug industry, but that only made things worse. The same problems that existed before, the lack of raw materials and qualified workers were coupled with the inefficiency and corruption that defined the end days of the American government.

There was no money to pay anybody and soon enough the money was worthless anyway, so after a while no one bothered to show up for work. The government arrested them for "job desertion," but there was no money to feed the huge numbers of prisoners or to pay anybody to guard them. After the collapse of the government, millions starved to death in the abandoned prisons.

When the drug supplies ran out completely it was about the same time the economy dissolved and nobody had money to buy them anyway, so I guess it really didn't matter.

CHAPTER 11

The early years after the collapse were tough in other ways, too. The closest thing to a plan most of the huddled masses along the crowded East Coast had for survival was to "head for the hills."

Well, I live in the "the hills" and we were struggling to survive as well. At first we tried to help, but they just kept coming and coming. We barely had enough for ourselves and there was certainly not enough to keep the millions that migrated from the cities alive too. Once we started to turn them away, they turned mean and tried to take it all by force. I lost a lot of good friends and relatives to those early social wars, mostly because at first we all tried to defend our homes by ourselves.

My family survived because I was a gun guy. "Back before," I had made my living as a writer for gun magazines and my recreation was competition shooting, so I had a lot of guns and ammo. I also had a lot of the supplies and tools needed to manufacture more ammo, or at least to reload the spent cases.

I had plenty of lead to cast bullets when the commercial stuff ran out. That worked fine for the pistol ammo and for some of the old rifle cartridges. But modern rifles, particularly the .223 Remington and .308 Winchester cartridges that we use for protection, need jacketed bullets. I could make them as well, using some dies that I made in my backyard machine shop before the electricity stopped flowing. But those bullets were not as good as the commercial stuff. They were okay for close-range fighting, but lacked accuracy for long-range shooting. The problem was with making the jackets that were needed to allow the high velocity of these cartridges. Pure lead is too soft for a high velocity bullet. It will not hold the rifling in the bore and will strip through without spinning, which makes bullets horribly inaccurate. Also, a few shots will incapacitate the firearm until the lead is cleaned out of the bore. To solve that problem, back in the late 1800s bullets were changed from all lead or lead alloy to a lead core wrapped with a jacket of much harder material. Of course, that material had to be softer than the steel in the barrels so it would not damage the guns. It also had to be malleable enough to take the shape of the rifling in the bore and spin the bullet so that it would be accurate in flight.

Commercial bullets use gilding metal for the jackets, which is ninety-five percent copper and five percent zinc. With no source of that material I had to make mine out of brass we salvaged from fired cases. It was tough to control the consistency of the brass, so the bullets were not as accurate as the precision commercial bullets. Still, they served their purpose. We kept the "store bought" bullets for hunting and any long-range work, while using the homemade stuff for everything from shooting cows to butcher, to protecting our homes.

What I couldn't make were the smokeless gun powders we needed to propel the bullets and the primers used to ignite the powder. I watched my dwindling supply of powder and primers very carefully. I also made it a point to trade for more powder and primers at every opportunity, even when I had to pay too much for them.

After Congress outlawed guns and the military was downsized, most of the gun and ammo manufacturers went out of business. The government confiscated all the guns and ammo in inventory, but not the materials. I had some good friends in the industry and back when gas was still available and the roads were relatively safe, my boys and I had twice made extended road trips to the ammunition factories to load up on powder, primers and bullets. My pals had the keys to the abandoned factories where this stuff was stored and we worked out a deal. I brought them a truckload of meat, to eat or barter with and they unlocked the doors.

Everybody told me I was just being paranoid, but it turns out that a little bit of foresight had helped to keep us all alive.

But, nothing lasts forever and the social wars had drained our ammo supply dramatically. I was dreading the day when I ran out of powder and primers.

Empty cases were never a problem as they could be reused multiple times. I had plenty anyway. After some of the bigger battles of the social wars my son, son in law and myself returned to the battlefields and filled the back of my pickup truck with empty cases time and time again. I built a storage shed just to hold all the empty cartridge cases. I just needed more of the powder and primers used to make empty cases into ammo again.

All my guns were double edged swords, because having those guns protected me and my family, but they also made me a target. It was never a secret that I had the guns. "Back before" I sold hunting books and booked hunting trips from my home office, so my address was published many times on paper and on the Web. It was easy enough to find me and a lot of people tried to take the guns away, starting with the government. Once the country collapsed and the Feds were gone, it was the gangs, the bandits and sometimes my neighbors. I was smart enough to hide most of the guns off the property and keep just what I needed to defend my home.

We were raided by the government within hours after Congress outlawed gun ownership, but I was ready for that.

The sneaky bastards passed the law at midnight on a Saturday, on a holiday weekend. "Tolerance Day" was our newest federal holiday, but those in power didn't show any tolerance for gun owners. They passed the total gun ban behind locked doors, in a back room of the Capitol without allowing any discussion. The president, who actually presided illegally over the joint session, signed it into law immediately.

They didn't even let the opposition vote. Armed Capitol Police kept the Tea Party lawmakers from the meeting. Later, the majority leaders claimed they had followed the rules, that the Tea Party was absent because they had boycotted. Nobody believed that was true, but there was nobody to stop them, so the law stood.

The Supreme Court had long since been compromised after the last few presidents had packed it with appointees they could control and who would do their bidding. Within hours, SCOTUS heard the case and ruled it constitutional. They ruled that the Second Amendment only applied to government employees because the militia was clearly a government entity in the eyes of the founding fathers. Later, when the raids started, the Supreme Court ruled without explanation or comment that the Posse Comitatus Act didn't apply to federal raids on gun owners. The press was so corrupt they didn't even bother to report on any of what was happening. If it were not for the internet v2.1, we never would have seen it coming.

The raids focused not just on gun owners, but also on Christians, conservatives, right-wing bloggers and anybody who still dared to fly the American flag. The conventional wisdom was that if they raided your place, they would find something to charge you with, even if they had to bring it with them.

It didn't matter if you owned a gun; the law gave them open-ended permission for unwarranted searches of any private property. All they needed to do was say they "suspected" there were guns on the property and centuries of constitutional protection for United States citizens were thrown out for good.

I was ready for the raids and all they got were a few rusty junkers I had collected over the years. They were enough to keep them from planting more damaging evidence, but were also guns I could afford to lose.

The rest of my guns, even those we used for daily protection, were safely hidden in a place nobody would ever find. It was a risk, not having any guns for protection, but I figured it would be better to risk a few months then, rather than the rest of our lives without any means to defend ourselves. I was pretty sure things would get a lot worse down the road and it turned out I was right.

The agents suspected that I had a lot more guns than what they found and tried their best to get me to tell them where they were, but I never did because I knew those guns were the only thing that would keep my family alive in the future.

After several days of painful "interrogations," they realized I wasn't going to talk, so they put me in jail. While the media back in the day focused on "water-boarding" and how horrible America had become because we used it on some terrorists, it was a joke. Everybody knew it never worked and they didn't even waste time using it on me. What they did instead was much worse. While there was no lasting or permanent damage from what they did to me, there are a lot of scars. I still wake up screaming at night with the memory of the pain they caused. They didn't try to hide what they were doing because there was nobody to stop them. My back, legs and arms will always carry the reminders.

They never found any more guns and never had proof that I committed any crimes. I was never charged with anything, I didn't have a trial and they wouldn't let me talk to a lawyer. Months later they got sick of feeding me, I guess, because one day my wife was waiting to take me home.

I was one of the lucky ones; I left a lot of good guys behind in that "Gun Act Violation Re-education Camp," most of them were never heard from again.

The Feds were watching me for a long time after that and I couldn't retrieve most of my guns. My cousin Randy knew where they were, so I asked him and his brother Scott to see if they could sneak a few to me; enough so we could defend our lives and property.

Getting to the guns was never a problem for them as my cousins were not being watched. They had voluntarily turned in their own guns the day after the ban. Of course most of their good guns were also hidden off site with mine, but they had a few, like I did, that they held back to give the government.

They were never "gun guys" anyway, so the government assumed those few beat up deer rifles and muzzleloaders were all they had. That collection actually was all they had, until they realized I was right about what I had been preaching all those years. They had quietly bought up more guns off the books and stored them in a bunker we had hidden under bedrock, deep in the woods.

With my consent, they also "gave me up" to the agents, pretending to be helpful and also pretending that in this age of power blackouts and spotty telephone service that they didn't already know I had been raided the night before.

This bought them a little trust with the government. Because the raids were so widespread, there were not enough agents to monitor everybody and by the time I was let out of prison nobody was looking at my cousins.

The world was on the verge of a global war, the United States was going bankrupt, there were no police and crime was out of control. Murder rates were setting records month after month, citizens were not safe on the streets or in their own homes, and the government kept saying that they simply didn't have the resources to police the streets or lock up the bad guys. But, oddly enough, they had enough manpower to keep four-man crew watching me 24/7. With the Federal Union-mandated labor laws ensuring a six-hour work day and three-day work week, it amounted to a lot of agents employed to watch over one citizen. As far as they knew, I had never committed a crime in my life worse than speeding. Technically, I had complied with the "Federal Small Arms Proliferation Act" in turning over the guns on my property. Yet, I was getting more attention than the little nut-job running China and threatening daily to drop a nuclear bomb on Washington.

CHAPTER 12

It was far too dangerous living in these times without some sort of protection and I needed some guns. I figured it would be better to live and to deal with the aftermath of using a gun and all the legal problems later, than to be cold and dead.

We still had sporadic television and Internet back then and every day the news was filled with people, often entire families, found murdered in their homes by roving gangs. Just as often too, there were reports of bodies found along lonely back roads. Bodies with gang tattoos and bullet holes. Nobody could ever figure out what happened. But then, nobody really tried all that hard. There was no state or local police left to investigate, only the Feds. When the towns and states started to go bankrupt, all the police departments in the United States were merged into one big federal agency. The official title was the "United States Federal Police Agency" but everybody just called them the "Feds."

For a while they concentrated on revenue-enhancing crime, like handing out speeding tickets. But once the economy started downhill, most people were no longer driving much. Those who did get tickets usually didn't have any money to pay them. They arrested them at first, but the jails were full with all the workers who had been arrested for illegal job abandonment and there was no room or money for more prisoners. So, the government declared that the "highway safety" program was a complete success, had achieved all its goals and they shut it down.

For the most part the Feds didn't work too hard. The courts were already clogged with citizens who had been arrested and the system could not handle any more. With union protection, most agents realized the best way to keep their jobs was to do nothing. If you arrested people, you got noticed. If you did nothing, nobody cared. So nobody worked very hard to solve the mystery of the dead gang members littering the back roads.

After those mysterious back-road bodies turned up, it was not uncommon to meet friends and neighbors at the local home supply and recycled building materials shop, getting replacement windows or doors. They would never look you in the eye, but just quietly went about collecting what they needed for repairs.

Of course, the act of self-defense was a felony by then in the "land of the free and home of the brave." Most of Europe had outlawed self-defense years before, as did Australia. Our law makers, who never had an original idea, followed suit. They reasoned that violence was never the answer (they were cut from the same philosophical cloth as my brother) and that we citizens should not be allowed to use any form of violence for any reason. They truly believed that by passing this law, all violent crime in the country would stop.

Those who did take the initiative of not allowing the bad guys to kill them, to protect their lives and the lives of their families, were arrested for their efforts. It didn't matter how cut and dried your justification was, if you reported it you were arrested and your property seized. So, the rule was you never talked about it. If you had to shoot some scumbag to protect yourself or your family, you simply dumped the body, repaired any property damage and hoped the incompetent Feds didn't suddenly get ambitious. I shared their thinking. But without any guns, I lacked the tools to protect myself and my family.

With these half-wits searching everything that came in or out of my property, it was a problem. Technically, what they were doing was still illegal under the Constitution, but who could I call? The same people ran every level of the government, law enforcement, the courts and all the judges—not just at the federal level, but state and local too. The concept of checks and balances was extinct. Anybody collecting a public sector paycheck had to play the game. If you made any waves, you joined the sixty percent of the population that was unemployed. Even most of the private sector lawyers were controlled by the government. Nobody was going to buck the system because I was being harassed.

I hoped they would be as lazy as all the other Feds, so we tried a few trial runs. What I found out was that clearly I was a "special project" and I had attracted the attention of somebody high up in the government—somebody with enough power to order these guys to lay siege to my property. Somebody they knew would protect them, but only if they actually did their jobs this one time. They were so scared of losing their cushy government jobs they did everything by the book.

I thought the first trial run was an inspiration. I was thinking of buying a cow and hired my cousin to transport it to my place for inspection. He stopped along the road and got it to swallow a plastic toy pistol by coating it with molasses. We figured more cows would be a good way to get some handguns past the Feds and wanted a test run. But, they used a portable X-ray machine that they hauled in on a big trailer and found the toy.

Of course they thought it was a real gun and pretty well freaked out for a while, calling in so many reinforcements that the road was filled with important looking vehicles with flashing lights and guys with shaved heads running around, looking like they were constipated.

After they cut the cow open and found out it was just a plastic toy gun, they were all pretty pissed. Of course, toy guns were banned as well. But we claimed we had no idea how this cow had come to swallow the toy. I had yet to make payment, so I didn't own the cow anyway and ultimately that's what got me off the hook.

It belonged to a lady in a bordering town, a government worker who pushed paper for the Federal Environmental Re-Education Enforcement Department. So, we got away with that one, but learned a lesson, which was kind of the point of it all anyway.

That lady sure was pissed off when the Feds declared the meat unfit for human consumption because of the proximity to the contraband toy plastic pistol. The entire cow had to be taken away by a hazmat crew and shipped by air for incineration at a government approved facility in Chicago, at her expense.

On the next try, we hid some metal crowbars in a load of manure that my cousin Scott was bringing to "fertilize my garden." We had it in a big stainless steel trailer designed for transporting maple sap. There was a cover, but we didn't bother to bring it, so this was like a giant brownie pan with three-foot sides, full of two tons of shit from several species. This sloppy mixture had the consistency of a thick, chunky stew and smelled worse than the bowels of Hades.

The trailer was too big to fit in their portable X-Ray machine. They tried a magnet, but as the tank was made from steel it just stuck to the bottom anyplace they probed. So, after much shouting and arguing, two junior agents donned fishing waders and shoveled every bit of the stinky, gooey shit off the wagon. Knowing that they would never load it back on, Scott brought a second wagon and insisted they move it there.

They found the crowbars, so it's safe to assume they would also find any guns we tried to hide in a wagon load of shit. Of course we had no idea how those crowbars, the very same two we had been trying to find for weeks, ended up at the bottom of the wagon.

We did take a lot of satisfaction in knowing that all the agents were splattered with a blend of cow, chicken, horse and pig shit. It hit one hundred degrees that August day and mysteriously the air conditioning unit in their trailer had sprung a leak; letting all the cooling agent illegally escape into the atmosphere.

By the time they finished filling out the paperwork for the "unauthorized release" of the air pollutants, they were several hours into overtime (which had required many phone calls to authorize) and the goo covering them had cooked into a crusty paste that smelled worse than a bucket full of putrid guts.

They were one agent short because one of them had fallen face-first into the three-foot deep shit that filled the first wagon. That happened after Scott "accidentally" left a shovel handle in his way, for which he apologized sincerely. The agent hit face first, sinking so deep that his head and body were completely submerged. He came up spitting shit and screaming incoherently.

Because he had ingested some of it, his buddies called in a federal hazmat medical team. I laughed like hell as they bagged him in a Tyvec suit head to toe, with just a breathing tube showing. Every couple of seconds another gob of shit came shooting out the end of the breathing tube as he spit chunks through it like a pea shooter. They put him in a government helicopter to Medevac him to the only remaining operational hospital in New England.

I wondered what they planned to do with him there. Boston, where the hospital was located, had been under a potable water ban for months. The Quabbin reservoir was lost after Windsor Dam breached and flooded several towns a few years before. The experts kept saying it was in danger, but nobody wanted to make a decision to fix it and so through bureaucratic dawdling they lost the water supply and thousands of lives. The Charles River still ran through the city of course, but the government refused to let them use the water because they felt it was too polluted, so they let people die instead. Residents were not allowed to shower or even brush their teeth. I doubt there was any water to wash the shit off him, short of tossing him in the ocean. But, that was illegal due to the anti-pollution laws. They couldn't treat him either. The only antibiotics available by then were on the black market and no government doctor would risk his cushy job by doing anything unauthorized.

I figured he would be just fine, at least medically. Psychologically, well, that's another issue altogether. He was just about catatonic when they bagged him.

The bottom line is that for generations famers in Vermont got shit on them; they just washed it off and continued on with life, no worse for the wear. Anybody with livestock still does. The difference is we will just hose it off, wash our clothes, take a shower and be done with it. It wasn't until the government decided to intervene that it became a huge crisis. I suspected the guy would be just fine, even without the medical care the government continues to promise, but can no longer provide. Of course nobody eats shit like he did, at least not on purpose. But still, other than perhaps suffering through a bout of the squirts for a few days, he would live.

The rest of the crew were dressed in the black ninja uniforms that all Feds wore in those final days. They were probably already incredibly hot, considering the mandatory body armor and the insulated "one style fits all" boots of the Federal uniform. The junior guys were also pretty stinky, as just about every inch was splattered in shit. In fact, the hazmat team had tried to take them to Boston. There was a big shouting match and I think the agents were on the losing end. But, the helicopter pilot pointed out that he was only authorized to transport one man and to move them all would take several trips. Nobody wanted to deal with getting authorization or with all the paperwork, so the hazmat team backed off and left them to deal with it on their own.

The Feds demanded I let them wash it off, but I told them my pump was broken and we didn't have any water. There is a stream that runs through my property, but federal pollution laws prevented them from washing there. Even swimming without showering first was a jailing offense. Ironic, when you consider that every time it rains every brook and stream within a mile of any livestock or wildlife is filled with floating shit. But then, I didn't write the rules.

Once the shit-covered Feds left and their replacements started their shift I found the problem with the pump, it seems a switch that's hidden out of sight behind a support beam in the barn got turned off somehow. I wonder how that happened?

In the end, we used a much simpler way to get some guns into the house. After months of dealing with this I had an epiphany. I put on a backpack early one evening and started walking down the road. Their thermal imaging picked me up right away, so of course the Feds followed me. At this late stage in the game, they were all either affirmative action hires to fill a quota, or they knew somebody high up in the government who got them a job. None of them were hired for their brains and with little money left in the government purse, they had very little training. Nobody thought to watch the back door.

With the Feds out of the way, my cousins came in the back way, dressed in camo left over from our deer hunting days. They stuck to the woods and in the shadows, and just walked up to the back door of my house.

They locked up the guns in the hidden vault in my cellar and left by the same route. I stopped at a neighbor's, filled the pack with summer squash and hiked back home. The Feds never suspected a thing. A few months later it all fell apart anyway and they were all unemployed, but I had guns to protect my family. So I guess it worked out

CHAPTER 13

Early in the first year after the collapse we lost some more guns when my wife and I were caught outside, working in the garden, by a couple of hundred people from New York City. The boys were hunting and my daughter was visiting a sick neighbor, so it was just the two of us with nobody in the house.

They only had sticks and rocks when they attacked, so we held them off with our handguns. But there were too many and they circled our flank, so we could not get to the house. We finally had to flee into the mountains behind our home with just our pistols and the clothes on our backs. I rallied some help and we drove them away a few days later, but the place was looted, including most of our guns and ammo. I kept a few hidden in the vault that they missed, but any we had out and ready for use were gone.

Most of the mob had moved on by then and there were only a dozen or so stragglers left behind. They ran as soon as they saw us approaching, so we didn't fire a shot. But, what we found was devastating.

Those assholes had killed all the livestock and pulled up everything in our garden. They raided our cellar, took every jar of canned food and preserves they could carry and smashed the rest. They stole all the dried meat and cleaned out all our stored foods. They also took our clothing, our cooking gear and my tools. Anything they could carry they lugged off. They smashed every window, broke all the furniture and tore up every book. They even killed my dogs. Nothing was left untouched. The bastards set the house on fire when they fled, but we managed to put that out with an old fashioned bucket brigade, leaving a lot of structural damage to one wall.

We didn't have to start over; it was worse than that. At least back when the world collapsed we had a foundation to build on. Now even that was gone.

Our friends and neighbors rallied and each of them brought some food, clothing and tools. Some even brought a few books. The men helped me repair the damage to the buildings, while the women helped my wife replant the garden. Even this late in the season, we hoped to get a few vegetables before the frost.

Randy brought a couple of laying hens and a few chicks. One morning I went to the barn and found a milking cow, two calves and three pigs in the stalls. To this day I don't know who put them there. But they saved our lives and restored our hope.

I think the thing that pissed me off the most was killing our dogs. While I mourned them like lost children, I replaced them as soon as I could. Dogs are our best early warning system and if I had not left them locked in the house that day they might have alerted us to the approaching mob in time for my wife and me to reach the house and our rifles. I traded some ammo for an adult male mixed breed named Clyde. One day a month later a female just wandered onto the place. Nobody claimed her except Clyde, and it wasn't long before we had a bunch of puppies running around. They brought with them a cheer that had been missing since the attack.

The bastards got a few guns, including a couple I really liked, but I had more hidden away off-site. Which is a good thing, because as it turned out that was just the start of things.

I vowed that scenario would never be repeated. Once again, having guns and ammo in multiple locations saved us. If I had kept everything we had on the premises, we would have been done, because in that decaying world if you didn't have a gun to protect yourself, you weren't going to be around very long. With guns going at a premium, some of what I had stashed also helped to fund the materials we needed to rebuild and to buy enough food to get us through the winter. It depleted the "principal" but we stayed alive.

A lot of Vermonters thought that their deer rifles would be enough to protect their homes. But, they were not. The rifles were designed for hunting, not home defense. The problem was there were just too many people. After the cities emptied, the highways became filled with wandering, aimless and desperate people. When word came down that there was a house with food, it wasn't dozens that converged, it was hundreds, sometimes thousands. Those with deer rifles could not reload fast enough and they were overrun and usually killed.

My family had better guns. We had drilled and practiced with them and had a plan for defense that we worked and re-worked until there were no flaws.

I realized that we needed a more defensible position. We cut every tree around the house for several hundred yards. My neighbors had moved and abandoned their house a few years back. We heard that they were all killed soon after they left, so we reluctantly tore it down, salvaged the lumber and filled in the cellar hole so it could not provide cover for the bad guys. To get to my place then, anybody had to cover four hundred yards of open ground in any direction.

My son, son-in-law and I spent several weeks traveling to farms in the area left empty after the owners left or were killed, collecting the barbed wire and fence posts from the abandoned fields.

We ringed the house, starting at the four hundred yard-line with a six foot high fence with ten strands of tensioned barbed wire, strung too close together to climb through and too high to step over. We then looped several strands of loose wire another two feet above that so that anybody trying to climb up the tensioned wires would not be able to make it over the top. Then we repeated that every fifty yards to the one hundred-fifty yard line. That meant we had six fences, one every fifty yards.

For the next fifty yards we scattered random coils of barbed wire, sort of like military concertina wire, for a tangle foot. In random places, we held it up a foot or so on posts or by stapling it to blocks of wood so that it formed a big mess that was impossible to walk, let alone run, through without stumbling.

We planted crops between the fences, but no tall growing plants like corn. I didn't want any place to hide.

I put signs every ten feet on the outside fence stating that it was private property monitored by armed guards and anybody approaching past the fence would be shot.

We installed gates through the fences using big thick steel pipe that I had traded for years earlier, set deep in concrete. I traded a thousand rounds of .223 ammo to a guy with a diesel-powered welding rig in exchange for putting the gates together. These gates were too big and tough to crash through with a truck. Besides that, we staggered the gates twenty-five yards off center, so that the second gate was twenty-five yards to the left and the third twenty-five yards to the right, or fifty yards apart. It was a pain in the neck for us, but with six gates to get through, this staggering arrangement would prevent any truck ramming the gates from building up enough speed to get through them all.

The gates were triple locked with the locks hidden under welded brackets so that they could not be cut with bolt cutters. When things started to get bad I had the foresight to order three dozen hardened locks. Half of them were keyed alike so one key opened them all and the other half all required their own individual keys.

The gates have spikes sticking up on top to discourage climbing over them and were strung with barbed wire. They were all easily visible from the bunker we made on the roof of the house, so we could shoot anybody trying to breach them. We kept a .50 BMG rifle loaded with armor piercing ammo at the ready to take out any vehicle. We also kept a bolt action sniper rifle in .300 Winchester ready to deal with anybody trying to cut through the locks. Plus, we all practice with our AR carry rifles out to five hundred yards. Any one of us could easily handle a problem along the fences with those rifles if the need came up.

We surrounded the house with a double row of sandbags to stop any bullets, leaving shooting ports at strategic locations. I welded up metal doors and window covers in my shop and installed them before it became impossible to get materials or electricity to run the welder. Of course, I had gun ports through them, which could be closed and locked from inside when not in use. We installed a double metal roof to prevent anybody from tossing a torch on the roof to burn us out.

When it came to our guns, we picked wisely. Each of us carried a semi-auto handgun and several spare magazines at all times. After that first incident, we also never left the house without a long gun. We didn't use deer rifles, even though I had a lot of them, or the shotguns that so many others thought were the answer. We picked AR-15 rifles because of their thirty-round magazines and the fact that the empty magazines can be replaced in about a second if you practice; giving you another thirty shots, so shooting was virtually uninterrupted. Our current guns were the best in my collection and they were tested to be sure they would keep running when they were hot and dirty.

We also had a few highly accurate bolt action "sniper" type rifles with removable magazines to handle any long range precision problems such as a sniper or some jerk on a machine gun. We kept several extra magazines with each rifle so it could be reloaded very quickly.

In addition to carrying one of these AR rifles whenever we stepped outside, we also kept at least one more in every room of the house and plenty of loaded magazines near each one. It was a risk because we might lose them again, but the benefits outweighed that risk.

More than once we ringed the property with bodies from the rioting masses trying to kill us and take what was ours, but finally word spread down the roads to leave us alone. The attacks slowed and finally stopped.

I knew that was not enough. We were doing okay, but too many of my friends and neighbors were being overrun. I helped them make their homes more secure and taught them how to defend against a mob attack. I explained to them about the best guns and helped them locate better firearms.

Together we organized the several towns in my valley. We kept lookouts posted on all the roads to watch for approaching trouble. That was their job. The rest of us provided them with food and shelter, everything they needed. There were a lot of people who wanted what they perceived as a "cushy" job just sitting around all day, but we picked carefully. We rotated them often to keep them sharp. These guys had our lives in their hands, so we selected only the best of the best.

Once the initial emptying of the cities had sorted out, about a year or so into it, the trouble came less often. But, it came better prepared. The wandering gangs that were left were organized and smart. We could do without the organized part, but we counted on them being smart – smart enough to understand that we would fight back and kill them all. That was an easy concept to grasp, even for a criminal.

At first, when we still had communications, our outpost spotters would call on the radios. But, nobody had made batteries in years and our supply ran out. Without them, of course, the radios were useless. So we resorted to a signal fired with a gun. Two fast shots then, exactly one minute later, a third. This was an old signal that my grandfather had come up with for our family deer camp. We were trackers and still hunters and tended to work deep into the mountains. If we shot a deer we would later fire this signal. It meant we needed help getting the deer out of the mountains. Of course, the joke was that if we heard the signal we would run the other way because dragging a big buck for miles was hard work. But, the reality was that we were a team and the system worked well. We used it, too, if anybody was lost at night. That happened often if a storm rolled in and cut visibility. The lost hunter would fire the signal and the camp would signal back. That gave the hunter a compass bearing to bring him home.

It worked just as well to protect our valley. The three shots were in a sequence that is not common in the world, so we could recognize it. As soon as we heard it, we repeated it using our carry guns, as did the next guy and the next, until it flooded the valley. We would all meet at a central location, figure out which guard had fired the first signal and then we would go to meet the threat.

At first we had a few battles and we lost some very good people. But, it proved to be so much better than each of us trying to go it alone to protect our property. One gang tried to decoy us by sending in a bunch of armed people from the south, hoping we would converge all our forces there while they brought in their main force from the east. It almost worked, but a sharp-eyed guard spotted the eastern main force from his lookout high up on a mountain and fired the signal. We left a handful of our best men to deal with the decoys and the rest of us met the main force. We didn't lose a single person that day, but we trashed those assholes so bad that they became our best advocates. They found religion in preaching the gospel of "leaving those Vermont guys alone."

Like I said, those gangs were evil, tough and vicious. But they were also smart, or they wouldn't have survived. It didn't take too long for word to travel throughout what used to be New England to leave our valley alone. There were easier pickings elsewhere. Places like Connecticut, Massachusetts, Rhode Island and New York, for years, had put a lot of restrictions on citizens owning guns, so even when guns were banned and the purges came most of the citizens were already unarmed. Most of those who still had guns handed them over when the laws were changed. So today, for the most part, their rural areas are unprotected. After a while, the bad guys figured it out and they left us alone and went to hunt less dangerous game.

I don't enjoy these fights by any means. But in every case, the people any of us shot were trying to kill us. All we wanted was to be left alone so we could try to survive and live our lives, but they decided not to do that and they paid a price. We had every moral right to protect our lives and we did. Those, like my brother, who chose not to fight died. There was no middle ground. We had the willingness and the tools to fight back, so trouble finally went off to find easier pickings. Now, it's been quiet in the valley for several months and "the boys," my son and son in law, could watch the place while I was gone. Hell, they were both better shots than me anyway.

I thought it would be safe enough to go look for my niece. But, clearly I thought wrong.

CHAPTER 14

My leg was hurting like hell, but it was getting easier to ignore with every swallow. Davy had found a bottle of good Kentucky bourbon, poured a water glass full and handed it to me. I was seeing how fast I could empty it.

As I sipped the amber warmth I focused on two important things. The first was how much I missed this wonderful elixir. Cider was simply not an acceptable substitute. But then, nothing really was. Good bourbon has always been my drink of choice and I missed it most on those quiet winter nights when I was sitting by the woodstove and reading.

The second point of interest was that the middle-aged lady picking the shrapnel out of my calf was not very good at it. She was much too tentative and even seemed a bit afraid. I asked if they had a doctor and she showed up. I don't know what she did to get by, but I was pretty sure she was not a doctor.

A searing pain shot up my leg and into my groin as she plucked at a nerve that was long enough to use for a clothesline and angry enough to go to war.

"Sorry," she said with an apologetic smile.

"That's okay," I grunted, trying hard to stay conscious, "I know you are doing the best you can."

"No, it's not okay," she replied through clenched teeth. "But, I don't know what else to do here. You have a lot of metal in your leg and it has to come out. It's just that I really don't know much about this. My husband was the doctor, but he was killed a while ago on a trip to Whester to deliver a baby."

"I am sorry," I said.

"Yeah, well, so am I," she said as her eyes turned glassy with tears.

"The ironic thing is that he had actually sewed up a bullet hole in that bastard who shot him just a few months before. Didn't even charge the guy. He knew everything the little shit told him about being attacked on his way to his mother's house was a lie and that he was more than likely a road bandit who tried to rob the wrong guy. But, Frank didn't make those kinds of judgments. He had taken an oath to help people and the guy would have died without medical attention. He fixed the bullet hole and I fed the little shit while he recovered in our house. We thought we were doing the right thing, but right now I wish Frank had let him die, or that I had poisoned his food.

"At least he is dead now, even though it's too late. Davy was on the security team traveling with Frank and he took care of that by putting a new bullet hole in that piece of shit, this time in a better place.

"Hell, it was just a fluke the bullet even hit Frank; it came through one of the shooting ports and ricocheted off the inside of the truck, catching him in the leg. It wasn't even that bad of a wound. Frank held on a few days, long enough to make sure the baby was okay, but he must have thrown a clot on the way home. He complained he was having trouble breathing and then he was gone.

"My guess is it happened because the bullet was still in his leg three days later and I am not about to let the same thing happen to you. It's just that I majored in liberal arts in school, not medicine. I have a masters in the humanities with a focus on woman's studies," she snorted. "Real helpful stuff in this life. I am trying to figure this medical thing out on my own, but reading about this in a book and doing it are quite a bit different.

"You are my first," she said with a forced smile. Then she blushed and added, "Surgery patient, I mean. At least the first one with car parts in his body.

"I guess because I have his medical books and instruments people thought I should continue his work. They just started coming to me after Frank died. I suppose they have to go someplace and I am trying. I have plenty to do all day and I read the medical books every night until I collapse, but being a doctor is apparently a tough thing to teach yourself. The books only can take it so far, after that I think it comes from actual experience and from others teaching you. There is nobody to teach me, but I am slowly getting the experience. Some of it I really wish I didn't have.

"I mostly take care of setting broken bones and cleaning up infections. I can sew up cuts pretty well, but I don't know anything about war wounds or actual surgery. We just don't see bullet wounds like we used to when the social wars were still going on. I can't even say I helped Frank then, because I didn't. I hid back in the village while he was on the front lines trying to help people who were defending their homes. I told myself that he had a nurse and didn't need me, but the truth is I was scared. Even after his nurse was killed, I just avoided it all and figured if I could pretend it wasn't happening, then maybe it wasn't. It took my husband dying to make me realize that this is all pretty damn real and that I was acting spoiled and childish."

I didn't know what to say, so I just grunted to let her know I was listening. She took that as permission to go on.

"I grew up in the city and my family had a little money. We weren't exactly rich, but I never had to work and my parents bought me everything I wanted. I never had to grow up and accept any responsibility. Look at college, for Christ's sake. Liberal arts? What's the point of that? I just did it because it was trendy and I thought it proved I was more intelligent than everybody else. It didn't teach me a damn useful thing or about how to survive in the real world.

"For that, I did what any rich Jewish girl would do, I married a doctor. I figured I was set for life. But, I really did love the guy. I didn't count on our own government, the same guys I voted for, screwing up the health care industry so much that my orthopedic surgeon husband would have trouble earning enough money to make ends meet.

"We moved up here for a job in a clinic near the ski area. Frank spent his time putting trashed knees back together and making less money than the guy down the road selling used cars.

"I was bitter about it and had turned into a nasty, spiteful person. I suppose that's why Frank worked so much, to be away from me.

"Regrets?"

"Yeah, I got a few," she said sarcastically.

I still didn't know how to respond, so I just looked at her and took another sip of whiskey. Seeing that I had nothing to say, she continued.

"After Frank was killed I realized, too late as it turned out, that I was not a nice person. I decided to try to change that and make myself useful. Truthfully, I was a pompous fool. I voted for the people who did this to us and I believed that socialism was the answer. I believed that the rich should be taxed until they were not rich anymore. I never understood that it would apply to me, too. It took me a long time to figure out that I was on the wrong side of just about everything. It's too late now, voting is a thing of the past, so I guess my change in politics really doesn't mean a damn thing, does it?

"Well," I said. "It gives us something to talk about while you go about doctoring."

I didn't bother to mention that she was doing all the talking. I realized she was nervous as hell and telling her life story was a way of blowing off energy, so I kept quiet and let her continue.

"My point is that you are my first gunshot surgery and I can see why real doctors practice on cadavers. I wish we had something to numb the pain, but we are out of everything except Davy's bourbon and I think he is hiding the rest of the bottle from you right now. I am so sorry that the train didn't have any anesthetic medical supplies. I know this hurts like hell and I know I am making it worse with my incompetence, but we have to get this stuff out of your leg.

"Hang on, I am locked on to something metal here and I am going to pull it out."

It is impossible to drink enough bourbon to dull the pain of what happened next, but I figured I should at least give it a good try. I drained the glass just before she pulled what looked like a piece of fuel injector from my calf.

She pulled seven pieces of metal out of my leg in total. One was clearly a rifle bullet jacket, but the rest were fragments from the car that broke off when the bullets hit them. The good thing was most of them didn't have a lot of power behind them and so they didn't penetrate very deep. Other than the top of the old style fuel injector which stuck in several inches, most were just inside my skin. They made a bloody mess, but didn't cause any structural damage. Once she cleaned out the metal and the little bits of cloth they dragged into the holes while passing through my pants, I felt much better. She irrigated all the wounds and packed them with some antibiotics. Then she gave me a handful of amoxicillin capsules to keep infection away.

A week later Davy and I had finished his bourbon, including his hidden stash. We'd told all our war stories at least twice and I was ready to travel again.

CHAPTER 15

I was sitting on Jack's front porch, staring at the moon and thinking dark thoughts. My plan was to head out at first light, but that was the extent of it, other than that I was just going to wing it, which was not good strategy. But, I was about out of ideas.

My guns were loaded and my pack well supplied. I had replenished my ammo supply from some Jack had with a promise to replace it on his next trip by my place. Now that he had fresh gasoline he would be meeting the train next month under a contract with another town in need of supplies. He made it a point to say he would be by to collect his steak dinner.

I heard the scrape of a boot to my right and I pulled my pistol from its holster and pointed at that end of the small porch.

"Whoa there partner, I mean you no harm," Davy said with a grin in his voice, before showing himself. "In fact, I come bearing gifts."

Once I re-holstered my 1911, he walked over, set two glasses on the railing, pulled the cork on a bottle and started pouring.

"I might not have told you the whole truth about the extent of my bourbon stash," he said. "But then, some things are worth lying about."

I grunted a thanks and thought about how much I needed this drink.

We sat for a long time without speaking, sipping our drinks and staring into the night.

"I am going with you," Davy said softly.

"The hell you are," I replied. "This one's my fight."

"Do you remember that story you told me about the tracker and the lions?"

"Of course. So what?"

"Well, I remember it too; let me tell it again, just like you did."

"There were lion tracks in the sand around the camp every morning when we woke up. They came in the night while we were sleeping, looking, as lions usually are, for something to eat.

"The window in my little hut had no glass or even a screen. It was only about five feet off the ground, so a lion could easily come through it while I slept. That had me a bit concerned, so I kept a loaded rifle in bed with me every night and another on the floor beside the bed.

"Sometime late in the night I woke to growling and loud African voices. I looked out the window and could see several moving shadows capped by a burning branch that was dancing in the dark night like a kid's sparkler on the 4th of July. Dressed only in my underwear, I jammed my feet into my boots, grabbed a rifle and a powerful flashlight and ran out to see what was happening.

"I probably should have stayed put, or at least showed a little more caution when I exited my cabin, because that's how you get eaten in Africa; charging blindly into the night when there are lions lurking about. But, I knew somebody was in trouble and needed help and I didn't stop to think.

"When I got close enough I could see a diminutive Shona tracker named Never waving a burning branch he had pulled from the campfire outside the trackers' cabin. Surrounding him were six lions, circling and moving, looking for any opening.

"I fired a couple of shots in the air with my .458 Winchester and shouted at the lions while shining my light in their faces. The biggest female looked at me for a moment as if deciding whether to eat me or move on. Finally she walked off, with an insolent, 'kiss my ass' slouch that would have made any surly teenager proud. The rest followed her into the night.

"What the hell are you doing Never!" I screamed at him.

"The lions, they take the meat from the bushbuck you give me for my family," he replied in English with his soft and melodious voice. "So I come outside to stop them."

"Are you crazy?" I shouted, still full of adrenalin and a bit pissed at the crazy little African. "Let them take it, I can get you more meat."

"It is my meat. Not the lion's meat."

"Well hell, at least ask for some help next time. You can't expect to take on an entire pack of hungry lions in the dark with just a stick, even if it is on fire."

"My meat, my problem."

"Never, don't be stupid, next time ask for help."

"Not your problem. My meat. My problem. I do not ask for help for my problems."

"Did I get that about right? Hell I should have, you told it to me three times in the past week."

"Yeah, so what? You still are not going with me."

"Take your own advice, you stubborn old fool. You can't go into the lion's den with nothing but a sharp stick. You need some help."

"Sorry Davy, but you are not coming. You have become a friend over the past several days and I owe you my life, but you are not coming."

"You really think you can stop me?" he asked, his voice rising in anger.

"Maybe, maybe not, but do we want to go there?" I replied softly, trying to keep my own anger in check. "I didn't come here to fight you and I don't think you want to fight me."

"I am coming."

"No, you are not," I shouted, finally losing my temper. "I don't need to be babysitting some damn fool with a death wish. I am not going to have your death on my conscience too, particularly when you orchestrated it yourself."

"That's what you think? That I have a death wish?"

"Well, don't you?"

He didn't answer, but just sat, staring into the dark and sipping his drink.

I did the same and enjoyed the scent of lilac from someplace in the dark. I always welcomed that smell because it meant that another brutal Vermont winter was behind us.

Time passed and my glass emptied. I thought he had given up and that I had really hit a nerve.

Then he spoke.

"Listen," he said softly. "I don't want to die. I want to grow old and I want to find a good woman to grow old with. I want to make a lot of babies and stick around to watch them make more babies. I want to have a family and a life I can be proud of having. But, I can't bring kids into this shitty world. It's just too messed up right now. Somebody's got to fix it."

"And you think you can fix the world?" I snapped back.

"No," he said softly. "But you can."

"What the hell are you talking about?" I asked him, shocked at that statement.

"Look, I know I'm not much good for anything but fighting and pouring drinks. But, you are going to change the world. Or at least what's left of it.

"I am good at one other thing, paying attention; and I know about the meeting the Farnsworth's have set up in Virginia. You guys are planning to start a new government. That's good, because we need that if this thing is going to work. We can't keep living like this, we need to bring civilization back to

America. We need a government that works, one that can establish a new economy and protect us from enemies, foreign and domestic, all that shit. Once we have that, we will have stability. That's all we need. When people feel safe again, when they believe there is hope for the future they will start to invest, to build. We can become a great nation again, but it has to start someplace. Most people just are too scared or don't know where or how to start. But, you do."

"What makes you think that?" I asked.

"Look at what you did during the social wars. Families were getting picked off one at a time. But not yours. You could have just protected what you had and the hell with the rest of them, but you didn't. You organized the people, gave them some leadership. You spanked the enemy and taught them to leave you alone. You made that valley safe. Nobody else would have done that.

"I rode that train before I came to work for Jack. I have been up and down the coast and I can tell you that you are going to be the smartest guy in the room at that meeting. They will listen to you. But, you need to stay alive."

"Bullshit," I replied. "There are some good leaders out there and some smart people. I don't know how in the hell you found out about the meeting, it was supposed to be a secret, but if you know about that, then you know who Tim Jackson is and what he can bring to the table."

"I knew Jackson well. He was one of the best."

"Was?"

"He's dead. Shot in an ambush a lot like the one you escaped from. He was out looking for his son who had gone after a loose horse. Seems somebody had opened the barn door and left it open. They shot him three times in the head and left his body in the road. Nothing was taken, his guns were still there with him. That sound like bandits to you?"

"Did his son come home?"

"They found his body in the woods, beside the dead horse."

"Shit. What about Peter Shaw?"

"They got him too. Lured him out to help a neighbor deliver a calf. Then made it look like bandits shot him on the road.

"They got them all. You and the Farnsworths are all that's left. Besides himself, Billy Farnsworth had planned for seven of you guys at that meeting and six of them are dead."

"How in the hell do you know all this?" I asked, suddenly suspicious of my new "friend".

"We have a pipeline of communications up and down the coast. After you got attacked I suspected something was going on, so I got a message to Billy Farnsworth and told him to watch his back. He and his brother went into hiding and sent the train to check on the other guys. He found out they are all dead, then he sent word back here. I just found out about ten minutes ago. Something bigger than we thought is going on here. That ambush had only one goal, to kill you. They haven't dared try while you are here as we are well fortified, or maybe they don't even know where you are. But the minute you step out on that road, they are going to try again. You need help.

"Billy is trying to find some more guys for the meeting, but they will all be second tier. He is a good organizer, but he is not a leader, nor is his brother. They need you at that meeting or it's all going to fall apart. So, you need me to keep you alive."

"You still are not coming with me. I am not getting you killed for something that's my problem."

"You never did tell me why you need to go to Easton."

"Nope, and I am not going to, it's my problem and you are not going with me. It's not that I don't appreciate the offer, I do and I can use the help, but Jack needs you here."

"Jack and I already talked about this and it was his idea for me to go with you. Besides, I am getting bored out of my skull here. I need some action!"

"I said no and that's final."

We sat quietly for a while and Dave refilled our glasses. I had about decided that he had accepted it when he spoke so softly that I barely heard him.

"I know where she is."

"What?"

"I know where she is."

"Where who is?"

"Sarah. I know where she is."

"How in the hell do you know about . . . aw hell, never mind. I know too, she is in Easton."

"Yeah, but I know where in Easton. I know which building and even which room and I know how to get us there."

CHAPTER 16

"How the hell do you know about Sarah?" I demanded.

"Well, you're a smart guy, figure it out," Davy said.

"Shit, the guys who got the message to me about them moving her to Vermont are part of your pipeline, right?"

"Bingo, give the man a cigar.

"Well hell, look at that; we are fresh out of cigars. Will a little more whiskey do instead?"

"I knew you would be coming for her and I was bored to tears hanging around here without much going on. So awhile back I took a couple of days off and made a recon trip to Easton. Remember there is a road from here that cuts through the mountains to that little berg. It's a longer trip from here than where we let you off, but it ends up in the same place. One more thing, they might not know where you are right now, so maybe they won't be expecting us from this direction.

"Anyway, I made it all the way to town and the only guard I saw was at the intersection of the roads, about a mile outside of town. He was bored and half asleep. I could have killed his ass, but instead I just ducked into the woods and got around him. Jack only gave me two days off, but I spent three in that town looking around. I slept in the woods during the day and prowled around at night. The town was deserted after the social wars, but it's filled with people now. Most of them look exactly like the guys who tried to smoke you.

"I went back while you were healing up. You were lousy company, bitching and complaining, so I told you I was on a run for Jack, but that was a lie. I was making sure they hadn't moved her after you dusted up their hit team.

"I probably should have told you about all this before. But, my plan was to come back here after dropping you off and then to head up the road to Easton and intercept you just outside of town. I guessed, correctly as it turns out, that you would never accept my help back where we dropped you off. So I was going to wait until you were close and once you found out about all the bad-ass dudes waiting in town you would let me come along. I never thought they would try to kill you on the way or I would have said something. I am so sorry that happened."

"How in the hell could you have known?" I said, letting him off the hook. "Anyway, you are right, I would have turned you down if you tried to get out of the truck with me."

"It took me awhile on that first trip," he continued as if I had not said a word, "but I found her. Not exactly where you would expect her to be and not in a place you can easily find before they gut you and put you on a spit to roast. I am not about to tell you where that is either, so like it or not, you need me and I am going.

"How do you know it's her?" I said. "You never saw her before. It could be a decoy."

"About five foot-six, thin and stacked, blond hair, green eyes. She is left handed and with a voice that could have made a fortune doing phone sex back before. There is a small mole on her lip on the right side, and her teeth are just a little crooked, but sexy as hell."

"Fine," I grumbled, "I know when I am licked, that's her."

We sat a while longer, then I quietly said, "Thanks."

"Don't thank me just yet, there's more I need to tell you and I am not sure you are going to like it much."

I felt something go dead inside me.

"What?" I finally asked, dreading the answer.

"Your brother is there with her."

"You mean he is not dead?"

"Nope, he is very much alive and looking well."

"You sure it's him?"

"Mid-forties, six feet tall, gray hair and clearly a gym rat as he is in good shape. Also left-handed and he has a small scar on the right side of his head that shows through his hair. Besides, she called him Dad."

The scar was the clincher. I had put it there when we were kids during a "sword fight" with wooden broad swords we made in our dad's shop. Our mother was mad as hell when she had to take Bradley to our small town country doctor for stiches. Dad chewed us out for using the table saw without permission. Then he chuckled in wonder at the swords we had made.

"You guys do show some promise with your craftsmanship. It's your judgment I worry about," he said.

I was ecstatic about this good news. I just couldn't sit any longer and I started pacing the porch, babbling like a toddler who just discovered talking. Davy let me go on for a while before he suggested I sit down again.

Then it dawned on me.

"What the hell did you mean when you said I am not going to like it much?"

"There's more," he said, avoiding eye contact. Then he just sat there saying nothing while I waited.

"God damn it, spit it out," I roared.

"Ok, well ... um ... he is not exactly being held prisoner."

"What the hell are you talking about?" I said. "If he is not being held prisoner, then what the fuck is he doing in Easton with Sarah?"

"It looks like he is part of the group. One of the leaders in fact, as best I could figure out. I hid in the rafters of one of the buildings and managed to listen to one of the meetings and he was leading it. The others were deferring to him like he was a big shot. Sarah seems to have the run of the place and is free to come and go. I am not sure what it all means, but I figured it was information you probably needed to have."

It felt like I had just been shot in the guts. I couldn't breathe, I couldn't think. I just sat there stunned by the implications. My entire body turned numb. Could my own brother be trying to kill me? I didn't know whether to laugh or cry, so I did both. Then I bellowed and roared. I smashed the chairs, kicked down the railings and bloodied my knuckles on the corner post. I screamed and I raged at the heavens.

Then I sat on the steps, buried my head in my hands and sobbed.

I had never lost it like that before. Through all the social wars, prison, even when they took over my place, I never lost hope. I handled the loss of everything, the death of loved ones and so much more but nothing had ever been this painful. Betrayal is the worst form of sin and betrayal by your own family is the worst pain in the world.

None of it made any sense.

What seemed like hours later I looked up and Davy was still sitting there on what was left of the porch.

"Pour me another glass Davy, and make it a big one. We are not going anywhere tomorrow morning and I don't much give a shit if I have a hangover or not. We need to figure this out before we step into another trap."

"I wonder how many dead cows you'll owe Jack to cover this damage," Davy said as he looked at the destruction on the porch. "I suspect he will be eating filet mignon for a while.

CHAPTER 17

"None of this makes any sense, Davy.

"Why would anybody want to kill any of us? It's clearly not coincidence and I doubt it's revenge. Most of us have never even met each other before so I doubt we have any common enemies. In fact, we don't have a damn thing in common other than that meeting Farnsworth was putting together."

"Well then," Davy said with a grin. "I ain't a rocket surgeon, but my best guess would be, it's about the meeting."

"But, why?" I asked. "We are not a threat to anybody. In fact, just the opposite; we are trying to make things better. They say follow the money, but I don't get it. What money? There isn't any money; there hasn't been for a long time. That's one of the things we were going to talk about, a new currency. We just want to get some sort of an economy back on track and try to start building a society again. How can anybody object to that? Hell, if they are going to make money, or even steal money, some form of money has to exist. There is nobody I know who would want to stop us from creating an economy just to keep things the way they are, because this sucks for everybody.

"I thought all our enemies were gone. The only ones who attacked without reason and for anything other than money or perhaps power, were the nutjob Islamic terrorists. But it can't be terrorists, that problem was resolved a long time ago."

"I remember," Davy said with a husky voice. "I told you I don't have any family left, right? Well, I lost most of them that day."

That "day" was the anniversary of 9/11. The terrorists wanted to bring America to its knees once and for all. They felt that in the aftermath of the original attacks America had become soft, divided and so afraid of offending the Muslim culture that we would simply take any blow they threw and turn the other cheek.

They thought the seeds they planted on September 11, 2001 had grown enough to be harvested, so they hit fifty major cities simultaneously. Most cities were hit in multiple locations, more than three hundred places in all. They hit transportation hubs, subways, shopping malls, airports, office buildings, concert halls, stadiums; anyplace with a lot of people. They set off multiple bombs in every location, and then machine-gunned any survivors as they ran for the exits. Almost a million people died. It was a rare American who didn't lose somebody in their family.

Our spineless president went on television that night to read a speech off his teleprompter calling for tolerance and calm. He said we needed to understand their culture and why they were so angry at America. He said that perhaps it was time to sit down and talk with the terrorists and to try to give them what they wanted so they would stop this continued cry for help.

The Mullahs and other Islamic leaders all expressed shock and sympathy when the television cameras were rolling and it looked like perhaps things were going to calm down. Then a series of undercover videos surfaced on the internet showing mosque after mosque across the country celebrating the attacks behind closed doors while they mocked the weak Americans. The American people erupted. Enough was enough; it was clear the government wasn't going to help so the people took over and solved the problem. They burned the mosques and shot anybody who complained. I have no doubt that some of those were good people, but this was survival and sometimes collateral damage occurs. Killing them was rationalized, not unfairly I thought, by the fact that not one of them, from the leaders on down, had stood up to condemn the attacks. Americans had been pushed as far as they were going to go and when they decided to fight back, it was over in days. The "official" Muslim population of the United States, according to our census bureau, soon stood at zero.

Once international travel went away, the terrorists had no way to replenish their ranks and the Islamic threat ended. Obviously, not every Muslim was gone, but those left behind either mingled into our society or were killed. There were a few "retaliation" attacks, mostly suicide bombers; but they soon ran out of dumbasses, which meant no more volunteers. The few underground Muslims left saw the light, considering that anybody connected to a terrorist bombing, not just the bomber, was killed. They were hunted down by the newly enlightened government using the resources available to find the "masterminds," then the government released their names and looked away. They were killed and in a few cases their heads stuck on pikes as a reminder. It was medieval, but it solved the problem.

"The only good that came out of that day was that America finally woke up and put that political correctness crap behind us for good," Davy said. "If the other Muslims had just worked with us and condemned what was going on it might have been different, but they didn't realize things had changed; they thought they could keep playing both ends against the middle and that America would continue to take the abuse. I guess they found out Americans can only be pushed so far before they push back. We are a pretty tolerant people, but there is a limit and they found it."

"But, that's all history," I said. "Besides, the guys who tried to kill me were not Muslims. They were speaking mostly English. One guy was screaming in French after I shot him in the legs, but all the commands were in English. That first guy I killed had a tattoo on his arm with words in German. Most of them looked like us, Western European ancestry. Nobody I got a close look at looked Middle Eastern or African."

"That makes no sense," Davy said. "Europe is pretty much gone. They had all the same issues we did. Their governments were dissolved along with the Euro currency. Hell, their social wars were worse than ours. Most of the citizens didn't have guns and ammo to fight back like we did and the bad guys were all armed. It was a goddammed massacre. Some of the guys we met in Montreal who work the transport boats told me about how it went down. It was like what happened here, the way everything just collapsed is scary. Once the fighting started, the bad guys seemed to have very good guns. They said the assholes in Europe were using military assault rifles. I wonder how in the hell they got their hands on top of the line AK, FAL and M4 rifles. Somebody had to be supplying them. But, who?"

"I don't know," I said. "By then most of Europe had banned guns completely, so the citizens had nothing to fight with. Hell, England had even banned knives and cricket bats."

"The guys on the boats barely got out of there alive and when the opportunity came to leave Europe, they took it," Davy said.

"They said that every European country is now without a government or a currency. They are all using a barter system, just like us. The Scandinavian countries and those that were the "New Europe," the former Soviet Bloc countries, seem to be recovering and that's where a lot of the stuff we are trading for is coming from. But, 'Old Europe" is a mess, with most of the population dead and the rest holding on day by day. They said that Russia is also a mess, along with Japan and Australia. Israel, the UAE and Saudi Arabia were done before this started, after Iran started that war and nuked them all. It looks like China is the only major country still holding on to their previous government and society. I guess the Chinese are hurting because they were so dependent on the world economy, but the old government is still in control, as we well know. Now that they have most of our country, they are starting to make a comeback. But, they only took what they believed was theirs and no more. They have made it clear that they want to be left alone. I don't think they are behind this."

"So who the hell is this trying to kill us?" I asked. "There are too many of them and they are too well equipped to be bandits. This has to be something bigger, but what?

"What are they afraid of here? That we will bring back America? Hell, it can never be what it was. The "superpower" thing is gone. We have no plans to bring that back. The military is gone, but so is everybody else's except China's and they have downsized dramatically. From what I have heard, other than the troops here, they only have a few left to guard the homeland. They just don't have any money to pay them. I heard Chinese troops beg to be stationed here because there is food."

The rumors leaking out are that they have started growing corn, beans and wheat again in the occupied Midwest. I guess it's better to be a well fed and broke solider here than a starving and broke solider in China.

"It's hard to be a superpower without nuclear bombs, but they have been gone for years and all the technology to build them destroyed. Hell, even I believe that happened worldwide and after all that's gone on I am skeptical of just about everything. But the monitoring was foolproof and every single country complied. The bombs are a thing of the past. After seeing what happened in the Middle East, we all know that's a very good thing. One little asshole with a few big bombs killed a lot of people in a very short time.

"So what the hell is happening here? The only thing that makes sense is if somebody wants to take this in a different direction. But what direction? Who are they and what do they want?"

"I don't know," Davy said. "And that's what scares the hell out of me."

"The first thing we need to do is to find your 'pipeline' guys and figure out just what side they are on and where they get their information," I said.

"That might be tough," Davy said. "I don't know where the guys we need to talk to are right now. I can get a message to them, but it might be several days before we hear back, if we hear from them at all. If any of them are part of this, we will just spook them off and they might pass on the fact that you are alive to the wrong people. I think it might be better to leave them all alone for now and let them think we haven't caught on. They might be a lot more useful that way. Let's get Sarah out and back to your place, then we can talk to those guys."

"Okay, I guess I can see that point," I said. "But how did they know Sarah was going to be moving to Easton? I've got a sneaking suspicion that they are more than just the messengers. I think maybe we have been played like a bad fiddle and I don't much like it.

"What about my brother? How does he fit into all this? I have been thinking about nothing else since you told me he is alive. I can't believe he would be a willing participant in anything like this. He is no killer. He is hopelessly delusional, but basically a good man. He would never condone killing. If he is part of this, I suspect he is being played too. If he is, that means somebody is using him and Sarah to get to me. It might also mean they killed his wife and son to trick him into going along. If these people killed my family, they are going to have to answer for it.

"You remember that line from the movie "Tombstone?" 'You tell them I'm coming and Hell's coming with me?' Well, this time Hell just got scared and chickened out, so I guess it's just you and me Davy. But, goddamn it, the way I feel right now, that's gonna be more than enough."

CHAPTER 18

It turns out we did leave the next day, but not until late afternoon; partly because we both were suffering from hangovers, but mostly because the plan was to hit the town after dark so we had a chance of moving without being seen. Besides, I had something to do that morning.

"Hello," I said when I walked into the doctor's office. "With the amount of 'anesthesia' Davy was pouring I forgot my manners and I never properly thanked you for helping me. I also neglected to introduce myself. I apologize."

"I know who you are," she said with a smile, "I am Emily."

She washed her hands as she spoke and after drying them on a cloth towel, extended a chapped and raw right hand for me to shake.

"Sorry, but latex gloves are a thing of the past, so is gentle soap and hand lotion. It's okay if you don't want to shake my hand. I have to scrub several times a day with homemade soap and then wash with alcohol, usually something we distilled, to try to stay sterile. It takes a toll on my hands. At night I soak them in lanolin that we get from the sheep, but it's not enough. I know it's not healthy for me or my patients to have my hands with open sores like this, but I am at a loss about what to do to fix the problem."

I took her hand as gently as I could and thanked her again for helping me.

"The next time Jack stops at my place I'll send you some steaks as payment. I also have some latex gloves in my shop. I used them back before to keep my hands out of the harsh solvents we used cleaning guns. When things started to go bad, I bought several cases of them; I'll send them to you. They are not sterile, but you can rinse with alcohol to take care of that. I hope your hands will heal soon after that.

"Thanks, but if it's all the same to you I'll take my meat as burger and roasts. I never did like steak. As for the gloves, well, I just can't thank you enough." She started to tear up and turned away from me. "You have no idea how painful and shameful these hands can be."

"Can I ask you a question?"

"Of course you can, you don't have to ask permission," She said with forced laughter that was meant to hide her embarrassment.

"When you were in college, did you backpack around Europe?"

She laughed. "Of course I did, it was just about mandatory to keep my membership in the spoiled rich girl's sorority."

I noticed a darkness cross her face as she looked away, blinking tears again.

"Sorry, I didn't mean to pry," I said.

"No, you didn't," she said. "I just had a flash of bad memory. That trip almost broke up Frank and me. He was pissed that I was going to Europe with my girlfriends for two months. We were dating then, but it was clear it was going somewhere. He wanted to go with me and I said no. I was being selfish and self-centered, taking him for granted. I left him behind to work at some crappy summer job alone, while I went off on my 'adventure.' A month into it, he had an affair with some girl he met in a bar. I don't know if it was to punish me or just because he was feeling lonely and neglected. Either way, it took me a lot of years to figure out that it was as much my fault as his. She got pregnant as a result, but he never told me. I found out a few years later about their son and almost divorced him.

"The girl had some big issues and was not dealing well with the boy. Child protective services was going to take him away and put him in a foster home. That's when Frank told me about his son and admitted he had been paying child support for years.

"I felt betrayed, still too self-centered to realize that it was both our faults, I actually filed the papers for divorce. I guess we were both just young and stupid when it all happened. But I realized that I loved him and that this was probably some of that 'better or worse' the preacher was talking about. It was rough for a while, but finally we decided that the best way to atone for our sins would be by helping make a good life for Frank's son. We knew we couldn't do that if we split up, so we decided to stick together and we wound up raising the boy, Jimmy, from the time he was six. I won't lie and tell you the first year or two was easy, because it wasn't. But, Jimmy was special; I think he helped to heal our wounds more than anything else, just by being Jimmy. I loved him like he was my own, maybe more. He moved to California a couple of years before the crash. It wasn't even some pipe dream about being an actor. He was a lot smarter than that. He probably could have been one, he was extremely talented, but he had other plans. He moved there with an academic scholarship for engineering and to be close to the ocean. He loved boats and he wanted to design ships. I have not heard from him in a long time, he probably doesn't even know his dad is dead. Hell, I don't even know if Jimmy is alive."

She stopped and wiped her eyes.

"Sorry, I am off babbling about myself again. Why did you ask me that?"

"I am hoping you picked up a little German while you were there, I need something translated. At least I think it's German."

"I can go one better than that," she said with a laugh. "My mother was German; she emigrated here after the war, a Holocaust survivor. I was a 'surprise' baby born late in life and she wanted to make sure I understood what happened. She always told me that it was a bunch of bad people who caused all the trouble, not the German culture. She explained that German history includes a lot of good things, but so many people in our lifetime focused on the Nazis and forgot that most Germans were just people like everybody else, trying to find a way to survive. In spite of it all, she was proud to be German and she made sure I learned the language. I could speak it like a native by the time I traveled to Europe.

"I never told Frank, but two weeks of my time in Europe I spent touring the Holocaust sites, alone. As a German and a Jew, I thought I had a vested interest in that history and I wanted to try to understand what happened and why. My mother had lost her entire family in the camps and she almost starved to death. She endured beatings, rape and other horrible things, yet she found the courage to go on, to immigrate to America and find a new life and a husband she loved. I wanted to see if I could find a few clues to what would inspire her to do that, rather than take the easy route and just give up.

"I never could figure it all out back then. But, now I think that with the war and the Holocaust, there are a lot of similarities with what we have experienced. I just can't put my finger on the root, the center of what makes people do these horrible things to other people. It's more than just power and money, it's something black, evil and perhaps beyond our ability to understand. There are a lot of things that keep me up at night, but none more than trying to understand why humans can be so goddamned nasty.

"I didn't find the answers I looked for in Europe, but I found some of them here in the past few years. I understand now how my mother could keep going, what inspired her. Everybody has to find their own way to fight back, or you turn to dust. Just living is defying those bastards and having a productive life is spitting in their faces. I am trying to do both. While I miss Frank every day, in some strange way, I have found a happy life now, just living and defying the bastards that did this to us."

She turned away and laughed that nervous laugh again. "Sorry, what is it you need me to look at?"

"Well, the German I need translated is from a tattoo on a nasty guy. But, he isn't hurting anybody now. He had a bunch of tattoos and one on his arm said something in German. I can't say it, but I memorized the letters and can write it down."

She handed me a pencil and a scrap of paper and I wrote the words I remembered, "*Treue zur Welt für ein größeres gut*" and turned the paper so she could read it.

Her lips moved a little as she read the words and her forehead wrinkled with the effort. "I have not used German in many years," she said , "so I am sure it's rusty; I think this means loyalty or perhaps fidelity, to the world, for a greater good.

"What an odd thing to have tattooed on your arm."

CHAPTER 19

Davy still had not told me where they were holding Sarah, so I didn't really have any specific plan figured out. At this point I don't think holding back had any strategic benefit for him. Hell, I had agreed to let him come with me and we were in this together. My guess was he wasn't telling me because of how much it pissed me off, which he seemed to be enjoying immensely.

We caught a ride in one of armored trucks to a point about a mile from the intersection of the two roads. We didn't dare go any closer because if there was a guard at the intersection, even a dope like the one there when Davy came by a few weeks ago, I didn't want him to hear the truck. So, we took the shoe leather express.

We were both carrying packs with enough food for a few days and some first aid supplies. We didn't pack much water because it's easy to find this time of year. Every brook is running full and there are puddles of standing water in every low spot. I had a filter with me like the backpackers used to carry back before.

When I saw this was all going to hell I bought up every one of the filters I could find. Boiling water might kill the germs, but the pollutants remain. The best of these filters removed most of the heavy metals, pesticides and other bad stuff from the water as well as the germs, protozoa and other bugs. It was one of the smarter moves I made, as we had clean water even in the worst of times. That turned out to be key to staying alive and healthy.

It's surprising how many people died because of the water. Not from thirst, hell, there is water everywhere in New England and all of the East Coast for that matter. They died from dysentery, giardia and other waterborne illnesses. With food in short supply, most people were stressed and unhealthy anyway and simple diseases that were easily survivable in good times were enough to push them over the edge. With no medicine to cure their problems, fatalities were high.

Take giardia, for example. I've had it three times in my life, after I caught it from drinking out of streams in the wilderness while I was hunting. The first time I had kicked through the ice to reach a stream on top of a mountain deep in the wilderness of Montana. I had been tracking a bull elk in the snow all morning and I was extremely thirsty. That water tasted like ambrosia. I remember thinking that I could probably bottle the stuff and make a fortune.

But two weeks later I was a quivering mass of miserable. I was shitting forty or fifty times a day, running a high fever and dealing with severe stomach cramps. This was before giardia was well known in our area and the test for it was notoriously unreliable, so it was misdiagnosed.

I was young, still in my thirties and in the best shape of my life, but it almost killed me. I got so dehydrated my electrolytes got out of whack and it affected my heart rhythm, so they put me in the hospital. Oddly enough, the first thing the nurse gave me to take was a laxative, but that's another story.

Once they figured out the problem and after a week of taking the prescription drug Flagyl, I was fine. The next two times I contracted giardia I had the pills with me and within a couple of days I was good to go. My point is that the first time it was so bad it almost killed me, I was a strong and healthy young man. Giardia will not go away if it's not treated and right now there are no doctors and no drug stores with magic pills on the shelves. These days, something like giardia, a waterborne illness that nobody died from back before, will eventually kill you.

Even those smart enough to boil the water were often ingesting a lot of pollutants that could make them sick. These attack the liver and kidneys and often leave permanent damage that can shorten life expectancy. With no advanced medical help around, it just made sense to be careful, so we filtered all our drinking water.

Davy and I each had a one quart bottle we could refill, using the filter, from just about any water source short of a failed septic tank. Even that might work, but I ain't drinking it.

Still, our packs were very heavy. That's because we had all the ammo and magazines we could carry as well as extra guns.

I remember what a good friend of mine, Patrick McHugh, told me about how he survived Vietnam after he was drafted and forced to go to war.

"I wasn't a very big guy," he said, "so I knew I was limited in what I could carry all day in the jungle. I had to decide between food and ammo. I left the food and took all the ammo I could carry. I was never hungry, because I got plenty of food out of the packs of the dead guys who ran out of ammo. I also came home while they did not."

I am a believer that lots of ammo can solve any problem. It's not always the outcome you want, but the problem can be solved. (I once said that to a buddy of mine from Austria who ran the U.S. sales division for one of the European sporting optics companies. "How about stinky feet?" He said with a smile. Then the smile disappeared. "Oh," he said. "I guess you can fix that too.")

I also believe that ammo is very possibly the one thing you can control as you go into a bad situation. There is no way to predict what is going to happen in a fight. Once the shit hits the fan, the splatter pattern is anybody's guess. But if you control any variable you can, the outcome is weighted more to your favor. If you bring a lot of ammo there is no guarantee you will win the fight. But, if you run out of ammo in the middle of a fight, it's a sure bet that you will lose.

My knees were complaining about the weight, but let them bitch. If they wanted to keep their jobs, we had to come out of this thing alive.

I still had my doubts about that happening, but I did know one thing for sure. If they wanted to see my dead body, they were going to have to wade through a lot of empty cartridge cases to get to it.

I was carrying my M4 semi-auto carbine and two pistols. One was my 1911 and the second was another 1911 Jack had loaned me. His was a compact gun called an "Officer's Model" and smaller than my pistol. But, like mine, it was chambered for the best fighting cartridge ever put in a pistol, the one the 1911 handgun was designed to use, the .45 ACP.

Actually, that cartridge dates back to a war the United States fought in the Philippines from 1899 to 1902. The U. S. forces were using double action revolvers chambered in an anemic cartridge called the .38 Long Colt. But too many of our fighting men were getting chopped to pieces with machetes even after hitting the drug crazed natives with every bullet in the gun.

This experience, combined with the dubious Thompson-LaGarde Test of 1904, led the Army and the Cavalry to decide that a minimum of 45 caliber was required in the military's new handgun. John Browning developed the .45 ACP in 1904 and it was adapted to the Browning designed semi-auto pistol in 1911.

That confirmed a concept that dates back to at least when Sammy Colt first sent his hoglegs west, a concept that most gun guys still believed in, "If you bring a handgun to a fight, make sure it starts with at least a four."

While both the pistol and the cartridge have undergone some modernization, the 1911 remains, at least in the minds of many gun savvy people, the best fighting pistol and cartridge team available. The only downside is the relatively small magazine capacity. The standard magazines I was carrying hold eight cartridges. Considering that some 9mm handguns hold as many as nineteen cartridges, that's not a big number. But, I'll accept the need to reload more often in exchange for using a handgun I shoot well and trust. Besides, I never saw the point in sending a swarm of little 9mm bullets to do what one grown-up .45 can accomplish.

The smaller Model 1911 pistol Jack loaned me could use the full size magazines I had for my gun; they just stuck out the bottom of the grip a little bit more. That means that the two 1911 pistols could feed from the same pool of ammo and magazines.

In my pack, I also had the Glock that I took off the dead guy along with another M4 carbine, also borrowed from Jack. I had considered bringing a pump shotgun, but from an ammo standpoint it didn't make sense. The two carbines can use the same magazines and ammo so they draw from a common supply. But the shotgun uses different ammo, bulky and heavy ammo. It makes no sense to have two long guns that use different ammo. Besides, if this fight is outdoors, which it probably will be, the short range effectiveness of the shotgun would be a liability. With the carbine I can engage bad guys out to five hundred yards or even more, but the shotgun is only good to about fifty yards at best with buckshot.

Davy carried two M4 carbines and a matched pair of Model P229 Sig Sauer pistols chambered in .40 S&W. He liked the big, blocky, indestructible pistols and with twelve-round magazines he had a bit more firepower between reloads than the 1911s.

We each carried a couple of knives; assisted-opening folders and fixed blades. Davy's fixed blade was a tactical design popular in the last years of America. I took a more traditional approach. I had a leather handled, Marine version of the Ka-Bar fighting knife strapped to my chest so it stayed with me when I dumped my pack. The knife had belonged to my father-in-law. He carried one through the Korean War, but lost it to another person's stupidity. He complained about the loss of that knife for forty years until I gave him a new one for Christmas back in the early nineties. I inherited it after he died and now carried it with me every day.

CHAPTER 20

The story of how he lost the knife actually ties in with this water thing. His Marine unit had been on the front lines of the war for months. It was deep into the cold winter and they were living in holes they dug into the side of a hill. They piled dirt in front of the entrances so the enemy, who was below them, could not shoot into their "homes."

One night somebody, Korean or Chinese; it didn't matter, they were fighting them both no matter what the U.S. Government claimed, sneaked into the hole next door to John's and grabbed his best friend.

They dragged him down the hill and tortured him all night while the Marines were forced to listen to his screams. Whenever a Marine poked his head over the top to try and shoot somebody, at that point even their buddy to end his suffering, the bad guys were ready and would shoot them. It was too far to throw grenades and just shooting blindly over the berm was ineffective, as most of the goblins were doing their nasty work behind cover. They lost a couple of guys before they realized there was nothing they could do but lie there and listen to the screams.

That's the nightmare that woke John up screaming for the rest of his life.

Still, he was the kind of guy who could usually find some humor in any situation and he laughed when he told how, about a week later, he was lying in his down filled sleeping bag with the knife on his belt.

"I dreamed they had me, when in fact I was just tangled up in that damn mummy bag. I wasn't going without a fight, so I started flailing with the knife, which I kept sharp enough to shave with. By the time I was fully awake I was standing hunched over in that cave, with the air full of feathers and my sleeping back in tatters."

He got another sleeping bag and a Colt 1911 to sleep with after that. "I figured if it happened again I would just punch a couple of small holes in the bag with the pistol, rather than slicing it to shreds. It was too friggin' cold to sleep without one."

A few weeks later they were all getting sick and nobody knew why, so John decided to explore a little bit. He walked up the little creek where they were getting their water and about a quarter mile upstream he found a dead and rotting body lying in the water. John was pretty sick, and now that he knew the cause, he decided to walk several miles to a MASH unit for some help.

The doc really didn't much care one way or the other and just gave him a handful of APCs, which stood for "All Purpose Capsules" The Marines told the troops that APCs would cure everything from a headache to the clap, but John insisted they were just aspirin. If nothing else, he thought that some decent food would help, so he headed to the chow hall. After months of eating C-Rations, some real food sounded pretty good. He had to get back to his unit, but figured he could grab something to go. The cook was a bit of a jerk and was always a little ashamed that he was a cook and not a "fighting Marine." He had coveted John's Ka-Bar knife and insisted he let him use it in exchange for some eggs. They worked out a deal where he could use the knife for a week and then send it back up the line to John.

John took his dozen eggs and headed back to his "home," the hole dug in the frozen dirt and lined with cardboard. A big transport truck stopped and offered him a ride, but it was full so he climbed onto the trailer hitch on the back.

A few miles down the road the enemy spotted the truck and started shooting mortars at it. The truck sped up and began doing evasive moves. It's not clear if John fell or jumped off, but he wound up in the road with mortars hitting all around him. He spotted an abandoned building and made a run for it. But they saw him and started machine gunning the building. He ran out the back just before a mortar round blew up the building. He ran into the woods, where he was able to evade the enemy and eventually make it back to his unit. Through it all he said his only thought was, "protect the eggs."

By then he was hungry as hell, so he decided to cook some eggs. When he opened the carton, eleven of the original dozen were broken.

He started his little camp stove and tenderly added the last egg to the mess kit frying pan. He tended it like a treasure, carefully cooking it until it was perfection. The smell of this egg cooking was driving him crazy and the anticipation was excruciating, but he refused to give into temptation and eat it before it was properly cooked. This would be his only fresh food in weeks and he wanted it to be perfect.

Then, just as he was about to eat the egg, a soaking wet sleeping bag came flying in through the entrance of his hole, knocked over the stove and dumped the egg in the dirt.

Seems his buddy didn't bother to take the time to dig his hole correctly, so it filled with snow and water and he was cold and wet. He knew John was meticulous about this sort of thing and he decided he would come and "share" John's sleeping quarters because it was warm and dry in there. Without his Ka-Bar, John had no way to gut the damn fool, so he let him stay.

The cook left the knife on a stove and burned the leather handle off it, so when John got it back it was useless.

After all the shit he endured in more than a year on the front lines of that horrible war, that ruined knife and the lost egg were what he bitched about the most.

So, I carry his knife today to remember him. I figured maybe he is upstairs telling his stories to the angels and trying to keep this knife in one piece. You never know, maybe a little of that guardianship might spill over to me.

Besides, the Marine Ka-Bar is still one hell of a fighting knife. I might be sentimental, but I am not stupid. I am going to carry the best gear I can find.

The problem is that if it comes down to fighting with knives, we have screwed up big time and are in a lot of trouble.

To hell with knife fighting. I am too old and slow for that shit.

That's why I have guns.

CHAPTER 21

As we approached the intersection the evening light was in that golden phase that sometimes happens just before the sun sets. This was where Davy had seen the guard on the last two trips and if anybody was watching they would see us if we continued on the road. So, before the last bend, the one that would expose us, we slipped into the woods and walked parallel to the road, hidden by the thick brush. After we were past that bend we belly crawled through the cover to the edge and, keeping low so the grass and weeds would hide us, crept out to where we could see the intersection. Then we used our binoculars to look for the guard.

The little shack the guard was in last time was put there, back before, for kids to get out of the rain and snow while waiting for the school bus. He probably had orders not to use the shack. If his commanding officer had an ounce of brains he would have told him to hide back in the woods and out of sight. But Davy said there was a cold wind that first day and the guard was in the shack to escape its bite. He must have liked it, because the same guy was in the shack the next time Davy came by. That indicated a lack of discipline and training. To draw this crap duty he was probably the low man on the totem pole, but he still should have stuck to his orders. I liked that he did not. It gave me a little hope about the kind of people we were dealing with.

The shack was empty today. So were the woods. We spent some time searching the shadows to make sure nobody was hiding beside the big maple trees and the old stone walls that lined the road. There were only so many places a man could hide and still see the intersection, and we checked them all until we were pretty sure there wasn't anybody waiting for us here. You can never be one hundred percent sure. If the guy was good he would hide and we wouldn't see him; or he may have wandered into the woods to take a dump, so we waited. After half an hour we decided the place was empty.

It really didn't matter, we could get around any guard pretty easily, but I wanted to get a feel for what was waiting for us, a clue about just how prepared these guys were.

Were they still expecting me to show up? My guess is they were short-handed with all the guys we killed or wounded at the fight near the bridge and couldn't spare anybody to watch this road. Or maybe they found all that blood I left behind and figured I didn't survive my wounds.

Still, we would keep to the woods for a while longer. We were on the north side of the road, which I realized was a mistake. To continue on to Easton we would have to go south, which meant crossing the road. I figured the smart move would be to backtrack until we could cross without being seen from the intersection. Even though we didn't see a guard, it made sense to be careful.

We belly crawled back into the brush and once we had enough cover to stand up I started back east. Davy grabbed my arm and stopped me.

I turned, a little annoyed that I would need to explain my strategy, but I was stopped by the shit-eating grin on his face.

"We are going that way," he said as he pointed to the north.

It'd been several years since I drove this stretch of road, but there was a time when I knew the country well. It took me a minute to map out the road in my head

"There is nothing but empty ground until you get almost back to the bridge where the fight was, that's over ten miles of empty land," I said. "All the farm houses were burned years ago."

"We ain't going that far," Davy said. "We are making a left turn in about two hundred yards."

"So, that's where they have her?" I asked, finally realizing where we were going.

"Yup."

"So why the hell wouldn't you tell me that before now?"

"'Cause, I like watching you bitch and pout. I ain't in this for the money, and I need to find my fun where I can. You ready to go?"

"No, I am not," I said. Then I sat down, leaned against a big oak tree and stared at Davy.

"Ah hell, you gonna have another one of your tantrums now?"

"Nope. You got me. I can live with that until I get you back. But, think about it. We need to go up the road. I have deer hunted all through this country and I can tell you the woods on either side of that road are full of ledges and thick briars. We can't get through them. They might have pulled the guard from here, but you can be sure they will have guards out someplace else. Which means they will see us if we walk up the road. It will be dark in an hour, we'll go then.

"My guess is the guards will be high in the ledges along the gulf. That's where I would be. With luck we will see them first, but that won't happen unless we go after dark. Let's eat something and you can tell me again about what a clever guy you are."

"Hell, you already know all that. Let's talk about where they are holding Sarah and what we need to do to get her out of there and back to your place."

And so we did until it was full dark and we started walking again.

The road wound up the mountain a couple of miles to a large bench about halfway to the top. The bench held an old Catholic monastery that for years was the home of the Easton Monks.

It was a popular tourist stop, back before. The faithful would come to attend Mass in the chapel, while the skiers and leaf peepers from the cities would come to act superior as they "marveled" at the "quaint" lifestyle of the monks. The monks made a killing, raking in money from the restaurant and souvenir shop. I read somewhere that they made more than a million dollars over the years with one T-shirt alone. It had some double entendre about sex and monks on the front, but damned if I can remember exactly what it said. Something about "Monks Do it With Their Mouths Shut" along with a suggestive photo of a person on their knees. It was about their vow of silence and praying, of course, while the rest of the world thought blow jobs. The monks pretended they didn't get the joke and smiled all the way to the bank.

Most people assumed that with their trusting, "believe in your fellow man" naiveté the monks would have been wiped out in the early days of the social wars. But, the Catholic Church was founded by Jesus and hadn't survived more than two thousand years in a hostile world by being stupid. Once things got bad, the bishop sent trucks and vans all over the northeast collecting the priests, monks and anything of value, along with most of the employees of the church and their families. They moved everything and everybody to a walled compound someplace in upstate New York.

The story we got was they defended it viciously against a couple of attacks from a bunch of low-life dirt-bags. If you believe the rumors, the priests used claymore mines and rocket launchers as well as full auto small arms. It didn't take long before the word on the street was that you didn't mess with the

"Fathers." I guess they figured out that the "turning the other cheek" crap can get you killed in today's "America."

Of course, that left the monastery empty. I suppose that like any building left abandoned, it was at some point occupied and trashed by squatters. Then when times got really hard, even the squatters disappeared. With the buildings still structurally sound, it wouldn't take long to clean it up and repair the damages.

It is an easily defensible position, isolated and open in all directions. A large mass of attackers would have to approach through a few hundred yards of open ground. As Davy had discovered, the small town of Easton, a few miles south, was filled with tough guys. But, there was no place to put the V.I.P. types who needed to be guarded. The monastery made the most sense for that. There wasn't enough room there to house a lot of people, so they likely quartered most of the crew in the buildings in town and just had a few guards to protect the honchos. I suspected that meant the best they had would be at the monastery waiting for us.

One more benefit; it's isolated enough keep the prying eyes of the troops away from Sarah. No matter who they are fighting for, soldiers are young, horny, guys; in their prime and very full of themselves. I suspect that if the rank and file had laid eyes on her, sooner or later there would be trouble. A smart commander would keep her isolated and make sure he could trust the men around her.

I had not been to the monastery in years, but it was coming back to me. The compound consisted of several buildings scattered over a few acres of land. The road split, going left or right as it entered the compound. On the left, before the fork, was a big parking lot. On the right was a meadow with a large man-made pond. Straight ahead were several larger buildings including a community kitchen, chapel, souvenir shop and a large meeting room. To the north of that, the dirt road is lined on both sides with cabins that were used as living quarters for the monks.

"There are six cabins. She is living in the first one on the right side." Davy said. "Your brother is in the one across the road. The other four are filled with men who seem to be important. There were people with trucks or cars coming and going all day, but at night it thinned. I guess most of them head back to Easton to sleep.

"The meeting I sat in on, the one your brother was running, was mostly about logistics. They talked about food supplies, medical shipments and something I couldn't quite understand about transportation for some kind of big gathering. I couldn't tell for sure, but I think they were planning to hold it here. What I did learn is that after the meeting they were planning to pull out of here and head south.

"Two other times there were meetings going on that I couldn't hear because I was outside, looking through the windows. In fact, that's why I snuck in and hid for the next one. I didn't think much about it until now, but your brother was not there for those first two meetings. They were run by a different guy each time, and those two are in the other two cabins on the left.

"There are two more cabins on the right and the largest cabin, the last one on that side, seems to hold the big dog, the guy in charge. He has some guy with him all the time. I can't tell if he is a bodyguard or some kind of assistant. He is a big, black guy, large enough to be dangerous, but he is oddly effeminate. He also keeps two guards in the cabin between his and Sarah's cabin all the time. They don't sleep there, just run guard duty and rotate every eight hours.

"I never saw the big kahuna leave his cabin. Those other 'important guys' all came to his cabin and they all seemed to get a little smaller when they stepped onto his porch. He kept the shades drawn and the lights low, so I never got a look at the guy, but I heard his voice and it's familiar. I just can't seem to figure out why.

"The chapel is set up as a barracks of sort and it looked like about twenty-five men were living in there. As far as I could tell, their job was to guard the place. They run three shifts. In addition to the guys guarding the boss man's cabin, there was always another in the bell tower, watching all three of the approach roads. Another is in the back, on the roof, watching the big meadow to the rear. Two other guys just roamed. They will be a problem, because I never could determine a pattern. They just rambled around with deliberate randomness and never stopped moving. It is impossible to predict where they will be, so assuming nothing has changed, we need to locate them first. We can't risk them wandering into the middle of things at the wrong time.

"When I first found this place, there were a couple of guys who liked to hang out close to Sarah, probably against orders, but on the last trip I didn't see them. That makes me think they learned their lesson after that dust-up at the bridge and are using reliable guys as guards up there."

CHAPTER 22

The moon was full and high in the sky as we made our way up the road. It looked so big in the clear air I felt I could reach out and touch it. I could see every crater and just for a moment believed that with my binoculars I might see the flag the astronauts planted in 1969.

It's odd what pops into your head, but that made me think about the congresswoman from Arkansas, Jackie Sheena Lea. She was best known for camping out for hours to get a spot near the rail just so she could get some camera time with the president on the night he gave his State of the Union address.

Once, while on a visit to NASA to celebrate the success of the Mars rover, she asked them if the Mars rover had taken a photo of the flag Neil Armstrong had planted there. When the NASA official explained that the flag was on the moon while the rover was on Mars, and that the two were separated by about two hundred-million miles, she got pissed and threatened to pull their funding.

She had a whole list of bonehead ideas, acts and statements. During the Clinton impeachment hearings she asked that the Constitution be entered into the congressional record. When assured it already was she said she doubted that and said that she would be conducting an investigation. She said many times that we won the Vietnam War. She supported selling F-16 parts to the dictator Hugo Chavez and she did about a million other stupid things. She was arrogant and proud of being stupid. She was rude to her constituents and racist against whites. Yet, the people of Little Rock kept re-electing her and Congress actually put her on several very important committees, including Homeland Security. It was people like her, and the morons who voted for her, that led us into this mess. Once we let the dumbasses run the country, it was doomed. She was the ultimate Congressional dumbass.

The moon was so bright we could see the shadows we cast as we moved, almost like a sunny day. If we walked up the paved road we would have been silhouetted against the solid background and easy for any sniper to pick off, so we kept to the edges. We had to be careful about making noise, as the gravel would crunch under our feet and there were leaves and sticks littered where the car tires didn't pass to sweep things clean. In some places, there were deep ditches on the side that were hard to see in the moonlight. Falling into one probably wouldn't cause any major damage, but it would make enough noise to give away our position. The brook running beside us might cover a small noise, but sound travels funny in the night air. Silence was the best policy. If there was a guy with a rifle waiting up ahead it would only take one small mistake to get us killed

We moved painfully slowly, aware of how much we had left to do and how fast the night was slipping away, until we finally came to the last twist in the road before the gulf. We stopped one hundred yards out. The ledges had a lot of places to hide and the last thing I wanted was to walk into another ambush.

Moving back into the woods for cover, we used our binoculars to look at the ledges that walled up either side of the narrow road. A brook had worn a deep crevasse in the rocks over the eons and when they built the road they had blasted the crack wider. High ledges rose on each side and there was barely enough room for two cars to pass here. The land to the north was filled with steep ledges and was impassable without walking several miles to get around them. On the south side there was a deep gorge with a large whitewater river at the bottom. There is a trail that will go over the top, but the only way to it is past a suspended bridge that hangs on cables high above the river. You must approach the bridge, go out onto it and then off the side through a gap in the rail to reach the start of the trail. I was sure the bridge would be guarded, and the only other way through was this road. The narrow funnel created here was a logical place to post a guard.

The guy who was at the intersection when Davy was scouting could cover all the angles because the road was the only approach to both. But he was gone and my guess is they pulled back and covered both approaches now that they knew I was coming. It's what I would do.

As Davy had proven, a smart guy could get around a guard at the intersection. But, there was almost no way to approach without going through the gulf or across the bridge, and getting around them was almost impossible. There is a road from the south, but to access that would have meant traveling down the main road through the town, a town infested with guys waiting to kill us, and then another ten miles out of the way before doubling back on the road that came back through the mountains to the monastery. No doubt that approach was also guarded. That's too far for a man on foot, so my guess is they would expect me up this road. One ace we had hidden in our boots is that they thought it would be just me and they didn't yet know about Davy.

The brook ran down one side of the gulf between the road and the ledges, so I figured most guys would stick to the other side rather than wade across and spend the night with wet feet, so I started my search on the dry side.

I had invested in one of the top of the line 10x42 European binoculars back when I was still doing a lot of big game hunting and have found them to be a huge asset now that most of my "hunting" is for people trying to kill me. The high quality optics gathered the existing light and brightened the ledges even more, letting me look back into the shadows. Still, I looked for a long time before I found him.

The guy had found a spot backed up into a crack in the rocks about thirty feet above the road. He was so deep in the shadows that he would have been hard to see even in daylight. His mistake was when he moved. His feet were sticking just outside the cubby he was hiding in and I saw his boot move when he shifted his legs.

Very few people can sit still for hours on end without moving. The very best snipers and hunters can do it when they are young. As they get older, their joints can't take the inactivity. Only the most elite, fit and well trained operative, maybe one guy in ten million, can hold perfectly still for more than a few hours and even those guys have their limits. Sooner or later everybody will move, it's just that some wait longer than others.

If he had been really smart he would have piled some brush in front of his hiding place to cover his feet. I doubt we would have found him then. I grabbed Davy's arm and started back down the road to a safe distance where we could talk.

"It looks like the reason they didn't have anybody at the intersection is because they have pulled back to watch the gulf," I said. "There is a guy high up on the right side, dug in and well hidden and he is probably not alone. We can't get to him and the only way to take him out is to shoot him with a rifle. But for that we need something suppressed, with sub-sonic ammo, which we do not have. Our guns are too noisy. Besides, if there is more than one, there will be return fire for sure. We are only half a mile from the monastery and any noise will let them know we are coming. That would be a huge mistake. It's been more than a week since the fight and they have to be wondering if I am ever going to show up. They probably think I died from my wounds and with luck they have let their guard down a little bit. If we shoot this guy, they will hear the shot; if he has a buddy with him they will hear a lot of shooting. Either way, we can expect a welcoming party after that. This is going to be tough enough to pull off if they don't know we are coming and impossible if they do. We need to find another way."

"The only other way is past the swinging bridge," Davy said. "But that was guarded when I checked before. The guy was dug into those boulders on the far side, well protected and armed with a rifle. The only way to the trail is to go over the north end of the bridge and he would pick us off on a bright night like this. We also can't get to him to take him out quietly, so again we would need to shoot him with a rifle. The river noise might hide the sound of the shot, but I think it's too chancy. On the other hand, we need to do something and I am running out of ideas here."

CHAPTER 23

"Did I ever tell you about the buck I shot up here in '97?"

"What the hell? You are going to tell me another one of your hunting stories?

"Really?

"Now?"

"Yes, I am. Shut up and listen.

"I found him on Wheeler Ridge. He was coming up the trail I was walking down, on my way to a mid-morning breakfast back at my truck. I don't usually do that, leave early, but it was wicked cold that day and my feet were numb. That truck heater was looking mighty good.

"Neither one of us was paying much attention and we each spotted the other at the same time. He froze for a second and I snapped a fast, front-on shot at his chest. I had a custom rifle that never fit me very well and I pulled low and left. I never did like that damn gun, but I had paid so much money for it that I kept hunting with it out of guilt. At least until this buck came along. I sold it after him. Anyway, I muffed the shot and broke his front leg."

"That was on the other side of the damn mountains, miles from here. Why are you babbling about this now?" Davy asked.

"I know where it is, I have been there many times, but like I said, you need to shut up and listen," I said with a big grin. I like seeing the frustrated expression on his face.

"It turned out to be one of the toughest tracking jobs I ever had in all my years of hunting. We had a light dusting of snow on that side of the mountain and he was bleeding at first, so it was easy enough to start. He headed for the road, but something must have spooked him and he turned around and came back at me. He caught my scent and got around me in the thick brush. Then he headed for the top.

"You will hear a lot of guys say a wounded deer will never head uphill, but this buck sure did. It was a long, steep climb through the beeches and oaks. Once we got in the hardwoods where the sun had penetrated, the snow disappeared. Sometimes the tracks were hard to see and often I didn't know if I was on the trail or not. Mostly I just kept walking without thinking, letting the shape of the land guide my feet. I figured he was doing the same thing. Once you get in tune with the woods things like that just happen in the back of your mind. If you try to think about it too much, you screw it up, but if you just let the reptilian part of your brain operate then eons of evolution are suppressed and the caveman in you will come out of hiding and turn you into a creature of the woods, just like the deer.

"I saw him a couple of times in the next few hours. Twice, I topped over a bench on the side of the mountain and saw him going over the next one. But, I could never get a shot.

"It was a very cold day and I was dressed for sitting, not hiking, which meant a lot of bulky, warm clothing. By the time I hit the top of the mountain I was drenched with sweat. It was so cold that the sweat would freeze as soon as it left my skin. My hair was longer then and it had icicles hanging off where the sweat had dripped and frozen, just like when they form along the roof of a house. My beard was frozen solid from the moisture in my breath and from the sweat dripping off my overheated head. Every time I moved my mouth it hurt like hell because the ice would pull the hair in my beard. I was sucking air so bad trying to catch up with that three-legged buck that my jaws were pumping and my face felt like little green goblins were plucking the hairs from my beard, a dozen at a time.

"Once we got over the top he quit bleeding, so all I had to follow were his tracks. The trouble was, there had been a lot of deer feeding in the acorns and there were a lot of tracks on the ground. If he hadn't been going downhill and hitting so hard on that good front leg I am not sure I could have followed him. But it was just as steep on the other side of the mountain and every now and then he would skid a little on the frozen ground, not much, just a couple of inches, but it would kick up a few leaves. If you knew what to look for you could sort them out from all the other deer tracks. The trick was to get low, right at ground level, so the leaves that were pushed up a little higher than the rest would show up. Sometimes I could line up several of these markers in a line, just like connecting the dots. When that happened I would pick out a tree at the other end for a marker point and run like hell for it trying to make up ground faster.

"He went all the way to the Millstone River at the bottom of the valley and hit it about two miles upstream from the swinging bridge.

"That damn buck crossed the river. My guess is he had been tracked before and knew some tricks. Not too many hunters would have followed him and if I had just been tracking him trying to get a shot I would have quit right there. But, I had wounded him and had a responsibility to clean up the mess I made. I never quit on a wounded animal until I have exhausted every possibility and this guy was still leaving something I could follow. So, I kept on him. I figured I owed that buck at least that much.

"That damn river was running high and fast and it was so cold the rocks on the bottom were coated with anchor ice. Anchor ice only forms in fast moving water when the air temperature is well below zero; something about super cooling the surface water until it forms ice which sinks and clings to the rocks. Never made much sense to me how it all works because ice floats, but I have seen it all my life and I know it only happens when it's goddamned cold.

"I took off my boots, socks, pants and long johns. I held them and my rifle above my head as I waded across that river barefoot, which I can tell you was no fun at all. About halfway across I thought I had made the biggest mistake of my life. I couldn't feel my feet so it was hard to tell what I was standing on. The current was powerful and the rocks were so slippery I almost fell about a hundred times in the first fifty feet. If I had fallen, I doubt I would be here. That water was so cold and so fast that it's likely sometime the next spring they would have pulled my frozen body out of Lake Champlain, fifty miles downstream. On the other hand my mother used to say I was so contrary that if I ever did drown she would tell the search party to look for me upstream. So, you never know.

"Once I hit the bank my feet were so cold they felt like half melted popsicles when I touched them. Before I finished dressing I could actually feel the ice crystals under my skin. I got dressed and took about three steps before the deer took off. That sneaky bastard was laid up behind a big bolder watching me the entire time, probably laughing at the naked, half frozen hunter. I am sure there was "shrinkage" so I guess I can't blame him for laughing. Anyway, I snapped a shot and hit a sapling, which deflected the bullet, so I missed the buck. At that point I was seriously considering tossing that damned rifle into the river and letting it bounce along the rocks all the way to Champlain.

"That tough old buck went about half a mile along the shore until it looked like he crossed the river again. His tracks led right to the edge and stopped. I could see where he stepped in the water and dragged his leg over the rocks, dripping water on them. It was so cold that it should have frozen in seconds, but this was still wet, so I had to be close. That should have given me a clue. He could not have made it across that fast, but I didn't think of that until later.

"There was no way in hell I was going to cross barefoot again, so I just waded in and let the cold water fill my boots and soak my wool pants. It took me a while to figure out what happened, but it turns out he hadn't crossed at all. There were some more deer on the other side of the river and he had walked to the edge to look at them. He probably wanted to join them, but knew he couldn't get back across that torrent again with his bad leg and weak condition. It turns out he slipped into the woods, out of sight and continued heading downriver. His tracks didn't show for about fifty more yards, which is another reason I assumed he had crossed again. I spotted his tracks going to the edge of the river and jumped to the conclusion that he had crossed. I should have looked a little more because then I had to come back across the river a third time.

"I was wearing boots with half-inch thick felt liners. Those liners soaked up about a gallon of water each and in half an hour were frozen solid. It was like walking in ski boots, big, heavy, cold, clunky ski boots. My pants froze solid too. I worked to keep them free at the knee so I could walk, but they were stiff as cardboard and as cold as a whore's heart.

"I stayed on that buck all the rest of the day, tracking him almost ten miles altogether, before it got dark and I couldn't see his tracks anymore. I walked out to a road and after a couple of miles, hitched a ride back to my truck. When that farmer picked me up on the road I think I was closer to death than the deer.

"I came back the next day, with a different rifle, one that had been good to me over the years and was quick to forgive me for abandoning it for that custom hussy I had been using. That pump-action rifle is chambered in .35 Whelen and it is a thumper. It also was a lucky gun when it came to cleaning up messes like this. Over the years more than one buck had been escaping, only to collide with its big bullet. Some rifles just have magic in them and that was one of them. If I had been using it the day before, I doubt I would have had to track that buck at all. When that Whelen hit them they usually only moved about two feet . . . straight down.

"I jumped the buck out of his bed in some thick alders just past where I left off the night before. My buddy used to say that stuff 'was so thick a dog has to back up just to bark.' I was trying to get a look at him when I got tangled up in the brush and plunged head first over the edge of a bowl scooped out by eons of flood waters. I fell six feet and slid another ten down into a basin full of tangles and driftwood. Meanwhile the buck escaped by running around the far end of the mess. There was no way to get through the ledges downstream and the deer was out of options. He jumped back into the river and made for the other side.

"My backpack had flipped over my head and damn near strangled me. Even with gloves on, I somehow cut my hand and was leaving a lot better blood trail than the deer. I clawed my way out of the pack and dumped it in the brush. I found my rifle, which had a different trajectory path than I did when I fell, and I started fighting my way through that shit to the river.

"I shot him on the other side as he was scrambling up the bank, dripping water from his swim. I'll always remember how he was backlit with the low morning sun so that it looked like he was shedding sheets of sparkling diamonds as the water drops cascading off him glowed from the sunlight passing through them.

"When the bullet hit him, the diamonds shattered. It was like those old boxing photos of the glove colliding with a jaw and a halo of spray surrounding the guy's head from the impact. That buck was surrounded by water spray that formed a rainbow over his back. Like I said, that Whelen hit them hard.

"There was no way I would wade that river again, so I had to go around to a bridge half a mile downstream and then back up to where he was cooling on the other side of the river. It was so friggin' cold that by the time I got to him he had frozen to the rocks. I couldn't get him off by myself and had to go to town to find my cousins to help. Three of us pulled all the hair off his hide while prying him off the rocks so he was as bald as my old aunt Beulah."

"What the hell," Davy said, his eyes wild in the moonlight. "We are about to get our asses killed and you are telling me hunting stories, are you nuts or just senile?"

"Well, you do need to know that I am one hell of a tracker. That's important.

"I am tough too, that was a hard day.

"But, my main point is I tracked that buck along the river and past the suspended bridge over the gorge. If we can get past the bridge there is a spur trail that will bring us out on top of the gulf."

"I know that, Davy said. "But if they have a guard on the road they will damn sure have one on that bridge too."

"Yes, they will. But we don't need to cross that bridge when we come to it. Pun intended, by the way. We just need to get past it. Most people think it's impossible to do that without climbing over the bridge. But, that buck knew a way and he was nice enough to show it to me. I thanked him by giving his back-straps a place of honor at my family's Christmas dinner later that year."

CHAPTER 24

"So what the hell was all that? You could have just told me you knew how to get past the guard at the bridge instead of making me listen to that pointless, endless story about what how wonderful you are at deer hunting."

"It wasn't pointless," I said, "and it has indeed ended. It actually served a very good point, which you clearly have not yet figured out."

"Well, other than me wanting to shoot you in the foot and go home, I guess I haven't. But, I suppose there is no way to stop you from telling me what I missed, now is there?"

"You, Davy, are purely a man of action, while I am a man of both action and of deep intellect. You are compelled to move, to press on and to charge ahead and I needed to keep that skinny, white ass of yours planted for a while. What better way than to entertain and enlighten you with an allegorical tale of great and wondrous feats?

"Ahab had his whale, Odysseus his journey and me, well; I am but a humble man with only a simple story of deer hunting to share with you. But we all serve a deeper purpose when telling our tales. Mine was to keep you rooted here until the moon grew closer to the western horizon. If we attempted to get past that guard with all this moonlight, somebody would no doubt end up with some extra holes. Since I am the bigger, slower target I suspect it would be me and I have already filled my quota for being shot this month.

"But, I just now see by the lunar position that we have just exactly the correct amount of time needed to get into place before the moon glides behind yonder mountain ridge and shades us with a few more hours of darkness in which we can continue our quest to rescue yon maiden."

Davy's less than articulate response was to silhouette his middle finger against the moon, which I had no problem seeing quite clearly.

CHAPTER 25

We approached from the up-river side of the bridge. The river was still wide here and the bed was twice as wide as the river, even when it was as high as it was now. That left deep flats on either side of the river choked with thick alders and willows. The deer once had trails through the brush that I hoped were still open. If so, it would be possible, not easy but possible, to approach through the thicket of brush and trees. I had not been in this jungle since tracking that buck a long time ago, but it looked like a few deer were still around and using the trails. That didn't surprise me. Back when the threat of nuclear war was going to end the world, people predicted that only coyotes and cockroaches would survive. I would have bet on the whitetail deer as well. They are the ultimate survivors and no nuclear war would wipe them out. They would find a little piece of land with some cover and food and start producing baby deer again.

The thing about deer is that as long as they have cover to hide in, it's impossible to shoot them all. I always figured a few survived the collapse, when everybody with a gun wanted to eat them. Now that everyone assumes they are extinct in Vermont and it's not safe to go wandering around alone, nobody is bothering them much and they appear to be making a small comeback. One thing they figured out is to stick to places like this, so thick, brush choked and inhospitable that any sane man avoided coming here. Never claiming to be sane, I simply thanked them silently for contributing these trails.

The trouble is that a deer is not as tall as a man, so often there is overhanging brush you must duck. To clear it with your backpack you must hunch over, bending deeply at the waist. This is an exhausting way to walk, yet there were few places where a man could stand up and move forward more than a couple of feet.

There were also a lot of blocked paths where the deer could easily jump over the blowdowns, but a man cannot. Plus, deer are streamlined. They are narrow and covered with slippery hair, so they slide through tight spots where a man hangs up. A man, particularly a man carrying a pack and a rifle, is not well suited to traveling these game trails. You will tangle in the brush and trip over the obstacles. The branches will whip you in the face, stinging so your eyes water. Then, when you can't see, they will poke you in the eye. The thorns will steal your hat, scratch your hands and trip your feet. You can't bully your way through and cursing does no good. Rage is the emotion you most feel, but you need to lock it down and keep moving in a methodical way, one step at a time. It is an exhausting, noisy affair, but with luck, the roar of the river as it pounded through the gorge below would hide any noise we made from the ears of the guard at the bridge.

The brush approaches the gorge along a wide flood plain carved between the mountains. At this point the river is perhaps one hundred feet wide, but just upstream of the bridge it enters a deep rock gorge and narrows to about twenty feet. It also starts to drop in elevation much faster. The result is all that water enters a narrow gorge between the cliffs then descends rapidly. It goes from a babbling brook, although a large one, to a roaring, raging, impassable whitewater hell in just a few yards. It continues that way for two more miles.

There were plenty of high willows growing along the edge of the river to keep us in cover until we were at the mouth of the gorge, just upstream of the bridge. It was still very bright when we arrived there, so we stayed back in the brush and found a comfortable spot to sit and rest our packs on the ground.

A pack can get pretty damn heavy when you have been carrying it for hours. But this close to the bad guys it was not a good idea to take them off. If we had to move fast there would not be time to put a pack back on. Carrying a heavy backpack in your hand makes running almost impossible and you won't have your hands free to fight. Our packs have most of our gear and several guns. To leave them behind would mean death at the worst or a failed mission at best, so we kept them on our backs. I found a low boulder that I could rest the pack on and sat down, so the boulder took the weight off my shoulders while we waited for the moon to pass below the mountaintop.

The gentle night breeze was in our face and the cooling thermals were causing the air to slide down along the contours of the land. Twice I could smell cigarette smoke, so I knew they had a guy waiting on the other side of the bridge. The bridge was the only defensible position and if trouble came at him, it would have to cross the bridge, giving him a clear line of fire. I figured he had to be there, but the smoke confirmed it. It always baffled me how those addicted managed to stay supplied with tobacco, no matter how bad things got.

I had been sort of daydreaming when Davy kicked my boot. I looked to the bridge and saw the glow of a lit cigarette from a guy standing ten feet out on the span and leaning on the upriver suspension cable that served as a railing.

The moon had dipped below the horizon from our perspective and it was getting dark where we were, eighty feet below the guy, but he was higher and still lit by the reflection from that huge celestial body. I could plainly see the barrel of a rifle sticking above his shoulder, where he wore it on a hunting style sling. These slings were fine for carrying a rifle, but most tactical guys realized long ago that they were very slow when you needed to deploy the rifle in a hurry. It is much faster to have a carbine hanging muzzle down on a sling so it is in front of you, resting on your chest. When adjusted properly, all the operator needs to do is slide the butt to his shoulder, raise the muzzle and start firing. The best can do that in about half a second. The way this guy had it slung over his shoulder he would have to remove it from his shoulder, in back of him, bring it to the front and then raise the gun into position. It would take several seconds to do that and nobody who is battle savvy has used that method of carrying a fighting rifle since the Vietnam War.

It told me this guy was not well trained. Smoking while on duty indicated he was not well disciplined, either. I could see a trend developing with these guys. I just hoped it was representative of the rest of the guys we would encounter.

CHAPTER 26

The guy on the bridge turned dark, changing from a man to a shadow as the moon dove deeper into the earth. A couple of minutes later I saw his cigarette flick out into space, leaving a contrail of orange sparks as it descended into the river. I could detect the shadows changing as he walked off the bridge. The cables were silhouetted against the night sky and I could see them jump up a few inches and then dance a bit as his weight left the bridge.

"Let's go," I whispered to Davy. "He is off the bridge. Stick close, it's a tricky trail."

It looked impossible to pass by the bridge from underneath, even in the daylight. But that buck knew a way. I remembered the trail was hidden between two huge boulders on the edge of the river. They looked like two giant eggs nested side by side. Tonight one of them was halfway in the water and the other tight against the cliff. With the moon gone, it was very dark, my eyes had not yet adjusted and I almost bumped into them before I saw the rocks. The passage was tight and the buck had to turn his antlers sideways to get them through. I had found this spot because the antlers had rubbed on the rocks and left white streaks. They had stood out like petroglyphs and when I walked over to see what the hell they were, I spotted his tracks in the gravel.

We had to remove our packs, and drag them behind us as we twisted sideways to get through. Still, it was a very tight fit for me at the choke point. I had to suck in my stomach and force my body through. When I shot that buck I was young and still dabbling with martial arts. I worked out five days a week and was in great shape. I was also aided by the fact the rocks were covered with a thin coating of ice from the river spray, which made them very slippery. Even then it was a tight squeeze. Five years ago when I was fat and happy, I never could have made it through. Tough times and the fact my food didn't come from a supermarket or fast food joint anymore had slimmed me down, but I was not sure it was enough.

I sucked it in and pushed hard, up and forward with my legs. I slid partway through, but as my body settled down into the narrow part of the passage, I was wedged in tight. My feet were barely touching the ground as the rocks held me up. I couldn't go forward or back and the rounded rocks were acting like two giant cams forcing me deeper with every breath or movement. The rocks were crushing my chest and pushing on my diaphragm. I struggled to get a little air in my lungs while I fought the panic that comes with oxygen deprivation, and lost.

Twice over the years I have found dead deer hung up in the crotch of a tree, just like I was now hung in these rocks. I never knew what possessed them to try to jump through the forked trees, but I was starting to understand why they died.

My vision was getting spotty and my legs week when I felt Davy pushing on my side. He had a rhythm going and I timed my efforts to his, so on the third joint effort I popped past the choke point and fell to the gravel below, smacking my left eyebrow on a rock. I could feel blood streaming down my face, but focused only on the sweet, wet air that was filling my lungs. The spray from the river was soaking me, but it didn't matter. In fact, it felt good.

"Get up old man," Davy whispered as he kicked me in the ribs. "We ain't got time for this shit."

I felt my pack bump my leg as he held it out for me to take and I grabbed the top handle. I scrambled a few more feet and was suddenly free of the boulders and on a small gravel bar on the edge of the river ten feet in front of the cliffs of the gorge.

We shouldered our packs and I came in close to the cliff and looked up at the night sky. The trail the buck used ran up the front diagonally. It was an old fissure in the rocks that had filled with earth over the eons and it provided a narrow shelf to walk on. In this total darkness it was hard to find, but I spotted the top by its shape against the skyline. I lined up with that and moved right, feeling with my hands until I felt the dirt. I reached up, found a hand-hold and pulled myself onto the trail. We climbed slowly, going mostly by feel for the next fifteen minutes. By then my night vision was starting to adjust and I could see shapes and shadows well enough to climb a little faster.

This trail topped out on a narrow shelf on the ledges about ten feet below the bridge and then ran on a slight incline until it disappeared under the bridge with about five feet of clearance. I remembered that it ended abruptly at the far side, seeming to strand anybody who made it this far eighty feet above the river. The buck had jumped like a mountain goat across the gap, to another tiny shelf on the cliff that supported the abutment for the bridge. Then he jumped three feet below that to another little shelf, barely large enough for a man to stand on. From there, he jumped the gap to the side of the hill that rose above the cliffs.

That buck had worked his way up the steep bank through the stunted hemlock trees. The ground was covered with several inches of dropped needles and loose rock and gave no purchase. I had to pull myself up hand over hand, using the trees. It was grueling work because there was no way to rest. It was so steep that my weight was always supported by one or the other of my quivering, spasming muscle groups. It was a brutal climb with arms, hands and legs that work and I marveled at how that buck was able make to it with only one functional front leg.

Like any true hunter, I recognize that sometimes you wound things that you hunt. That's part of hunting. It's one thing to rationalize it in your mind while quite another to live with it and I always feel bad about wounding game. But, I remember that I felt my worst as I struggled up that hill and thought about what the buck was enduring to stay alive.

I don't mind shooting animals. Man was meant to be a hunter and like they say, if God didn't want us hunting them he would not have made animals out of meat. There is a reason we have canine teeth. Humans are meant to eat meat and getting that meat by hunting is the most honest way possible. But I took no joy in causing anything to suffer. I recognized intellectually that sometimes things don't go as planned with all the variables in hunting wild animals and wounding is part of hunting, but that doesn't mean I have to like it.

I remember one "First Nations" guide we had while hunting moose in British Columbia some years ago. My friend had wounded a moose. I saw the bullet hit the bull too high. I was pretty sure we could find the bull, although it would be a long, tough day before we did. But the guide only followed the tracks a short distance before giving up. I protested that we had clear tracks in the snow and a decent enough blood trail and that it was much too early to quit.

"It's just a moose," he said, with a shrug of his shoulders. "We go find another."

I never could accept that attitude and I didn't that day. Any hunter owes the animal he shoots a huge debt he must pay. It is your moral duty to do everything you possibly can to recover the wounded animal. Leaving it to suffer and die a horrible death because it's inconvenient is wrong on so many levels. So you stick with them, no matter what.

As I moved through the dark I very clearly remember following that buck. Climbing this hill had taken a big toll on me physically and psychologically and made me ask myself uncomfortable questions.

Now as I prepared to do it again, I couldn't help but wonder if this repeat performance was part of a bigger plan.

CHAPTER 27

I suppose my mind was on that day so long ago, rather than where it should have been. But, even if I had been paying attention I doubt it would have happened any differently. I was leading along the ledge, with Davy close behind. The land rose slowly as we approached the bridge and we had to duck down to move under the first support beam. The ledge was just barely wide enough to support my boot as we inched along and I was focusing on not falling.

Something, I don't know what, a coyote or maybe a raccoon, came charging out from underneath the bridge in a blind panic. It was right in front of our faces and it actually knocked my hat crooked on my head and stepped on my shoulder as it scrambled up onto the bridge. It would have made more sense to run off the end of the bridge and up the trail, but instead it scrambled across to the other side. We stood perfectly still as we listened to it, claws clicking across the wooden planks above our heads, knowing this wouldn't end well.

I had expected to hear shots, but instead it was shouts. I occurred to me that if the guy had been guarding the bridge long he probably had seen whatever this was coming and going. So he knew something was living or feeding under the bridge and recognized the shape as it charged across the planks. But, unless he was completely stupid he would also realize that something or somebody had spooked whatever the hell it was out of its hiding place.

"Reach up and grab on to something and hang on," Davy said. Then he grabbed the straps of my pack and swung himself past me on the ledge. Once past, he ran out to the end, climbed up onto the bridge structure and waited.

We heard cautious footsteps on the bridge above our heads as the guard approached. He leaned over the railing and tried to look under the bridge.

"Anybody there?" He shouted again as he leaned even farther over the rail.

"Why, yes there is!" Davy said.

The guy paused with that "aw shit" look on his face for just a split second. But, that was more than enough.

I have never seen anybody move as fast as Davy did right then. He uncoiled, reached up and grabbed the guy by the front of his shirt and tossed him into the gorge so fast it was nothing more than a blur of movement. As the guy fell Davy snagged his rifle's sling and pulled the gun off his shoulder. The guy grabbed the rifle butt and held on with both hands, swinging from the gun as Davy held the other end. Davy had one hand on the sling and the other over his head holding on to the bridge. His feet were planted on the narrow ledge. The guy looked to be about fifty pounds heavier than Davy and I was amazed at the strength he had to hold him with one hand. The guy was screaming and cursing and threating to kill Davy if he let go. That is, until Davy gave a quick yank on the rifle and the guy lost his grip and fell into the abyss.

The river was running high, so I figured he had a fifty-fifty chance. He hit in rushing water that was about ten feet deep, so unless he landed at an odd angle and broke his back, he probably survived. If he was smart and knew about whitewater, he would turn on his back, point his feet downriver and ride it out. The gorge is about two miles long and it would be a brutal ride. He would lose some skin and maybe break a bone or two, but he should squirt out the other end alive.

Or not.

I really didn't care. He would have shot us on sight. That made him my enemy, so I had no qualms if he died. Either way he was out of it for at least a day and no longer our problem.

With him gone, it didn't matter if we showed ourselves and now we didn't have to take those risky jumps in the dark, trying to land on a sliver of shelf and then make that brutal climb back up through the trees.

Davy handed me his pack and then climbed up onto the bridge. I held onto a support cable with my right hand as I swung the pack with my left. He grabbed it as it reached the apex of the swing. Then I did the same with mine.

"Holy shit!" Davy said. "What the hell you got in this thing, bricks?"

"Just some pretty rocks I found on the trail," I said. "But, there might be a sandwich in there too and I am hungry. Let's eat."

I scrambled up to the bridge, then after digging out some food to eat on the way, we stepped onto the trail up the hill.

A mile later we hit the road to the monastery, just above the gulf, and half a mile past that we could see its lights. We kept to the edge of the meadows on the right of the road, so we would be invisible against the dark background of the trees.

Unless, of course, they had night vision or infrared. If they did we were screwed. I half expected a bullet to hit me at any time, but none did.

There was a large pond taking up about half the meadow, with a thin strip of open land between it and the woods. The pond drained through this strip and was the start of the brook that ran parallel to the road until it hit the Millstone River near the valley floor. Part of this was wet, filled with cattails and blocking our path. The only alternative would be to go around the pond, which would have left us exposed for way too long, so we just waded through, being very careful not to make any sucking noises as we pulled our boots out of the mud with each step. It was slow, painful work as we were often off balance and in danger of falling in the mud. The heavy packs on our backs made that even worse, but one mistake here could make enough noise to alert the guards, so we just worked slowly and held on to each other's packs for stability. As one guy stepped, the other would stand still to anchor him. Then the first guy stood still while the second stepped. Back and forth we went. It was probably only one hundred yards or so across the wetlands, but I was completely exhausted when we finally got to the high ground on the other side. I lay on the grass, sucking air and waiting for my legs to stop shaking. It did my heart good to see that Davy was doing the same thing.

CHAPTER 28

"Wait here." Davy said, and then before I could respond he disappeared into the dark. I found a big maple tree and made myself comfortable at the base while I hoped I wouldn't regret turning him loose without adult supervision. I must have dozed off because the next thing I knew he was squatting beside me.

"Wake up old man, it's time to go rescue the damsel in distress. I couldn't find any dragons to slay, but I did take care of the guards in the bell tower and on the roof. I even found one of the roaming guards. That means there is still one more out there someplace wandering around, but what the hell, that just makes things more interesting. Let's go see if we can avoid him, get the girl and get the hell out of here."

A few minutes later we were outside Sarah's window. It was dark and when we didn't hear any sounds after ten minutes we figured she was sleeping. We made our way around to the front and then onto the porch and to the door. I was trying to figure out how to get her to open it without attracting attention when Davy tried the handle. It was unlocked, so we slipped inside and shut the door behind us. I lit a match and used my hand to block most of the light while I found the bed.

It was empty.

I had not seen working electricity in a long time, so when the lights snapped on it surprised me, as it was about the last thing I was expecting. I turned to see Sarah sitting in a chair and my brother standing beside her with his hand on the light switch. Beside him was a very large black man in a business suit.

"Hey bro'," I said with a calm that I hoped was masking the fear I was feeling. "I heard you were dead."

"Sorry about that," Bradley said. "It was the only way we could be sure you would come."

"What the hell are you talking about?" I said. "What do you mean the only way? You could have just come to my house and asked me to come here and you know I would have."

"We tried that. You didn't respond well."

"What? When? You never came to my house."

"Not me, I was still in the city, but they sent Reggie here to ask you to a meeting and you told them no, and then ran him off at gunpoint."

"What, when? No. Nothing like that ever happened. I don't know what the hell you are talking about, nobody ever came to my house to talk to me about anything to do with you or Sarah. I am pretty sure I would remember a seven-foot tall, three hundred-fifty pound black guy with a shaved head. He doesn't exactly blend in my neighborhood. The first thing I heard from anybody was that you, Samantha and Brent were dead and that Sarah had been kidnapped. I got that information from one of the guys working on the Farnsworth's train. He has red hair and relies on high-heeled cowboy boots to hit five foot-four, so I am pretty sure it was not "Reggie here" who told me anything."

"What we are doing is radical, it's going to change the world." Bradley said, seeming to ignore me. "In fact, we are going to save the world. Like I said, we needed to get you out here, so we could talk to you without the poisoning influence of your comfort zone. I told them you would never agree to help, that you were too rigid in your thinking and that they were wasting their time. But, the top guys all seemed to think they needed you. That you had something to contribute. I told them they were wrong, but in the interest of consensus I agreed to help them get you here so they could show you the plans."

"What plans," I asked?

He ignored me again.

"After you ran him off, Reggie came up with the idea of telling you that I was dead and Sarah was kidnapped because we knew you had a hero complex and could never just leave it alone. You would 'have' to charge off on your white horse to rescue her. 'Don't mess with my family,' right? That's what you always said. So what better way to get you to do what we wanted than to mess with your family?

"It would have worked if you hadn't done your usual 'John Wayne' thing and shot the guide we sent to help you find us. But then, that's always been you: shoot first, ask questions later. Mr. Macho, always gotta be the alpha dog."

"Are you talking about the guy in the old hardware store?"

I was choking back my anger and starting to see what was happening here. I knew rage would just get me killed; I had to stay calm and think.

"That asshole started shooting at me first. I didn't have any choice but to kill him. He was not there to be my guide, he was there to be my executioner."

"Like hell! He was just trying to help you and you shot him."

"What about the thirty or so of his friends who showed up a couple of minutes later and did their best to kill me, were they friendly 'guides' too?"

"What the hell are you talking about," Bradley shouted. "There weren't any other people there. Just you and Connor. That's was his name, Connor, the guy you killed. I figured you should know that. He was my friend and he would never hurt anybody."

The big black guy in the suit spoke for the first time, "Yes well, about that, Bradley. We really couldn't tell you, because you would never understand. The truth is Connor was paid to be your friend and he actually hurt a lot of people."

I noticed that Reggie had a pistol pointed at my brother.

"His primary job was to control you. Your purpose was to lure your brother out for us so we could indeed shoot him. But, he proved to be more resourceful than we expected. He not only shot Connor, but he managed to deplete the assets housed in Easton by a pretty high number and then make off with one of our trucks. He even managed to drop out of sight for a while.

"You kept saying he would come, that he was too much of a knight in shining armor to let Sarah go un-rescued. Turns out you were correct. I really wish you had told us how dangerous he was, too. This is a knight who carries a very sharp and well used broadsword. He cost us a lot of time, money and aggravation.

"I assume," he said, looking at me, "that the guys we left to guard the road are no longer part of the team?"

I didn't answer, just stood staring at him. I thought it best not to reveal too much and the less he knew about how we got there, the better.

He held my stare for a couple of seconds, and then with a smirk he turned back to my brother.

"But now, Bradley, we have a dilemma. You indeed got him here and so it would seem that your usefulness for our cause has expired. Be thankful that you can die knowing it was for the greater good of mankind. I am sorry that we can't put that on your headstone so future generations can believe you were a hero, but history doesn't always recognize those who truly sacrifice. The best I can do is an unmarked grave in the back meadow, one that you can share with your brother and his surly looking sidekick. I will, however, look after Sarah once you have gone. In fact, a lot of our 'assets' have expressed an interest in looking after her. I think I will make a present of her to them, so that they can keep their morale high and their libidos satiated.

"Gentlemen, if you please," he said, pointing the gun at us, "put your weapons on the bed. Do it slowly and do it one at a time. Just put them down and then step away to that wall where you will keep your hands high over your head where I can see them. You go first Handsome," he said, pointing at Davy.

Davy dumped his rifle on the bed, followed by his backpack with his spare long guns. Then he took his pistol out of his holster.

"I assume there is a second pistol under your vest. Take that one out, too. Now the knives, both of them. That's a good boy. Now step back away from the bed while Hero here gives me his guns."

I didn't see anything else to do but comply. Once I had all my guns and knives on the bed I stepped back against the wall.

He turned to me and said, "You have thought for some time now that your brother was dead. Well, tonight I am going to shoot him first so that when you die, which will be very soon after him, you will go to the great beyond secure in the knowledge that this time he is truly and completely dead."

He turned the pistol to my brother, pointing it right at his face. But, before he could pull the trigger Davy broke into a blur of motion. He pulled one of the loaded rifle magazines from his vest and hurled it, spinning like a buzz saw, at Reggie's head. A fully-loaded, metal, thirty-round AR-15 magazine weighs more than a pound and is all edges and corners. When a bottom corner hit the guy's temple, there was a loud crack and a hole appeared in his skull, white for a split-second and then red as it started spurting blood like a gusher oil well. He went down like a steer hit with a poleax.

Davy and I both jumped for our guns. I grabbed a rifle and covered the door while he put on his backpack and holstered his pistols, and then he did the same for me while I got my gear back on. By the time we had our kits all back in place the guy was just starting to wake up. I put my knee on his chest, grabbed the back of his head and pulled until his chin was on his chest. I stuck my knife deep into the back of his neck at the base of his skull and twisted the handle back and forth, severing his spinal column. He went limp and stopped breathing without a sound.

"We used to do that to alligators we hunted in Florida before we brought them into the air boats," I said. "We couldn't have them thrashing around, breaking our legs with their tails, so we needed a fast, quiet way to turn them to Jell-O. I always figured it would work on men as well as reptiles but, with this guy, I think that question is still unanswered because he was more snake than man."

CHAPTER 29

"Put on some boots," I said to Sarah. "Grab a jacket. If it's waterproof, all the better. If you have any food here in this cabin, put it in my backpack. Hurry! We need to move fast."

She put on a pair of lace-up leather boots and grabbed a backpack from the closet. She filled it with food from a small cupboard in the corner. I was impressed with her efficiency, just like she had been planning for this moment.

My brother, on the other hand, just stood there.

"Come on," I said. "We need to get the hell out of here now. Move! Help Sarah! We gotta get all the shit we can packed and get the hell out of here before anybody figures out this didn't go like they planned."

"I am not going anywhere until I understand what is going on here," he said with that peevish voice that has always made me want to slap him.

"What's going on here is you have been played for a fool. They are trying to kill me and they are going to kill you and Sarah if you don't drag your ass and get moving."

"Not until I talk to him."

"Who?"

"I know you never liked him and that you didn't agree with his politics, but you just need to be educated. You are smart, you will understand. He is a great man, a true leader. He is the one who will lead us out of this mess. I need to talk with him. He will explain. This has to be a misunderstanding."

Before I could stop him, my brother opened the door and started outside. A shot rang out and he spun back into the room with his left arm bleeding where a bullet had passed through his forearm.

Sarah screamed as Davy pulled Bradley away from the door. I kicked the door shut and pushed her to the floor. Bullets erupted through the door. I could hear them hitting the walls of the cabin as well, but the thick logs were stopping them. I belly crawled to a corner, dragging Sarah with me. I noticed that Davy had dragged Bradley to the opposite corner. He already had his first aid kit out and was covering the wound with a QuikClot sponge to stop the bleeding and securing it in place with an elastic bandage. Bradley sat watching him and gritting his teeth.

"I think we just found our missing guard." Davy said.

"That's how they knew you were coming," Sarah said. "He noticed that the other guards were missing. So he told Reggie. He and Dad got here just before you showed up."

"There is just one guy out there now. He was probably standing by to mop up after Reggie had his fun," Davy said. "We gotta move fast because all this shooting is going to attract attention. Don't forget there are always two more guys in that cabin to the north. I figure they are in play now, too. It's going to take a couple of minutes for the rest of them to get here from the barracks. So, I think that's three guns we need to deal with for the moment."

Davy grabbed a broom from the corner and broke off a section of the wooden handle. He wrapped that as a support splint to Bradley's arm. Then he yanked down the curtains and made a sling. Then he gave him a morphine shot from his first aid kit.

I was astounded that he did all that in about a minute.

"What the hell Davy, were you some kind of super medic in another life or something?" I asked.

"When you work the transport trucks you learn to move fast. If I didn't fix up the guys and get the bleeding stopped, they would die. But if I screwed around too long, I was not on the guns shooting assholes. I told you we train hard; well, this is one of the things I trained to do.

"Sorry, that's the best I can do in a hurry," he said to Bradley. "We will fix you up better later. It's going to hurt like hell because I only gave you a half-dose of pain killer. I need you mobile because we got to get the hell out of here."

The simple one-room cabin had a door in the center with a window on each side. The problem was that there were also windows in the back.

"Give me your spare AR," Sarah said. "I'll cover the back."

She must have seen the look of doubt on my face.

"Don't worry, I know how to use it and I want to get away from these bastards. Dad was always a true believer, but not me. They are evil posing as saviors. I have always expected them to kill us. I told Dad that, but you know how he is, he just wouldn't listen."

I motioned to my back and she pulled the extra M4 from my backpack. She locked the bolt back and pulled the magazine to make sure it was loaded. "Right side," she said as she looked at the top cartridge. Then she slammed the magazine back in place and hit the bolt release to close the bolt. She pulled the magazine, looked and said, "Left side, so one is in the chamber." She replaced the magazine, smacked it hard with her hand, switched off the safety, put the butt on her shoulder and aimed at the back windows. This took about three seconds, just long enough for my jaw to hit the floor, figuratively and literally. I was already lying on my belly, so it only had to drop an inch or so.

"Don't look so surprised Uncle," she said, never moving her focus from the windows. "I had a cop boyfriend who was on the SWAT team. We went shooting all the time. I loved it! Plus it really pissed Dad off. You know what a pacifist he is and how much he hates guns. When I was dating Colin and we were shooting every weekend it used to make Dad foam at the mouth, sort of like he is now. But back then I was just having some fun. This is a bit more serious. Now, let me worry about the back while you guys clear a path out that door, I want to get the hell out of here, now!"

I got set under my window, which was missing the glass, as Davy did the same under his. He stuck the barrel of his rifle up and broke the glass. That drew a couple of shots. Then he stuck the gun up and out the window and fired three fast shots, which were also answered. I figured they were focusing on him, so I got up into a squat below my window with my rifle ready. Davy stuck his gun up again and fired as I stood up. I saw the muzzle flash as the guy shot at Davy's rifle, so I held just under it and fired five rapid shots. There was a little ambient light from the cabins and I saw the guy fall.

Then I noticed two more coming around the cabin in front of us. I shot the one on the right as I heard Davy's gun shooting to my left. They both fell, but the one Davy shot didn't look right as he did. I shot my guy in the head and just as I did the other guy rose to his knees and fired a three-round burst at me. One of the bullets hit my left shoulder and I fell back into the room. Davy's gun barked twice and I heard bullets hitting meat outside the cabin. My shoulder hurt like hell and was spraying blood everywhere, but I flexed my arm and it seemed like it still worked okay.

"How bad is it?" Davy asked. "You better still be in working condition old man, because we are out of time here."

CHAPTER 30

"Let's go," I said. "Head north. They won't be expecting that. I know a trail up over the mountain that can get us out of here."

Bradley was on his feet and moving with us, any illusions about them not wanting to kill him gone for the moment. He had a dopey grin on his face from the morphine Davy had given him, but he was coherent and moving well.

Davy headed out first, with Sarah next, then Bradley and me. We ran up the dirt road, which ended in a large meadow.

By now dawn was hinting in the eastern sky and I knew we had to get across the meadow before somebody saw us. The trail ran off the northwest side of the meadow about two hundred yards from the north end, where we were. It was an old stagecoach road back in the early 1800s when this entire mountain had been cleared of timber to make charcoal. But now the mountain was choked with tall trees and thick underbrush. Most of these old roads had been kept open by the snowmobilers. But the monks would never allow them to ride on their property, saying the noise polluted their calm or some such shit. So, with this road leading only to the meadow, there was no reason to ride on it and no reason to keep the trail open and marked.

When I was sorting through his stuff after my grandfather died, I had found it on an old topographical map from back in the 1920s that he had squirreled away in his gun cabinet. I carried the map with me while hunting that fall to help keep my connection to the old man alive. After I had filled my deer tag I still had a few days off so I decided to find the trail. By then, it was nothing more than a faded path, full of blowdowns and impassable in places. But I managed to walk all the way to the monastery.

I bought a burger and a Diet Coke at their little shop and laughed at the monk waiting on me. He didn't hear any car drive up and he kept going to the window to look in the parking lot to see how I got there. He was too polite to ask me, or maybe he was one of the silent ones, but I could see it was driving him crazy.

I knew he would watch me leave, so I walked down the road until I was around the corner and out of sight, then I circled around through the woods back to the trail. I hoped that guy was now an old monk enjoying his last years in a secure compound in upstate New York and pondering the question still.

I remembered that there was a huge, dead elm tree on the edge of the meadow. Like most elms in Vermont it had been killed by Dutch elm disease back in the '70s. But, elms are tough trees and decades later a lot of them were still standing dead on the stump. I had used this one as a marker to find the trail that day. I remembered the trail started one hundred yards north of the tree.

I was looking through the gloom of the emerging day, trying to see that tree and wondering why I could not. It was a huge tree, stuck out twenty yards into the field and all by itself. It should have been easy to see even in this light. To miss the trail is to miss the only way up the mountain. The rest of it is simply too choked with brush and covered with steep ledges and cliffs. The other side is cut off by a deep gorge where the Millstone comes down from its source in a series of beaver bogs along the top of the mountain.

We must have missed the tree as I could hear the Millstone on the south end of the meadow growing louder. But how? I kept the treeline silhouetted against the sky and that old elm was the biggest tree around.

Knowing that time was getting short, I turned back. We had been splitting the meadow on a diagonal, moving south, while looking for the tree. My plan was to cut as much space as possible until we found the tree, then head straight for it. But, we had hit the south tree line already and still no elm. I turned north and headed along the stone wall that lined the west side of the meadow. It was getting light fast and soon they would be able to see us. My shoulder hurt like hell and I could feel blood dripping off my hand as I ran. But there was nothing I could do about it right now.

We ran hard. I noticed that Bradley was keeping up in spite of his smashed arm. I guess all that time at the gym and on his mountain bike counted for something. Still, I was starting to get winded. I hoped it was just age and fatigue and not blood loss that was causing it.

Then, suddenly there it was. The elm was gone. It had probably fallen down in a wind storm and the monks, never wasteful, had collected it for firewood. I know that they disdained modern ways and cut their wood with a hand saw and split it with a maul and wedges. God bless them, because they earned their heat that winter. Elm is the toughest wood to split that God ever created. It is stringy, tough and refuses to split when it's dry. Back when some of the trees were alive you could cut it green and let it freeze in the dead of winter, then it would split. But, these old, dead, dry trees were more work than they were worth, unless you had a gas-powered hydraulic splitter. Doing it with a maul and wedges like the monks no doubt had, would have been a lot of work. A lot of cussing too, for most people. As it's impossible to split elm without cussing, I have to wonder how they handled that, particularly when most of them had taken a vow of silence.

What remained was the stump. It was six feet in diameter, far too much work for the monks to dig out of the ground and finally I knew where I was. I ran with the renewed energy of a saved man. I found the subtly different rocks in the wall where somebody had filled in the gap left from the road after they stopped using it. They had done this many years after the original wall had been built and had clearly used field stones from a different source. The rocks used to fill in this section of wall were the same shape, but either because of the age and the time exposed to the sun, snow and rain, or the fact they were buried in different soil for the past million years or so, they had a slightly different color to them. It's not something most people would even notice, but hunters notice little things and I had spotted this after I had my burger all those years ago.

With that section spanning almost exactly the width of an old stage road, I knew I found the right place. But, the fact I could see the subtle differences in color so easily told me that the morning was far too advanced for us to be out in the open like this.

We climbed over the rock wall and I spotted the faint difference in the vegetation that defined the old trail. Now that we had cover, we were safe for a while. I collapsed under a giant white pine tree to catch my breath and to deal with my wound. I figured, like that monk years ago, they wouldn't know where we went and would never think of this trail. It would be a long, hard hike, but it would eventually get us back home. There were a series of snow-mobile trails, old abandoned roads and foot paths that would bring us right to the front porch of my house. But it was about twenty miles by road home and I am guessing at least twice that using the trails.

I figured the bad guys would be patrolling the roads looking for us. They had vehicles and gasoline, so that would be the logical thing to do. If we stuck to the back trails we could avoid any vehicle accessible areas. If they were smart, they might have some foot patrols out looking on the trails, but we would deal with that when the time came. We still had plenty of guns and ammo and three of us could, and would, fight.

I hoped it was still dark enough to cover our escape when we were out in the meadow. As it got lighter we were against the treeline and harder to see. Damn few people in the world knew about this trail, so I thought we were going to be fine. My guess was that they would think we headed into the woods and would circle around to hit the road above the gorge. They thought the guards at the gulf were dead, so they would assume we would leave down the road. By the time they figured out we went a different way, we would be miles away.

CHAPTER 31

I shucked out of my pack and found my first-aid kit. Sarah came over to help me bandage my shoulder.

"It's not as bad as it looks," she said. "There is a furrow dug out of the muscle on your shoulder. It's going to need stiches when we get home, but there is nothing important damaged. However, it's a bleeder. Your arm is covered with blood and your shirt is soaked. It's covered your pants, too."

She cleaned up the wound and put a QuikClot Sponge on it. Sam Farnsworth brought a couple of cases of them with him on a trip last year. It's a product that was initially developed for the military to stop bleeding and it saved a lot of kid's lives during the war in the Sandbox. I knew about the Sport version from my writing about wilderness first aid and survival. The sealed packs have a little mesh bag in them filled with a mineral called kaolin, along with white aluminosilicate, which I think is a binder or vehicle agent. The kaolin will interact with the blood and make it clot much faster. I wished we had had them during the social wars, because they would have saved some lives. So when Fansworth offered them for sale, I made sure I had some now.

Some redneck scavenger down south found a couple of cases in an abandoned sporting goods store in South Carolina and traded them for food. Keeping with the theme, I traded several pounds of moose steaks for both cases.

My wife actually gave me hell for trading for so many of them, thinking the worst was behind us and we didn't need them. But right now, I was thinking that given what was happening, we didn't have enough. On the other hand, it seems like life recently is learning to live with 'not enough' of just about everything.

What we really needed were bandages. We didn't have enough of them to start and the social wars depleted our supply. Our first aid kits had bandages we made out of old cotton shirts that we cut up, washed and then boiled to sterilize the cloth. We wrapped them in plastic sheeting to keep them clean, but it was stopgap. The truth is, our first aid kits were pretty pathetic. Other than the homemade bandages and QuickClot, we carried whatever medicine we could get from Jack. Most of it was outdated, over the counter stuff like common pain killers and antiseptics. I was thinking that if we got out of this I needed to put Jack to work on finding more medical supplies, particularly bandages, because I had a feeling this trouble was not going to end soon.

For now, the goal was to get my shoulder to stop bleeding. Sarah squeezed the gaping wound shut while Davy slapped some duct tape on it to hold the edges together.

Wonderful stuff, duct tape. You can use it to fix just about anything, even gunshot wounds. I am so glad I bought a couple of cases of the stuff before the crash and I dread the day we will run out. Sarah and Davy worked in unison to add more tape until the wound was secure. The bleeding had stopped and the pain was not too bad yet. But, I was horribly thirsty and I had an odd metallic taste in my mouth. I had not yet recovered from the blood lost when my leg was damaged, now this additional leakage was taking a greater toll.

Years ago, when the government was running the health care system, I caught Lyme disease from a tick bite, but the moronic doctor misdiagnosed it as hemochromatosis, which is a disease that causes too much iron to accumulate in the body. They treat it by drawing blood. The problem was compounded when they turned me over to an equally incompetent nurse who drew so much blood in the next few months that she almost killed me. It took almost a year for me to recover. One thing I remember vividly from that mess is that whenever she took too much blood, I wound up with this same metallic taste in my mouth, the same consuming thirst and the same lack of energy.

I found some Tylenol tablets in my first aid kit and washed them down with the last of my water. I was thinking about this trail ahead and how it didn't pass any water source until we got to the top of the mountain, several uphill miles from here. Everybody else needed their water too, so I would not ask them to share. But, I was as thirsty as I have ever been in my life. That includes the time we got lost while hunting Cape buffalo in Zimbabwe in one hundred-fifteen degree heat. We walked ten miles without water until we found a road. Then, after sending a tracker up the road for the truck, we waited six more hours in that heat for him to return with something to drink. That was bad, but this was worse. Or at least it seemed like it was. Time softens most memories and this was fresh.

"Here, drink these," Sarah said. "They are too heavy to carry anyway."

She was holding two quart-sized bottles of Gatorade. While it might have been a gym rat's drink of choice, it's also not a bad thing for a shot up old man. That's because Gatorade contains electrolytes to help replace what I had lost with the blood that leaked out. It also has some sugar to restore energy.

I drank the first one without pausing to breathe. Then I dug out another sandwich and after eating that and drinking the other quart of Gatorade I felt better. It didn't occur to me until later to ask where in the hell she found Gatorade. The last bottle of that stuff I had seen was well before the collapse.

"We have a problem," Davy said. "We have movement on the other side of the meadow."

I got my binoculars out of my pack and crawled up beside him to peek over the stone wall. There were about a dozen well-armed guys working their way across the meadow, three hundred yards from us. One was in the lead, watching the ground as he walked. Two more flanked him, twenty yards out and slightly back. They kept their rifles ready while the rest followed well behind.

Every now and then the guy in the lead would stop and motion the other two back. Then he would backtrack before turning and moving forward again. Twice he repeated that. Then he stopped and stood still for a few moments. He walked back one hundred yards to a stick somebody had pushed into the ground, and moved ten yards to the side. Then he slowly walked forward fifty yards. His head was always moving, sweeping the ground, always looking. He stopped, walked back until he was even with the stick, moved another ten yards to the side and then began slowly moving forward again.

I knew that movement pattern well because I had done it hundreds of times while looking for wounded game. It's called a grid search. He was blood trailing me and had lost the trail.

"We need to do something about this," Davy said. "We can't let them follow. How are we going to do it? There are way too many and they are too far away. Besides, they are not that far into the meadow, so they can run back for cover before we can get them all."

"How's this sound?" I asked. "We stay hidden here and let them get closer, say halfway across the field. Then if they try to run, they are in the open for one hundred-fifty yards or so. If we stay in cover we should be able to get them all before anybody escapes. That will give us a little time to get some ground behind us before the next wave starts after us."

"You can't be serious!"

Bradley had crept beside us unnoticed. But he was hard to ignore now, shrieking in my ear.

"You can't possibly be talking about murdering those men in cold blood!"

His voice was much too loud and I told him to pipe down.

"No, I will not. I am not going to stand by and let you murder those human beings."

"Well then, professor, what do you suggest we do?" Davy hissed at him. "They are going to try their motherfucking best to kill us and the only way to prevent that is to kill them first. I am really starting to not give a flying fuck about you, but I do want to get out of this alive, so unless you have a better plan, I am going to kill all the assholes I can right now."

"If you will just tone down the tough guy act for a few minutes," Bradley said in his most condescending tone. "I can go out there and reason with them. Once I explain that we are just trying to leave and mean them no harm they will back off and let us go. The mind is mightier than that gun you have and I'll prove it to you."

CHAPTER 32

Before any of us could stop him, Bradley stood up and jumped over the rock wall. He started walking toward the group of armed men, waving his good arm and yelling at the top of his lungs.

"HELLO! Hey guys, we need to talk. You all know me and you know I am unarmed. Please hang on; I just want to explain something to you."

The first shot was rushed and hit the dirt in front of his feet. I think he was so stunned that those guys were shooting at him he froze like a deer in the headlights. After that, they all opened up on him.

What saved him was probably as much a lack of training and discipline on the part of the guys with the guns as it was Davy. They all stood up, shooting off-hand on full-auto. Full-auto guns don't work like in the movies, where the hero stands there and hoses the bad guys, usually holding the gun in one hand. In real life, the muzzle will climb with each shot. It takes a very experienced and very strong man to hold a full auto rifle on target while it is shooting. That's why the best machine-gunners practice trigger discipline and fire three-to five-shot bursts before pausing to realign the sights. These guys were just holding the trigger down and emptying the magazine. Most of the shots were going into the trees well over Bradley's head. If just one guy had gone prone, taken a careful sight picture and squeezed off an aimed shot, it would have been all over.

Davy looked like a panther as he glided over the wall. He grabbed Bradley by the back of the shirt collar and yanked him off his feet. Bradley started to howl about how much that hurt his arm and what a bully Davy was, but Davy didn't pay any attention; he just dragged him back to the wall. By the time he got there I was over the top and grabbed Bradley's good arm. The two of us heaved him over the wall and then dived in behind him.

"If you stand up again, I will shoot you myself," Davy yelled at Bradley. "Just lie there and keep that fucked up head of yours down until I tell you to move."

I stuck my head over the rock wall and could see that most of the guys were reloading. Some were still shooting, but nobody was moving for defensive cover. I aimed high on the center of mass of the guy who was doing the blood-trailing and shot him in the chest. Then I moved on to the next guy to the right and shot him. I kept picking out targets and shooting. Beside me, to my left, I could hear Davy and Sarah shooting. I centered the crosshair on the next guy, but before I could shoot, a bullet impacted his neck. So I moved to the extreme right of the group. I knew Davy would go to the left, as that's the side he occupied. I hoped Sarah would understand the tactic and work the center of the group.

Some of the guys were starting to realize how much trouble they were in and began running for the trees. Letting even one escape would be bad because they could provide information about where we had headed. The bad guys were going to figure it out anyway, but the longer we could delay them, the better. A survivor who could lead them to the start of the trail would speed things up rather than force them to take time to figure it out, time that might just make a difference whether we lived or died.

So, I started shooting at the running figures. They were far enough away that I had to lead them a little and I had a couple of misses before I got the hold right. Then the next two shots dropped the guys I was shooting at; both hit the ground and skidded to a stop. I could see that Davy had the same idea and he was also shooting at the guys running away. Sarah was working on the group still standing and shooting. That was good, as they needed to understand that they couldn't keep doing that.

Several of the guys in the group had gone prone, I think to provide a smaller target rather than for a better support while shooting. It was clear these were just a bunch of guys with guns, but without real training or experience. A couple of the prone guys were covering their heads with their arms, their guns lying in the dirt beside them. I left them for the moment and shot the two who were shooting at us, and then I went back and shot the two cowering behind their arms.

I moved the gun back and forth, looking for more targets, but there weren't any.

"Did we get them all?" I asked.

"I don't know," Davy said. "One guy made the tree line, but I had two bullets in him before he did. I am hoping he is dead."

A shot surprised me and I turned to look at Sarah.

"I need a fresh magazine," she said.

"What? Why are you looking at me like that? That big guy was trying to stand up and aim his rifle; I had to shoot him again. Look, there is another and I am out of ammo."

Davy shot the guy before he could shoot at us.

"Ordinarily I would say let's shoot them all again. But it's a long way home and we are going to need all the ammo we have," I said to nobody in particular. "It comes down to this: Do we go over there and make sure they are all dead and waste the time? Or do we get the hell out of here now and hope for the best? Unless somebody is playing dead, none of them are going to come after us. Even if they are alive, they are hurt. Besides, those guys clearly don't know what they are doing. My guess is that none of them has any real military training, so I can't see one of them playing hero and chasing us all alone. Even if he is alive, he will wait until help shows up. I vote we use that time to get the hell out of here."

Nobody objected, which kind of surprised me, considering Bradley was in the party. Instead, we just reloaded and started up the trail.

I took the lead because I knew the trail. Davy took the rear to deal with any followers.

Bradley took the bitch position.

CHAPTER 33

He just would not shut up.

"I can't believe you killed those guys in cold blood."

"What the fuck, dumbass?" Davy replied. "Did you not notice that they were shooting at you?"

"They were just shooting to scare me, most of the bullets went over my head and the others hit the ground in front of me. They were not trying to hurt anybody. You didn't have to kill them. No wonder the social wars lasted so long. Nobody bothered to use their intelligence. Of course, that's assuming that any of you had any, which, given the evidence, would be a stretch.

"All you macho guys over-compensating for your inadequacies with your big guns would rather just shoot each other. Once you jerks have guns in your hands you turn into killers. All the studies show that the only reason you pick up a gun is so you can kill somebody. A gun empowers you and turns you into a murderer, that's why the government banned them. Clearly you are both criminals, too, as I can see you didn't turn in your guns as ordered. Now you have infected my daughter. You gave her a gun and it's made her a killer, too."

That's when Davy punched him in the back of the head, knocking him to the ground.

"Shut the fuck up, you ungrateful asshole. We have saved your life twice in the last hour and if I hear one more word from you I am going to break your jaw so you can't talk. I am tired, hungry, grumpy and feeling pretty fucking unappreciated right now, so don't mess with me. Be smart, and keep that over-educated mouth of yours shut.

"You have two choices, you can shut up and keep up, or you can head back down that trail alone right now and take your chances. Those are your only options. If you try to 'reason' with me about any others I will beat you until you shit your pants. Am I clear?"

Bradley glowered at him, but was smart enough not to say a word. He just got up and started walking.

"Hey dumbass, that's not the trail," Davy said.

Bradley still didn't say a word, he just walked back, stepped in about two feet behind me and stood there staring straight ahead.

I guess that was my cue to start up the trail again.

It was so overgrown with brush it was hard to follow in places. But, even so, I knew if we didn't stick to it we could not get over the top of the mountain.

The key to identifying the old road was to look at the type of brush. The growth was younger than that surrounding it, so the trees were smaller and for the most part a different species. Near the stone wall just off the meadow, big white pines dominated. They actually kept the trail open, as they formed a canopy overhead that blocked the sunlight so most plants wouldn't grow. There were a few young hemlocks and other shade loving species, but it was easy enough to walk around them. That lasted for a few hundred yards until we started to climb. Then the vegetation along the sides turned to maple, birch and beech. The trail was filled in with small, one- to two-inch diameter maple whips we always called striped maple because of the color striations on their bark. In most places it was impossible to move through them, so we paralleled the road instead.

In other places, the deer trails kept things open so we could make our way. Apparently this area was remote enough that, given the number of tracks and droppings I was seeing, there was still a decent population of whitetail deer. I would keep that in mind if we survived this and I'd come back for some venison. It'd been a while since I'd had roasted venison backstrap and I missed it desperately. From the look of things, taking a couple of deer out of the herd here would probably benefit them, as there was a lot more sign here than we saw along the river. They were probably overpopulated for the carrying capacity of the habitat, which meant a bad winter would decimate the herd. Shooting a few would actually help the many. Not unlike managing the current human herd, at least if we could thin out a few of the assholes trying to kill us right now.

The deer had been using the road for as long as it was here, so when the vegetation started to grow in, they kept the trails open. Deer trails are pretty narrow to get through with a backpack, but it was still the easiest way.

The entire trail was filled with blown-down trees. Sometimes we would go several hundred yards before encountering one. Other times the road was filled with them stacked up every few feet. They really slowed our progress. Often the deer trails would provide a path around the blowdown, but not always. Some of them were in brush so thick that going around was not an option. The deer would go under the logs suspended above the path, or simply jump over them. Most of the logs were too low for us to duck under and too high to step over.

One option was to hook one leg over, lean over on our bellies to balance the weight of our packs and jump until we were straddling the log and resting on our crotches, which was not comfortable. Then, shifting our weight, we would tumble to the ground on the other side. With luck we would catch ourselves on the leg that landed first and remain standing, but more often than not, we wound up falling as our trailing leg skidded along the log and threw us off balance.

The other option was to get on our bellies and crawl under the logs. It seemed like they were never high enough to get under with the backpacks on, so we would have to take the packs off and drag them by their straps under the blowdowns. Then we had to put the packs back on our backs. I know it doesn't sound like much and it's not, until you do it two hundred times.

Both approaches were exhausting and left us wet and muddy.

Once we got above two thousand feet in elevation, the hardwoods gave way to hemlock and spruce. When the land flattened out at the top it became wet and the trail was filled with alders.

To get here we passed over a cut through the top of the mountains. The peaks still rose high on either side, which meant they drained into this basin. The bedrock was close to the surface here, so the water just collected in a big, dark muddy mess. In a few places we could recognize the trail through these wetlands by the corduroy road.

A corduroy road is a series of small logs about four inches or so in diameter laid side by side, ninety degrees to the trail to form a hard surface. This was done years ago when labor was cheap, probably by the Civilian Conservation Corps during the Great Depression. The CCC was one of Roosevelt's New Deal, make-work projects and we spent a lot of tax dollars on foolish things like corduroy roads that led nowhere. The CCC only employed young, single men from families on relief. They paid them thirty dollars a month, but it was mandatory that twenty-five of it went to the parents. I suppose it bought Franklin a lot of votes, which was the most important thing, right?

The result formed a bumpy road; hence the name, as the texture was not unlike a giant piece of corduroy fabric. The logs were now covered with green moss and only the tops still showed, but they kept our boots from sinking into the mud. I was thankful there was a slight breeze and it was cool enough the mosquitos and black flies were not active. Perfect hiking weather, actually. But, this was not hiking, this was running for our lives and I was feeling like I was going to collapse any minute. My shoulder hurt like hell and my head was fuzzy. I was dizzy and the loss of blood had really taken a toll on me.

I had to sit down.

CHAPTER 34

I guess we were all ready for a break as everybody found a tree and sat down, leaning against the trunk and nobody, not even Bradley, complained. We had been there about ten minutes when a whitetail doe came running up the path and splashed past us in a blind panic.

"Go, go," Davy hissed as he motioned us down the trail.

Then he just melted back into the trees. I gathered up Sarah and Bradley and we started running down the trail. We had only gone about one hundred yards when a shot behind us was followed by multiple machine guns shooting all at once.

I tried to swallow my panic and keep going, knowing that Davy had probably given his life to buy us a couple more minutes. Then I heard a two-shot double-tap, followed by another, then more machine gun fire and I knew he was still in the game.

We ran flat out until we were out of breath, then we slowed to a stumbling jog. I desperately wanted nothing more than to lie down and suck air, but I kept going because there wasn't any other option. I was so oxygen starved that lights were dancing in my eyes, but my only concern was getting Sarah to safety. We needed to open the distance as much as possible while Davy fought a delaying action.

I was feeling horrible. My muscles were not getting enough oxygen-carrying blood, because so much blood was gone from my system. I knew that if I stopped we died, so I kept putting one foot in front of the other, not thinking about anything beyond the next step.

It had been quite some time since we had heard anything, I am not sure how long, as our perception of time changes when things like this are happening, but I thought it had been about fifteen minutes. We had gotten our breath back and were moving at a more reasonable and less panicked jogging pace.

The trail had opened up a little and was now a single lane snowmobile trail that the clubs used to keep free from brush. Of course, recreational snowmobile riding is a thing of the past and nobody had worked on this, or any other trail, in a long time. But, the path was a lot clearer than the old road that had about six extra decades to fill in with brush and blowdowns.

With the lack of shooting, I had started to think they must have killed Davy and were back on our trail. Then I heard another single shot followed by a sound I had heard many times when hunting big game, the thump of a high-speed bullet impacting a body.

This time the shot was close to us, less than two hundred yards behind. That was followed by another shot, then another, obviously being fired by somebody picking targets and conserving ammo. I heard the impact on all of them and one was followed by a human scream that stopped abruptly five seconds after it started, just as another shot echoed through the hills. The answering machine gun fire was diminished compared to what it was before, clearly there were a lot fewer guns firing. But, this fight was moving close to us and we didn't have enough reserves left to keep running.

"Let's go," I said. "We can move to the side and let them pass. Then I'll come in from behind them and help Davy. Be quiet, they are close."

We turned off the trail and started cutting around the end of a large beaver dam. That's when I noticed Bradley running out along the dam. It took all I had to catch up with him.

"What the hell are you doing?" I asked.

"I am going to swim out and hide in one of those beaver houses. I saw it on the History Channel years ago. Some mountain man did that and escaped the Indians who were chasing him for trying to steal their land."

"Forget it, won't work, let's go, we don't have any time to waste."

"Always gotta be in charge, don't you. You always think you know more than anybody else. Okay, I'll humor you. Why won't it work Mr. Expert?"

"First off, you probably won't make it to the beaver house. The water is about forty degrees and you only have one working arm. You have no idea how to find the entrance and if you do it will be big enough for a thirty pound beaver, not a two hundred pound man. Even if you could make it inside the hut, there are beavers in there. This is an active colony and they will be very pissed at the intrusion. How are you going to fight them off with one arm inside a cramped hut with just enough room for your head? Their teeth are three inches long and they can bite through hardwood trees, believe me they will make short work out of your face. On top of that, you will probably die of hypothermia and if you don't that arm will become infected from being submerged in dirty water that's full of beaver shit and you will die a painful death in a couple of days.

"But hey little brother, you do whatever you want to do. We are going up into those ledges and hide behind one of those big boulders."

I noticed that he was crowding my back the whole time we were running up the hill.

As soon as we got behind the boulder two guys came down the trail below our position. I was going to let them pass, so that Bradley and Sarah would be safe to stay here. Then I would take up the trail and ambush them from behind. The strategy was that they would not be expecting me to come from behind and if I stayed quiet they would never hear the bullets that killed them. By not giving away our position, nobody would know Bradley and Sarah were hiding behind this boulder. Any other bad guys would run past them, down the trail to the sound of the guns, where I would be hiding and waiting, to shoot them too.

It suddenly occurred to me that our tracks would show that we left the trail and I felt a moment of panic. But they didn't seem to notice. The two guys just kept sneaking along with their guns on their shoulders, knees bent, guns swinging from side to side like the bad guy troops in the old movies. They never even looked down at the trail or at the tracks.

As I watched, one humped over like he had been punched in the guts. He dropped his gun and then fell to the ground, just as I heard the shot. The other one started spraying machine gun fire in a circle, just dumping ammo as he spun round and round in a blind panic. We were high enough on the hill so that all the bullets were going below us and some of them were hitting the beaver house.

I figured with all the noise nobody would hear my shot and be able to tell where it came from, so I centered his head in my scope and shot him in the face as he made his third spin.

Then I waited, standing perfectly still, not wanting to give away my position. That's one advantage of a semi-auto rifle. It reloads itself instantly and the sound of doing that is masked by the noise of the shot. With a bolt action rifle, you need to work the bolt to reload the gun and that can give away your position.

I guided bear hunters in Canada for a couple of seasons and several times we had the same thing happen. The hunter shot and the bear dropped instantly.

As soon as the hunter worked the action, the bear knew where the danger was coming from and got up and ran off in the opposite direction. The hunters always insisted they hit the bear, but I never found any evidence. There was never any blood or hair to indicate a bullet strike. My guess is the bears instinctively dropped to the ground at the noise of the shot and froze, waiting until they could pinpoint the source of danger before running away. One time a guy had a semi-auto rifle. During the pre-hunt talk I had told him if that happened he should shoot again, but he ignored me because he wanted to brag about a one-shot kill to his buddies. He watched the bear for a few moments before he decided to climb down from the treestand. As soon as he moved his feet the bear was gone.

It's the same while fighting assholes. Often one shot is hard to pinpoint, particularly this one, which I fired while the guy was rocking and rolling with his machine gun. But it will put anybody out there on high alert. If I make a sound, even moving my feet and scuffing the rocks, he will know where I am and have something to shoot at. I just hoped Bradley didn't decide to take this time to be an idiot again.

I waited a long time without moving. Something didn't feel right and while I didn't know what it was, I learned a long time ago that when you are not sure what to do, it's best to do nothing. I could feel somebody out there, but I just couldn't see him. I kept my eyes scanning the trail, confident that Sarah and Bradley would see anybody coming from behind. My little voice never lies and it kept telling me somebody was there. The tension inside my body was building, as was my frustration. My arms were starting to shake from the stress of holding the rifle; a drop of sweat was stinging my eyes. I was standing on a narrow ledge and one leg wanted to do the sewing machine thing from holding my weight on my toes for so long. As the agony increased, I was thinking that something had better happen pretty damn soon.

A pine cone hit the boulder above me and just missed my face as it bounced back. I turned in a panic to find Davy standing ten feet behind me, grinning like a fool.

"I suppose you are proud of yourself, sneaking up on a guy who is half deaf," I said, trying hard not to show how pissed I was. "It doesn't take a lot of skill, you know. Besides, where the hell is my wing man, or wing woman or wing idiot or whatever the fuck these two are supposed to be? Sarah, you are supposed to be looking out behind us; I shouldn't have to tell you this shit. What if that had been somebody other than Davy? We might all be dead right now."

I noticed she was laughing and surprisingly, so was Bradley.

"I saw Davy coming up behind you a long time ago. He shushed me with his finger and so I didn't say anything. He got really close; you gotta admit he is pretty damn good."

What I had to admit was that I didn't much like the way she was looking at Davy.

"Hey old man, thanks for taking care of that last one. My trigger finger was getting tired and I really, really, really needed some help," Davy said.

"That's all of them. You shot number eight. I think that is probably all they could spare from the monastery. I am sure they kept a couple back there to guard the big, important guy your brother thinks is so special, so that's probably the end of their pursuit until they can get some more guys from Easton. I suggest we be long gone before they show up, 'cause I'll bet some of them are going to be really pissed when they find out their buddies are worm food!"

We took a few minutes to drag the bodies off the trail and to gather up the guns. Everybody took another rifle and several extra magazines while Sarah also grabbed a belt with a holstered Glock. Everybody except Bradley of course, who refused to touch, let alone carry, a gun.

The rest we hid under the roots of a blown down tree about one hundred yards above the beaver pond. A black bear had made a winter den in there and lined it with leaves, so it was dry and protected from rain. It was on the hillside with bedrock ledges, so any running water would drain. Just to be sure, we piled some rocks to keep the guns and ammo up high off the ground. Then we threw a few hemlock branches over the top. I made a mental note of the spot using a big boulder with a streak of quartz through it as a marker, with an idea of coming back here to collect the guns at a later date.

If we survived.

CHAPTER 35

As we walked along I tried to explain to Bradley that simply touching a gun was not going to damage his brain waves and that we could use some help with carrying the extra weight of these new firearms.

"I will never touch a gun of any kind again," Bradley snorted.

I tried to point out that there are (or were, back before) about three hundred million guns in the United States alone. Only a fraction of a percent of the owners ever committed any crime with a gun. But, Bradley never listened and he damn sure was not listening now. There is no reasoning with a closed mind and his had been closed for years, ever since he started college. Before that he was a pretty reasonable guy, but all those years behind the ivy towers had poisoned his ability to think. I knew I was probably wasting my time, but time was all I had as we hiked. Besides, it was kind of fun to poke him with a sharp stick now and then and watch the reaction.

"No problem was ever solved with a gun," he said.

"What about the two world wars? Stopping the rise of fascism? How about stopping the Holocaust and ending the murder of millions of people? What about stopping the genocide in Bosnia? What about keeping your dumb ass alive for the past several hours?"

"Without guns, there would not have been the wars. I am not sure I believe in the Holocaust, and all you did was kill a bunch of innocent men trying to do their jobs.

"Without guns there would be no wars? Did you not study history in all those years of going to school? What about the bow and arrow, the spear, the sword? They fought a lot of wars with them before guns were invented."

"Those were just the guns of their day. They only led to developing more efficient ways of killing each other. A man in medieval England with a sword was no different than a man today with a gun."

"So the noble knights of King Arthur's Round Table were possessed by their swords and lances and were just lunatic killers?"

"Fuck you!

"Besides, the Knights of the Round Table were a myth."

"Did they teach that articulate vocabulary to you in graduate school? As to your second point, what about King Richard's knights? They were real."

"They were murdering bastards and he was nothing but a repressed homosexual bully."

This was getting nowhere fast, so I decided to tell him about something that had happened in an African village I had visited years ago.

In a dispute over a woman, one man shot another and killed him. His defense was that the gun was possessed by evil spirits and it made him kill the other man. He claimed the gun was "witched" and it would kill again.

So, the village elders loaded the gun and put it on a table. They placed a man beside it 24/7 and watched it for one month. When at the end of this time nothing had happened, they decided the man was guilty of murder and they hanged him.

"You've got it all wrong," Bradley said. "Only a heathen would think that a gun is capable of having a spirit inhabit it. The real problem is with humans themselves. Once they pick up a gun they cannot control themselves. They get sick with the power a gun represents and they turn into killers, just like you."

"Remember that old Clint Eastwood movie?" I replied, ignoring his bait.

"I never watched that drivel; his films were another example of using violence to solve every problem. The man should have been banned from making movies."

I continued, "Clint had a quote in one of the Dirty Harry movies. 'Nothing wrong with shooting as long as the right people get shot!' Bradley, you need to understand that I never shot anybody who didn't deserve to be shot. I only did it to protect my life and the life of others. If they didn't want to be shot, they should have left me alone."

"Nothing justifies taking another human life . . . nothing."

"They were trying to kill me, Bradley. It's nothing more than self-defense."

"Self-defense is a myth," Bradley said. "If we had just outlawed self-defense like the other civilized countries, and people followed the law, then the violence would have stopped. If a robber knew you would not kill him, he would have no reason to hurt you. But, with these damn guns a person's mindset shifts and he becomes a killer. Even today, if we outlawed guns, like the government tried to do back before, and if we forced people to comply, all this violence would stop and the world could move on in peace. That's what he was trying to do and now you have ruined everything."

"He, who?" I asked. "Who the hell are you talking about? The guy in the cabin back there? Who is he? You said I didn't like him as if he was somebody I know. That guy tried to have you killed, Bradley. He used you to lure me out so he could kill me. Can't you see that?

"What's going on here, Bradley?"

But he clammed up. Set his jaw, fixed his eyes straight ahead and refused to talk any more. I knew that look too well. When he was losing any argument he would take one of two approaches: he would start calling me names, or he would just refuse to argue anymore. He told me once he knew he was right and when it became apparent there was no changing my mind, he simply chose to stop participating. I pointed out that he only did that when he was losing the argument, but he just shut up that time too. I truly believed that when he got into that mode, no force on Earth could change his mind. If you looked up stubborn in the dictionary, my brother's photo would be used to illustrate the definition.

Sarah caught my eye and mouthed the word "later" to me. So, I let it go.

CHAPTER 36

The trail took us past several old stone foundations. These were homes back in Vermont's early years, places where people lived and loved. There was a little community here of half a dozen cellar holes, which probably meant an extended family.

They no doubt started as homesteaders living off this bony, unforgiving land. They probably located here, high in the mountains, to get away from the disease bearing mosquitos in the low-lying, wet valleys. They were tough and relentless people, I know, because that's the only kind who could survive here. My guess is they were also proud, independent and beholden to nobody. I am sure that once the road came through, they were also entrepreneurs. This little settlement is at the junction of two old roads. They are only faint footpaths today, but in the time when people were living in these houses they were major roadways. One continues on and eventually goes to Easton, while the road we had just traveled breaks off to the east and to the monastery. This is the height of the land and from here all roads go downhill. Or if you are traveling to get here, uphill. This location is in a natural resting spot and I am sure that there was a place to eat and water the horses for a fair trade in the coin of the realm. Maybe there was even a room or two to rent so a weary traveler could spend the night after a long toil up the mountain.

This family had survived for a long time grubbing in the earth, but they had no doubt prospered when fortune, or perhaps their own foresight in picking this location, brought commerce their way.

The cellar holes had all been dug by hand in this rocky, bony soil. Any ground here was once covered with a mile-thick glacier and when the ice melted it deposited millions of rocks ranging from the size of a pea to as big as a house. The eons buried them and any man trying to dig a hole earned every cubic foot with blood, sweat and cuss words.

The foundation walls for the houses were made by piling up the stones to line the cellar hole. Once they used up the rocks they had dug out, they found more and hauled them in by hand or, if they were lucky, with a horse.

They built the houses with lumber they sawed by hand and they pinned it all together with square nails that were hand-forged, one at a time. It had to be brutal work. But no more so than the work it took to clear this land for the apple orchards and fields to grow livestock feed. All those rocks had to be moved and the timber cut. Each tree left a stump that had to be dug out by hand, hauled off and burned. Then the holes left behind were filled in with dirt hauled from another location. They didn't have bulldozers or excavators. They had a crude shovel, a double bitted ax and the Yankee work ethic. But, that was enough. They built something important, created something from nothing.

I am sure, knowing the type of people they were, that it was not for themselves that they worked so hard, but because they thought they were planting the seeds for a better life for future generations. All they wanted from their toil was to be rewarded with something more, something better for their descendants to enjoy.

But, now that the future generations are here, look at this place: abandoned, tumbled down and rotted away. All that work, all that heartache, all the pain, for nothing more than a few old rock lined cellar holes and a weed infested cemetery on the hill beside them.

These people had epitomized what made the 14th state, the first to join the new nation after the thirteen original colonies, so unique. Brutal winters, short summers and a rocky land that fought back against attempts to tame it was about all the state offered. But, the stubborn residents took it as a challenge. If they could survive and thrive here, then they had nothing left to prove.

Vermont has a proud tradition of independence and self-reliance. It was an independent country before it became a state and it once was a place populated with hard and independent people. Vermont had one of the first written constitutions in North America and was the first place on this continent to ban slavery. Vermonters stood alone, asked for nothing, knew their word was their bond and believed in themselves. It was people with those qualities who built this place, who built Vermont; strong, self-reliant people with conservative values. The state didn't have a lot to offer the new country, but the people did. What Vermont brought to the newborn United States of America was a can-do spirit and a stubbornness to never give up.

"Make it do, use it up, wear it out." That was our motto. Self-reliance was our doctrine. Vermont was an inspiration for a new country and a role model for all the tough minded people who built America into the greatest nation in the history of man.

But Vermont had taken a left turn, some say a wrong turn, late in the twentieth-century. The independent, self-reliant and free-thinking people that defined Vermont for nearly three hundred years were replaced by aging hippies, entitlement bums and socialist politicians. In some ways we were again ahead of our time. As it turned out the entire country was following the path we explored. I suppose, history was repeating as once again, our tiny state led the way. But I could take no pride in that. Not this time. Not the way it all ended.

There were several apple trees growing around the old homesteads. No doubt the offspring of the twenty acre orchard that was just over the hill. Some bird or animal had ingested the seeds and then shit them out here. They landed on a patch of dirt where they could take root and sprout in the open, sun-filled area that was once a little village. I figured there had to be a lesson in irony here someplace, about how we all are at the mercy of a random drop of shit, or something like that. But it escaped me today. As my mood grew blacker I was less inclined to humorous musings.

These people had worked hard, perhaps to an early grave; to create a village, a home, something of value. But now all that was left were a few cellar holes that were filling in so that in another couple of decades they would be hard to even find. When you look at the inevitable end, any sane man has to ask, "What's the point?" Why bother, it's all so hard and if this is how it ends, it's not worth it.

The reasons why it happens are always different at first glance, but when you dig deeper, perhaps not so much. It's always because of human greed. Not just for wealth, but a thirst for power. My guess is these homes emptied after the forest around them was laid to waste. In the early eighteen hundreds every tree on this mountain was cut so the wood could be used to make charcoal. After that, they brought in sheep to graze on the plants that grew in the open lands. Once the sheep ate what remained and there was nothing but dirt and rocks, everybody else left.

That didn't leave anything for the people in these houses to survive on. There were no more travelers to spend money. The woods were gone, so they had no firewood for heat or anyplace to hunt for food. The streams were so polluted with wood ash and runoff silt because of the overgrazing that all the fish died. The grazing was gone, turned to sheep shit, so their cattle starved. A garden and apple orchard were not enough to keep the families alive. Due to no fault of their own, they lived alone in a wasteland without warmth or food.

These people worked hard to build something, but it was probably just one man, a guy named Silas Gifford, who dominated the timber industry in southern Vermont back then. He also owned all the charcoal plants and the sheep herds. He got rich off the timber that was cut and if the stories are true, he got off on the power he had over the local workforce. He was mean, brutal and evil, a bully who enjoyed hurting people. Once this land was raped and pillaged, Gifford moved on to exploit other places and if they were too stubborn or too broke to move, the folks who had lived for generations in places like this one probably starved to death.

Isn't that how it happens? The only difference is the scale. No civilization in the history of man has lasted and they all died the same way. Once the goals of peace and prosperity are achieved, the people get complacent and foolish. That, of course, allows the wrong people to rise to power because the masses believe the lies they tell. Or at least they convince themselves they believe them because they want to keep their cushy lifestyles. But, of course, they don't want to work too hard to do that. So the people turn over the day-to-day details to the politicians and blindly expect that they will keep the best interest of the people in their hearts.

Soon enough, decay and corruption sets in and it all falls apart. Sometimes death comes slowly, through economic decline and social collapse, but sometimes it's as quick as a mushroom cloud. The delivery system really doesn't matter, does it? The end result is all the same.

So, why are we bothering? The world will never be free from tyrants and evil. There will always be people out there trying to control everybody else, not caring who gets hurt so they can feel powerful. Why? Their time here on earth is just as short as everybody else's. Why waste it and all that effort just to say you are the boss? What drives men to exploit others? It has to be more than wealth, as often the people doing it have more wealth than they can spend already, but still they continue. Why is it so important to some people to have absolute control over others? Why can't they just live their lives and leave others to live theirs? Life would be so much better if we all just minded our own damn business.

That's all I ever wanted out of life, to be left alone. I try not to impose myself on others and ask only that they give me the same consideration. But, from the nosy neighbor who didn't like the truck I drove to the politicians who sold America down the river, there was always somebody trying to take over and tell me what to do.

It's exhausting just trying to live.

To be honest, in some ways I enjoyed life after the collapse. It was what I always craved, self-reliance and freedom. Once the social wars ended and for the most part the bandits had been controlled, life consisted of what I wanted to make it. I liked that, but here again somebody is stepping in and trying to take over and change it all. This time it's a bit extreme; trying to kill me is over the top in my book. But in a lot of ways it's no different than that neighbor who thought I was ruining the planet by driving a pickup truck. I know the neighbor sounds benign, but in reality it was people like her who used environmentalism and trumped up science to create many of the laws that helped trash the American economy. While we laughed at them as greenie whack jobs, they turned out to be just as dangerous as any enemy with a gun or a bomb.

Now, it's apparently all back. Some asshole is trying to control me and probably the rest of the world, for all I know. I don't know what is going on here, but the one thing I do know is that it's a long way from over. I just want to go back to my home and be left alone, but somehow I don't see that happening.

Still, I look at these cellar holes, understand the ultimate result regardless of what happens and think that maybe this fight is just not worth it anymore.

CHAPTER 37

For the next several miles the hike was downhill, which is not necessarily easier. The pack is just as heavy and the trail is so steep near the top that it forces your feet forward in your boots. This crushes your toes and it wasn't long before I could feel mine blistering and cramping. It also puts a lot of stress on your knees and thigh muscles and mine were still protesting the lack of blood in my system. About the time my legs planned a total, sit-down strike, the trail flattened out a little. It was still downhill, but now it was easy walking.

The sun was getting lower on the western horizon and I had a place in mind where I wanted to spend the night. So we pushed on. All talk and banter had ceased a long time ago. Everybody had the same blank stare as they just put one foot in front of the other.

Even Bradley had stopped complaining.

I remembered his wife once saying that if he ever stopped bitching we should check for a pulse.

So, that's what I did.

He still had one.

He also had a high fever. His eyes were glassy and sweat was pouring off his soaked head. I touched his arm and I could feel the heat through the thick bandage at the site of the bullet wound.

I called for a rest and we all stopped. I made Bradley drink some water and swallow a couple of aspirin to help with the fever. Then I had him eat a few pieces of jerky and a hunk of bread. We all needed rest, but he needed a doctor.

I think that standing up and starting back down the trail was one of the hardest things I have ever done. It would have been so easy to just sleep there. It probably would have been fine, too. We could have pulled back into the woods so we couldn't be seen from the road and sacked out on the ground. But, I knew the importance of keeping good morale. We still had at least two more days of hard hiking to make it back to my place and I had to keep tomorrow in mind. If we spent the night here, nobody would sleep well and that would slow us down tomorrow, sapping our strength and messing with our mental health. It would also dull our senses and with a better than even chance of running into more guys with machine guns, we needed to stay sharp. So, we got up and got going.

I was worried about Bradley. There was no way he could stand up to two more days of hard hiking. He was going downhill fast.

A couple of miles down the road we came to another cellar hole. While it was the same hand dug design and the walls were built by piling rocks without mortar, the ashes and charred timbers that filled it were much newer. It had once been our family deer hunting camp, built in a group effort on an old cellar hole from an abandoned homestead.

That old building had been filled with a lot of good memories; some of the best days of my life had been spent in this place. But it belonged to my uncle, who was a two-pack-a-day kind of guy. Once cancer finally took him, the camp passed to his son who didn't hunt and lived too far away to bother with the camp. After that, things were never the same and we just stopped staying there. It stood for many more years until some kids out riding dirt bikes and drinking beer thought it would be fun to burn it down.

We could not have stayed there, anyway. By now the trail had become a road; not much of a road, but one you could drive with a good 4X4 truck. There were some bad people looking for us and the idea of sleeping beside a well-known and navigable road didn't fill me with a warm and fuzzy feeling.

What most people didn't know is that just a half-mile back in the woods was another camp. This one had no road to it and over the years the footpath used to access it had grown in so it just looked like another deer trail.

But rather than turn onto that trail, we kept going down the muddy road. Our footprints were clear and it was easy to see that a group of four, three men and one woman, had walked down this road. We continued for another half a mile, where the road turned to hard packed gravel. Our footprints wouldn't show on this surface to anybody other than a very skilled tracker. My hope was that they only had one of those and I had put a bullet though him early this morning. With luck, anybody looking for us would think we had continued on down the road.

We turned off to the side of the road at a rocky spot that didn't show tracks and climbed down a steep bank, being careful not to leave any tracks in the leaves. Then we crossed a wide brook by jumping from rock to rock and made our way up a deer trail on the other side. I went last, brushing out the tracks on the deer trail as best as I could with a spruce branch. It wouldn't fool a good tracker, but it might fool a fool.

I didn't think anybody would ever be able to locate where we had left the road. But, if they did, they probably would not risk a dunking in the brook to look at this trail. Just looking from the other side of the brook might let them recognize a boot track if we left any behind, but they would not know what the marks from the branch were. A good woodsman would be curious enough for a closer look, but I suspected woodsmen were scarce in the bunch that was hunting us.

No matter, it was the best we could do; if they found us, they found us. We still had our guns and it hadn't gone well for any other group that caught up with us.

I took the lead again and soon had us on what was an old logging road that ran along the hillside through the forest. It was grown up and covered with leaves from the surrounding hardwoods. They were old and matted from the winter and for the most part we could walk without leaving any footprints that would look like they came from a human. I cautioned everybody to avoid any muddy spots that could show a boot print as we backtracked south.

We came in above the camp, as I knew we would, and hit a small brook where it exited a series of beaver dams. We followed the brook downstream and around the second bend was a two story camp. The door was locked, but I knew where the key was hidden.

We found a broom and swept the mouse shit off the beds. Then we found clean sheets and blankets packed in mouse proof plastic containers with locking covers. Sarah made up the beds while Davy and I went outside to roll over some rocks and logs. We collected the earthworms we found underneath, putting them in an old tin Band-Aid box that was on a shelf in the bathroom. I found a couple of fishing rods in the back room with #10 hooks on the lines. The room had no windows, so it was dark in there where no sunlight could penetrate. Because of that, the line on the reels had not deteriorated too badly.

Bradley seemed better, so I asked him to get the makings for a small fire collected and ready to be started in the wood stove. I asked Sarah to help him wash the frying pan we found hanging from a support post in the camp. I knew he had the skills from all the camping trips we made together as kids. He would know to use very dry wood to keep the smoke to a minimum and to scrub the pan using gravel from the stream bed until it shined.

Davy and I headed up to the beaver dams to try to catch some supper.

CHAPTER 38

I had cut a branch off a maple tree, leaving a wide fork on one end to use as a stringer for the trout. We would run the sharpened end through one gill and out the mouth, stacking the fish against the wide fork which held them from sliding off the end of the branch. Right now the stringer held fifteen of the little, six-inch brook trout, lying in the water to keep them cool.

They came out of the brown, tannin-filled water of the beaver dam with a golden hue along their sides. Their dark green, almost black backs and dorsal fins are filled with wavy lines of lighter green called vermiculations, which make them all but impossible to see from above and protects them from predators. Along their sides, the green lightens and the wavy lines turn to round spots. Interspersed from gills to tail, along their golden sides, are random dots of bright red, circled with blue aureoles. A gleaming white belly is streaked with an orange-tinted red where it meets the green and gold sides. The bright red/orange fins have a white leading edge and a thin black stripe to separate the two. The fish come from the water with their eyes bright, their spirits full of fight and I think that these wild brook trout are quite possibly the most beautiful fish in North America. But, within minutes after death, this beauty fades and they start to blanch to a sickly white.

I again am reminded how nothing lasts forever, but some things just disappear faster than others. These trout were wild, free and beautiful. But, once they are captured they seem to accept that it's over and all that beauty fades away in the blink of an eye.

Still, the meat inside would be pink and firm; the nourishment remained and that's what we needed.

We had a few more minutes until dark, so we would stay and try to add a few more trout to the stringer.

I was stretched out against a big hemlock, watching the bobber I had made from a piece of dry branch off this very tree. Davy had a similar pose against the tree next to me.

"You ever been married Davy?" I asked, more to pass the time than with any real interest.

"Yup."

"What happened?"

"She cheated on me."

"Ah, so she is married to the other guy now?"

"No, he could no longer satisfy her needs."

"Happens a lot."

"Not like this!" he said with a smile.

"Yeah? Well, we have some time to kill, so tell me about it."

"Okay. I love telling this story.

"I was working two jobs and fighting on the weekends trying to save enough money for a down payment on a house. I worked all day as a mechanic in a Tampax factory and then went to the gym at night to train other fighters.

"The training actually paid pretty well, and I worked out a deal with the gym owner where I picked up my own clients and paid him twenty percent of what I earned.

"Once I started winning my fights and I made a name for myself, I was in demand, so I could raise my prices and still be booked full. I was seriously considering going full-time at training. It was getting to be too much with all the guys wanting me to train them, and I was often at the gym until midnight or later. I started my day job at seven, so I wasn't getting a lot of sleep. But the bank account was starting to grow and I knew it wasn't forever.

"I didn't see much of her. We talked about that, how I was working for our future, trying to make a home for her and she always said she loved me for doing it and didn't mind that we didn't get a lot of time together.

"No sleep and long hours finally caught up with me and one night I was so sick with a cold that I cancelled my classes and headed to our apartment for some rack time.

"I came into the apartment quietly so I wouldn't wake her, but what I heard told me she wasn't sleeping. She was in the kitchen, on the table, screwing a guy I thought was my best friend."

"Every man's nightmare," I said. "So what did you do?"

"Pretty much want every man fantasizes about, but never does.

176

"You beat the shit out of both of them?"

"No, much better than that, my friend. I just stood there staring at him."

"Ohooooooo, what a badass you were. You are right, that is much better than punching the dickhead."

"Hang on, it gets better.

"Staring at him was freaking him out, so he started talking very fast. At first he was a little scared of me and very apologetic. But, within a couple of minutes he found his courage and that changed. I guess he took the lack of response as fear on my part and he started to grow braver and began to get belligerent.

"Had him right where you wanted him then, right?"

"You gonna shut the fuck up and let me tell this story?"

"Maybe."

"He started in with that bullshit about how I was using fighting to compensate for my lack of manhood and how I could never keep her happy because I wasn't a sensitive man like him. Called me shit like a Neanderthal, insulted my intelligence and claimed I was compensating for having a little dick by beating up people. Nothing original, but it was still pissing me off.

"We were friends since first grade and just stuck with it as we got older, even though he grew up to become kind of a prick. He always blamed everybody else for his problems and he thought that all people were like him, weak and afraid to act. I guess he thought that would protect him. He figured I might sue him or something like that, but would never do anything physical, because it would never occur to him to do that. Or maybe he was just too self-centered to even think about the consequences. I know he always thought he was the smartest guy in the room and I guess he figured his way was the only way. I don't really understand all that pop psychology bullshit and I really don't care.

"I stood there listening to this asshole insult and attack me after I caught him screwing my wife behind my back, and the absurdity of the situation started to sink in. Here he was, stark naked with a bulging hard-on. He was getting in my face, screaming at me and giving me shit, all after he was caught in the ultimate betrayal of trust.

"I think that arrogance got to me a lot more than the fact he was fucking my wife. I listened for a couple of minutes and every second that passed he got bolder and louder and more insulting.

"Finally I had enough. I had an assisted-opening knife in my pocket, so I snatched it out and with one fast swipe I cut off the last three inches of his dick. Which, believe me, didn't leave much behind."

"Holy shit!" I said, not able to stop myself from interrupting his story. "That's pretty damn extreme!"

"Yeah well, I was an angry guy back then. He should have known better than to keep pushing me," Davy said without a hint of humor.

"The blood was unbelievable. I had heard that happened because of the hard on and all the blood that the body is pumping in there to keep it stiff. Years ago I had a buddy who was a fireman and his station was beside a city park. Some drug dealer was getting a blowjob in the park when he shot his wad in a crack whore's mouth. She got mad and bit his dick off. He staggered across the street and bled to death in a couple of minutes at the fire station house door. I called it bullshit, but my buddy claimed it was true. After watching Tom bleed all over my kitchen I started to think he was right.

"I ran to my garage and grabbed a fly rod. I made a slip knot with the 10-weight line, flipped it over his dick and pulled it tight to make a tourniquet. Then I tied it off in a bow. That stopped the bleeding and I didn't have to touch anything that wasn't mine. I really didn't give a shit about him, but I didn't want to be arrested for murder if the asshole bled out. The bow I tied in the fishing line got a chuckle from the EMT guys that showed up to take him to the hospital."

"Wait a minute," I said. "I gotta call bullshit on this one. No man can keep it up while all that arguing with another man is going on; this doesn't ring true."

"I thought about that myself later on," Davy said, "So one day when we were in the lawyer's office I asked my ex about it. Seems he had trouble getting it up and was a Viagra addict. In fact, he would usually double up on the dose. That's another reason he bled like a hog with its throat cut, that stuff dilates the blood vessels. She told me that one time he took so much his blood pressure crashed and he passed out in the middle of screwing her.

"Trust me, that was info I really didn't need."

"Well, the knife was obviously sharp," I said with a chuckle. "So the cut was clean. They sewed Bobbit's back on and he went on to become some kind of porn star. How about this guy? Did they sew it back on?"

"No they did not," Davy said with a chuckle. "There was not much left that would hold stitches.

"I thought you said you cut it off with one swipe?"

"I did. But we had this little female Welsh Corgi that was a food whore. That dog would beg whenever anybody had something to eat and would catch anything that we threw to her. She would crouch beside the table during dinner waiting for anything we dropped. When any morsel of food hit the floor she would pounce and that's what she did when his dick hit the tile. In the confusion of trying to keep the asshole from bleeding to death in my kitchen, we didn't notice. The dog grabbed his dick and ran into the bedroom and hid under the bed. For whatever reason she didn't swallow it, but used it like a chew toy. By the time we figured out what happened and got it away from her, it was pretty well shredded.

"So how come you are not in jail?" I asked.

"The attorney general was a divorced and emasculated man. I told him that I believed that Tom was threating me with bodily harm. He laughed a little and then ruled it self-defense. Oddly enough, nobody challenged that ruling. Most men thought Tom got what he deserved for screwing another man's wife and a lot of women thought any guy getting his dick cut off was justice. Tom was too embarrassed to bother to appeal.

"I got a severe warning and they kept my knife, but that was all. I did some digging and found out the AG had also caught his former wife cheating and I suppose he let me go to strike a blow for men everywhere.

"I do miss that knife, though. It was a custom made Emerson that cost me a bundle.

"Anyway, I divorced the bitch and of course she got half of everything I had busted my ass to earn. She cashed out and headed to Oregon and I have not heard from her since. Last I knew, Tom was working as an aid to Vermont's junior U.S. Senator. I have no idea what happened to him after Washington fell to the mobs, but I suspect it didn't end well for him.

"Once this hit the news my work at the gym took off and I went full time. The reporters called me unstable and the MMA guys love that shit. But, nobody wanted to talk about what I did.

"You remember how it was after Lorena Bobbit cut off her husband's dick and it made them a national joke? You would be with a bunch of guys, drinking and telling jokes. Everybody is laughing and having a good time, and then somebody starts telling Bobbit jokes. Hell, I still remember a few."

John Bobbit tried to sue Lorena but failed.
The evidence would not stand up in court!

What did Jeffrey Dahmer say to Lorena Bobbit?
"Excuse me; are you going to eat that?"

He supposedly wasn't a bad actor, but they fired him because he would freak out when the director yelled 'Cut!'

"When anybody told these jokes, everybody would laugh, but it would be a little less after each joke. Finally there would be an uncomfortable silence. After a while, somebody would change the subject, but the mood would be gone. Every guy in the place was thinking about some crazy bitch cutting his dick off and nobody felt like laughing anymore.

"It was like that at the gym. Every guy thought it was very cool to take care of an asshole that would screw your woman, but nobody wanted to talk about it."

CHAPTER 39

I had a chunk of bacon in my pack that I cut into strips. We used the grease to cook the trout, putting the cooked bacon strips aside for breakfast. I never liked fish much, but these fresh, wild brookies tasted fantastic and I ate more than my share. After eating, I could barely keep my eyes open and I could see that Davy was not far behind. We had been up about forty hours straight at this point and our full bellies triggered the sleep mode.

Sarah offered to take first watch. I showed her how to climb up on the roof through a skylight that opened. We placed a chair so it straddled the peaked roof and was back against a low dormer and hidden by the branches of a huge hemlock growing next to the building. She had a 360 degree view of anybody trying to approach, but was hidden from the sight of anybody on the ground. She had one of the full auto M4 carbines we took off a dead guy, along with the Beretta 9mm pistol he also had donated. She had half a dozen extra magazines for each in a tote bag we had found in the camp.

"If something starts you get the hell down from there," I said. You will be a sitting duck once you start firing and they can see where you are. Don't shoot unless you absolutely have to. If you see somebody coming, sneak over to the skylight and get back down here with us. Understand?"

"Of course I understand, you have told me six times already. Go to bed and get some sleep, I got this. I'll wake you in four hours."

But she didn't. Davy took the next watch, even though we agreed it would be mine. On the other hand, ten solid hours of sleep made me a new man.

I wish I could say the same for Bradley. He was looking worse. Even though we had blankets piled on top of him he was shivering like a naked Eskimo in winter. He was talking in his sleep, but when I woke him up he said he couldn't remember dreaming. Then he called me by our dad's name. I explained that it was me, but he insisted he was talking with Dad, who has been gone for a decade. Bradley's forehead felt like it was burning up and when I unwrapped the bandages his arm was red and oozing yellow pus. I got him to drink some water and take a couple more aspirin from my medical kit. I squirted some antibiotic cream into the wound and then bound it up again, putting a clean bandage against the wound. By then, Bradley was coherent and being his usual pain in the ass self and bitching about having too many blankets on top of him.

Sarah had found a large, unopened vacuum packed can of coffee in one of the cupboards and had a pan of water filled with a big handful of grounds boiling "cowboy style." The aroma was maddening. It reminded me of better times and I had to work hard not to slip back into depressing thoughts.

She also had water from the brook at a full boil in a bigger pan. She had put cups, plates and silverware inside the pan of boiling water.

"They had mouse shit on them and I didn't have any soap to wash them properly. I scrubbed them with sand from the brook but I want to sterilize them before we eat. The food will be done in about fifteen minutes, but the coffee is ready now. I presume you all take it black?

"The menu this morning includes your choice of breakfast meats: bacon or jerky. We also have cold, fried trout that has seasoned overnight in a marinade of congealed bacon grease. I found some bread in my pack that was mashed into a ball. I am frying the pieces in bacon grease to make a savory toast. Davy went for a walk by the beaver dam this morning and found two mallard nests. I have seven duck eggs which I will cook to order, as long as fried is what you order.

"But wait, there's more! Back in the storage room a red squirrel has piled up a couple of bushels of butternuts, which I thought was mighty nice of him. If somebody will help me find a hammer to crack them open we can have a butternut appetizer while we wait for our breakfast to cook."

Then with a fake Southern accent she said, "Ain't we fancy, we's just like one of them there big city restaurants from back before!"

"Wow," Davy said. "She cooks, she cleans, she shoots and she is good looking too. Damn near the perfect woman. Her only flaw is that she is too friggin' cheerful in the morning. But, I can fix that."

"The hell you can," Sarah said with her eyes twinkling and the same fake accent. "This here cheerfulness is permanent. It's part of the package, partner and there ain't nobody going to change a damn thing, take it as it is or leave it behind."

"I'll have to think about that," Davy said. But, his crooked smile made me believe he wouldn't have to think too much.

Bradley was staring at him from across the room and the fire in his eyes was from a lot more than a fever.

CHAPTER 40

We had wasted a lot of time at the camp, but I think it was worth it. Everybody's mood had improved dramatically, including mine. That happens with rest and food. But we had a problem. I motioned for Davy to join me outside where we could talk.

"I had planned to stick deep in the woods, following old snowmobile trails until we hooked up with the Long Trail. That's part of the Appalachian Trail."

"I know what it is," Davy said peevishly, clearly wanting to get back to the food and the girl.

"Well anyway," I continued, "the Long Trail passes less than half a mile from my house. That would keep us off the roads and hard to find. But, it's not a very direct route, so it's forty more miles on grown-in trails that have not been maintained in a long time. Bradley is not up to walking in rough country for two more days. Hell, I am not sure I am up to it myself. With all the blood I've lost I feel like about half of me is missing and I am in a lot better shape than he is. We need to get some antibiotics into him fast or that bullet wound could turn mean.

"I think the best bet is to head for your place in Moultrie. If we get back on the gravel road we left yesterday and follow it for another mile, it hits the paved road I initially planned to follow to Easton before the shit hit the fan at the bridge. If we go two miles up that, I know an old snowmobile trail that breaks off and will take us over the mountain and dump us in town about a quarter mile from Emily's place. Bradley can really use her help right now.

"The problem is we have to go those two miles up the paved road, as it's impossible to run parallel in the woods. It's just too thick and rough. It means we would be exposed. I would prefer to do that at night, but we can't afford the time. What do you think? Is it worth the risk?"

"What risk?" Davy said. "Sounds like a plan, let's go."

Bradley was moving pretty well but I could tell he was hurting and not hitting on all cylinders. Hell, it didn't take a psychic to figure that out; he was quiet. The only explanation when Bradley is quiet, other than that somebody cut out his tongue, is that he is sick and hurting.

We made good time back through the woods to the gravel road. I stayed back with Bradley and Sarah while Davy went ahead to scout the road. It wasn't long before he was back, grinning, as Gramp used to say, 'Like a dog that ate the jonnie cake'.

"We have some company at the end of the road. Must be they are watching all the major outlets from that trail we ran, because there are two guys with a truck parked at the junction with the main road. They look bored. What do you say we go liven up their day a little and give them something to do?"

We left Bradley and Sarah behind, well hidden off the road in some thick brush. She was mad as hell and wanted to come with us, but I explained that somebody had to keep Bradley under control and on a leash. She suggested I do that. Well, she actually suggested I do a lot of things, some of them I think are pretty much physically and anatomically impossible. The girl has a temper! But, she also has passion, so I understood and didn't take a lot of offense. She craves action, but I think it's more that, like a lot of type "A" people, she just doesn't think anybody else can handle things as well as she can.

Plus, I think she really wanted to go with Davy.

One guy was sitting in the driver's seat, reading a comic book. I hadn't seen one of those in years and it made me wonder where in the hell he found it. The other guy was twenty feet away, with his back to the truck, taking a piss. I motioned for Davy to sit tight and I headed into the woods.

I made my way closer to the pissing guy, working along through the brush. I broke a few sticks because it was impossible not to, but that was also part of my plan. I wanted him to hear me moving around and get curious. When I was about thirty yards from him I hid behind a huge boulder. These rocks were dumped here by the glaciers and are called "erratics" by the geologists, because they are completely different than the local rocks. But I just called this one a damn good place to hide. I peeked around the edge, using brush to hide my face and I softly mooed like a cow.

"Did you hear that?" the guy said, back over his shoulder.

"I didn't hear nothing," the other guy said. "And we ain't gonna hear nothing. This is a shit detail, nobody is going to show up here. Besides, I don't want them to. Those guys killed a lot of people yesterday. Hell, I heard they killed more than twenty guys. They said it was only two guys that did it, but I don't believe that shit. They must have had like a platoon or something waiting in the woods. I don't want nothing to do with them. I can take two fuckin' guys on my own without breaking a sweat, but I ain't fighting no platoon."

"Shut the fuck up, will you. I heard something in the woods."

I mooed again, low and soft.

"Shit, I think it's a cow, or maybe a moose, I don't know. What's a moose sound like?"

"How the fuck would I know that a moose sounds like? I'm from Jersey for Christ's sake. You ever see a moose in Jersey?"

"How would I know? I ain't ever been to Jersey. Who in their right mind would want to go to Jersey? Besides, it ain't any moose. A moose would have heard you running your mouth by now and run away. I think somebody's cow got loose. Their loss. I can smell the steaks grilling already. Man, we are going to eat tonight."

"Hey," he said, with a slobbery snicker that sounded like his mouth was full of spit, "Maybe it's a fuckin' Jersey cow."

The guy didn't even bother to get his rifle into position as he came walking toward me, he just had it hanging at the end of his right arm. I slipped back behind the rock and waited. He was trying to sneak, but wasn't very good at it, so even my scarred old eardrums could follow his progress.

He was moving too far to my right, so I broke another stick to help direct him to the rock. When he walked past, he spotted me, but it was too late. I was squatting down so I swept his feet with my right leg, flipping them out from under him. When he hit the ground I pivoted on my hands and brought the heel of my left boot down on his solar plexus. He sat up to gasp for air as I came back with a round kick from the same left leg to the side of his head. My instep hit him hard just above the ear and he was still.

"What the fuck you doing out there?" his buddy called. "Hey, come on back. You know we ain't supposed to leave the vehicle. There ain't no fucking cow. Come on, get back here, you're going to get us in trouble."

I had hoped he would come over to investigate, but clearly he was not going to leave the truck. Instead he got his rifle out and braced it on the door mirror. Then he yelled for his buddy again.

"I don't think he is coming back," Davy said.

I could see him in front of me, walking toward the truck. He must have moved in there while I was dealing with my guy, but I didn't hear a thing. How in the hell did he keep doing that?

It really pissed me off.

The guy at the truck jumped out of the seat and started to raise his rifle.

"Don't do that," Davy said.

Then in his best Danny Glover voice he continued, "I don't wanna kill you and you don't wanna be dead."

The guy started to say something and Davy cut him off.

"Look buddy, if you move again, the platoon hiding in the woods behind me will shoot you."

The guy thought about it, then made the wrong choice. He started to move his rifle again, but it got caught in the mirror.

"Last chance," Davy said.

The guy yanked the rifle free and a split second later a bullet hit his forehead.

"You can't say I didn't give you fair warning," Davy said as he rolled the body over with his toe.

"Did you see that?" he asked, looking at me.

"The guy thought he could fight a platoon.

"What a dumbass."

CHAPTER 41

We dragged the unconscious guy back to the truck. I dug around in their tool box and found some rope which I used to tie his hands and feet. I also tied him to the roll bar on the right side of the truck, so he was sitting upright in the back seat like a passenger. I threw his guns and extra magazines in the back of the truck and noticed several boxes.

We got all the guns and ammo off the dead guy. I checked his pockets, but I didn't find anything else. After my experience at the bridge I checked again, doing a thorough pat-down. No blinking transmitter this time. Actually I didn't find much of anything on the guy, just a dull Swiss Army knife in his pocket, which I put in mine. We dragged his body off the road, stuffed it under a big log and covered it with branches.

The truck was some kind of SUV. It was smaller than the old Hummers the military had back before and with the engine under the hood where it belongs, rather than in back taking up passenger space. There were no markings of any kind to show who made it and I did not recognize the design.

In the back, beside the boxes, we found a cooler full of food and bottled water. Also, there was a large box full of loaded rifle and handgun magazines. A quick count found fifty of each. There were also a couple thousand rounds of extra 5.56 rifle cartridges and at least as much 9mm handgun ammo. It was all military grade stuff with a Lake City headstamp. The next box was full of hand grenades. The last box had rocket propelled grenades. I looked up and clamped to the roof inside the vehicle was a launcher.

"Holy shit Davy, these guys meant business," I said in a hushed tone. "What the hell is going on here? What do they need with RPGs? Who the fuck are these guys and what have we gotten ourselves into?"

"Shit, I don't know," Davy said as he opened the cooler. "But, I am hungry again, let's eat."

He munched on cold fried chicken while I drove the truck up the road to get Sarah and Bradley.

"Well, I suppose you killed a bunch more guys to get this truck," Bradley said. He was so sick that he was slurring his words like he was drunk, but he still just could not resist jabbing at us.

"Nope, just one," Davy replied. "We left this one alive."

"He doesn't look very alive to me."

"Did you forget what I told you yesterday? Two choices here; shut the fuck up and get in the truck, or start walking. That's it, two. Pick one of them now."

Bradley crawled in the back seat across from the guy we had trussed up and promptly fell asleep.

"Damn, that's effective," Sarah said. "I wish I thought of it years ago. You have no idea how many times I wanted him to 'shut the fuck up.' I mean, he is my dad and I love him but there are times when I wish he came with an off switch installed."

Then she laughed.

"What," Davy asked?

"Somehow, though, I think it's your delivery more than what you are saying, so it probably won't work for me."

"Don't worry about this guy. If he wakes up I'll keep an eye on him," she said as she got in the middle in the back seat and pulled her pistol out of the holster. Davy took shotgun and I drove.

The plan had changed now. We would drive down the road to the bridge where the fight was and then get on the highway back to Moultrie.

The temptation to head home from there would be strong as I really missed my wife, but we needed to get Bradley to some medical help.

About a mile down the road I could see a truck coming the other way. Davy reached into his pack, took out the hats the guys with the truck had been wearing and put one on me and the other on his own head. Then he scrunched down a little bit.

"You two in the back, get down. Leave the unconscious guy, he is okay."

Sarah pulled on Bradley until he slid down the seat below the door line. He didn't even wake up. Then she ducked down so she was out of sight.

We met the other truck and Davy just waved at them like he was their best buddy. There were two guys in the truck, both wearing the same black hats we wore. They waved back and kept going. I figured they would turn around and chase us, but nothing happened.

In fact, nothing happened for the rest of the trip until we were two miles outside Moultrie. There was a bad stretch of road there that was notorious for bandit activity. Jack had pretty well cleaned them out in recent years, but my little voice was telling me that maybe he didn't get them all.

I stopped well before we got to it and started looking with my binoculars. After about ten minutes one of the guys there got itchy and shot at the truck. He missed and hit the road in front of us. He probably had an AK-47 or one of its variants and we were at least four hundred yards away. He simply didn't know enough about ballistics to understand the shot was too far, or at the very least he had to hold high. He probably didn't know much about being a bandit either, as he had just given up his chance to surprise us.

"Well, what now?" I asked.

"Screw them," Davy said. "I am tired, hungry, grumpy and I have guns. Besides we have been on the road long enough, I want a drink and my whiskey is just a couple of miles past those assholes. In fact, if you listen you can hear it softly calling my name. It's lonely, I am thirsty, let's go."

"We don't know how many there are waiting for us. Don't forget this thing is not armored like the truck you usually ride in."

"Yes it is.

"Armored, I mean."

I turned around and the guy tied up in the back was awake.

"Push that red button on the dash."

"Why?"

"Just do it."

Davy got out of the truck and pointed his pistol at the guy's head though the open window. "If anything bad happens, the last thing I will do is put a bullet through your tiny little brain," he said.

"Just push the fuckin' button."

So I did.

Panels slid up into place over all the windows, the windshield and the rear hatch.

"Go ahead asshole, shoot me now," the guy said through the panel to Davy.

"Look guys, I ain't ready to die today. I can see there is trouble ahead and I know it's not my buddies, so there is no percentage in me helping them. I figure my best bet right now is you guys.

"Those are special lightweight armor panels. They got Kevlar or some such shit in them. They will stop a rifle up to a .308. The entire truck is covered with it, even underneath in case we drive over a bomb. They just keep these down so we can see. All the glass in this thing is bullet proof, but it won't stop a rifle. I guess the glass for that would be too heavy, so they have these pop-up armor plates. They got slits to look through in the windshield so you can still drive, sort of like in a tank. Just try to sit off to one side so if a bullet comes through one, it misses you. They told me the glass should stop pistol rounds and most carbine rounds, but a big rifle like a 30-cal can get through. But it has to hit square on; anything at an angle will not penetrate. They gave us a school on how to sit and look from the side, but it's not that complicated and you are pretty smart guys."

"By the way," he said looking at me. "You hit pretty fuckin' hard for an old man.

"Anyway, the tires are filled with some kind of self-sealing gel so they won't go flat. Even if they do, they are designed to run flat. The engine compartment is shielded so they can't shoot the motor or the radiator. Just put it in four-wheel drive and go through. Unless they have an RPG or a tank, they can't stop you."

"Thanks, buddy," Davy said.

"You can thank me later with a sip of that whiskey you were just talking about."

"We'll see how it goes. For now I ain't saying no."

By the sounds of the bullets hitting the truck there were four or five bad guys, but they didn't do anything other than use up ammo.

"A bunch of amateurs, by the looks," Davy said. "We need to come back here tomorrow and cull these bastards from the herd."

We made it through without a problem, got Bradley into Emily's hands and had a drink in ours, all before the hour ended. I noticed when Davy was pouring he had a glass for the guy with his hands tied together.

CHAPTER 42

"Oh shit," Emily said. "This is bad. He is close to being in septic shock if he is not already. Obviously, I can't do a blood gas or white cell count to confirm it, but his heart rate and fever are both high. Plus, to use the accepted medical terminology to describe his wound, that's some really gross shit. Something nasty must have gotten into that bullet wound. If we were in a hospital I would just start him on IV antibiotics and operate on his arm to clean out the gunk. Then I would send him to intensive care. But, we are not at a hospital, we are at the house of a scared, middle-aged lady playing doctor and trying to get by without training and little or no supplies."

"Well we gotta do something," I said. "He is a pain in the ass, but he is my brother and I can't let him die. Besides, we have to help him survive so I can kill him later for getting us into this mess. I don't know anything about gunshot wounds other than how to make them. You are the closest thing we have to a doctor, so please do the best you can."

I took her hand, looked into her eyes and said, "I trust you and have faith that you can fix this."

Emily gave a nervous laugh as she pulled her hands away. "Then you are not as smart as you think you are."

"Can I help?" Sarah asked. "I want to learn. I had planned since I was a little girl to go to medical school. Then the world fell apart, so obviously that never happened. But I still want to learn all I can about medicine. Someday this will end and the world will need doctors again and I figure if I can get a head start it can't hurt."

"I appreciate any help I can get," Emily said. "But, you should know I am not a doctor and never had any training. I just read my husband's books after he died. There is so much I don't know and that's what scares the hell out of me. Like what to do for him. He needs antibiotics, but he is unconscious and can't swallow. The easy answer is to put him on an IV and deliver the antibiotics that way. But, I don't have any antibiotics other than in pill form. I know that grinding them up and injecting them into his bloodstream, even with an IV, is not a good idea. In fact based on the little bit I do know, it will probably kill him."

"What if we injected the antibiotics into his muscles?" Sarah said. "I know that method was used a lot with penicillin in the early years of antibiotics. I remember reading about it in a book."

Then she giggled like a little girl and said, "I think it was how they fixed you if you caught the clap. The book said that they shot the penicillin in the buttock muscle because it was the biggest. I remember, too, the article said it hurt like hell when they did that."

"Well the closest thing I have right now is some ampicillin. It's not even human grade, it came from a vet supply. But, the human stuff is pretty well picked over these days. Somebody remembered that they used a lot of the same drugs on animals and the last time Jack made a run to the train they had this. Billy Farnsworth told Jack he could have sold it a dozen times on his way up here, but he saved it just for me. He didn't even charge for it. Just said he would take it out in trade next time he needed doctoring. Anyway, I guess one of the scavengers he trades with found it in an old vet office. Or hell, for all I know the scavenger stole it to sell to Billy. But I came by it honestly enough and right now I am glad I did. It outdated about four years ago, but it's in a sealed jar, so I think it will be okay.

"It will have to be okay, it's all I have."

I watched as she emptied two of the 500mg capsules into a small cup.

"We need to make some sterile water," Emily said.

"I am on it, I replied.

I took some of her boiled drinking water and ran it though my filter two times. Then I put it in a clean pan and boiled it again for five minutes. I tossed a clean spoon in to boil and sterilize as well.

Once it cooled a bit Emily took a teaspoon of the water and mixed it with the powder from the capsules. She put half of the solution into a nasty-looking syringe with a wicked-looking needle sticking out the front. The thing looked big enough to give a T-Rex a shot.

"This is from the same vet supply. I think it's for giving shots to horses. Maybe even for the clap. Can horses catch the clap? Hell, I don't know. How would they get it, by visiting a horsehouse?"

She stopped to chuckle at her own lame joke. I looked over and Davy was laughing so hard he was about pissing his pants, which made me think he had not been sharing his bourbon drink for drink.

"I think this thing would hurt like hell," Emily said as she prepared the needle.

Davy seemed to like that. At least for a moment, then he realized that Bradley was unconscious and wouldn't feel a thing and his grin disappeared.

Emily continued, "Sarah, I am out of alcohol, so grab some of Davy's bourbon and pour it on your dad's butt to sterilize the injection site.

"Hey, hang on a minute there, that's good whiskey, don't be wasting it," Davy said. "In spite of his nasty disposition and the way he treats me I am willing to donate, but let's compromise. You can have my whiskey after I filter it through my kidneys. I'll even deliver it personally."

Sarah laughed as she poured at least a shot of the precious fluid on my brother's bare ass. Emily scrubbed it around with a sterile bandage and asked for another dose. They repeated the process, but when she asked for a third dose, Davy grabbed the bottle out of Sarah's hand.

"That's enough. He can live or die on what he has and I'll plan to do the same on the little you have left me."

"The hell you will," I said. "Half that's mine. You can bill me later."

Emily injected the mixture into Bradley's butt, being careful to get the full dose into him. Then she mixed up the second dose and injected that into the other cheek.

"Now what?" I asked.

"Now we wait and see."

"If he gets better and wakes up, I'll get some fluids into him and starting feeding him antibiotics by mouth. If he doesn't, and he is still breathing, I'll give him another injection in about four hours.

"Meanwhile I am going to try to clean out that bullet wound and stitch it up."

"Good idea," I said. "I looked at his arm this morning and it was nasty."

"Not his, yours. He will be sleeping for a while and I want to give those injections a little time to work into his bloodstream. I'll get to his bullet hole, but later. You sit down and get that shirt off, we need to check you out.

"Is that duct tape? Really? Well, that's different.

"It looks like somebody thought you were a heating vent pipe or something."

"Doctor Sarah and Master Sergeant Davy applied that battle dressing under very difficult field conditions," I said with my best general's voice.

"Nice work," Emily muttered. "But keep your day jobs."

Turning to me she said, "Next time don't leave it on so long, your skin needs to breathe. Let's get that off you and have a look."

She gently peeled the tape off my wound and for the second time in recent memory started to treat a gunshot-inflicted wound on me.

"Well at least this time they shot you with a proper bullet instead of a damn greasy old carburetor."

"Fuel injector."

"What?"

"It was a piece of a fuel injector, not a carburetor. Same job, different parts. Actually, fuel injectors replaced carburetors in the eighties as a fuel delivery system for the engines used in cars. It was an innovative and dramatic change as the carburetor had been used since the invention of the gasoline powered internal combustion engine in the 1880s. The carburetor is a wonderful device, works off the Venturi effect. The air is sucked though the carburetor by the manifold vacuum until it hits a constricted area. This speeds up the air, but at different rates because of the shape of the constriction. That creates a vacuum and . . ."

"Will you shut up! I can't concentrate and I really don't much care for a lesson in auto mechanics today. I will have had quite enough education trying to figure out how to deal with two different bullet holes and a major infection."

"Okay, sorry. I think that little splash of bourbon you left in the bottle after scrubbing Bradley's ass has released the Irish in me and I'm babbling. Happens a lot when somebody gets near me with a knife"

"No, I am the one that's sorry," she said as her face softened.

"It's just my latent bitch surfacing. I try to keep it caged, but every now and then it claws its way to the surface. I guess I am worried about Bradley and hoping I didn't make things worse by improvising. But, I do feel compelled to point out that I was only using this "knife" which is actually called a scalpel, to remove the duct tape, which should be painless enough so that a tough guy like you will survive the process.

"I gotta say, duct tape, that's a first in my short medical career. But it looks like it worked. This thing is in a lot better shape than your brother's bullet hole."

The wound on my shoulder was a deep gouge. The duct tape had held the edges together and it had already started to heal.

196

"If we don't stitch it up, it will just pull apart now that the duct tape is not holding it together," Emily said.

"Davy go get another bottle out of that hidden stash you keep under the horse stall in your barn. He will need to have another drink or two because it's going to hurt and I don't have anything else to numb the pain. I will also need a little to sterilize the wound.

"I guess we are lucky I have some sutures. Although they are veterinary grade, I am sure they will work just fine. Hell, in the past I have used fishing line and even dental floss, so dog stitches are a step up.

"Nothing but the gold standard for my patients."

CHAPTER 43

Two days later we were in Davy's old barn, where we were keeping our prisoner.

"So how we going to get him to talk?" I asked Davy.

"Well, the uninspired way would be to torture me," the guy said.

"What the hell happened to the Brooklyn accent and the dumbass vocabulary?" I asked him.

"That was mostly just me going along to get along," he replied. "I'm not the smartest guy on the planet, but I am a lot smarter than those morons I was working with.

"Although, I must admit, I really did think you were a cow," he said with a smile.

"Anyway, the name's Mike, but everybody calls me Mickey. I came from upstate New York. I lost my family in the social wars and wound up joining a gang in Albany. That was the only way to stay alive and it worked for a couple of years, although it's really no way to live."

"So how did you wind up on a remote Vermont road waiting to kill us?" I asked him.

"One day a guy showed up, said he was looking for soldiers for this new army he was building. He said that we really didn't have to fight anybody, that we would mostly just work as guards. He promised three meals a day, a roof over my head and some of the new money he had. He said it was going to become the world's currency. I figured what the hell, no future in the gang. Particularly when the leader didn't like me and I knew we were headed for trouble. So, I signed up.

"That was about two months ago. They took me to that little town about five miles up the road from where you guys found me. They gave me a little bit of training like the school on the armored truck, but hardly anything on things

I would have expected, like shooting or fighting tactics. I mean, I can fight; I boxed and besides, you had to learn how to fight if you wanted to stay alive in the gang. But, I wanted to learn the stuff the army teaches, about big battles, shit like that. To tell you the truth, I am not sure they knew any of that themselves. They didn't have anybody who seemed to know much of anything about running an army.

"Mostly I just sat around and waited. I exercised in their gym, stayed in shape and we had a few shooting schools to make sure we could work the guns, but we only fired live ammo one time and they only gave me five cartridges. They kept telling us to be ready, but nothing much happened until you guys showed up.

"Now about getting me to talk. Yes, I do know quite a bit more. No, I will not tell you yet. Yes, you could torture me, but I'll hold out a long time and I'll scream bloody murder so everybody in town will know what you are doing. Besides, you guys don't seem the type. Or you can just do me a favor and after that I'll tell you everything.

"Do you a favor?" Davy said. "Why the hell would we do that?"

"Hold on," I said. "Let's at least hear what he wants."

"What I want, old man, is a rematch."

"Well, let me tell you something son, if you keep calling me old man, you will get one. Davy, you take note too. That old man shit is getting old. I am not yet an 'old man' and if you little bastards keep calling me that you will find that out the hard way."

"Whoa, calm down," Davy said tying hard not to smile. "What's got your panties in a wad this morning? I was just having a little fun."

"Not me," Mickey said. "I apologize if I offended you, but I wasn't poking fun and I still want a rematch.

"Why?" I asked.

"I am embarrassed that you took me out so easily. I know it was just because you surprised me and I want a chance to even the score. Then I'll tell you everything."

"What if you lose?" Davy asked

"I won't lose. But, if that's what you are worried about I'll still talk; win, lose or draw. I keep my word."

"Okay," I said. "You got it."

"Wait a minute," Davy said. Then he dragged me over to a corner and out of earshot of Mickey.

"He is a lot bigger than you and while I ain't calling you old, you are at least thirty years more experienced than him. This is a really bad idea."

I just walked over to Mickey and cut the ropes from his hands and feet with the Swiss Army knife I took off his dead partner. I could tell by his eyes he recognized the knife. He could probably tell by the way it sliced the ropes that I had sharpened the blade. I put it back in my pocket and waited until he had worked the blood back into his extremities.

"You ready?" I asked.

"Yup."

I hit him.

I was standing with my left shoulder leading, like a guy planning a round-house right would do, but with my hands down at waist level. The guy was looking at my right hand, which was a mistake for a couple of reasons; the biggest one being that I am left handed. I brought my left up from my beltline with a stinging backhand to his nose that he never saw coming. I knew that would make his eyes tear up and would hurt like hell. It also caused him to pick up his hands and leave his middle unprotected.

I shifted my hips for power and brought a straight right into his solar plexus, which still had to be sore. I finished by shifting my weight again and coming back with a hard left hook to his bottom ribs, hearing one of them crack with the impact. The three hits took less than two seconds.

He hit the ground and laid there gasping for breath, with his eyes bulging and rolling back in his head.

"When he can move, take him to Emily to patch up," I said to Davy.

"Then we will have a talk."

I left to get a second cup of coffee.

CHAPTER 44

I had not tasted coffee in several years before Sarah discovered that big can in the cabin. The trouble was nobody else had, either. I didn't realize how many "friends" I had until they came begging for a taste. The can was emptied fast and this cup in my hand might well be the last one I would ever have. I was sitting down on a stump trying to savor the experience when Emily came storming out of her house with bitch written all over her.

"Every time you show up my medical supplies are drastically depleted," she shouted at me, interrupting my serenity.

"Did you have to beat the hell out of the boy again?"

"No, I probably didn't have to; it was his choice, not mine."

"Well you broke his nose and I am pretty sure cracked two ribs. For what? To show him you are a big man?"

"No, actually it was to see what kind of a man he was."

"I heard it was a pretty lopsided fight, so I am guessing he was not what you had hoped."

"I really don't know yet."

"What's that supposed to mean?"

"Has it occurred to you that we have a problem?"

"We have lots of problems; you will have to be a lot more specific," she said, her shrill voice rising to shatter what little was left of the morning's stillness.

Then she stopped and checked herself, and when she spoke again the anger was gone.

"By the way, there is just enough coffee left for two more cups. One is mine, you want a refill with the other?"

When she came back she had two cups of hot coffee with milk in them and she had calmed down considerably.

"I think I see what you are talking about. It's Mickey, right? We are not equipped to handle prisoners. I know you won't kill him in cold blood and I think we can agree that letting him go is a very bad idea. So, I am guessing the problem you are talking about is, what do we do with Mickey?"

"That it is."

"So, what are you going to do?"

"I don't know yet. But, I have an idea. He made me a promise. I don't expect you to understand because it's a guy thing, but that promise is one that a lot of men would have trouble keeping right now. I want to see how he handles the situation."

"Davy told me that he promised to tell you what he knows, no matter if he lost the fight. Is that it?"

"Yes."

"So, what's the problem?"

"Clearly you have a lot to learn about the male ego. He is a young, macho guy who expected to mop the floor with me. He is bigger, stronger, younger and fancies himself a fighter. The last thing he expected was to lose that fight.

"He might have accepted it if the fight had gone on awhile and he had gotten in some good licks, managed to hurt me and then lost. But for me to take him out in two seconds without even so much as a scraped knuckle on my part . . . that is going to be hard for him to handle, particularly considering it's the second time I did it in three days. He has survived by being mean and right now he feels like a pussy.

"He had to still be hurting from the beating in the woods and not too many guys would want another fight just a couple of days later. Most would find an excuse that they could live with to not try again. He didn't. That tells me he has an ego, but it also tells me that he is tough. I think he is smart as well, but what I don't know is what kind of man he is.

"He was put into a very bad position at a very young age and he made the best of it to survive. He hooked up with some nasty people with a gang in New York and probably did some bad things. But when he saw a way out for what he thought was honest work, he took it. I think that after he got to Easton he realized the situation he moved into was not what he was promised, but he was stuck with it and had no place to go.

"He says he can tell me a lot. That might be total bullshit. But, if it's true, my guess is he had plans of some kind and was not going to stay where he was for long. The only way he could know information that will be useful would be if he was doing a lot more than just being a good soldier. He had to be spying or at least getting himself into positions where he could listen to things the soldiers were not meant to hear. He could have planned to use the information to move up in the organization, even though he knew it was corrupt and evil. In which case, I have no use for him. Or he might have been gathering information that would help him get away.

"Right now he is scared and full of self-doubt. What he does next will tell me a lot about his character. Most guys will turn asshole, be combative and uncooperative. I embarrassed and hurt him and not many men would be inclined to cooperate after that. But he made a promise and he told me he keeps his word. I guess we will see if that's true."

"Well, now is your chance," Emily said. "When I went back to the house for the coffee he asked to see you when you were done drinking yours."

CHAPTER 45

When I went into the house Mickey was lying on a cot. He tried to rise, but I could see his ribs were hurting.

"Just stay down, it's fine," I said.

"Do you have something to tell me?" I asked.

"Yup, I told you I would and I told you I keep my word. But, I have another request."

Anger and disappointment flared as I started to speak, but he stopped me before I could.

"I'll wait until we are done to ask it. Don't worry, I am not going to try to make conditions, we had a deal and I am not going to change it. It's just that when we are done I want to ask you something. You can say yes or no, I know that's your choice, not mine."

"Well then, ask me now," I said. "I'll think about it and give you an answer when we are done."

"Can you teach me?"

"Teach you what?"

"I want to know how you did that to me. Before I ran into you, I never lost a fight in my life. I figured the deal in the woods was because you surprised me, but this time I should have been ready. I thought I was fast enough to block anything you could throw at me. I know I am faster than you. No disrespect. But I am a lot younger and I know I am fast, even with guys my age. Yet, when you hit me, I never saw it coming.

"My dad was a Golden Gloves fighter. He was good, real good, and I wanted to be like him. I studied the best boxers in the world. I read all the books and I watched the fights. I was just a kid but I knew that the best guys like Ali and Sugar Ray weren't great just because they were fast and tough. Lots of boxers were fast and tough. Those guys took it to a new level because they were smart. It's pretty clear to me you know a thing or two and I respectfully ask you to teach me. Or at the very least, tell me where I went wrong. I think I know, but I want to hear it from you."

"We will see," I grumbled.

"I know I have no right. Hell, it was my job to kill you guys. You probably don't believe me, but I wouldn't have done it. I am no angel, but I am no killer either; not that way. I didn't know what I was going to do if you showed up. I thought about shooting that dickhead they stuck me with and asking if I could join you but, like I said, I am no murderer. I thought maybe I could just get the jump on him, tie him up or something, but mostly I just hoped you wouldn't show up. I know it sounds like bullshit and like I am just trying to blow smoke up your ass because of the situation, but I don't lie. I owe that much to my dad.

"Anyway, I want to say again, you hit pretty fuckin' hard for ... ah ... um ... a guy my dad's age."

His eyes went dark and he mumbled, "Or at least his age if my dad was still alive.

"Ah shit, I didn't mean it like that. I wasn't trying to call you old again, damn it. This is not coming out right . . . I want to start over, okay?"

"Don't worry about it, I am old. Just try not to point it out too often. It pisses me off. Now, tell me what you know."

"It's not good, I can tell you that," he started.

"I didn't figure it would be."

"When I got to town it was pretty clear that things were not like the guy told me they were going to be. They had the new money and they were building an army, that much was clear. But it wasn't to help bring back America. It was also pretty clear to me that things had not been going according to plan. They seemed to be having a lot of problems."

"What kind of problems?"

"I am not sure, but I heard them arguing all the time about how things had gotten out of hand and how they lost control, stuff like that. They never mentioned specifics around me. But, I got the impression that they had some grand, master plan that had gone bad and they were trying to get back on track with it. I was just muscle, so they didn't let me into any of the meetings, I just picked up bits and pieces."

"I played dumb around the other soldiers to fit in, but when I had a chance I let the guys in charge know that I was a little bit smarter than the rest of those fools. But, not too smart, so they didn't see me as a threat. I played to their egos and soon enough they started to request me as their bodyguard. That let me hear some things. I am not going to pretend I know everything that's going on, but I will tell you what I know and what I suspect."

"So who is the guy in the cabin at the end? The guy Bradley thinks is so great," I asked.

He started laughing. That hurt his ribs and his face grimaced.

"Something funny about that question?"

"Yes there is, actually, you will never believe the answer."

"Bradley acted like I knew him; he said something about how I never liked his politics. Was he a local politician or something, back before?"

"You don't have a clue, do you?" Mickey said with a grin.

"Apparently not, but I also don't have a lot of patience today either, so how about you just keep talking."

"Oh, you know him all right, the entire world knows him. He was our first Muslim president."

The shock left me befuddled for a minute. The guy he was talking about caused most of this mess. A Democrat, he was a one term congressman from Michigan before running for president. He was black, but we had elected a black man before. He was also a proud Muslim. So many fools voted for him for that reason alone. A lot of neighbors and half my family said they voted for him because they "wanted to be part of history." They said that it was time to show we were beyond the hate. That it was "their turn." Never mind that they voted against his opponent because he was a devout Christian.

It was an odd campaign, to say the least. The press pounded the Republican because of his Christian faith, but when anybody brought up the fact that the Democrat was a Muslim, one with radical Islamic views, they screamed that religion was off the table. They called the opposition bigots, racists and worse. In the end, the smooth-talking Khalid al-Hazmi became president of the United States and the slide into decay and ruin that had been happening for years rapidly accelerated.

Hell, he could never even prove he was born here so he probably wasn't even a legitimate president. But, by then the laws were pretty much being ignored by anybody in power and Article II of the United States Constitution was never enforced.

By the time his first term was over, the country was a mess. The Republicans were running a weak candidate, as they always did, but with unemployment high, the dollar in the toilet and three major wars going on, the

Muslim was not polling strong and it was thought he would lose. Then he came out of the closet as a gay man.

I'll never forget watching him read the speech off his teleprompter as he shocked the nation and the world. He said his wife and children were just part of an attempt to appease a bigoted and homophobic country and that while he loved them, he was not "in love" with his wife. He made the case that it was time to stop punishing people because of who they loved. He twisted the fact that he had lied to the nation so he became the victim, and somehow he was able to make it sound like he was noble in doing that. Once again, he pushed the buttons of guilt in this country's foolish voters and they gave him a second term.

His performance during his first term didn't seem to matter. The country was a shambles, but all that was important with our voters was to be politically correct. Well, that and his promise to give everybody something for nothing. Money, education, housing, whatever, he promised it all and it worked. By then the takers outnumbered the givers and most voters were too stupid and greedy to realize he had nothing to give them.

By the time his second term was over it was too late to save the country. We held another election and the token Republican easily won. A year later the radical Islamics executed the largest mass murder in American history. The American people, with the constant urging of the press, blamed the current president for all their troubles and a year after that, they stormed the White House.

Until now, nobody knew what had happened to al-Hazmi as he had traveled to Europe to make a speech the day after he left office and dropped out of sight.

CHAPTER 46

I broke out of my daze to realize that Mickey was still talking.

"I'll tell you something else. Everybody at the monastery and in town thinks he is the head honcho, but he is not. I noticed that he was getting messages almost daily and one night a car showed up about two in the morning. Three guys got out and went into his cabin. I sneaked closer and tried to listen from outside the window.

"He was clearly submissive to them and they were ordering him around like a hall monitor bosses a second grader. They were talking about you and they were pissed that you were still alive. From what I gathered, there are a bunch more guys on the East Coast they killed. I didn't know who you were at the time, but they were not happy you were alive. They also were pissed off about two brothers named Farnsworth who they were trying to have killed. They kept saying shit like you guys were the only obstacles left before they could launch their big plan. They were saying that they needed the population to be leaderless and running without a rudder before they offered them a choice. But, I never could hear what the choice was going to be."

"What was the big plan?"

"I don't know, I never could figure that out. But, from what I could tell they really were building up an army. They were talking about troop numbers and how many tanks and APCs they had coming on some ship. From what I gathered, they have about a thousand guys training and getting ready for something. I think the "something" is on hold until after you and the Farnsworth brothers are killed."

"Where is this army being held?" I asked.

"I don't know. All I could get was that it was someplace south of here."

"Did you recognize any of the three guys?"

"I did."

"Well then, spit it out," I said, trying hard not to let my temper get ahead of me.

"One was the president of Germany before the crash."

"They call them chancellors, not presidents," I said.

"Whatever, who cares. He was the guy on the television all the time shouting about how America was dragging the world down and how we should be stopped. I remember how my father would stare at the television and sometimes when he didn't know I was watching I would see tears in his eyes."

"Another was that Turkish asshole with all the money. You know the one who funded all the Democrat campaigns and put all that money into the left wing website? I can't remember his name."

"Robert Servro?"

"Yes, that's him. I can't put my finger on the last guy, but I think he is familiar. I know I saw him on television back before. But, I was just a kid then and never paid much attention to politics."

"Tell me what he looks like."

"He is probably in his sixties, but he is in great shape. He must spend time in the weight room, because he's pumped. His head is shaved and he has a gray goatee beard. He is not tall, about five-eight. His teeth are crooked and yellow. There is a big scar on one side of his face from a knife or something"

"Does he speak with an accent?"

"I could tell he was trying to hide it, but it slipped out now and then. Plus his syntax was off sometimes. Remember those old Rocky and Bullwinkle cartoons? You know the little short spy who had the tall, hot chick with him? He sounds almost like him when he slips up."

"Boris and Natasha, I remember them well. She was a hottie. Although, her head was too big. In fact, her character was the former Miss Transylvania. They were from a fictional place called "Pottsylvania" but everybody knew they were Russian. Remember, that show ran during the Cold War and the Russians were our mortal enemy.

"The guy sounds like he might be Mikael Gostrovavitch. He was the president of Russia for eighteen years until the people finally rose up and kicked him out. The news said he was killed, but nobody ever found a body.

"He was as corrupt as they come; even in Russia where corruption was a way of life, he was a snake. He was the head of the KGB in its last years and used that position as a stepping stone to make a run for president. After the election, he stayed in office for several more terms by bribery and intimidation

212

and if the rumors are true, murder. Russia claimed free elections, but it was a joke. I always thought he had some outside help to keep his job. Things always broke his way with the press. The UN, EU, Amnesty International . . . none of those fraudulent groups ever once made a claim of human rights violations.

"The U.S. sent that decrepit old potato-farming, former president to 'monitor' the elections and he declared them to be free and fair. But, the world knew they were not. Somebody was pulling the puppet strings, but I never could figure out exactly who.

"Once the world went to hell, Gostrovavitch seemed to almost give up willingly. In the old days he would have machine-gunned the people protesting in front of the Kremlin, but instead he let security lapse and all but invited them to storm the place. Of course the press reported it much differently, but back then the Internet was still up and running and the truth found a way for those willing to look for it.

"That is an odd mix of people. The German chancellor you mentioned is Norvan Heitzeman, and he and Gostrovavitch hated each other. I wonder what the hell they are doing together, especially with that lizard Servro."

"I'll tell you something else," Mickey said. "You know that big, guy you killed, Reggie?"

"What about him?"

"He is, or was, al-Hazmi's boyfriend. That skinny Muslim is going to be seriously pissed at you and believe me, he just ain't right.

"How so?" I asked.

"al-Hazmi runs around half naked most of the time with a big African shield and a little, short spear. He keeps ranting about how he is the reincarnation of some dude named Shaka Zulu. He looks ridiculous with those skinny arms and his sunken chest. He goes off on these rants about how he is going to fulfill the destiny that was denied this Shaka guy, only with the entire world, not just Africa. He was always talking about, join or die and the horn of the bull or some such shit. Said he was going to use the same tactics as Shaka to get things done."

"Shaka Zulu was the leader of the Zulus in South Africa in the early eighteen hundreds," I said.

"He was a brutal dictator who would invade a village and give the men a choice: join him or die. He meant it, too. Anybody who resisted was slaughtered. Before long word got ahead of him so every village just surrendered when he showed up and the men joined his soldiers. He amassed a huge army and used it to conquer a big part of Africa."

"Before him, warfare was almost a joke. They would hurl their spears and insults from a safe distance. Then they would pick up the spears and go home. Nobody got hurt very often. Shaka invented a big shield and a short spear called the 'iklwa,' which is pronounced to imitate the sound it made as you pulled it out of a body. He trained his guys to run in close and use that big shield to hook the edge of their opponent's shield and pull it away to expose their ribs. Then they stabbed the guy with the short spear.

"Shaka also came up with a military tactic that is used even in modern times called the horn of the bull, where the troops hook around the flanks of the enemy like the shape of a Cape buffalo's horns.

"He was a brutal, bloody son of a bitch who controlled a lot of southern Africa before he was done. He was also completely insane, a total nut job. After his mother died he ordered thousands of his own people killed to show his grief.

"He was a bastard child and they said he was picked on for having a small penis, but who knows what set him off? He killed a lot of people in his quest to rule the world as he knew it. His own half-brother finally killed him to stop him from murdering more of his own people."

"Well then, this guy is truly carrying on the legacy," Mickey said. "He gets crazy. More than once I watched him kill somebody with the spear for no reason. He tried with your brother, but missed. Bradley screamed like a little girl and ran away. Sarah grabbed al-Hazmi to stop him and I thought for minute he was going to stab her with that big knife on a stick. But she stood up to him. She is tough, I'll tell you that. They stood eye to eye for a long time before he backed down.

"He went into those rages without warning and I figured sooner or later it would be my turn. I planned to take that pig sticker away from him and shove it up his ass if he tried. I caught Reggie watching me look at him after al-Hazmi killed another guard for bumping into his shield and the next thing I knew I was out on that shit detail, watching the road."

CHAPTER 47

"Why do they have gasoline?" I asked. "They have trucks and generators that are running and we found some fresh gas on the truck we captured from them."

"The word is they took over a refinery in New Jersey and brought it back on line. They have some ships bringing in oil from overseas and they refine it into gas. Some of our trucks are diesel and they seem to have plenty of that as well. I know it keeps longer than gas, so I suppose it could be from back before. Nobody knew for sure, but I think they are making that, too."

"How in the hell are they getting stuff like Gatorade?"

"That I don't know, but I think they stored up a lot of food and supplies before things fell apart. My guess is they knew it was coming for a long time."

"What's with the tattoo I found on the guy trying to kill me? It was in German and said something about fidelity to the world for a greater good. Do you know anything about that?"

"They were constantly preaching to us about how they were going to create a new world order, how it would be for the greater good of mankind. One world government, stuff like that. They demanded our loyalty to that cause and a lot of guys bought into it. Not me, I have read enough history books to know where all that shit leads, but some of the guys were pretty desperate to belong to something. I guess it filled a hole in their psyche or some shit like that. Most of them came from bad backgrounds and crappy childhoods and these guys worked that, making out that they could be their new families, stuff like that. I played along because I had to, but I didn't get the tat. They were free for anybody who wanted one. The rumors were that they were going to be mandatory in a few weeks. Some of the guys liked how the Germans almost pulled off ruling the world in World War II, kind of a modern day skinhead thing, and they thought it would be cool to have their tat written in German. None of them that I knew spoke the language. I used to fuck with them, tell them I could read German and what it really said was, "I am gay and wish to suck dicks."

"You are talking about Americans, guys recruited from the gangs," I said. "But I heard some German being spoken I think, and I know one guy was screaming in French when I was in the shootout at the bridge,"

"They brought in some ex-special forces, former military types from Europe to help with our training. Actually, they were pretty pissed off after you killed most of them, because it messed up their plans for training the guys they recruited. I think that French guy was pretty important to them. He was an asshole, I hope you made him scream a lot before he died."

"What else do you know?"

"Not much, I pretty much told you everything. It's a lot, though, it should count for something. At least you know who is trying to kill you right now."

"How many more guys are there in Easton?"

"Where?"

"Easton, the town where you were staying before you went up to the monastery."

"So that's the name? They called it New Hope.

"I don't know for sure, but I think they were moving a lot of them south after I left. At least that's what I heard. When they sent us out to watch the roads there were only about twenty guys, I think that might be all that's left."

"Okay," I said. "You let me know if you think of anything else. I'll consider what you asked me to do and get back to you in a day or two."

I didn't think they would attack my place or try to kill or kidnap my family. That strategy had not worked too well for them so far. But, I had asked Jack to send word to my wife that I was okay and would be home as soon as possible. He had insisted on sending ten of his best guys to keep an eye on the place. I sent my wife a note to butcher a pig and to feed them well while they were there. Also, to make sure they had enough guns and ammo to get the job done.

Emily had cut open Bradley's arm and dug all the crap out of his wound. There were pieces of his jacket and shirt in there as well as some dirt and debris that he probably picked up while he was writhing on the floor after being shot. I looked at the wound and figured it was from a full metal jacket, non-expanding military style rifle bullet. That was a good thing, as they do far less damage than an expanding hunting bullet. Back before, the military had to use non-expanding bullets because of the agreement made at The Hague Convention of 1899, which outlawed expanding bullets for war.

Only politicians could come up with the concept that it's okay to shoot the enemy, but you must use bullets that don't hurt as much. Oddly enough, the military bullets are considered inhumane for hunting because they wound more often than kill. In Bradley's case it was a good thing; mine too, as the same type of bullet hit my shoulder. Like me, Bradley would heal with little permanent damage. If he had been hit with one of the violently expanding, hunting-style bullets most of us use now, he would have lost his arm and probably bled to death.

He was awake and doing a lot better. The infection was almost gone and he was healing. I was pretty sure Emily was going to cut his throat if he didn't get out of her house soon.

I was in her kitchen refereeing yet another squabble between them when Davy showed up with the sawed-off, redheaded cowboy and another military-looking guy. Davy and the redhead were both bloody and dirty. The other guy looked fine; clean, well groomed and with new clothes that looked a lot like the uniform the assholes who tried to kill me at the bridge were wearing. Not exactly the same, but close enough.

"This here is Pete," Davy said pointing to the red-haired guy in the cowboy boots.

"I know who he is," I said, while considering how I was going to rip his head off.

"Now don't go getting all growly on him. He ain't part of the problem. He was just given a message to take to you, that's all. He and I have already gone over that pretty extensively and I believe him. I might also note that he is a lot tougher than he looks. Seems he took offense to my accusing him and we had to discuss the issue back there beside the road."

"What are you telling me?" I asked. "That you couldn't whip that little shit? Why, he isn't much bigger than Emily."

"Well, of course I could whip him, the trouble is he wouldn't stay whipped. He kept getting up and whacking on me some more. He just would not quit. After four or five times of whipping him I got tired, so we agreed to call it a draw."

"Then why did you bring him here?" I asked.

"Well, you said you wanted to talk to him, so here he is, go ahead and talk."

"You gonna accuse me of being one of them assholes in Easton too?" the guy snarled. "Because I ain't taking any shit from you, either. I gave you a message, that's all; that don't make me one of them. I don't care who you are, if you call me a liar we are going to fight. I ain't afraid of you. Let's go outside so we don't mess up this lady's kitchen."

"Whoa there Pete, I didn't say a thing yet. I'll believe Davy when he says you are okay. But, I do want to talk. Can we do it here in the kitchen? It's a lot more comfortable sitting at the table than rolling around on the ground outside. Maybe Davy can get us some of that amber magic he keeps hidden away."

"You talking about whiskey? Thanks, but no thanks. That stuff affects my pleasant disposition and makes me surly. One drink and all I want to do is fight."

The guy sat down and Emily brought over some fresh milk and offered it to him.

"Now you're talking, this is a man's drink," he said while wiping the cream out of his moustache.

Davy poured a shot of bourbon for each of the rest of us, including Emily. Until now the other guy had not said a word.

"So, who are you?" I asked him.

"I am the guy who brought Pete the message," he replied.

"So then you are telling me that you are part of that outfit in Easton?

"Yes, I am."

My first thought was to draw my pistol and shoot the son of a bitch in the head, but it occurred to me that Davy must have had a reason for bringing him here.

"Okay, mister, right now I am listening and you better explain. You don't look dumb, but you just admitted to being part of the bunch that keeps trying to kill me. So, either you have a death wish – or, and I am guessing it's this one – you have a story to tell me. Spit it out."

"First a little background. I am, or was, part of the CIA. The name's Bob Smith.

"Ground rules," I interrupted. "One more lie and I shoot your balls off.

"Now that you know the rules, are you sure you didn't maybe misspeak about your name?"

"Nope, that's my name. No shit; I am a spook and that's my real name, the one my poor sainted momma gave me when I was born. Not even Robert, just Bob, no middle name, Smith. Kind of ironic, don't you think?"

"Yeah, it's fuckin' hilarious," I said. "But, you haven't told me much of anything that will prevent me from shooting you in the face yet, so keep talking."

"Okay," he said, backing his chair away from me a few inches. "At least we have upgraded the target from my testicles to my face. That's progress.

"We were keeping an eye on those guys well before it all turned to shit. After it did, I just stuck around hoping that sooner or later I could find a way to stop this madness.

"I was working for Servro while in deep cover. I could see what they were doing, but the problem was nobody would listen to me back at Langley. It was just too much for them to believe. I could have gone over their heads, but I didn't know who to trust, so many in the government were part of it I didn't think I could trust anybody. Probably my boss was deep in it and that's the real reason he ignored my reports. I just don't know.

"A lot of the problem was most of the guys I was working with were career bureaucrats and their goal was not to stop crimes, but to fly under the radar until they could retire. The top brass were political appointees who were probably in on the deal. Or at least they answered to the guys who were in on it. I didn't dare talk to them, so I just kept it in the chain of command. That way, my ass was covered. It's not that I embraced their thinking about CYA, but in my line of work if you color outside the lines somebody will shoot you. Some of the guys had to be honest, but most of them said they didn't believe me because it was too big to accept. I think it was mostly the fact that if they acted it would have ended their careers. You know how it was back then. The only jobs around were with the government and nobody dared rock the boat. Those assholes I worked for thought they could ride it out and let the next guy deal with the problem. The dumb shits let them end the world instead."

"What the hell are you talking about?" I asked.

"Sorry, I have been living with this for so long I forget that most people don't know. They did this on purpose."

"Did what?"

"This! Everything. The end of the dollar, the end of our government, the world collapse. It was all part of the plan, it just got away from them."

"Whoa, slow down. This was all planned?"

"Well not all of it, like I said it got out of control. They thought they were the smartest people in the world, but in the end they were not. They really had no idea what they were doing. Among other things, they forgot about the human factor. They never counted on people reacting like they did. Riots in the streets, shit like that. But, yes, it was all planned. At least the economic part of it was."

"By who?"

"Well, it's my understanding that you know about four of them, Khalid al-Hazmi, Robert Servro, Norvan Heitzeman and that asshole Mikael Gostrovavitch. There were six more at the start.

"Who were the others?"

"Mohammad Abdul Khaliq, for one."

"The Saudi Arabian king? He's dead. He was killed in a plane crash."

"Yes, I know. I crashed it."

"Why?"

"Following orders."

"Whose orders?"

"Servro's."

"Why? I thought you said they were partners. I also thought you said you worked for the CIA. Why were you murdering people under Servro's orders?"

"They were, and I did. The King got greedy, so the partnership dissolved. I got orders to take him out from Servro and the CIA approved. The King was a very bad man, responsible for a lot of dead people, I did the world a favor. It was one order I didn't mind following.

"Also, there was Claudious Dumbaba."

"The Secretary General of the United Nations?"

"The same."

"Did you kill him, too?"

"No, but I know the guy who did."

"Any others I would recognize?"

"You know them all."

One by one he listed world leaders, all dead.

"I only killed the one, but Servro was behind all the deaths except one. Your own president. He was part of the plan and Servro was going to have him murdered. But, before he could, he was killed just like you think he was. The American people beat him to death in the streets and hung his sorry carcass from a tree. They had no idea how guilty he really was. So was that bitch he was married to, although she was not one of them. She knew; she wanted the power and never lifted a finger to stop it."

"What about the U.S. Senate Majority Leader Nancy Boxmier? You named her. She was also ripped apart by a mob of people."

"That was our mob. She was a target.

"That dumb bitch should have been removed from the gene pool years earlier. Letting her breed was a mistake."

"So her kid, the congressman from Georgia, was part of it too?"

"No, he was too stupid to be part of anything except his five hundred dollar haircuts and his hookers. He just happened to be standing beside his mommy when the mob showed up. Fortunately he didn't breed, well at least not officially, so the bloodline ended when he died."

"The four who are left had a pact from the start. It was always going to be just them and I think the killing is done. At least the 'them killing each other' part. The real killing is just getting started."

CHAPTER 48

I pulled my .45 from my belt holster and pointed it at his head while I pushed the safety into the off position.

"We still have a problem here," I said.

"You admitted giving Pete the message. That was intended to lure me out so I could be killed. You fucked up, buddy."

"I figured you would take it that way. But, how about holding off on pulling the trigger until you have heard me out. Deal?"

"Okay, but I think I'll leave my gun out. Davy, please check him for a gun."

"Already done, big dog," Davy said as he showed me a Smith & Wesson M&P pistol.

"Nice choice," I said.

"Thanks."

"Look, I gave it to Davy without him asking, as a gesture of good faith. I need you guys, hell everybody needs you guys."

I looked at Davy who nodded a "yes."

"Okay," I said, lowering the gun and putting the safety back on, but keeping it on the table in my hand, "this does seem a bit obvious and I can't believe you are that stupid. So again, continue to explain why I shouldn't shoot you."

"I did deliver the message, but I didn't know they wanted to kill you. In fact, I never found out until after you guys shot up the place a few days ago. Like your idiot brother, I thought they just wanted to talk with you.

"Sorry, I didn't mean to insult your brother, that kind of just slipped out."

"It's okay, sometimes he really is an idiot."

"I suspected what was going on, but didn't know they planned to murder you or anybody else until just recently. I gathered as much info as I could, but when it was clear they were starting to suspect me I took off and headed here.

People they don't like tend to have very bleak futures. I took a truck, but ran out of gas two miles short of getting here. So I started walking."

"I ran into Davy about a mile farther down the road. I first noticed him when he put a rifle bullet between my feet."

"Normally I would have put it between your eyes," Davy said. "But I was tired and couldn't hold the rifle high enough."

"He was sitting there with Pete, wiping blood off his face and trying to catch his breath," Bob continued. "That's when I offered my gun and told him that we needed to talk. The bottom line is these guys have some very nasty stuff planned if we don't do something to stop them."

"It seems to me," I said, "based on what you have told us, they have already done some pretty nasty stuff. Did you miss the social wars? Maybe you didn't notice the people starving to death or freezing in the winters? Or the shit the gangs did to people? You knew they were planning this?"

"Well the truth is, I pretty much planned it. Not everything, I am a money guy, so I helped with the events that led to the economic crash. That's why they trusted me, I knew stuff. Some of it the CIA was feeding to me, but I am pretty good with world trade and economics. "The thing is, I never believed it would be implemented. The plan was to keep feeding them rope and then when the time was right, to choke them with it. Dummy me, I actually thought the system would work, that my bosses would listen to me and the government would step in before anything bad happened. I was wrong and I live with that every single day of my life."

He stopped a moment and looked down at the table, clearly trying to get a grip on his emotions. Davy and I just sat and waited for him. After a bit he continued.

"Trust me on this, it's going to get even worse. This was about taking over the world. I know that sounds like Saturday morning cartoon, mad scientist, James Bond shit, but it's true. They wanted to destroy the world economy so they could introduce a world currency as a first step to a world government. One with them running the show, of course. It was never going to be about wars and famine, just a new form of money. Remember that's how they started the European Union, it was just going to be a common currency. But, it turned into a lot more than just the money. They used the EU as a model; first get the world on a common currency and then gradually gain control until they were in charge of a one-world government. They had a ten-year plan that could have worked. The problem is they were not as smart as they thought they were. They lost control. It got away from them and millions died."

"This is hard to believe," I said. "The truth is, the factors that led to the crash went on for decades. The creep of socialism in our schools and government, the escalating debt, the entitlement programs, the decline of public education. The Islamic attacks. Are you telling me that was all part of a big master plan?"

"The attacks were done by some useful idiots. They had backing, but not from these guys. As far as I know, the rest was just the decline of society and nobody planned it. At least not one big central plan. I think that lots of smaller groups planned portions of it. But, mostly it was just a free society following the same path to destruction that every free society in history has walked. These guys saw it happening and recognized it as a big opportunity. They helped it along in the last few years, here in the U.S. and in Europe, Russia and several other places. For example, the Fed printing all that money? The president and Congress spending us into unprecedented debt? Greece going bankrupt? It was all part of the plan. Once the major economies of the world crashed, the rest just followed.

"But then it all fell apart. They couldn't control the events as they unfolded. They never gave up on the idea of running the world. They just formulated a new plan. This one is a bit desperate and is going to be very bloody.

"That's why it's taken so long to get started again. They wanted to wait for things to get bad, for people to be suffering. That way they would grasp at any straw handed to them. I suppose, too, they waited for a lot of people to be dead, because with fewer numbers it's easier to take control.

"Now they have a plan to bring it back to them. It's no longer just a plan to control the economies of the world, that ship has sailed. So they regrouped and decided to use force to gain control of the world, starting with the eastern United States. Once they have full control, then they will rebuild the economy. Or at least that's their plan. Me? I think that once again they'll ignore the human factor in the mix and they will fail. But as a result, the world will remain a dark and dismal place for a long, long time. Even if they succeed, the world will not be a good place. These guys will make horrible dictators. I see only misery and death."

"So how are they going to do this world domination thing?" I asked. "Every evil dictator in the movies had a master plan, so they must have one too."

"Theirs is pretty simple and pretty antiquated. Well, at least the idea is old and antique, but it's worked before. They think this time they can use it on a global scale. They figure the timing is right. The world has never been weaker or more vulnerable than it is right now. They believe the conditions are perfect for them to take over.

"They have built a small army by recruiting from the gangs in the remains of the American cities. They scrounged up a few ex-military types from Europe and Russia to train them. But, you killed most of them. They don't need a lot of men to start, because they also have a plan to grow the army exponentially. They are going to use the same strategy as Shaka Zulu. Join or die.

"I heard," I told him. "That's old news around here."

"Yeah? Well, I didn't know about that until a couple of days ago. I didn't realize it until the end, but they have been keeping me out of the loop for several months. I guess they didn't trust me as much as I thought, or maybe they finally smelled a rat. I stuck around, mostly because I didn't know what else to do. Now I need your help.

"I am kinda in over my head here, guys. I can't do this alone."

"Keep talking, we will let you know," I said.

"Anyway, the new strategy was to remove the top guys in the communities first so the people would be leaderless. The idea was that without strong leaders they would be disillusioned, fractured and divided. That would make them easier to convince. They have been taking out people all over the East Coast. They started with the weakest first and planned to end with those of you who were strongest. But, you monkey wrenched all that."

"Well, excuse me, if I had known how important it was to kill me I might have had a different view of things. Take one for the team and all that."

"Yeah, I guess somebody should have taken the time to explain it all to you before they started shooting," Bob chuckled.

"The communities that have survived and done well all had strong leaders," he continued. "Leaders who inspired them to fight the hordes during the social wars and later the gangs. Leaders who showed people how to trade and barter. Leaders who helped set up structure and governments. But, these guys didn't want any leadership. They know a leader that people respect will inspire them to fight, even for what appears to be a lost cause. Hell, just look at the American Revolution. Fight the British? That's insane, they could not be defeated. But we tried anyway, didn't we?

"These guys listened to their military advisers when they told them if anybody fights back, it will not only slow the sweep, which depends on speed and swiftness, but it might also inspire the next town to mount a defense. From there it would snowball and pretty soon they'd have a war on their hands.

"The last thing they want is a war and they believe that success depends on moving fast to control the entire eastern side of the continent as quickly as possible. They will not give anybody time to think, only time to act. With the leaders dead and the options gone, they figure the people will be intimidated and would join rather than die.

"They were going to wait until winter, so they could build and train the army some more and so that the people would be cold and hungry. But, I guess when they found about the Farnsworths' plan to bring the seven strongest community leaders all together and form a new government they panicked and started killing everybody. Still, it might have worked except you screwed up their plans by not getting killed and then warning the Farnsworths, who, I presume, are now in hiding.

"They are adaptable and I overheard the new plan before I took off. They are going to hit some of the communities where they already killed the leaders. They figure to wipe out everybody in the first few, hoping that word will spread that they are ruthless and mean it when they say join or die, even though the first several towns will never actually have the option, they will just die. As the terror spreads, they will begin to offer the deal, with the hopes that a few towns will want to fight so they can wipe them out too and make a point, teach a lesson. Have a "teachable moment" as that crazy African likes to say. They want the word to spread and the fear to start brewing and poisoning the social fabric of the people. They want so deep a feeling of hopelessness that the people will believe the only way to survive will be to surrender. That way there is little resistance. If they hit hard, move fast, they grow in numbers with each community that joins. The army grows and the territory expands, then it will fracture off into several armies that will all grow as they expand their territory. According to their plan, in three months they will control the entire East Coast. Then they hit Canada, the West Coast and Mexico. They plan to blockade the Central and Western states controlled by China and starve them out. Once they have North America under control and an economy established, they believe the rest of the world will follow. It if will not, they'll take the horror show on the road, starting with Europe.

"I am not saying it will work or even that they are sane, but I am saying they are going to do this and a lot of people are going to die. If they do succeed, I don't think the world will be a nice place to live in the future.

"They are not having much luck killing you, so they are initiating the plan and leaving you for last. They believe, and I think they are right, that by the time they get to this part of Vermont they will be so strong that they will just wipe you out without breaking a sweat.

"Maybe we can stop them, but I need your help. Some very bad shit is about to hit the fan. If you shoot me, I won't be much help to you. How about we talk a deal? You help me stop these bastards, then after we do that you can shoot me if you still want to.

"In fact, I'll supply the bullet."

CHAPTER 49

"Well, suppose we agree," Davy said. "They have an army, we are just a few guys. Besides, we don't even know where they are keeping that army."

"I do," Pete said.

I noticed that Emily had brought him a homemade donut.

"Where?"

"P-Town."

"Where the hell is pee-town," I asked?

"Massachusetts you dumb shit. Provincetown, out on the tip of Cape Cod. Didn't you go to school?"

"Pete, I am starting to see why you get into so many fights."

"It's 'cuz people don't like my red hair, that's why."

"How do you know where they are?"

"Hell, traveling on that train I know where everybody is and what they are doing. When the train is moving we ain't got nothing to do but talk. Everybody knows everybody else's business. Gathering up a thousand men and a bunch of tanks and shit is not something you can hide for long. A buddy of mine was out in his boat fishing for stripers between rides and he saw them. Damn, them fish are good eating too. I traded fifty shotgun shells for one he caught and consider it a bargain. Grilling them is best, on account of they are a little greasy ... "

I cut him off before he got too far into his fish cooking story and lost focus.

"Why there?"

"Well, the way I hear it that peckerhead al-Hazmi used to go there for vacation afore he was president. Didn't take his wife with him, neither. It wasn't a female-friendly kind of place, if you catch my drift.

"It's way out on the tippy-tip of the land where it's pretty skinny and I guess he thinks that the roads are easy to defend. I think they did something to make a harbor so the ships from Europe can bring in the tanks and guns and shit like that."

"Okay," I said, "one problem solved. But the other one is a lot bigger. We are just a few guys."

"And one girl," Sarah piped up from the other room.

"Two," Emily said. "You need a medic and I have a gun."

"No matter," I continued, "there are not enough of us. We could try to raise our own army, but most guys will not leave their families unprotected while they rush off to tilt at windmills. Nor will I ask them to. It would be suicide for all of us. Besides, by the time we got everybody organized, equipped and trained, they would get word and head out to meet us. They have tanks, most of us just have a rifle. Only a fool brings a rifle to a tank fight."

The room was quiet as everybody thought about the situation.

"Right now this looks hopeless," I said, "But, let's not give up, let's use our brains, there has to be a way."

"There is," Bob said. "We nuke them."

"Oh sure," Pete said. "Or better yet, Bobby, why don't you call in the mother ship and have them hit the place with a plasma ray?"

"Besides, where're we going to get a nuke? They have been gone from the face of the earth for several years now. I might be wrong, but you said you were a money guy. Do you also have a degree in whatever the shit you need to build a bomb, too? Because if you do, great, I'll just tell Sammy Farnsworth to start keeping his eye on the lookout for some extra plutonium. That way you can build us a bomb and we are good to go."

Emily started giggling and she turned red. The rest of us just stared at Pete. I thought he was the most combative person I had ever met in my life, but he was kind of growing on me.

Then again, cancer and fungus can both grow on a person too.

"Work with me here," Bob said. "For the sake of argument, let's say I can produce a nuclear bomb that we can deliver. Would you use it?"

"It seems pretty brutal," Emily said.

"It's a brutal world," I replied. "What they have planned for us is brutal."

"Let's put it in context. We would not hesitate to go after them with rifles. Dead is dead, what difference does it make how it happens?"

"This is the same dilemma that Truman faced with Japan," Pete said.

"No it's not," I replied. "He was faced with wiping out cities full of innocent people, we are just talking about killing those who want to kill us and a lot of other people. His was a much harder decision.

"Truman knew that dropping those bombs would end the war and save hundreds of thousands of lives, many of them American lives. It is also often neglected when discussing his decision that Japan started the war. If they had left us alone and not attacked Pearl Harbor, they probably would not have been nuked. Truman made the right choice, but this is different.

"We are talking about a military target," I continued, "one that has been constructed for the sole purpose of killing us and taking over the world. Even if we take out the selfish context of all of us wishing to live a little longer, it's still an evil force that will do great damage to the rest of the world. We have a moral obligation to stop them and to protect the people who cannot protect themselves. We have no way to stop them right now. But, if we are given one, I think it would be in our best interest and in the best interest of what remains of the world to take that option."

"Couldn't we just warn them that we have the bomb and tell them that if they don't cut this shit out we will use it?" asked Sarah.

"What's to prevent them from hunting us down with an overwhelming force, then killing us and taking the bomb away?" Bob asked.

"We could hide the bomb."

"We could, but then they could still kill us. With us dead, the bomb is no longer a threat because there would be nobody to use it against them. There are a lot more of them than there are of us. We would not stand a chance against that many men. Especially if they have tanks and other heavy weapons. I think we all know that trying to reason with these people is not a viable option."

"*Are you people insane?*" Bradley roared as he stumbled into the room. "*You are talking about the deaths of thousands of human beings here.*"

"They plan to kill thousands themselves," Davy said.

"Then they will have to live with that."

"What, you think it will bother their conscience? You think that is somehow a fitting punishment? You are one whack-a-doodle nut case. I am not going to let anybody kill me or Sarah, or even you, just so they can suffer a guilty conscience. Those guys are stone cold killers who think they have a right to kill other people. Do you think Stalin or Pol Pot had trouble sleeping at night?"

Davy was just getting warmed up. He stood up and took a couple of steps toward Bradley. Bradley's eyes went wide with fear, but to his credit, he didn't back down.

"You are a complete head case," Davy continued. "They already killed your son and your wife, now you will let them kill you and Sarah too? What the fuck is wrong with you? You must have taken a lot of drugs when you were younger to have a brain that is this fucked up."

"They didn't kill Samantha or Brent, street gangs did that."

"You fool, can't you see it was a setup?" Davy was shouting now. His face was red and his eyes were bulging.

"They came sweeping in at the last minute and rescued you and Sarah, right? You think that just happened? The people who killed your wife and son worked for the people who you think 'rescued' you and Sarah. They probably all went out for a drink after they were done and had a good laugh at how easy it was to fool you. How much will it take to get that through your thick head? They sacrificed your wife and son just so they could use Sarah as bait to lure your brother in and kill him. They have no respect or regard for any human life.

"Look at your arm, you have a bullet hole through it and they tried to put a lot more in you. How fucking blind can you be? For Christ's sake, Reggie flat-out told you that you were set up, that it was all a lie and then he tried to shoot you. How are you even alive? Nobody can be this stupid and still have enough brain power to remember to breathe."

Bradley stood there for a minute and then burst into tears, collapsing on the floor.

"Aw shit, now he is going to cry like a little kid. How in the hell did this guy survive this long?"

Emily and Sarah helped Bradley stand up and tried to move him back to his bedroom, but he shook them off.

"Do you have any idea what it's like to have your entire belief system collapse around you?" Bradley shouted.

He was blubbering and smearing a mixture of tears and snot around his face with his hands.

"Do you know what it's like to have your whole world turn into a lie overnight?

"This was all I had, it defined me, I couldn't be wrong. To admit I was wrong would be to cease to exist. I hoped if I ignored it, the situation would sort itself out, then I would be right again. I believed in al-Hazmi. I voted for him, I campaigned for him. I thought he was dead and when he showed up on my doorstep to tell me he had a plan to save the world I believed in him. I was honored that he wanted me to be part of it."

"So, little brother," I said softly. "What changed your mind?"

"I have known deep inside that I was wrong for a while. But, I laid there in bed listening to Bob tell you about the army and it started to come together. I always knew in my core that al-Hazmi believed that non-violence was the only way. I had rationalized his thing with the spear as just a manifestation of the great pressure he was enduring. But building an army, importing tanks and guns from Europe? That was cold and calculating. I started to see that he is not who I thought he was.

"Believe it or not, I never made the connection with Samantha and Brent until Davy so eloquently pointed it out. That was the turning point. It just clicked in my head, that they were callously murdered by those assholes just to manipulate me. What's worse is that it worked. How could I be so stupid?

"I am not going to lose Sarah too. You get a bomb and nuke those motherfuckers. In fact, I'll push the button myself. I would rather burn in hell than lose her. I still don't believe in taking another human's life. But I think it would be a stretch to call those bastards human."

CHAPTER 50

I poured another few fingers of Davy's bourbon and wandered out the door. The sun was setting and twilight was working its magic glow. This is my favorite time of day and I sought out a big maple tree that was some distance from the house to sit under and think.

I was sitting on the ground, leaning back against the tree with my eyes closed. I was enjoying the glow from the drink and the smell of springtime in Vermont. We had a big problem, but for now I didn't want to think about it. There would be time enough for that. Right now I wanted to just be alive and enjoy that simple pleasure.

I didn't hear Bob as he approached on the matted grass. But, I sensed his presence, yanked my 1911 from the holster and pushed off the safety as I pointed it in his direction. Back when I was competing I could draw and shoot in one second, but when my life is on the line the motivation makes me even faster.

"Will you stop pointing that fucking cannon at me," Bob demanded. "I am getting pretty sick of looking down that road culvert of a barrel. I told you that you can shoot me later if you like, but for now keep the thing out of my face, okay?"

"Well then you would do well to announce your approach in the future," I said. "I don't hear all that well and if you surprise me I get a bit territorial."

He sat down against the smaller tree a few feet away. For a long time he said nothing, then, quietly; "I do have one, you know."

"One what?"

"A bomb. A nuclear bomb. A suitcase bomb. Actually, I have three."

"Impossible," I replied. "The verification process was foolproof. After that little shit in Iran did his thing we got rid of every bomb in the world. Don't insult me."

"I am not trying to, but don't be naive either. You don't seriously think there was full compliance, do you?"

"Actually, yes I do. I am the last guy to trust any government, but that plan was brilliant. There was no way to beat it, no way to hide a bomb."

"There was if nobody knew you had it. If it never existed, they couldn't very well find it, now could they?"

"What are you saying?"

"Think about who I worked for. You don't seriously think that every weapon the government ever produced was 'on the record,' do you? I was a 'go to' guy, the guy who got stuff done, the guy who found what couldn't be found and the guy who knew how to keep it all off the books. The CIA was never on board with the idea of getting rid of all the nukes. It was our superior arsenal that kept America the top super power for years. The concept of mutual destruction kept the war from happening, but mostly it was the fact that for every one they could hit us with, we could hit them with ten. That was our strength. Like my buddy T. R. used to say, 'walk softly, but carry a big stick.' Those nukes were our big stick. Hell, by the time the Democrats got done trashing our military, it was our only stick."

"So, how'd you do it?"

"Easy, we made our own bombs. It wasn't a big deal to find a Korean guy willing to trade an easy rest of his life in the tropics for a year's work. I found the materials on the black market. There was a lot of shit available from the Middle East back then if you had the money. I had a blank check for an account filled with taxpayer money, so I didn't even haggle. We set the Korean up with a lab and he made us five bombs. We had a couple of American experts watch over him to make sure they were done right. Hell, we even tested one of them up in the Arctic."

"You said you have three. He made five; you tested one, where is the other one?"

"Ah, now we are getting to a big part of why I don't sleep so well at night. Actually, we tried that bluffing thing. Well, some of my co-workers did. It didn't work out all that well. They are fertilizer now and we lost the bomb."

"That can't be good. Any idea where it is?"

"Yup, I found it again."

"Yeah, where?"

"On a truck in Easton, packed up and ready to head to P-Town. That was two days ago, so I suspect it's already on site."

"Any idea what they plan to do with it?"

"Yup."

"Care to enlighten me?"

"Well, they want to make a big splash right? Scare the shit out of people, make sure they knuckle under? What better way?"

"I figured that, but where?"

"Well Vermont doesn't have anything they need. No natural resources to speak of and the farmland is marginal. In the last years your only marketable product was tourism. Not much call for ski vacations these days. But, Vermont does have one big pain in their ass that they need to get rid of. Blowing this place up makes the statement they need to make and it makes sure you and Davy and company don't bother them again."

"Well then," I said as I drained my glass. "We can't let that happen now, can we? Just where is this bomb of yours and how do we get it?"

"You ever spend any time up in what they call the Northeast Kingdom of Vermont?"

"Of course, lots."

"You know about that nice, winding, paved road behind the locked gate that takes you to the abandoned buildings on top of the mountain?"

"Yup, I used to moose hunt off that road before they locked the gate. The site was a radar base back in the Cold War. But, they say it didn't work right, something about the terrain or the magnetic interference from all the granite. I never could get a straight story about why, but they abandoned it pretty fast. Only the government would build a big, wide, paved road to the top of the mountain to a radar site that didn't work."

"That was never any radar site," Bob said. "Those buildings were abandoned the day they were finished."

CHAPTER 51

"I always thought that place had to be a cover for something," I said. "The federal government's approach to failure would have been to keep pouring money into the site for years."

"It's a missile silo. They are not all in the West, we have plenty in the East. A lot of them are in the cities, right up the center of the skyscrapers. The dumb shits that did it never knew, but when they took out the Twin Towers they buried two ICBMs with nuclear warheads. Why do you think we were so eager to start the clean up? We had to get them out of there.

"Same thing with the federal building that white supremacist supposedly hit in Iowa City. Although, that was our own president ordering the bombing to take the heat off the corruption scandal that was about to take him down. It worked too, got him reelected. But the dumb shit forgot there was a nuke in the building and nobody had the balls to remind him. That's why we had bull-dozers in there within hours to clean up the mess.

"Anyway, we have them all throughout the country hidden in all kinds of places. The people who picked the sites were pretty creative. Another one is in Eldorado, Texas. Maybe you have heard of it?"

"As a matter of fact, I have."

"Probably because of that weird Mormon offshoot cult that was there. Remember they put the leader, Warren Jeffords in jail for raping underage girls? It was all over the news for months, back before."

"I remember. But, I know about Eldorado because I have been there many times. In fact, I actually took a photo of that pedophile son of a bitch inside the compound when he was hiding in there.

"I was in town deer hunting on a nearby ranch. After lunch one day we drove over to the compound gate to check the place out and snap some souvenir photos. I had just focused my camera when he walked through my viewfinder.

The FBI stopped my truck a couple of miles down the road and tried to confiscate my camera. We had one hell of an argument. I finally let them download the digital files. They got some good deer hunting photos off that SD card.

The photo proved he was there and let them get a warrant. The trouble was, he had seen me and he was smart enough to bug out, so they missed him. They caught him in Canada as I recall, about a year later; put his ass in jail forever.

"I did a lot of hunting there, deer and turkeys, but I shot a few rattlesnakes too. That's rough country and the snakes loved it. I am guessing the missile silo is that huge abandoned radar station you can see from just about anywhere in town, the big triangle-looking thing?"

"You would think so, but no, that really was a radar site. It never worked right. Just like you said, the government dumped money into it for years before claiming satellite technology made it obsolete so they could save face and abandon the site.

"The missile silo was the church the cult built. The one they thought would levitate when God ended the world. Little did they know!

"We made a deal with Jeffords, but he got arrogant and tried to sell the plans to the Chinese, so we took him down. I heard he starved in prison after the guards abandoned their duties."

"I can't generate much sympathy for a traitor who would sell out his country," I said quietly as I stared at my empty glass.

"He was guilty as hell of the rape charges too. He loved his little girls. But, we needed him so the government looked the other way for years."

"Let me guess," I said. "Using the old silo helped you slide past the global radiation detection satellites? I thought they were foolproof."

"They were, but all those sites have some residual radiation. We shielded the living shit out of the bombs. It's not possible to completely block the radiation from the satellites, but if we could make the levels match the residual levels, it washed out and the satellites didn't detect anything abnormal.

"As you know, they created a world map of radiation sites: hospitals, dump zones, power plants, etc. If the level of radiation changed with any of them, the satellites sent out a warning. So we had to get it perfect, which was not as hard as it sounds. But, it's the reason we blew up one bomb."

Those radiation-detecting satellites had been key to the entire program. They even found all the nuclear bombs that had disappeared during the breakup of the former Soviet Union. Most of them were in the Middle East. The technology was amazing. It could find anything giving off more radiation than a watch dial. With the use of super computers they were able to map the world. The side benefit was that they also helped to locate a lot of previously unknown uranium deposits. That drove down the price and it was thought that we could build more nuclear power plants to supply electricity to the world and the energy crisis would end. But, the environmental nut jobs tied it all up in court for years and then after the world collapsed it didn't matter anyway.

"So why did you waste a bomb?" I asked.

"Blowing shit up is fun," Bob said with a laugh. "You never outgrow that. Real men love to blow things up, but blowing up stuff with a nuke is the ultimate. I'll tell you, it was a rush watching that thing go off.

"But the real reason we blew it up was because we could only find four suitable sites to hide the bombs from the satellites, so we had to get rid of one of the bombs. The satellites picked up on the blast of course, but I blamed it on the Koreans trying to dispose of a bomb they failed to register."

"I remember that," I said. "It caused quite an international incident, we almost had a war."

"Almost only counts in horseshoes and hand-grenades. Besides, that little puke, Kim Dum Shithead, who was running the place needed to be taught a lesson. Notice we didn't have any trouble from him after that?

"Anyway, I have one of the nukes hidden in the Kingdom. I need you to help me recover it and save the world."

"Cue the theme from James Bond!"

It was Davy who said that. He had sneaked in behind without either of us noticing. It pissed me off, but it pissed Bob off even more.

"How come you don't yank out that big pistol and point it at him like you do me?"

"Well, mostly because he shoots back and you don't have a gun."

"Yeah, well, I think it's time you gave it back to me. I am feeling kind of exposed here."

Davy stepped in between us.

"Just for the record guys, nobody is going anywhere without me. I haven't had any fun lately and I am in favor of a road trip. Actually, I have that rig the assholes donated to us ready to go. I changed the oil, topped off all the fluids and filled the tanks with some of that nice fresh gasoline they gave us. I loaded ten more five-gallon cans for spare fuel, plenty of guns and ammo and a candy bar just in case the old guy here starts to get grumpy when his blood sugar gets low."

CHAPTER 52

It was a two hundred mile round trip and we discussed at great length how to approach it. Bob argued for having one of Jack's armored trucks clear the way, while Davy thought the speed and agility of the APC we captured would be much better alone. In the end Davy won out and at first light the next morning, the three of us headed north.

We left Mickey handcuffed to the bed with a chamber pot and a sincere promise to behave. Bradley was still not doing well, so he was in bed. Sarah was madder than hell that she couldn't come along. But, I pointed out that Emily needed somebody who could protect the place. I left her with her guns and a very bad attitude. I also walked in on her and Davy kissing goodbye in the garage. Now that Bradley was in a killing mood, I hoped he didn't catch them too.

I didn't know where Pete wandered off to; he had left with Jack hours ago and Emily had been moping around ever since. It was getting like a goddamned soap opera around there and I needed to get the hell out.

We ran into several washed out sections of road as we traveled through the mountains. Most had been half-assed filled in by nature or some locals so we could make it across with the four-wheel drive truck. Others we could go around where somebody had cut trees to open a path through the woods. We did get hung up once at the bottom of a deep washout when the angle from down to up was so steep the truck just breeched between the two. We used the winch mounted on the front to pull the truck up and out of the hole. In one spot we had to use the chainsaw I had the foresight to include (now that we had gas again) to drop a couple of trees across a ravine so we could cross, using them as a bridge. Jack's trucks could never have made it through most of those places. Besides, on the open road we could run at a much higher speed than

Jack's overweight armored trucks, so I was very impressed with this vehicle and felt like we made the right choice.

Until we hit the first roadblock. It was about thirty miles out, just before the last town we had to cross before we hit the old Interstate 91 highway north. Most of the towns we had passed through were empty, with only a few people on the streets. While everybody was armed, nobody gave us any problems. Most pretended they didn't see us, but a few waved. Of course, the fact that Davy had painted "*The 14th is Back in Business! Vermont is Getting it Done Again!*"in big, bright red letters on both sides and on the hood might have given them a clue we were the good guys.

Then we ran into trouble.

We sat back about a quarter-mile, checking it out with binoculars. Somebody had piled a bunch of rocks, trees and old telephone poles in the road. We could see several armed men behind the barricade, waiting. After about ten minutes one guy came around the pile of debris and started waving for us to come forward.

"What do you think," Bob asked? "Is it a trap?"

"No," I laughed, putting my binoculars down between the seats. "I know that guy, it's okay. Just go ahead slow and easy."

Once we moved close enough to shout, I asked Bob to stop the truck and I stuck my head out the window.

"Hey buddy," I shouted at the guy holding an AR-15 rifle. "You had your ass kicked in a pistol match lately?"

"I know that voice," he said, "the answer is 'no,' and you never beat me even on your best day. Come on down here. How the hell are you? More important, what are you doing out here?"

"We're on a mission from God."

"Yeah, well the last time we met, you looked a lot more like Belushi than Aykroyd. This stuff's been good for you. You have lost weight, you look good."

"Look, I can't tell you much now, but if it works out I'll explain later. Right now we gotta get up the Interstate to the Kingdom. What's with the road block?"

"As you probably remember we had some guys come up and talk with your people about how to handle security a few years ago. We did what you suggested and we thought we had the bandit problem licked, but it's started again. This worked before, so we are using it again. Back then we stopped them from coming into town. Most just turned back, those that didn't we dumped in the river. I don't know what's got the problem stirred up again, but this time they have better guns and they look a little cleaner. To be honest, they seemed more like a scouting party than bandits. I think they were testing our defenses rather than looking for loot. That was about a week ago. We haven't seen anybody since, but you know it's like Jefferson said, 'the price of freedom is eternal vigilance,' so here we still are.

"You know anything about those guys?"

"Yup, a little. That's a bad bunch. We have had a few run-ins with them ourselves and it's gotten pretty bloody. The truth is, that's exactly what they were doing, checking you out. They will be back. The good news is that it's going to be a while. The bad news is that when they do they will be bringing very big guns and a lot of their buddies, unless we can stop them first. Keep your eyes open and don't believe anything anybody but me tells you. With luck, they will be gone soon."

"Need any help?"

"Not right now, but keep the offer on the table, because I might later. How many guys you got?"

"Well, I have about twenty-five people who can fight, but they are not all guys. Six of them are girls and two of them are my best shots."

"I know what you mean, I got one back home like that myself. She is mad as hell she is not with us. But, she is protecting the nest and God help anybody who messes with her.

"What's the news up the road? We are going up north of Saint J."

"Last I heard, there are some bad dudes hitting vehicles up around the Woodsville exit. There is a rough patch of road and they have some old vehicles off to the side where they hide and wait. When you slow down they will hit you. They're mostly dumbasses with pistols, shotguns and a couple of old SKS rifles. Just local scumbags trying to play bandit. Other than that there's nothing I know about. There was never much to steal up in that part of the state to begin with. Everybody was struggling way before the crash, which means they were already pissed off and they all had guns. Most serious bandits have headed south for easier pickings."

"What about south? Any word?"

"You heading that way?"

"Maybe."

"How far?"

"Far enough."

"Well, the news travels slow these days. But, I hear some bad things are still going on around Lawrence, Mass. Of course Boston is still a mess, just like any city. Can't say about anything beyond there. You going farther south than that?"

"I don't know. But, if we do, I guess we will just have to wing it."

"Where on earth did you get gas for all this travel?"

"Told you, we are on a mission from God, and as you know, God will provide."

"Pull to the right of the roadblock, Jimmy is dragging that pole out of the way with his draft horse. Go on by, let me know how it works out.

"When you talk to God again, ask him to send us a little gas."

CHAPTER 53

"Who was that guy?" Davy asked as we drove off.

"I can't remember his name, but he used to be on the shooting circuit and we squadded together in a bunch of matches."

"You know what they say, right?"

"What's that?"

"Your memory is the second thing to go when you get old."

"Fuck you."

"You sure you remember how?"

"Besides, that's the first thing to go."

We went through town and hit the entry for the Interstate, but it was blocked by a fallen maple tree. So we drove around it on the grass and up over the shoulder. There probably hadn't been a vehicle on this road in years, but out of habit we all looked both ways before entering the road. Then we all burst out laughing at the same time.

We drove along at an easy forty miles per hour. That let us see the bad stuff, like giant potholes, in time to stop or steer around, but we still made good time. When we got to the Woodsville exit we found the spot we had been warned about and put up the window shields. Davy wanted to shoot the bandits, but I pointed out that we didn't have time. Besides, if one got lucky and hit one of us with a bullet it would be bad. We had a lot more at stake here and could not afford to risk losing anybody just to deal with a few home-grown bandits.

It didn't matter as there wasn't anybody there, so we just drove on past without any problems.

Davy seemed disappointed and sulked for the next ten miles.

We got to the silo just after noon. In the old days I would get up and drive here to hunt, making it in a little over two hours. Today it took seven. Bob went inside alone, insisting we wait in the parking lot. I wasn't too pleased about that, but figured it would take too long to argue my point. He was back in twenty minutes, pushing a handcart with a Pelican case about the size of a big suitcase.

"They weren't kidding when they called them suitcase nukes," I said. "I expected something bigger. Besides, I thought a suitcase nuke never really existed."

"Oh, they are real enough, and the technology evolved way beyond what any government was admitting. This nasty little fella here weighs a hundred pounds, but it can wipe out a city. It's a one-megaton payload. The second bomb they dropped on Japan, Fat Man, was the bigger of the two and it had a twenty-thousand ton yield, this one has a one million ton yield. That means anything within five miles in any direction is gone instantly. Any building in the next ten miles will be flattened. We need to be at least thirty miles away when it blows, and I would feel a lot better if is fifty miles.

"That's from a ground blast. It's also designed to fit on a missile delivery system and if it were exploded above the earth we can just about double the blast radius.

"The best part is they have developed technology that reduces the lingering footprint, the radiation. The idea is to blow the thing, but not still be killing people with a radiation cloud two weeks later and two hundred miles away. They thought that if they could make a bomb that is deadly when it explodes but doesn't leave all the radiation behind, then it would be a much better tactical weapon. This is one of the last generation designs and probably one of the last bombs ever made. It utilized every bit of the advanced technology, so it leaves a very small radiation footprint. With a strong west wind it will blow out into the Atlantic and dissipate. Nobody will die from that. The only real change is that Cape Cod will be a few miles shorter. But in ten years, it will be safe to live there again."

"What about the other two," I asked?

"I have them hidden safely away in two other locations. Trust me, nobody will ever find them. Even if they do, they won't have a clue what they are. The bombs can't be fired without several failsafe codes and right now I am the only man alive who has access to them all. The codes are locked in my brain and when I die, they die with me."

"What about the bomb you lost?" I asked. "If you are the only one who can arm it, it can't be a threat."

"Unfortunately, all but one failsafe was implemented. We wanted the bomb armed so they would know we were serious. It would take just four more numbers to make it go boom. It was the last four numbers from my agent's mother-in-law's social security number. They might have tortured that information out of my guy, or not. He was trained to resist, but everybody breaks sooner or later. Or, if they can get access to one of the old super computers, they can probably break the code. Either way, I would like it back or at the very least, destroyed. If it's on the ground in the blast radius when this one goes off, it won't detonate, but it will be destroyed."

I thought about the incredible power in so small a package and about the morality of using it. But then I remembered that every person in that blast range was going to try to kill me, my family and all my neighbors. There were no innocents this time, they all were guilty. If Bob was right they were going to use the lost bomb to kill us, so this was as clear a case of self-defense as ever existed in the history of mankind. If we failed to stop these people, they would kill all of us, our family, friends and a large portion of the remaining population of the country.

Like I said before, I would shoot every one of them given the chance, so how was this any different? Intellectually it wasn't, but the mind thinks what the mind wants. One megaton is a lot of power.

"So, how're we going to pull this off?" I asked. "You said you had a plan. Now might be a good time to tell us about it."

"We need to get to Gloucester."

"Gloucester, Massachusetts?"

"The very same."

"Okay, but, that's two hundred miles south of here."

"No problem, this truck is pretty much a rolling gas tank," Davy said. "The main tank holds one hundred gallons. There are two auxiliary tanks that hold thirty gallons each, plus they even have a bladder tank in the roof that we found. It holds another ten gallons. Whoever designed this vehicle had the end of the world in mind, as it's designed to cover a lot of ground between gas stations. Plus, we have another fifty gallons in the back in jugs."

"I just hope we don't catch an RPG or something," Bob mumbled. "If those tanks blow we will make an East Coast Grand Canyon."

"Mickey told me all the tanks in the truck are isolated and shielded," Davy said. "He said they even split the main tank into five twenty gallon compartments and that they all have some kind of heat sensing fire suppressing foam that is instantly released when a fire starts. It's technology they developed for airplanes and it is supposed to keep the fuel tanks from all blowing up at once."

"Remember, though," I said, looking at Davy, "those cans in the back don't have any of that shit and even a five gallon bucket will make a bigger fireball than I want to deal with, so let's try to keep this thing out of trouble."

"What? You turning pussy in your old age?"

I didn't bother to take the bait.

"Once we get to Gloucester," Bob said, "I'll handle the transportation. I have a boat stashed there with lots of fuel. It's one hundred miles of ocean from there to P-Town. My boat can make that in two hours easy. Less, if we are in a hurry."

"How did you know where they would be far enough in advance to stash a boat?"

"I didn't. I told you, the CIA had a blank checkbook. The agency had boats and vehicles stashed in lots of places. I just shifted some of them around once this all started. By then, there wasn't anybody to tell me I couldn't.

"I figured they needed a harbor to get gear in from Europe. Gas was pretty hard to find until they got that refinery up and running a few months ago, so I knew they would stay close to the water. They seemed to like the Northeast, so I figured they might end up in Boston. I had a boat there, but I didn't want it trapped if they did move in, so I moved it to Gloucester a couple of years ago. Got a guy taking care of it for me. I also have boats near New York, Washington, Virginia Beach and so on, all down the coast. But this one is the best, it's my baby. Like I said, the taxpayers were generous.

"Besides, boats are much easier to move around unnoticed than a truck. Got a couple stashed out in the Great Lakes too. When I needed to go some-place, I always used a boat if I could."

"What about pirates?" Davy asked.

"Wait until you see this boat. Those dirtbags don't have anything that can come close to catching it. It can hit eighty knots, which is more than ninety mph. If they did catch it, which would happen only if I wanted them to, I have a Ma Duce 50-caliber BMG machine gun, two M240, 30-caliber machine guns and several RPG launchers."

"After we save the world," Davy said. "Can we go find some pirates with your boat and ask them to come out and play?"

"I don't see why not."

CHAPTER 54

The first part of the drive took us down the old Interstate 93. After a few miles, we left Vermont and traveled into upstate New Hampshire. When the cities emptied, the Interstates were the natural corridors for all those poor souls whose only survival plan was to "head for the hills." As a result, most of the early battles in the social wars happened along these highways. The roads changed the country after Eisenhower created the Interstate system, but they changed it again after everything went to shit.

As a result, most of the people living along the highway were either dead or long ago moved on. Traffic ground to a halt over the years and so with nothing left to prey on, the bandits moved on as well. Now they were usually on the secondary roads outside the smaller cities and towns as they branched out looking for prey.

The farther south we moved, the more the devastation increased with every mile. That direction brought us into what had been increasingly denser and denser population centers. The land from Boston to D.C. had been pretty much one big mass of humanity and so as the cities sprawled, the people moved west or north, but mostly north.

The sprawl had not reached the far northern areas closer to the Canadian border by the time of the collapse, so populations were still sparse there. But the closer to the cities, the denser the population became.

When things went to hell and the cities emptied, many of the hordes of desperate people moved north looking to get food any way possible. The social wars started outside the cities and worked their way north or west. The coast was to the east and the way south was already full of people. By the time the remnants of those hordes hit the North Country, much of the population was dead and they started encountering citizens who were prepared and willing to fight. So, eventually it all ended. But in the first miles north of the population densities of the eastern United States, a lot of death and destruction occurred. I live about halfway between Boston and Canada and well off the path of the Interstates and I know how bad it got there. I can't imagine how it must have been for those poor souls living closer to the cities and along the travel corridors of the highways.

We were following that path in reverse, so the theory was that, due to the horrors of the social wars, the farther south we went, the fewer people we would encounter. At least until we hit the cities like Boston and the surviving suburbs where gangs still ruled. At least that's what we heard last. For all I know, every gang member still alive was waiting for us in Provincetown and the cities were now empty. It's not like we still had Fox news to rely on for information.

I had hoped that some people had held on, but every small town we passed was wiped out and empty. Perhaps some miles back into the land, away from the highway, things were better; but it was clear that living close to the Interstate had been a death sentence. We had been warned about Lawrence, just across the Massachusetts border from New Hampshire, but based on what we were seeing we expected little trouble before then. While we didn't leave the highway to investigate, even Concord and Manchester had looked empty and abandoned.

The first fifty miles or so of our ride was uneventful. Most of us had lapsed into our own thoughts and the truck was quiet other than the drone of the motor and the tires on the broken pavement. The road was in remarkably good shape and other than the need to go around an occasional roadblock left over from the days when the bandits ruled this part of the world, the ride was monotonously boring. I suppose the lack of traffic cuts down on the wear and tear and keeps the potholes from forming.

My mind was going in all kinds of directions and for a while all the talk about boats made me think about mine. I had grown up around boats, water skiing and fishing, but I didn't get a powerboat of my own until I was in my late twenties. My wife and I had bought a twenty-foot I/O bow-rider shortly after we were married. We got it from a guy who needed money for an adoption that happened faster than he had expected. The boat had eight hours on it and I got it for sixty percent of the retail price. I paid it off in a few years and just never got around to getting rid of it. I used it for fishing back then, but once I got into competitive shooting it just sat in the driveway because I was busy on the weekends. Later when my kids got big enough, they started using it for water skiing, fishing and socializing with their friends. Now it's parked in a barn. I suppose if gasoline is ever available again and we can make the world safe, I might take up fishing once more. I'll bet without anybody on the water for the past several years it will be good, the fish should be big and populations strong.

As we rode along I lost myself deeper in the good memories of the past as I thought about the day we got the boat, a beautiful Saturday morning in July. It was late afternoon before I had everything ready, but I was so wound up about owning a boat of my own that I just had to get it wet. My wife was working at the local hospital, so I planned to meet a buddy at the old Lake St. Catherine marina in southwestern Vermont, where he kept his boat moored.

You exited the marina on a small canal that passed under the state highway. The bridge was very low and the water was high from recent rains. My boat had a stereo, which I used to crank up Steppenwolf's "Born to be Wild" as loud as I could. Leading the way, Hagan ran his smaller boat under the bridge and out into the main lake. But, when I tried to follow, the windshield of my boat was too high and wouldn't clear the steel girders supporting the bridge. I was strong then and pumped full of adrenalin, so I just grabbed the girder and pushed up on it until the windshield cleared and the boat slid in under the bridge. But, no matter how hard I tried I could not get under the next girder. Maybe it was lower than the first, I don't know, but I could not get past it. By the time I tried to go back I was exhausted and could not push hard enough to clear the first girder under the bridge. I tried and tried, but I was stuck.

I was trapped under this bridge, looking foolish as "Born to be Wild" screamed from the speakers. A crowd from the nearby beach started gathering to laugh at me. After a while I just started laughing with them and we all sung along with John Kay as he belted out,

"Like a true nature's child
We were born, born to be wild
We can climb so high
I never want to die

Born to be wild
Born to be wild!!!!!!"

There were girls in bikinis dancing to the music, guys saluting me with their long-neck Budweisers and within minutes it felt like a party.

Finally a bunch of the guys took the offer for free beer and jumped into the boat to ravage my cooler. Their weight sunk it enough to get under the bridge and set me free.

For just a little while, it was absurdly fun.

Somehow, I didn't think this next boat ride would leave the same warm memories.

CHAPTER 55

We were going past the exit for Battleboro, New Hampshire when we finally ran into a problem.

It figured; that town was a haven for every fool on earth back before, so it stood to reason that anybody who still lived there could be counted among the "dumbasses of the world." It's probably some kind of karma thing, the earth sending out a force field that attracts stupid people. That town even issued an arrest warrant for President George W. Bush and Vice President Dick Cheney during the Iraq war for "crimes against humanity." I had always hoped that they would show up and tell the locals to "bring it on" but sadly they never took the bait. It would have been fun watching the Secret Service mop the streets with a bunch of aging hippies.

Looking back, it was just fitting that the dregs of society would set up there. This liberal town not only attracted old hippies trying to recapture the glory days, their easy attitudes about law, order and drug use also attracted a lot of lowlifes.

As we passed the first road signs announcing the town I couldn't help but wonder if there was anybody left here and if they still embraced "diversity and acceptance." That was the town motto. Except of course, for Christians and conservatives. Those groups didn't count as human beings within their hypocritical "we are the world" mentality.

Then I remembered that Battleboro was one of the first towns to be pillaged and burned and there was nothing of value left. When a place is full of gun-hating old hippies, it's an easy target.

We had not seen another vehicle the entire trip and clearly it would be a lonely life of crime waiting to rob travelers passing through. So there was no reason to expect any problems. Why would there be any here? The highway was empty, the town pillaged and empty, what was there to attract bandits?

That's why we were caught off guard when the attack started and why there was no time to debate their motivation.

They were hidden in some abandoned cars that were scattered on the highway. They had left enough room to drive between them, but staggered the cars like an obstacle course, so we had to slow. As soon as we started to slow down they opened up with rifle fire.

They concentrated their firepower on the tires and the engine compartment, which probably saved us. No doubt that had worked before and probably accounted for some of the abandoned cars used in this ambush. But, ours were shielded. That gave us time to raise the window shields too, so we were completely protected. We just drove on through.

If anybody else had been driving that would have been the end of it, but Davy had taken the wheel about twenty miles back when Bob said he wanted a nap. Davy raced out of the road block, built up speed, hit the parking brake, spun the wheel and executed a perfect bootleg turn. That reversed our direction. Then he released the brake and stomped the gas, so we were running right back at the cars at high speed. We skidded to a stop just before we hit the first car. Davy's door flew open and while hiding behind the shielded door he threw three hand-grenades, one left, one right and one up the middle. Then he slammed the door just as they went off, spraying the truck with shrapnel.

Three guys with rifles ran out from behind one abandoned car and started across the median strip that separated the north- and southbound lanes of the highway. Davy dove out the truck door with an M4 carbine and took them down with three quick shots. Two more broke out on my side, one of them spraying the truck with a full auto AK-74 as he ran. As soon as he ran out of ammo and was struggling with a magazine change, I stepped out of the truck and shot them both. I got back in, shut the door just as Davy slammed the left side door, and we waited. After about two minutes a guy stood up through the open sunroof of an SUV about ten feet in front of us and fired a full-auto burst at our truck. Davy waited until the guy ducked back down, opened the door and tossed a grenade into the sunroof.

A few minutes after it went off he stuck his head out the door and yelled, "Anybody else out there?"

A voice yelled back, "Yes sir, just me. I am the only one left alive. Please sir, don't kill me."

"Stand up, let me see you. If you are not armed, I will not kill you."

The guy that stood up looked like a mean son of a bitch, but he had the demeanor of a whipped puppy.

Davy walked over to the guy and punched him hard between the eyes. Then he jumped on top of the guy's chest and carved a big, wide "A" in his forehead with his fixed-blade knife.

"That stands for asshole," Davy said when the guy stopped screaming. "I usually kill assholes, especially those who just tried to kill me. But, in a weak moment I promised not to kill you. I am a man who always keeps his word. So, instead I am hiring you. It don't pay much, in fact it don't pay anything at all, except you get to live, so this is an offer for employment that you would do well to take. Your job is to head south and to tell every other asshole you meet about us. Tell them to leave us alone or I will make it a personal quest to cut their balls off and shove them up their ass.

"Got it?"

The guy whimpered something to the effect that he did.

"Furthermore," Davy continued. "I am spreading the word. If you have that 'A for asshole' scar on your forehead and you commit another crime, even something like talking rude to old ladies, you are to be shot on sight. You already had a chance and it's one more chance than you deserved, so you'd better mend your ways and behave."

While Davy was busy with that guy, Bob and I checked the rest of the vehicles for survivors. We found seven more bodies. One guy was still alive, but was missing an arm and he bled out before he could say a word. My guess is the guy Davy was decorating had no idea he really was the only one left alive, because he couldn't see most of his buddies where they were hiding. He was probably hoping one of the other guys would come to his rescue. But that was not going to happen.

I watched as he pulled off his dirty T-shirt and wrapped it around his head to stop the bleeding. I noticed his body was covered with tattoos that were all crude and homemade. Prison tats they called them. He looked about forty-five and I had no doubt he had done time.

"Were you in Newport,"? I asked him.

"What's Newport?"

"The prison in northern Vermont."

"No."

"But you were in prison, right?"

At first I didn't think he was going to answer, but when Davy pulled his knife out again, he got pretty chatty.

"I did federal time in Colorado. That's where I met most of these guys."

"So what are you doing here?"

"Easy, I made my living holding up businesses and robbing people. Out west, too many people have guns. That's bad for your health in my line of work. So, I came home to Massachusetts where nobody carries a gun, except me and my buddies. It was a much safer place for guys like me. The crash happened right after we got here. It was pretty sweet for a while because we ruled down in South Boston for the first year or two. Then the pickings got thin with everybody worth robbing dead or gone, so we took it on the road. Even that wore out and now we mostly just go around and find food in abandoned houses that are so far off the main roads they were missed before."

"So why are you still here?" I asked.

"This part of New Hampshire has been pretty well picked clean, so we were heading west. We try to avoid any other people because it's not like it was. Now everybody has a gun and they are all pissed off. Man, they just start shooting as soon as they see you. Assholes!"

"You find enough to eat that way?"

"We eat well. Well enough to stay alive anyway, but I can tell you that lately I am getting really sick of canned beans. The trouble is, this life? It's boring. I think I liked it better back in prison."

"What were you in the federal pen for?"

"Running drugs across state lines. They caught me with a bunch of heroin I was taking to Vermont, but the judge let me go. The feds were pissed, so they charged me because it was Interstate and that asshole lawyer they gave me let them convict me."

"Boo-hoo, poor, poor pitiful you. Did it occur to you that if you didn't commit crimes, you would not go to prison?"

He didn't answer me.

"No, I suspect not. You're probably too fucking dumb to do the math. When did you get out?"

"My sentence was for twenty years, but they ran out of money and let me go after two. Technically, I am still on probation. What a fucking joke, right? I am supposed to be wearing one of them bracelets so they can identify me. I guess your buddy found a new way to take care of that problem."

"Enough chit chat," Davy said. "Time you were heading south. Start walking, buddy, before I lose my charitable mood."

"Walking? What about my truck?"

"What truck?" I asked.

"My truck, the one I drove here."

"Are you telling me you have a vehicle that still runs?"

"Yeah, that black truck up the road is mine, I parked it there because I didn't want it all shot up."

"How much gas do you have?" I asked while fighting the temptation to put a bullet through the "A" on his head.

"A full tank and a couple of extra cans in the back."

"Where did you get that much gas?"

"Same place I got the truck. Some guys came through here a few days ago with a big convoy of trucks, most of them looked like yours. They spotted the smoke from our campfire, I guess. We haven't seen anybody in a long time, so we were sloppy. They sneaked up on us and when we went for our guns they shot Tommy.

"Then they told the rest of us about you guys. They gave us that truck and some more guns and ammo. All in all, it wasn't a bad trade. Tommy was an asshole.

"All we had to do in return was wait here and kill you guys. The truck was in case you made it through the trap, we were supposed to chase you with it. The thing has a Hemi in it and goes like a raped ape.

"They told us to shoot the driver, but we had better luck over the years with taking out the vehicle first. After it couldn't move we would shoot the guys inside because they had no place to run. I guess I should have listened to them, right? They told me the truck had armor, but I thought that was bullshit. That thing looks like something a soccer mom would drive, not a tank.

"Remember them, the soccer moms? Some of them were pretty hot and they were always easy to grab, they never fought back. They just begged me not to hurt their kids. I never did. Hurt the kids, that is. I didn't hurt the moms much either, just took their money and their rides. If they were really hot I would fuck them a little. Most of them liked it. Besides, nobody armor-plates tires, right?"

I just stared at him in amazement. Before I could say a word, he was back to his stream-of-consciousness babbling.

"They said if we failed, or ran off, they would find us. One skinny black guy smacked me in the face with some weird African shield and poked a spear at my chest. He said he would personally take care of me if we didn't kill you guys. He looked like somebody I used to see on television. He reminded me of some old movie star or something. Somebody I know, I don't know who, I can't remember; but I'll tell you one thing, he was batshit crazy. The black guy, not the movie star. Well maybe the movie star was crazy too, I don't know because I can't remember who it was … "

"Are you the leader of this band of assholes?" Davy asked, interrupting the guy.

He stopped talking and looked around with a perplexed expression on his face.

"I was. Not much left to lead now."

"Well, then take the reprieve and get your ass out of here. You drive down this highway and you tell everybody you meet about us. I was going to send you walking, but now I know you have a truck that's even better.

"Spread the word to leave us alone and trust me, if you fuck up, you will wish it was that crazy African after you and not me."

We searched his truck and found several guns and two cases of ammo and thirty-seven cans of Bushy's baked beans in a box that probably held a hundred at one time. I made the guy lug everything down to our truck, including his extra gas and put it in the back. I suppose we could have driven one or the other closer, but I liked watching him work up a sweat.

"Keep them beans, I am so sick of them I will puke if I try to eat any more. But I need a gun, it's suicide to go out there without a gun."

"Buddy, right now, it's suicide to keep arguing with me," Davy said. "Shut up and get out of here before I change my mind."

"How far do you want me to go?"

"You run down this road until you hit I-95. Then you turn south and keep going until you are out of gas. Once you are out, stay by the truck and wait for us. When we come by, I'll give you a gun and some more gas. If you ain't there, I'll come find you. This old fella here with me? He is the world's best tracker … just ask him. He will track you down and I will cut off your balls. So just stay with the truck, okay?"

CHAPTER 56

"You think that will help?" I asked.

"It won't hurt," Davy said. "Besides, he will have a long wait. We are not staying on this road that much longer. Your buddy told you there is trouble in Lawrence, so we should bypass that area. In another few miles we can get off the Interstate and from there it's all back roads to Gloucester."

There were a few more tense moments as we approached obvious road-blocks, but they were all old and abandoned so nothing happened. Even on the secondary roads most of the towns were empty. Twice, I noticed guys stand-ing back in the shadows watching us as we passed. Both were armed and made sure we saw the guns. I don't know if they were good guys or bad guys, but we didn't bother to slow down for any stop signs in case they wanted trouble. I fig-ured if a cop caught me, I would just pay the ticket.

It was getting pretty late by the time we pulled into the driveway of an abandoned looking building built on a small cliff so it hung out over the ocean. I noticed that the building itself dropped well below the surface of the water, so I figured there must be a boathouse underneath.

As we turned into the driveway, a garage door opened and we pulled inside. The door shut behind us as soon as the truck was clear.

The guy working the door looked like he was right out of central casting. He was tall and lean with flowing white hair hanging down his back. In front, his equally white beard dropped nearly to his belt. He wore a faded and torn red-checkered shirt with the sleeves rolled up and tails out, over faded blue jeans. Heavy, lace up boots completed the ensemble. His face was all crags and crevices, without a smooth spot anywhere. His eyes were a faded blue under bushy white eyebrows. He wore a dirty black watch cap, even though it was a warm night. The yellow fingers of his gnarled hand held a lit cigarette that looked like he rolled himself.

"Where the hell did you find this guy?" I asked Bob before we got out of the truck.

"He was a fisherman back before. Never married, it was just him. I asked around and they said he could be trusted, so I set him up in this house and gave him some guns. I send food when I can and he keeps the boat ready in the boat-house underneath."

The guy crushed the cigarette on the cement floor of the garage and was already walking through the door into the house by the time we were out of the truck. "Don't smoke in the house," was all he said.

We followed into a spotlessly clean kitchen where the guy was putting old jelly glasses on the counter.

"Heard you drink bourbon," he said with a strong New England accent.

"You heard right my friend," I said, liking the guy already.

"All I got right now is some Jack. I bought up several cases before it all went to hell. I stocked up on the good stuff too, but that's long gone. This ain't the best, but it'll do, I suppose."

"I suppose it will."

"There is some shit I just ain't gonna live without," he said to nobody in particular. Whiskey's one. Need a smoke now and then too."

"Where do you find tobacco?" Davy asked.

"Can't. I hafta' grow my own at another place I got a few miles from here. Use that shade-grown stuff they growed in Connecticut. Not my first choice to smoke, but it does okay growing here."

"Name's Jamerson," he said as he handed me a glass with a couple of inches of whiskey in it.

"First or last?"

"Only.

"It's just Jamerson. That's all anybody ever called me.

"The boat's ready, but I didn't have but five gallons of extra gas after I topped off the tanks."

"That's okay," Bob said. "We have plenty in the truck. Will you help me lug some stuff down the ramp? One package is heavy, so we need the hand-truck."

Bob looked at me and Davy and said, "Grab some shit from the fridge and make some sandwiches. Lots of them, this might be a long night. If he has lobster, make sure to get some of that for me. Love that stuff. But, you gotta wonder how hungry the first guy to eat one must have been. They look like a big bug. What there says 'eat me?'

"Anyway, don't forget to grab all the water jugs in the garage and follow us down the ramp to the boathouse. We are also going to need plenty of guns and ammo, so get all of ours and bring that stuff we collected off those assholes who tried to kill us. I do not want to run out of bullets in the middle of a fight.

"But before that, so we won't forget, go through those doors into the living room and grab four of the backpacks I have stacked up in there. Doesn't matter which four, they are all the same.

"I have had those bug-out bags ready for a while. It's about time we get to use them. By the way, each one has a 1911 pistol in the front pocket with lots of extra ammo and magazines, and no you can't keep them. But, if you need to shoot somebody, feel free to borrow them. There are also some space blankets, MREs, a small solar still, a sleeping bag and some other survival stuff in each bag. Some of it might come in handy. If not, we can just put them back in the living room when we return. While you are doing all that, Jamerson and I will be prepping the nuke and getting it strapped down in the boat."

"Nuke, what fucking nuke?"

"You mean a nuclear bomb?"

"You have a fuckin' nuclear bomb?"

I was starting to think we had a problem, then grinning like a twelve-year-old, Jamerson shouted, "How cool is that shit?"

Looking at Bob, he asked, "Where'dja get it?"

"Hang loose, I'll explain everything on the way. We need you to captain the boat anyway and there is no time to explain now."

"Okay. We gonna blow something up?"

"Yup."

"Cool."

"I thought we were just going to run down there, drop off the bomb and run back. Why do we need all this stuff?" Davy asked.

"I learned a long time ago that it's better to have it and not need it than to need it and not have it," Bob said. "Especially on the water. Things never go like you plan. The best laid plans of mice and men, all that shit. If we wind up adrift in the ocean for a couple of weeks because we got chased and ran out of gas, I want some water and something to eat."

Davy didn't answer, he just looked like he felt foolish as he started grabbing handfuls of food out of the antique fridge with a big, dripping block of ice in the top compartment. I made a mental note to ask Jamerson where he was finding ice.

The place was well lit with kerosene lanterns and I noticed that all the windows were blacked out with plywood so the building looked unoccupied from the outside.

The place was clean and smelled like fresh wood. There were books everywhere you looked, and decoys. Hundreds of wooden duck decoys. On the way to find the backpacks we passed a small room that was full of wood and wood shavings. There was a work bench in the back with several decoys in various states of finished from wood blocks to finely detailed ducks with every feather defined. There were knives and tools everywhere. While the rest of the place was neat and organized, this room was total chaos.

The decoys, though, were amazing, I thought some of them were alive. Clearly this guy was a very talented artist.

"That was one of my hobbies back before," Jamerson said from behind me. "I would carve at night out on the boat. Just kept on doing it after everything fell apart. I could pick up some extra spending money selling them at the outdoor shows and DU banquets back before. No market now, but it keeps me busy. 'Bout all I got to do these days, that and read."

I picked up a decoy with an incredible amount of detail in the feathers.

"Did you burn the wood to get that shadow effect?" I asked.

"Yeah, been experimenting. I did that with an old coat hanger that I pounded flat with a hammer. I heat it in the lantern flame then use it to burn the color into the wood. Had to do something. Gettin' hard to find paint. I make some of my own, but it's dangerous to go out in the woods to gather the stuff I need. So mostly I stay here and try to figure out different ways to make do."

"It looks like you have made yourself a nice home here," I said.

"Yeah, I suppose so."

"I got a gravity-feed spring, so I have good water. I keep a bait station with fish and meat scraps down under the boathouse so I get lobsters and fish without going outside. The tide takes bits of bait out into the ocean and they follow their noses back to my traps and hooks. I get so many that I can't eat them all so I built a pen down there to hold the extras and keep them alive. They are good trading material.

"I keep a low profile here, so I don't trade too many, just a few with my brother for firewood and some with an old lady that lives a couple of miles from here for vegetables and shit like that. Sometimes for pussy. Well, actually the truth is we were bumping nasties a long time before things got bad. Not as much now though. She is getting a little long in the tooth and starting to lose interest.

"Guess we both are."

He was quiet for a long time. Then in a voice so low I could barely hear him he said, "It ain't the worst life."

CHAPTER 57

"Where is Jamerson?" Davy asked a few minutes later.

"I don't know, I haven't seen him for a while."

We stepped into the garage to see if he was having a smoke and heard voices outside.

"This can't be good," I said. "We need to make sure this truck is still here when we get back. If we get noticed, there is a very big chance it will be gone. No matter what happens, keep it quiet. No point in attracting more vermin. So, don't shoot anybody! Think you can handle that?"

"I ain't making any promises I can't keep."

We went through the small door that dumped us outside, around the corner from the driveway. We walked softly on the paved path until we could see two big guys arguing with Jamerson in the driveway. One appeared to have a baseball bat. But the light was fading fast and it was hard to see a lot of detail.

"We heard that truck, old man," one said. "We want it. It's a long way to Provincetown and I don't plan to walk."

"Hey, you got food?" the other one asked. "I am hungry, I haven't eaten all day."

"I'll give you some food," Jamerson said. "But then you go on your way. I don't have any truck. I told you, I am just an old man who wants to be left alone."

"Enough of this bullshit," the guy with the bat said. He stepped at Jamerson and swung at his head like he wanted to bounce it off the green monster wall at Fenway.

Jamerson ducked just enough for the bat to miss. The guy was off balance, but he recovered and swung again, lower this time. Jamerson jumped back so the bat missed him by inches.

This went on for a while. Jamerson never attacked, he just kept dodging the bat. They repeated this dance several times until the guy with the bat was huffing and puffing.

"Let's rush him," the guy with the bat said to his buddy.

"I ain't rushing shit, that guy knows something. Let's just go."

"Last chance," Jamerson said. "I asked you to leave me alone. That's all I ever wanted, to be left alone. Why can't you do that?"

"Fuck you, old man," the guy screamed as he charged.

Jamerson sidestepped to the left and caught him in the throat with the leading edge of his gnarled right hand. Then spinning with amazing speed, he came around with his left with a hooking knife edge strike to the side of the other man's neck. The guy went down in a heap. Jamerson grabbed the bat from him as he fell and threw it like a spear, hitting the other guy on the nose. Then Jamerson stepped to him, kicked him in the nuts and when he bent over Jamerson snapped a kick to his face with his heavy work boots. I heard bones break and the guy fell in a pile with only his left foot twitching.

"I guess we ain't needed here," Davy said.

"Well, actually you are," Jamerson replied. "Help me get these assholes off the street. They are big and heavy and I am a feeble old man.

"I imagine that one's dead," he said, pointing to the second guy. "Broke his neck. But that first guy is going to wake up in a bit. He probably won't be able to talk after that hit in the throat, but he can still make trouble."

"Where did you learn all that shit?" Davy asked.

"All those years of being alone? They can make a man mean. I took my aggressions out in the Dojo. Fourth degree black belt in Taekwondo. Third degree in Jiu Jitsu. Old school, none of that Brazilian bullshit. Those two make a good mix, complement each other well. Trust me, you practice your moves for twenty years on a boat that's bobbing around on a good chop and you learn about balance and timing.

"Those two were actually knocking on my door," Jamerson said. "They heard the truck and were going door to door, trying to find it. They heard us talking inside. You guys still haven't told me what is going on, are they part of it? What's this about P-Town?"

When I bent over to pull the first guy into the garage he grabbed my shirt, yanked me down and head-butted me. I was able to duck my face at the last second so he hit the top of my head and didn't get a solid blow, but it still hurt like hell. I fell as he got up. I rolled away from him and got to my feet just as he charged in, throwing roundhouse swings with both arms. I ducked under his punches and planted my Ka-Bar in his chest. I yanked it out and used the back end to smack him on the back of the head as he staggered past me. He went down, spurting blood with every remaining beat of his heart.

Both of my ears were ringing and my head felt like it was going to explode. Luckily he had hit the top of my head, not the center of my face like he planned.

I get mean when somebody hits my nose.

"Wow," Davy said, "it's retro night at the fights. Hell, I know when I am not needed. You old dudes can clean up your own damn mess. I am going to get another shot of that Jack.

"Bob asked me to tell you that he wants to hit the beach about four in the morning. Something about the Art of War and some Chinese dude named Sunny Sue or some such shit. He claims the guy told him the best time to attack your enemy is early morning. I really don't know what the hell he was talking about."

"You really need to read more Davy," I laughed.

"Yeah, Bob said you would know what he was talking about and would probably say something like that. Anyway, we leave here at one a.m. I am going for that drink and some shuteye. Let me know when it's time to party."

"So what do we do with these two?" Jamerson asked me. "I guess Davy isn't going to help."

"I think he is a little pissy about being the only guy here that didn't get any action," I said. "He would have been welcome to mine. My head hurts like a son of a bitch.

"First thing, let's make sure they are dead. I don't want any more surprises. Then let's get them inside and see if we can figure out who they are and if being dead creates any problems for anybody except them."

We dragged them into the garage and got a couple of lamps. I checked their pockets and all I found was a map to P-Town and a handful of money. I didn't recognize the money and assumed it was some of the new currency we had been hearing about.

I held the bills under one of the lamps to get a closer look. They still called them dollars, but World Dollars, not U.S. Dollars or the newer "One Earth." The five had a photo of Khalid al-Hazmi. The twenty had Mikael Gostrovavitch. They didn't have any other bills in their pockets, but my guess is that Norvan Heitzeman was on one of them too, probably the ten. Servro liked to be a behind-the-scenes player and I doubted he would have his face on the new money.

I thought it odd that these guys didn't have any guns. Their only weapon was the baseball bat. Nobody travels today without guns. In looking closer they both had bruises on their faces that looked to be at least a few days old and not from their final fight. I assumed somebody took their guns from them. In this world it's unusual that anybody would steal their weapons and not kill them.

We wrapped both guys in a plastic tarp and put them in the boat. When we got far enough out to sea we would dump the bodies overboard. I got a couple of buckets of water and washed the blood off the driveway. Then I used Jamerson's shower to wash the blood off my clothes. I hung them to dry and had another whiskey. When it was gone, I laid down on the couch in the living room and tried to get a few hours of sleep. But I knew it was a lost cause.

I had been gone too long. I missed my wife, I missed my kids and I missed my dogs. I had traveled all over the world while hunting, but this always happened after a few weeks away. If I did sleep at all I would have horrible nightmares about my wife leaving me.

She was always such a bitch about it, too.

CHAPTER 58

We idled the boat out into the bay. The engine was surprisingly quiet and I doubt anybody could hear a thing. When we were half a mile out Jamerson powered up. When the boat was on plane he took a compass reading and headed south/southeast.

The boat was a thirty-foot, sleek-looking thing with a small cabin under the deck, an open cockpit and a whole lot of horsepower. The disappointment was the sound. I love the throb of powerful engines while going fast, but this thing hardly made a sound.

"It's muffled and shielded until it sounds like a damn rowboat," Bob said after I asked about the lack of sound. "Can't say I like it, but it does help for this type of work."

"Anybody else hungry? We have some cold lobster. There is even hot butter for dipping. I have this little gadget that plugs into the power outlet on the boat. It's made for heating a cup of water for coffee, but it works great to melt the butter too. God, I love this stuff. It's the food they serve in Heaven. Gotta be, or else I don't wanna go there."

We sat like kings on a golden chariot, eating the food of gods and washing it down with cold spring water. I would have preferred an ice cold beer as that's the proper drink with lobster, but I haven't tasted good beer in a long time."

"Years ago I loved to fish," Bob said between bites. "Me and a couple of buddies decided to drive out to Montana to fly fish on the Yellowstone and some of the other rivers. The rancher we stayed with wouldn't take any money, but he did ask us to send him a lobster or two when we got home. We FedExed some to him, but somehow it didn't seem like enough.

"So, the next year we decided to do it up right. One of the guys owned a small store that sold seafood. He had a trailer that was basically a huge rolling

271

cooler that he used to run up to the Maine coast to get his lobsters. We packed that thing full of ice and live lobsters, hooked it to my truck and pointed the grill west.

"Our luck was shit and we were fighting storms all the way. Somewhere in South Dakota, we hit a patch of black ice. I was in the back of the SUV sleeping when it flipped. I don't know how many times it rolled, because I was ejected the first time over. Nobody wore a seatbelt back in those days and everybody was tossed out of the truck before it was all over.

I remember lying in the ditch with my back broken, watching the flash-lights through the fog as the state police looked for survivors. Suddenly one of the cops started screaming like a little girl. Then he pulled his gun and started shooting at the highway.

"I suppose the last thing a cop in South Dakota expected to see on a dark and stormy night was fifty alien-looking green and orange bugs crawling through the rain and fog. He said later he thought we were a crashed spaceship or something. Once we realized nobody was dead, we all had a good laugh and agreed that what happened in South Dakota, stayed in South Dakota. That cop and his crew ate lobster until they puked. Nobody ever explained why several of the claws had 40-caliber holes in them."

His smile faded as he added. "My back healed up fine, but I never got out to Montana fishing again."

We could see the lights from several miles out and figuring it had to be our guys, we steered a course to them. A mile out we powered down and at a half mile we switched to the auxiliary electric motor. The tide was moving to high and the waves were very low, so the approach was easy. When we were close to the beach, Davy and I slipped overboard. We waded in with the nuke between us until we were hit land.

We could see the camp just a few hundred yards away, but it looked quiet. I suppose if they were looking for trouble they expected it from the land, not the sea.

We moved in behind a sand dune that would provide cover while we worked. Each of us manning a shovel, we dug a hole right on the edge of the water. Bob said the bomb was completely waterproof. The plan was to bury it in the sand and as the waves moved up the beach with the rising tide they would hide where we dug. Lapping back and forth, the water would soon make the sand look like all the other sand. Twenty minutes after we buried it there would be no way anybody could find the bomb.

It would be under an inch or two of water when it blew, but that hardly mattered. When the hole was three feet deep we placed the bomb and set the timer for two hours. Then we filled the hole and started wading back out to the boat.

Before we got far there was some shouting from one of tents and a lot of guys started running around, waving their arms and yelling. We got back to the boat and, using the electric motor, ran out half a mile before stopping to watch. We couldn't see much because it was still dark, but the camp was now lit up and there were people running everywhere. We kept low in the boat, just in case they had a sniper with night vision.

After a few minutes another boat came roaring out from the back side of the point of land. The spray it was flinging was backlit by their lights and looked like ghostly curtains fluttering in the wind. The boat was accelerating rapidly as it headed northeast and I could see a skinny, half-naked black man standing on the deck.

We gave chase, and got close before they started shooting at us with a .50 BMG machine gun and an RPG. It was hard to tell if it was the choppy ride that threw off their aim or if they were just lousy shots, but they missed with everything. We shot back and then dropped back. It might have been the old "mutual destruction" argument or more like the pre-Shaka fights in South Africa where everybody threw their spears from a safe distance, but it was a gut reaction, one that probably cost us. Then we came to our senses and realized we needed to stop that boat, danger or no danger, Jamerson pushed the throttle back to the peg. That couple of seconds of hesitation had opened up the space between us, but now we were closing in fast.

Then, with a roar that rattled the night, their boat put on a burst of speed that had them pulling away even though we were at full throttle. We were riding in their wake where it was smoother and we were losing ground.

"Hang on," Jamerson said. "It's going to get rough."

Then he turned our boat to the port side, riding up over their wake and nearly flipping our craft as the air came in underneath and threatened to send the bow skyward.

Jamerson was a master, I'll give him that. He finessed the wheel and the throttle to bring the boat back under control, then without hesitation he pegged the throttle forward again.

"Out here in the chop we won't have as much drag on the hull," he shouted. "It should be a little faster."

He worked the trim levers to find the sweet spot, using every trick in the book to pick up a few miles per hour. The motor was eerily quiet, but the wind was roaring in our ears and the spray was soaking us like a torrential rain.

We were skimming the tops of the waves at a crazy ninety-six miles per hour, way past a suicidal speed on the rough ocean. The waves pounded the hull with a loud rhythm, each one seeming to hit harder than the last and I wondered how much the structure could take before the hull was pounded into pieces.

Jamerson took that boat to the limit and past, extracting speed from it that I doubt any other man could have found, but in the next two miles the matter was settled.

They were gone. We lost sight of them. We turned off the boat and listened and we could not hear them either. Their wake no longer showed and we didn't have a clue where to look. They had simply roared into the dark night and disappeared.

"Holy shit," Bob said. "That's the first time this baby was ever outrun. I didn't think anything was faster than H-A. I wonder what's in that boat to push it that fast?"

"What's H-A?"

"The name of the boat, Homarus americanus. It's the scientific Latin name for lobster."

"You named your boat after a lobster?"

"Not me, the guy who had it originally. He told everybody it was because lobster fishing paid for it. Of course, the truth was running drugs is what bought the boat, which is why the government now owns it. Well, at least they did back when we had a government. I suppose it's mine now. Anyway, I never saw a need to change the name, I kind of like it.

"Or at least I did when I thought it was the fastest boat on the East Coast. That's the first time anybody outran it. Those guys have really pissed on my parade."

CHAPTER 59

"Enough!" I shouted.

"Shut up! Listen to me! Turn the boat around and head back to the shore."

"Are you crazy? There is a bomb that's going to go off there soon," Bob shouted back.

"No, it's not. Trust me. Can you stop the countdown?"

"Of course."

"Then do it. But don't let anybody see you. I'll create a diversion."

"It's going to be daylight soon and we can't get it finished before then, those assholes will see us and start shooting for sure."

"I don't think so. I have a hunch, go with me on this."

"Are you insane?"

"Probably."

"Listen guys, I have an idea. Maybe we can get out of this mess in a better way. There is no time to explain. Will you all trust me on this?

They all indicated they would, but I heard Bob mutter under his breath, "This crazy old fool is going to get us killed."

"You said I could shoot you once we planted the bomb, anyway," I said. "So what are you bitching about? Why do you care who pulls the trigger? Maybe I'll give somebody in that camp my proxy."

We came in quietly, anchored the boat and waded to shore near the bomb, which was out of sight from the camp behind the sand dunes. Once it was light the boat would be visible floating offshore, but for now the darkness was hiding it from the camp. I noticed the lights were all on and most of the guys would not have any night vision to see a boat several hundred yards away.

But, that would change fast. I figured we had half an hour before the boat, and all of us, would be visible. But that was the least of my worries. There was not much time before this part of Cape Cod was scheduled to turn into a fiery hell, I hoped Bob was right when he said he could turn off the bomb's timer.

There were a few moments of panic as we tried to find where the bomb was buried. The surf had done its job and everything looked the same. Luckily, Davy had picked a few landmarks when we were burying the thing and he triangulated with them to find a spot about ten feet into the surf. When we drove a shovel into the water and hit the hard plastic case, everybody's heart rate dropped dramatically.

While Bob and Jamerson dug out the bomb, Davy and I walked quietly along the shoreline. There didn't seem to be much activity along the water as most everybody was in the camp about a hundred yards away. We passed a lot of gear stacked up on shore, which helped to keep us hidden. Once we reached the docks we climbed into a boat that was tied to the first of a series of docks and waited.

After a few minutes a guy emerged from behind a stack of crates twenty yards away, zipping his fly and looking distracted. Davy mooed like a cow, and then turned to grin at me.

The guy walked closer to the boat and said, "Hello, anybody here?" Davy mooed again, kind of low and soft as we hid ourselves by tucking in tight to the gunnels, trying hard not to laugh. The guy looked puzzled as he moved close enough to look down into the boat.

Davy grabbed the front of his shirt as he leaned over and dragged the guy into the boat before he had a chance to react.

That's when I noticed another man back near the tents watching us.

"Make it fast, Davy," I said. "Somebody saw that."

"Listen up, asshole," Davy said to the guy lying on the floor of the boat. "Tell the truth and I won't hurt you. Where are your guns?"

"I don't have any guns."

"Does anybody in camp have any guns?"

"Hell no," the guy said. "Those jerks said we were an army but they never gave us any guns. In fact, they took ours away before we even got here. They said, no private guns allowed. I lost a sweet Glock and an AK. We had to turn them all over before we could get in the trucks to come here. They even took our knives away."

"They disarmed everybody?" Davy asked.

"Some guys cried bullshit and refused to get in the trucks, but they took their guns anyway. They threatened to shoot them if they refused so most everybody handed them over. They did shoot a couple of guys who still said no. Everybody handed over their guns after that. But, those assholes pounded the shit out of the guys who gave them trouble. I heard one of those European dudes tell them they could still join up, but now they had to walk to get here as punishment for mouthing off. Most of those guys told them to fuck off, but a lot of them showed up later. Where else they going to go?"

"Okay, I didn't ask for your life story," Davy growled. "I just want to know if anybody in camp has guns. I don't want to get shot here."

"No, nobody has any guns that I know of. The only guys that were armed were those shithead European body guards and I think they all left on the boat. At least that's what everybody is saying."

With that news, I jumped out of the boat and climbed up on some crates piled at the end of the dock. I wanted to be seen easily, but I hoped I wasn't just giving somebody a clear target. I also hoped it wasn't as stupid an idea as it felt like at the moment. How smart could it be to try to control a thousand guys with just four of us? But, once I was up on top in plain sight, it was a done deal.

I shot half a magazine into the air at full-auto with my M4, and then shouted, "Listen up, guys! Everybody get your sorry asses down here, we need to talk!"

I waited until I had a crowd gathered. Then I continued.

"You have all been had. Your leaders just ran out on you and you know why? Because we planted a nuclear bomb that is going to wipe out this place in a few minutes."

They started to murmur and grumble so I fired another full-auto burst into the air and shouted, "Shut the fuck up and listen and maybe we can all get out of this alive."

By then the crowd had grown very large. The men were stacking up from the docks all the way back to the tents and more were joining every second.

"I know you are not armed," I shouted. "But I believe in the old Reagan concept of 'trust but verify.' I need to make sure nobody has a gun hidden on them. We don't have much time, so move fast, do exactly what I say and we can sort the rest out later. If you do not, we all will die before the sun comes up."

Davy had climbed up on another stack of shipping crates on the other side of the dock. He fired a burst in the air and shouted, "Do what he says and do it fast. I will shoot the first guy who gives us any shit. We don't have time to argue here and I have a lot of bullets. So pay attention if you want to live."

"I want everybody to strip completely naked," I continued. "Leave everything where you are standing and head to the water. Go until you are shoulder deep, and then spread out arm's length from the guy beside you. Form a line from that dock on your left until you are even with the boat up there floating off the beach. Then the next line will go to waist-deep water and so on until the final line will be knee deep. Don't fuck around, do it fast. When you get there, put your hands on your head, face me and wait.

"Do it now!"

They complied and while there was some confusion at first, by the time the sun was up there were close to a thousand naked men standing in the surf of Provincetown, their clothing lying scattered along the beach.

The irony didn't escape me and I wonder if that fulfilled somebody's fantasy of this place from back before.

CHAPTER 60

"Okay guys, here is the deal. It would have been a lot easier to just kill you all. In fact, that was the plan. We planted that bomb almost two hours ago and we were going to be back in Gloucester by now, sitting on the dock, enjoying a drink and waiting for the ultimate fireworks show to start. But, after your leaders bailed on you, I had a little change of heart. At least for the moment, but it will not take a lot for me to flip the switch on the bomb again and get the hell out of here. So, it's best to keep your mouths shut and do what I tell you. I am still not completely sure that not killing you all is a good idea. So don't piss me off.

"You may not know it yet, but that's what you would have been doing to us in a few weeks. Killing us, or at least trying to kill us. That's why you are all here; those guys had a plan to take over the world. This army was the start and they planned to use you guys to kill a lot of people. You would not have had a choice. If you didn't do what they told you, they would have killed you.

"But you can thank a guy named Mickey for convincing me that you are not all bad guys. You might also thank the two bodies floating in the ocean about fifty miles from here for making me take the chance that none of you were armed. After dealing with those two assholes, I suspected that the control freaks running this show would not trust any of you with guns until they were ready for you to do their bidding. Guess I was right.

"So now, what to do with you?"

"If it were up to Davy here we would still kill you. After all, that's the safest approach and I am not so sure but what he might be right.

"But, I am not gonna do that. At least not yet. That choice, the choice to live or die, is going to be yours.

"Here's the deal. Some of you are going to be in the ocean for a while, so plan on being sunburned and soggy. You will come in here when I call you, one at a time to start. I am going to pick at random, and so if you are picked last, tough shit, I don't want any bitching. If you bitch, I will shoot you. If you talk, Davy will shoot you. If you move or give us any shit, both Davy and I will shoot you."

By now, Jamerson and Bob had walked up from the beach. They were well armed with rifles and handguns. Bob even had an RPG with him that he must have pulled out of the boat somewhere. I don't know what he planned to do with it, but it was intimidating as hell when he pointed it at the assembled men in the ocean. I used the opportunity to remind them again that we would not tolerate any bullshit.

We brought in the first guys, one at a time. Davy watched over the rest of them with the RPG while Bob and I questioned them, before giving them to Jamerson to lock up.

Well, the truth is, I watched while Bob questioned them. He was clearly very experienced at extracting information. Most of these guys were scared to death and willing to cooperate, so getting the information was not difficult. Making sure that they were telling the truth and not just saying what they thought we wanted to hear was a little tougher. But Bob seemed to have a built-in truth detector and when somebody started bullshitting, he cut them off fast.

We explained to every one of them right from the start that only the truth would be accepted. We warned them all, but of course there were some who just had to try us. There are always a few guys in every bunch who think they are smarter than the rest of the world. But they were no match for Bob. The first couple of idiots who lied got their faces broken. They had been warned and now they knew we were serious. We parked them, tied to a chair, in front of the door the rest of the guys had to come through when they got there. After that, things were a lot easier.

We questioned the first fifty guys, one at a time, before locking them in a building with Jamerson standing guard. They all told pretty much the same story. They were in the gangs in the city when some guys showed up with an offer. Clearly some of them were monsters; after all, the gangs were not run by altar boys. But, it became obvious to us that the makeup of the gangs had evolved and changed. Most of the bloody turf wars were over and these younger members had missed them. They were kids when things were really bad, yet now through events probably beyond their control, they were caught in in the gangs. A lot of them were clearly victims of the circumstances and trying to survive the best way they could. There were really no surprises in their stories, but I wanted to be sure. Once I was, I climbed back up on the packing crates and again addressed the huddled mass of scared, naked, and shivering young men.

"Okay," I shouted, "Where are the tattoo guys, the ones who were doing the free tats?"

Three guys raised their hands.

"Come here," I told them.

"Here's how it's going to work," I said to the rest of the guys. "We are going to tattoo you with a big red 'A'. We all know that stands for asshole, but you can tell people whatever you want. Me? I would say it stands for 'Army.'

"Davy thinks we should put it on your foreheads and looking at you guys, I think it would be an improvement for most of you."

There were some chuckles, but not many.

"But, I am going to put it on your right shoulder. If you already have a tat on that shoulder, I will pick another spot. My choice; if you give me any shit it will be on your forehead.

"When we are done, you can find your clothes and head on out of here on foot. No more than three at a time. If we can find some food, we will give some to everybody. But, no guns. You guys leave here unarmed. I know it sucks, but that's the way it's got to be."

"Now I can't stop you from gathering up later and causing some problems. But, here's the deal. I am giving you a chance. Those guys who just ran out on you were planning to use you to sweep through the country. At every town they would present a choice to the people living there, join them or die. That's it. No choice to live free.

"Well, I am giving you a chance to make the decision to live free. But, it's a one-time deal. If anybody fucks up in any way while wearing this tattoo, they will be killed on sight. Not just by me and my boys here, it's going to be the law of the land; anybody can shoot you and be free and clear. If you alter the tattoo or remove it, you will be killed on sight.

"You are going to hate that mark and probably some of you will be killed unfairly. Tough shit, it's still better than all of you being blown up by a nuke."

CHAPTER 61

"I am going to give you a chance to use the mark to improve your life as well," I continued. "Things are going to change around here soon. There will be work, food, prosperity. We will be spreading the word about you guys, the truth, all of it, but in addition to telling everybody to kill you if you fuck up, I am also going to ask everybody to think about giving you a chance to prove yourselves. I am going to ask the citizens of the new United States that you be given special consideration because of that tattoo. I am asking that you be given a chance, one chance. That's what this buys you, so don't screw it up. I am asking that you be hired first when somebody needs a worker. It's not a handout, it's a chance to prove you are not an asshole, what you do with it is up to you. But it's your only chance.

"If you want to continue the gang life you will be hunted down and exterminated. If you steal, cheat, lie or even forget to smile in church, we will kill you. But work hard, stay honest and you can become part of the new America that's coming.

"I won't lie to you, it's not going to be easy and most of you probably won't make it. I know, too, that I will have some regrets for not just killing everybody here and being done with it. Some of you will no doubt hurt some innocent people, people that would not have been hurt if we had killed you. But, I believe that a lot of you guys are just stuck in a bad situation. Life has been lousy for a long time and I understand that some of you have just been trying to survive. This is your chance.

"I also understand that some of you like this life, you are lazy, mean, stupid or all three and you like hurting other people. If you do, I will find you and make sure that you are hurt a lot more before you die. That's my promise to you: If you hurt innocent people, you will be tortured to death. This man here with the rocket launcher was with the CIA and he knows every possible way to

283

inflict pain. It's going to take a long time to die and it's going to hurt more than you can possibly imagine. Brutal? You bet, but it's your choice. Leave people alone and people will leave you alone. If you choose to test us, you will be killed publicly so the world can watch and it will take a long time to die. By the time it's over you will be writhing around in your own shit, choking on vomit and begging to die. This is a new world now and it's going to be fair and just, but it will not be granting second chances. At least not for you guys.

"You guys gave me a tough choice here today: Kill you all, or try this approach. Frankly, I am starting to have doubts. It's been tough these past years and I am tired. It might have been easier to just let the bomb go off. It would have fixed a lot of problems.

"But I am hoping that some of what made America the greatest country in the history of the world is still running in your blood. I am trusting you guys to be the new pioneers, the rugged individualists who are going out to tame a wild land. I am also trusting you to self-police. If you stand by while somebody else commits a crime and you do nothing to stop it, you will be killed. I know you think that's unfair, but remember, you chose to be here. Also remember the alternative is to kill you all right now. Given the circumstances I think I am being goddamned fair.

"That's the deal; it's more than you deserve and the only one you will be offered. If don't you want it, raise your hand and Davy will shoot you now."

Not one hand went up, but a lot of guys found something very interesting to look at in the sea close to their feet.

I lowered my voice, the fire and brimstone gone, and I sounded like the tired old man I was.

"Look guys, I am pretty sure most of you have not been happy with the way things have been for the past several years. Why would you want to go back to that? This is a chance at a real life, something you didn't have an hour ago. Think it over, choose wisely. Don't disappoint me. I don't want to live with knowing I made the wrong decision in trusting you guys. Who knows? Maybe someday that tattoo will be a medal of honor, proof that you were here when it started. Proof that you were part of the few who stood up and rebuilt America. Maybe in some odd, twisted way, you guys will be the new founding fathers."

CHAPTER 62

It took three more days to process everybody. There had been an order issued for everybody to get a mandatory tattoo for identification. But, that was not yet started, so we had plenty of ink and supplies. We did find a lot of food, so nobody was hungry. I figured out pretty quickly, too, that I couldn't leave them standing in the ocean. So we brought them in five at a time. We filled up every building that had a lock on it and even had some tied out with chains like dogs. As far as I know, none of them escaped.

Bob found a ledger listing their names, but we had processed a hundred or so before that. We accounted for all the remaining names and ended up with one hundred-seventeen names unaccounted for. But, to be honest, I wasn't counting. Maybe we had done that many, maybe a few got away. In the end it probably didn't matter.

Bob and Jamerson had taken a truck down the road, traveling back and forth from the bridge at Sagamore and P-Town, making sure they were not grouping up. But, at some point it was out of our hands. We had to trust that we had made the right choice.

"You think this will work?" Davy asked as we watched the last three limp down the road, their feet sore from being wet for so long."

"Hell, I don't know," I said.

"If one of them rapes and kills some little girl I am going to regret the decision. But, you could see, they weren't all bad guys. Most of them thanked us for doing this and a lot of them were crying.

"We couldn't just kill them. Not after their 'leaders' ran off. Hell, without those four shitheads to spur them on, they were no longer a dangerous army. At least not yet. They might have formed into something very bad in a few days. When we got here, things were happening fast and they were confused,

285

I saw a chance and I took it. Sometimes, you need to have a little faith in your fellow man."

"How are we going to enforce it?"

"The people will have to do that. They can either bring some law and order back or they can continue living like it's been. We can't force them. All we can do is put the tools in front of them and hope for the best."

"So what was all that 'things are going to change around here' shit?" Davy asked.

"Hell, I don't know. I was just winging it trying to figure out a way to keep everybody alive."

"Well, you know now that you ran your big mouth, you will have to back it up. Somebody has to take charge and get this organized. We need to make sure the people know the deal you made and they need to know it's real and that somebody has their back. Somebody has to pass out the tools. So was that you volunteering?"

I just stood staring at the three guys until they were out of sight. Then I turned and walked to the dock and sat down.

Davy walked with me and changed the subject, "I was talking with some of the guys who were waiting and I figured out what happened."

"They had one of those radiation detectors that the enforcers used. Remember? Right after the nuke ban the government was handing them out like candy. Every police department got at least one. The thinking was that the more out there, the better the chance of finding any bombs. Remember the slogan, 'If you find something, say something?'

"Well they had the signature of their bomb blocked in the meter, so when the alarm went off, they knew we had another bomb. They must have known that somebody still had a few after Bob's guys tried to negotiate with the one they had. I am sure the guys made it a point to tell them that it was not the only one and they probably put two and two together. They didn't waste any time looking, they just jumped into their boat and ran like the little pussies they are. They took all those European, ex-special forces types with them. At least, the few that were left after you got done with them. The good thing is they left their bomb behind. Bob just found it, and it's in the boat with its sibling now. It looks like the good guys won this one and made the world safe for democracy once again."

We sat looking at the ocean for a long time.

"I am tired, Davy," I said. "Let's go home."

"Cool! Can we look for pirates on the way?"

EPILOGUE

We actually found some pirates, but they were pretty pathetic. They had been adrift for two weeks and were not in any shape to plunder.

They said their motor had thrown a rod and several days later, right at first light, they saw a huge ship headed their way. They thought they were saved, until this big brown boat came out of nowhere and intercepted the ship. Four of the guys they described getting on to the ship met the descriptions of the four horsemen who had escaped. A skinny black guy with a shield and spear put to rest any doubts. They said the brown boat headed south while the ship turned around and traveled east. Neither one paid them any attention.

We gave them water, a little food and a paddle. But not until we marked them each with a big red tattoo, took their guns and explained the new way of life to them.

We slept almost a full day at Jamerson's place. Then we gorged on lobster and fish until we couldn't walk. After two more days Jamerson started to complain about the damage to his whiskey stash, so we decided we had overstayed our welcome. It was time to go home.

I promised Jamerson that I would replace his whiskey with some from the train, good bourbon if I could get it. I had plans to send some guys to check up on him in a few weeks anyway. At least that's what I told him. The truth is, I figured by then I would be ready for more lobster. Besides we needed some people to head to P-town and collect all the military gear waiting there.

Bob and Jamerson stayed at Jamerson's place, while Davy and I took the truck home. After a long and loud argument, they kept one bomb and we took the other. Bob gave me the arming codes for ours.

We made it back to Moultrie without a single problem, which put Davy in a foul mood. At least until he saw Sarah in the doorway, then he was fine. Hell, he even wagged his tail a little bit.

Emily had turned Mickey loose after we left, as I expected she would. He turned out to be a good kid and a hard worker. He was already building a new room to expand the clinic. I looked at his work and he was a good carpenter. I told him to come and see me after things settled down. I would answer his questions and put maybe put him to work. I had some expansion plans of my own.

Apparently, Emily and Pete had tried dinner, but it didn't work out. I guess Pete couldn't deal with the fact she was an inch taller than him. Sarah told me Bradley had asked the next day if Emily would have dinner with him and she agreed. Against all odds, they hit it off. For now he was going to sleep in her spare bedroom.

Sarah and Davy went off by themselves for a few hours. When they came back, Sarah said she was going to stay at Davy's place for a few days and "see what happens." Bradley stood with them and made no attempt to "reason" with Davy, so I guess they had his blessing.

Like I said, it a goddammed soap opera at that clinic.

"I am quitting Jack's operation," Davy said to me as I was packing to leave. "Things are going to be tame now and it's no fun. When you guys start this new government, you think you can find a job for me?"

"What new government?" I asked.

But he didn't answer. He just grinned and walked away.

I drove the truck to my place, arriving early in the morning, just as the sun was coming up. As I unlocked the first gate, Clyde came out to meet me. He was barking and growling and all bristled up until I said, "Who told you that you were tough?" He immediately recognized my voice and started to wiggle and wag so hard I thought he would turn inside out.

By the time I got to the house my wife was on the porch. She seemed happy to see me too, but didn't do much wiggling or wagging.

Later, as I was drifting off to sleep she said, "The Farnsworths would like you at the train station early Saturday morning. They have another meeting scheduled in Virginia and say they can't do it without you.

"I'll pack a lunch, you are going to get hungry trying to rebuild a country."

Six months later, we were making good progress when the first reports came in that a huge army was sweeping through Europe, gathering soldiers and laying waste to those who resisted.

ABOUT THE AUTHOR

Bryce M. Towsley is an unrepentant gun nut and is an avid, world-traveling hunter. He competes in several shooting disciplines, including 3-gun, IDPA and USPSA.

As a full time writer for decades, Towsley has published hundreds of articles in most of the major outdoor and gun magazines and is listed as field editor in several of the top publications.

He has published six hunting or gun related books and contributed to several others. This is his first novel.

Towsley lives in Vermont with his wife Robin in their empty nest. Their children, Erin and Nathan, are grown and doing well in the world.

Clyde is real and lives with them, although sadly he has not and never will father any puppies. His best friend and housemate is a food-loving Corgi named Gypsy Rose.

For more info check out: www.brycetowsley.com

Made in the USA
Lexington, KY
18 March 2013